PRAISE FOR
TIM GREEN'S PREVIOUS NOVELS

THE LETTER OF THE LAW

"Taut...page-turning...Green's best novel to date, and that's saying a lot."
—*USA Today*

"Classic Green, with tense courtroom scenes, a smart woman lawyer, and some gruesome killings...another winner."
—*Orlando Sentinel*

"Realistic dialogue, great characters, and an intelligent plot...one of those books that pulls you in from page one."
—**Nelson DeMille, author of *Up Country***

"A top-notch writer....This book moves fast and hits hard."
—*Tampa Tribune-Times*

"Green scores big!...Highly recommended."
—*Library Journal*

"A fun read....Green keeps the pages turning."
—*Booklist*

"Interesting characters...an intelligent plot...a page-turning legal thriller."
—*Tulsa World* (OK)

more...

"Entertaining…suspenseful and exciting."
—*Wichita Falls Times Record News* (TX)

DOUBLE REVERSE

"Over-the-top…absorbing."
—*Entertainment Weekly*

"Green keeps the suspense building and the reader continually off guard throughout the book…explosive…a quick and entertaining read."
—*Chicago Tribune*

"Plot twists as complicated as a double reverse play….Green, whose writing is ever more polished, scores a touchdown in this one."
—*Atlanta Journal-Constitution*

"Fast paced….Green knows the territory and leads us briskly right through the bloody, satisfying climax."
—*Publishers Weekly*

"A highly entertaining novel….Green is at his best."
—*BookPage*

"Green delivers another gritty story of violence and greed…great action."
—*Library Journal*

THE
FOURTH
PERIMETER

Books by Tim Green

Fiction

Ruffians

Titans

Outlaws

The Red Zone

Double Reverse

The Letter of the Law

The Fourth Perimeter

The Fifth Angel

The First 48

Exact Revenge

Nonfiction

The Dark Side of the Game

A Man and His Mother: An Adopted Son's Search

THE
FOURTH
PERIMETER

TIM GREEN

WARNER BOOKS

NEW YORK   BOSTON

The events and characters in this book are fictitious. Certain real locations and public figures are mentioned, but all other characters amd events described in the book are totally imaginary.

WARNER BOOKS EDITION

Copyright © 2002 by Tim Green
All rights reserved. No part of this book may be reproduced in any form or by any electronic or mechanical means, including information storage and retrieval systems, without permission in writing from the publisher, except by a reviewer who may quote brief passages in a review.

Cover design and art by Tony Greco

Warner Books, Inc.
1271 Avenue of the Americas
New York, NY 10020

Visit our Web site at www.twbookmark.com

 An AOL Time Warner Company

Printed in the United States of America

Originally published in hardcover by Warner Books

First Paperback Printing: February 2003

10 9 8 7 6 5 4 3 2 1

*For my love Illyssa, my dream Thane, my joy Tessa,
my pride Troy, and my inspiration Tate*

ACKNOWLEDGMENTS

I would like to thank the following people who helped to make this book possible: my agent, Esther Newberg, for her invaluable guidance; my editor, Rick Wolff, for his constant instruction, advice, and hard work; Sara Ann Freed, for her valuable editorial help along the way; Mari Okuda and Roland Ottewell for their special attention to the manuscript; Caroline Dignan, M.E., for her insight into forensics; my parents, Dick and Judy Green, for their careful reading of all my manuscripts; Warren Miller for his expert insight into scuba diving; Bob Brown for his knowledge of private aircraft; Sergeant Pete Patnode for insight into police work; also Captain Michael Kerwin, who once again made himself available to me day and night.

A very special thanks to Larry Newman, who served in the Secret Service under Presidents Eisenhower, Kennedy, Johnson, Nixon, Ford, and Reagan, and without whom this book could never have been written.

THE
FOURTH
PERIMETER

PROLOGUE

It was the taste of metal wiped clean with gun oil. It was the taste of horror, of death. Collin's teeth bit instinctively into the gun's barrel, and he closed his eyes against the coming blast. In the brief instant before it came, his mind replayed the events leading up to this crisis. In vivid slow motion he was afforded the opportunity to regret a million moments that he could have rewritten to prevent what was about to happen.

Pernicious fog, heavy with the moisture from the warm river, shrouded the old brick buildings, casting gloom on their normally cheerful wooden signs. The cold spring's last dying gasp had rushed down the eastern seaboard from Canada and so everything was obscure and ill defined. Collin Ford rolled slowly down King Street under the hazy yellow light of ancient lampposts in his pewter Toyota 4Runner. He might have been any young man in any American city. Most had renovated areas of bygone commerce that hugged some once-vital body of water, and most were teeming with young professionals at night. But Collin wasn't just any young professional, and the capital of the United States wasn't just any city. Collin was an agent in the Secret Service.

Unlike with many of his young counterparts, money was of little concern to Collin. He had a substantial trust fund. But that was something he neither relied upon nor talked about. His concern, rather, was one of distinction. Collin had no desire to outdo his father in business, even if he could. As well off as the Fords were, Collin's father had taught him from an early age that while wealth could be beneficial for certain things, it wasn't something to strive for. So instead Collin had set his sights on rising in the ranks of the Service and surpassing what even his ambitious father had accomplished before he left the same Service to develop a high-tech business.

Collin found a spot for his truck on a side street and hunched over to pull his jacket closed before slouching up the brick sidewalk to a place called Harpoon Alley. A pleasant amber glow spilled out of the large mullioned windows. Collin spotted his friends inside in the midst of the crowd hunkered down at the bar. He slipped through the door into where it was warm and dry and dodged his way through the throng. He ordered a Coke from the bartender and greeted his friends with a timid smile.

"You're late," Lou said, looking pointedly at his Rolex. Lou was tall, handsome, and blond, a former college swimmer. Collin was his opposite in looks as well as demeanor. Lou was the kind of guy who introduced himself to strangers with total ease. Collin, while singularly intelligent, was reserved, average in height and build, and dark-haired, with hazel eyes.

"One of my kids needed a ride home," he said with a shrug.

"Your kids?" asked Allen, a preppy-looking lawyer with stylish glasses who was better acquainted with Lou than with Collin.

"This guy is like the original saint," Lou replied, taking a swig of beer. "Instead of using his trust fund to travel Europe in style, he buys uniforms for a kids' basketball league. Instead of working for his old man in a Manhattan high-rise, he hoofs it all over the country sleeping in Motel Sixes waiting to take a bullet for the president.

"It's a good thing," Lou continued, raising his hands in the air. "Don't get me wrong. But I'm just not prone to a guilty conscience or else I wouldn't be able to stand hanging around with you."

"Like handicapped kids or something?" Allen inquired, blinking behind his glasses.

Collin looked at him out of the corner of his eye and took a drink of the Coke that had just arrived in a pint glass. "They're at-risk kids," he explained, satisfied that Allen wasn't trying to poke fun at him. "And we just won the City League Championship for ten- and eleven-year-olds . . ."

Collin was beaming now and he looked at Lou expectantly. Lou knew better than anyone that Collin had gone into this not knowing the first thing about basketball. A couple of months back, when the two of them were on their way to a party, Lou had asked for a breath mint. Collin distractedly told him to check in his brief-case and that's when Lou discovered the book on basic strategies of the sport that Collin had borrowed from the library.

"Hey," Lou said now with genuine admiration, "that's great, Collin."

"I know it," Collin said with a self-deprecating grin. "But these kids worked so hard. You should have seen their faces when I handed out the trophies. The trophies were as big as the kids."

"Now that calls for a real drink, by God!" Lou said, signaling the bartender for another round. He pointed to Collin and told the bartender, "And make his a pint of Foster's.

"You can certainly have one or two to celebrate," he said brightly as the glasses arrived. "I mean, that's really great."

Effusive over his victory, Collin gave in and raised his glass. It wasn't long before he had two pints under his belt and was working on his third. He was demonstrating his zone strategy with balled-up cocktail napkins on the bar when he caught sight of a familiar face across the bar. He stopped speaking in midsentence.

Lou followed his gaze and emitted a low whistle. "Wow," he said.

"That's her," Collin heard himself say. He was suddenly and acutely aware that he was wearing his old jacket rather than the new double-breasted Italian blazer his father had given to him at Christmas and that he'd forgotten to brush his teeth before he came out.

"Who?" Lou asked.

"Her," Collin said, buttoning and then unbuttoning his jacket. "The girl I told you about. The one I see in my coffee shop. She's—"

"Incredible," Lou said. Allen nodded appreciatively and uttered his concurrence.

Her hair was black and straight and her eyes a striking incandescent yellow. They were almost feline and hinted of Asia. But her high cheeks, thick red lips, and long straight nose were more reminiscent of the Mediterranean. Her skin was bronze, and her tall, striking figure was snugly ensconced in a cashmere turtleneck and pleated black slacks.

She had taken the one empty stool on the opposite side of the bar and ordered a drink. She was alone, and while nearly all eyes were on her, she seemed unaware. There was something delicately innocent about her; Lou knew in an instant why she had been the first woman in over a year to distract Collin from the girlfriend who had dumped him for an NHL hockey player.

"Go talk to her," Lou urged.

"No," Collin said. "I can't. Look what I look like."

"What are you talking about? You look fine," Lou said.

"I don't even know her name," Collin said weakly.

"I thought you said you've talked to her," Lou protested.

"I've said hello and things like that," Collin replied, taking a nervous swig from his glass. "But I haven't *really* talked to her, and I don't know her name."

"Dude, she's looking right at you," Allen said, nudging him in the ribs.

Collin looked up and smiled foolishly. The girl smiled back and gave an embarrassed little wave.

"Go!" Lou hissed, surreptitiously grabbing Collin by the back of his blazer and urging him away from them.

Before he knew it, Collin was standing there in an empty space, his friends jerking their heads at him like idiots and the girl smiling patiently from the other side of the bar. He took a deep breath and worked his way through the crowd.

By the time he got to the other side, it was too late. A big guy with a gold watch wearing a dark Armani suit had wedged himself right up alongside her and was already making his pitch. Collin dipped his head and slipped past as if he were really on his way to the restroom after all. He was struck by the strong smell of the man's cologne and further reminded of his own tousled appearance. But as he passed, the girl reached out and tugged him toward her. Collin stumbled and bumped into the guy sitting on the next stool.

"Excuse me," the girl said abruptly to the interloper, "this is my husband."

Collin met the other man's hostile glare with a confused look. Then, without thinking, he bent down and kissed the girl on her cheek.

"Hi," he said, then straightened up and gave the other guy his best forbidding Secret Service look. The man opened his mouth as if to speak, but his resolve visibly wavered and he quickly melted away. Collin turned to the girl with a grin.

"I never saw that before," he said.

"It worked," she told him. "I'm Leena."

"I'm Collin," he said, taking her hand. "Collin Ford. I'm the guy from—"

"The coffee shop," she said with a suppressed smile. "I know. I was wondering if you were ever going to talk to me."

"You were?" he asked.

Leena nodded and said, "I'm not very good at meeting people. I'm new here. I guess you've been here for a while. I saw your friends . . ."

"About three years," he told her. "Originally from New York."

"The city?"

"Close by," he said. "Now I'm with the Secret Service."

"Not very secretive, are you?" she said archly.

Collin blushed despite himself.

"Your friends are staring at us," she added with a smile.

He gave them a dirty look, but all that did was incite them. "They're morons," he said.

"Want to go someplace that isn't so . . . crowded?" she suggested.

"Sure."

Collin led her out into the fog. She had a dark full-length coat over her arm and she stopped outside the door to put it on. Collin helped. The shapeless coat hid her spectacular form and left Collin eager to get to someplace warm where she would take it off again.

"Thank you," she said in a soft tone that thrilled him. She was almost too sweet.

He started down toward the water but she said, "No, let's go this way. I know a good place."

He shrugged and walked along with her in the mist past storefronts, restaurants, and bars.

"How about here?" she said, pointing around the corner to an out-of-the-way place. They went down a small set of stairs into what was once a cellar. It was darker than Harpoon Alley, darker and dingier, yet Collin felt remarkably at ease. They found a pair of empty stools at the long bar in the back corner.

"Can I take your coat?" Collin asked.

Leena pulled the garment tight to her shoulders and with a feigned shiver said, "No, thanks. Maybe after a drink."

A lanky bartender who wore two silver hoop earrings as well as a thick dark beard ambled over and asked what they wanted.

"How about a vodka?" Leena said, looking at Collin expectantly. "I'm not much of a drinker, but sometimes I think it's the best thing in the world to take away a chill."

Collin hesitated, but only for a moment. "Sure."

"Two doubles," she told the bartender, "straight up."

Collin fished out his wallet and slapped a fifty-dollar bill down on the bar without comment. He never noticed that while the bartender filled his glass with vodka he gave the girl nothing but water.

When the drinks came, Leena held hers in the air and touched Collin's glass. "To new places, new friends," she said, and with a mischievous smile added, "and secret agents . . ."

"I said Secret Service," he told her, smiling also. He liked her sense of humor. And in fact, as they talked, he found he liked everything about her. Leena was remarkably similar to his ex-girlfriend. They both had fathers who were bankers. They both had studied fine arts, rode horses, and loved the symphony. The similarities didn't even bother him. For nearly a year now, anything that reminded him of Amanda had caused a pang of regret. But Leena was like an improved version of his old girlfriend. She had none of Amanda's haughty and sometimes frigid nature. Leena was warm and open. Before Collin knew it, he was dead drunk.

He was buzzing comfortably when she finally said in a bashful whisper, "I'd like to go home with you."

He looked at her, stunned. Tears were welling up in her eyes. "What's wrong?" he asked.

Leena blinked and looked up at him through her long lashes. "I'm just so lonely. I haven't been with anyone in so long. I'm sorry. I know it's not right, but I can't help it. I've seen you now for weeks and I think about you all the time. I can't help wanting to be with you . . ."

Collin almost choked. "No, no, no," he slurred. "Don't you worry. I don't mind. I'd love to have you come home with me. Please, come . . ."

She smiled tentatively and stood up. Her coat fell open, and the sight of her perfect body thrilled him. But when he rose, Collin staggered half a step backward. Leena helped him into his jacket like a mother sending her son off to school. She pulled her own coat close around her shoulders and tied it tightly at the waist. Then she hooked her arm through his and led him through the bar with her head slightly inclined so that the curtain of dark hair hid her face until they walked up the dirty stone steps and out into the cool damp night.

"Where's your car?" she asked.

"This way," he slurred and walked unevenly around the block, relying heavily on her much steadier gait. When they arrived at his truck, she asked him if he was all right to drive.

"It's not far," he said.

Collin could drive better than he could walk. Without a word, Leena let her hand drift to his thigh. His blood raced, and in less than ten minutes they were in front of an expensive row of town houses right next to the water. He led her up the brick walk. Inside, he flipped on a couple of lights and his sound system before directing her to the couch. He found a couple bottles of Bud Light in the back of his refrigerator, left there by Lou months ago when they had a small Super Bowl party.

He sat down on the couch next to Leena and offered her a beer. She sipped it, then put it down on the coffee table. They continued to talk, and Collin continued to marvel at how similar, but better, this girl was than the one to whom he had sworn everlasting love, the one who had deserted him. And as the minutes passed and he finished not only his own beer but hers, it seemed to him that he was immersed in some blissful dream.

"Do you want to go upstairs?" he asked her, his head starting to nod.

"Yes," she said quietly. "I'd like that."

Collin led her up the stairs to his bedroom, a spartan place with a large bed on a bronze frame resting in the middle of the hardwood floor and a view that normally let him gaze across the river at the lights of the capital. With maternal tenderness, Leena helped him out of his clothes and pushed him gently back onto the bed.

"I have to get something from my purse," she said. "I'll be right back."

Collin frowned as he watched her disappear down the stairs. If he weren't completely drunk, it would have seemed ludicrous to lie there like that, stripped naked with his clothes in a pile on the floor. On the night table lay his gun. Drunk as he was, his training didn't allow him to do anything careless with his weapon. It was the first thing he'd removed. He recalled a joke from his past, something about a gun in bed, but the punch line escaped him. He chuckled drunkenly and sighed.

Downstairs, Leena took the beer bottle she'd touched and put it into her purse. She turned off all the lights. Then from the same purse she removed a handkerchief. She draped it over the lock and the handle of the front door and opened the door into the misty night. After waving the handkerchief back and forth several times, she pulled the door shut without latching it. Quietly she climbed the stairs. Collin was still there, lying where he should be. She crossed the room and smiled at him as she picked up his clothes.

"Let me fold these for you," she said.

"No, no, don't worry about that," he slurred. "You're too sweet. Forget my clothes."

Behind her, Leena could hear the stealthy footsteps of two men ascending the stairs.

"I'm going to turn out the light before I undress," she said calmly. "Then I'll be there."

What happened next came fast. The light went out and two dark figures entered the room. Quickly they pinned Collin to the bed. Leena hastened across the room. From its holster on the nightstand, she extracted the big standard-issue Secret Service Glock 9mm, jammed the gun into Collin's screaming mouth, and pulled the trigger. The men stepped back from the bed and she calmly handed one of them the weapon before hurrying out of the bedroom and down the stairs, leaving them alone with the choking, gurgling sounds of death. In the front room, she pulled back the curtain and scanned the walk up and down as far as the fog would let her see. There was no one and nothing to be seen or heard. She left the house without any apparent urgency, walked around the corner, got into a black Jeep, and drove away into the murky night.

CHAPTER 1

It was late Saturday in upstate New York, a perfect early summer evening on Skaneateles Lake and not the place one would expect to receive tragic news. On the water, an occasional boat droned past through the light chop that had been kicked up by a pleasant breeze. The sun had dropped behind the towering hills and already overhead the brilliant three-quarter moon danced with tattered clouds. Jupiter winked nearby, and the soft hum of crickets played background to the rustling leaves of a tall willow. On the broad covered patio of the Glen Haven Inn, groups of people sat around circular tables covered with white linen tablecloths and adorned with fresh-cut flowers. Peals of soft laughter drifted across the veranda as if the patrons too were blooming in the first true warmth of the season.

None, though, seemed happier than the couple that sat by themselves at a table by the railing on the edge of the night. The man was in his late forties. His posture was effortlessly upright and his shoulders subtly muscular. Though he had been dark-haired as a youth, his asymmetrical face was now weathered and crowned by a full head of hair frosted by time and care. Either side of his irregular visage by itself was uninspiring, but together they were somehow pleasing. His dark brown eyes were a constant contradiction, brooding fathomless pools one moment, smiling and luminescent the next.

He had the look of a man who had seen much, yet had somehow retained at least some of the joy of youth. He appeared both rugged and gentle, with the outward demeanor of a man whose livelihood relied more on his hands than his mind. The labels inside his clothes could betray his wealth if he hadn't removed them all for comfort's sake. So could his gold watch, but only on the rare occasions that he remembered to put it on.

The woman looked younger by ten years or more. Her wavy light brown hair was highlighted with long golden strands and it fell past her shoulders in wild bunches that might have given her an unkempt appearance if not for the meticulous demeanor of her clothes and the perfect features of her face. Her eyes were the color of blue glass and bright, unspoiled despite the disappointments life had shown her. Her smile too was as animated as it had been when she was a young girl, and she was always ready to laugh, even at herself.

She was laughing now while the man recounted for her the verbal abuse he had taken earlier in the day from his sister. Gracie was much older than he, and the two of them had a unique relationship. It was she who for years had helped to manage the domestic affairs of a man who seemed to care very little for money although he had vastly more than most. It was Gracie who ruled the mansion in Greenwich, if not the lake house in

Skaneateles and the massive penthouse apartment on Central Park West in the city. The younger woman was quite familiar with the sister's austere demeanor as well as her unabashed and biting criticism of the many things that didn't please her.

". . . So I said to her," the man continued between gleeful gasps, " 'Gracie, if I didn't know you better, I'd say you have a thing for that man!' "

The woman, Jill, let out a shriek of mirth. "You didn't!"

The man laughed even harder, barely able to catch his breath. "And then she said . . . she said," he howled, bursting into tears of delight. "She said . . . 'Don't forget, Kurtis Andrew, that I used to change your diapers!' "

Jill shrieked again, wiping tears from the corners of her own eyes.

"Holy shit!" Kurt bellowed, still crying. "Can you believe she said that? Oh God, she sounded like my mother . . ."

Together they emptied their laughter into the night, unconcerned with the stares they drew from everyone around them and the embarrassed smile on the lips of their waiter, who pulled up short of the table with their coffee and dessert. When they had quieted, and the waiter had moved on, Kurt reached into the pocket of his blazer and felt the velvet box he'd hidden there. He gazed lovingly across the table, moving the flowers to the other side of the candle so he could see his companion's face without obstruction.

"My God, I love you so much," he said with quiet urgency. Reaching out across the table with his other hand, he grasped her fingers tightly.

"Oh, I love you too," she said fervently. "Kurt, I love you so much."

The mirthful tears in his eyes turned sentimental. He thought of how long it had been since he had allowed himself to really love a woman, more than twenty years. The last had been his wife, and since then, although after a while there were other women who had occupied his mind, none of them had ever truly been allowed to find a place in his heart.

Even so, he chided himself for being so apprehensive. His intention had been to present the ring when the champagne arrived, but for some reason he'd come unnerved. Maybe it was because that was too formal a time. Their relationship was more casual, born out of friendship, although lust on his part had been present from the moment she walked into the boardroom with her flushed cheeks and her wild hair falling all around the padded shoulders of her trim business suit. That first jolting impression was what prompted him, but it was the person beneath that he fell so deeply in love with. She was brilliant and kind, and she seemed to adore him too.

Somehow, it seemed more appropriate to him now that he give her the ring, a seven-carat canary yellow diamond, over coffee and apple strudel. He was certain, or almost certain, that she would accept. Maybe therein lay the problem. He was either certain or he wasn't, and if he was almost certain, then he wasn't certain, not really. They had never talked about getting married, not in any concrete sense. Oh, there had been romantic whispers deep in the night about the enduring nature of their love. And it had seemed for a while now that what free time either of them had, they spent together. But they'd never really gotten down to the business of it.

She had been married once before. A mistake. Her husband, Kurt knew, had been possessive, selfish, and generally unkind. They had argued frequently and he was irrationally jealous. Then they learned that he was unable to give her children, something she had always wanted. The tempestuous nature of their relationship only worsened. He became abusive—not physically, but verbally and emotionally. Nevertheless, Jill fought hard to keep her marriage alive. She had confided to Kurt early on that she considered divorce an admission of abject failure.

Even so, Kurt had been able to become a part of Jill's life, a confidant and a friend. And, although they were truly just friends, Jill's husband finally had a palpable target for his burning jealousy. Jill was working for Kurt's company, then and now, as a scientist. It wasn't long after they started to become close that Jill quit without a word, right in the middle of the development of the project that had first thrown them together.

Kurt was no scientist himself, but he was the source of almost every successful idea the company had developed. Whenever a new product or a line of business was being pioneered, he would be heavily involved until things were up and running smoothly. That's how he had built Safe Tech into a billion-dollar business and that's how he intended to keep it that way.

But when Jill inexplicably left, Kurt forgot all about business for the first time since his son had gone away to college. He moped about for a week or so feeling sorry for himself, going through the motions of being the important CEO of a major corporation. Then he literally just went and got her. She was coming out of her house in Long Island, sharply dressed in a dark brown business suit, her wild hair tightly constrained with clips and a comb. She looked sad and beautiful and was so preoccupied that she was in the middle of the driveway with her hand on the car door before she realized he'd pulled up to the curb and was walking toward her.

"Kurt?" she'd exclaimed in a voice laced with fright. "Why are you here?"

"I had to see you," he told her. "You just left. Why didn't you say anything to me?"

"Can we go somewhere?" she asked, looking nervously around.

They went to a nearby diner and had coffee until it was time for lunch. She told him everything that day, and he had been her true confidant ever since. She'd been his as well. But even though he was able to save her, so to speak, the marriage ended quite messily. Her husband dug in and made everything as painful as possible. And although she returned to Safe Tech, she insisted on keeping their relationship purely platonic until her divorce was final. While that time had seemed agonizingly slow, Kurt thought now that their relationship was even more special for having been built on the solid rock of friendship and genuine respect.

That was more than three years ago. Of course she

would marry him, Kurt told himself. She was still young enough that they could have children. He would do that for her. He had always sworn to himself that he would never have another wife and certainly not another child. But . . . well, he really believed that it was what Annie would have wanted him to do. He never told anyone, not even Jill, but instead of talking to himself, he talked to Annie, as he had done since the day she died. And so he knew that she wanted him to do this, to marry this wonderful woman—to make himself happy, and to make her happy as well.

The tears were now close to spilling from the corners of his eyes. *Oh God, Annie,* he said to himself. *You know I wouldn't do this if I didn't think you really wanted me to.*

"Jill," he said out loud, closing his fingers around the velvet box and taking it from the pocket of his blazer, "I have to tell you something. I mean, I have to ask you something . . ."

She gave him a puzzled look, which transformed into something between fear and excitement. He opened his mouth to speak, then stopped.

"I just . . ."

"Yes?" she said softly.

"I love you so much," he said, exhaling his words as he fumbled with the box, "and I want to know if you'll marry me . . ."

He placed the black velvet box on the linen tablecloth in front of her and opened it to reveal the enormous yellow gem.

*   *   *

Jill felt an indescribable numbness. It was unlike any other combination of emotions she'd ever known before: pure joy mixed with a sense of relief so strong it was almost painful. This was exactly what she wanted. It was what she'd hoped for, even though lately she had begun to despair.

As her good friend Talia always told her, she was smart in everything but men. The two had been friends since high school, and they were roommates at Cornell. Through the years, Talia would openly marvel at Jill's ineptness when it came to relationships with the opposite sex. "Your IQ drops from a ski size to a shoe size," she was fond of saying.

And until this moment, because of her past, Jill had irrationally suspected that something with Kurt was about to go wrong. Their relationship had matured to the point where the next logical step was marriage, but that seemed almost too good to be true. Part of her apprehension came from the notion that she was getting old. She was secretly desperate to have a child, and time was running out. She felt the panic of a final exam coming to a close with a dozen pages left to finish. The unwarranted thought of having to find someone new and start all over from the beginning again filled her with horror.

All that was annihilated in an instant. Tears streamed down her face. Words backed up in her throat, but a bubbling laughter escaped in their stead and she nodded her head vigorously and left her chair to throw her arms around his neck.

Kurt laughed too and said, "I guess that's a yes . . ."

"Of course it is," she said, embracing him with all her might.

"Then can I kiss you?"

Jill kissed him, gently at first and then passionately before breaking, rising up from his lap and composing herself as best she could. She put the ring on her finger. Then they clasped hands over the table and beamed at each other in silence for several moments.

"Are you happy?" he asked.

"I've never been happier," she told him. "When can we be married?"

Kurt laughed tolerantly and replied, "Whenever you want. Tomorrow."

"Kurt, really," she said, her smile reaching up and touching the corners of her eyes.

"I mean it," he said. "Whenever you want."

"Mr. Ford?"

Kurt swung his head around with the smile still fixed on his face.

"Mr. Ford," the manager said in a distressed, apologetic tone. "I have an emergency phone call for you, sir."

Jill saw the alarm on Kurt's face, and her stomach dropped a million miles. She'd never received such a phone call, but she knew Kurt had. Its meaning was written clearly on the manager's face. Her expression was a universal sign. The harbinger of death.

"You can take it in my office," the manager said under her breath. The Glen Haven Inn was at the far south end of the lake, where the steep ridges of the lofty hills prevented the use of cell phones.

Kurt offered Jill a faded smile and gave her hand one last gentle squeeze before he rose from the table and followed the manager inside. With a blank face, Jill watched him cross the veranda. She fought against it, but her instincts told her that, like a young girl being rudely awakened from a dream, the most magical moment in her life was now over.

CHAPTER 2

Kurt entered the office and picked up the phone. It was his sister Gracie.

"Oh my God, Kurtis," she said, wailing into the phone, her words broken into sharp fragments. "Oh my God . . . my God . . . he's . . . dead. Oh, Kurtis . . . I'm so . . . sorry. It's Collin . . . Kurtis . . . our little . . . our little boy is . . . dead."

Kurt solemnly gathered up Jill and raced back up the lake to his own house, where two New York state troopers were waiting with Gracie. The night wind whipped through his hair, and Kurt was oblivious as the boat smashed its way through the thickening chop on the water. His mind was filled with Gracie's words about their little boy.

In truth, Collin had been Gracie's boy as much as Kurt's. When his mother died, the child was only two. Kurt was in Dallas then, a young agent, learning the basics of his craft out in the field. And being an agent in the Secret Service meant that he was constantly in the rotation of the protection detail. He would be gone for weeks at a time following the president, the vice president, or foreign heads of state all across the country, activities that weren't conducive to rearing a little boy. Several months after Annie's death, Kurt's supervisor called him in and kindly asked if he still planned on making a career of the Service. If he did, then he'd have to make some accommodations.

Gracie was in upstate New York at the time, living with their sick mother and working as a bank teller in Albany. In eighteen years she had never ended a day with a drawer that didn't balance, not once. She was happy to tell you about it too. Kurt had been the youngest of seven. Gracie was the oldest and had never been married. She was a devout Catholic; everyone always wondered why she hadn't simply become a nun. Her spirit was strong—all you had to do was cross her to find that out—and she was reclusive and showed little interest in men.

Kurt was too young to know about any of that growing up. He just thought of Gracie as a kind of second mother. She had been ever since their mother had fallen into a protracted illness when Kurt was just a baby. Their father worked fourteen-hour days for the railroad until he died of lung cancer when Kurt was only six.

When that happened, Kurt's second-oldest sister, Colleen, had assumed the care of their sick mother. Gracie, however, had always coveted Kurtis Andrew. She didn't show it outwardly, but Kurt was convinced that she welcomed the move to Dallas. He even caught her on occasion whistling cheerfully to herself. That's how he thought of Gracie in those early days, dressed in a gray cotton shift and an apron, taking clothes down off the line in the backyard and whistling to herself. It seemed that a baby of Kurt's was just as good as one of her own.

So that was how it had been, the three of them, a somewhat untraditional family unit, with Gracie doting on Collin when Kurt was away, and Kurt doting on him when he was home.

Kurt pulled deftly into his boathouse and ran up the walk with Jill trailing silently behind him. The two state troopers were waiting for him in the entryway. The sergeant offered his sympathy and gave Kurt the number of a police detective from Alexandria, who proceeded to tell Kurt something worse than he had ever imagined: The boy he or Gracie would have killed for . . . had killed himself.

"You're wrong," Kurt told the detective bitterly into the phone.

"I'm sorry, Mr. Ford," the man replied. "It was pretty conclusive . . . I'm sorry."

"You don't know my son. My son wouldn't kill himself, Detective," Kurt said, his blood rising. "So you just get your head right from here on in about that. I know how this goes. I was in law enforcement, Detective. You see something that looks a certain way, but I'm telling you I know my son wouldn't kill himself. Never."

"Mr. Ford," the detective said calmly, "we'd like you to come down here. We're in the process of trying to get your son's fingerprints from the Secret Service, but we'd like you to make a visual identification if you would."

"I'll be there tonight."

"I don't know if you can get a flight this late—"

"I have access to a plane, Detective," Kurt said insistently. "I'm on my way. In the meantime, would you please tell your captain that I would like to see him and let him know that I'm a former Secret Service agent. Tell him I'm coming down there and I want to see him and talk to him. I want this investigation to proceed like it's a murder. My son would never kill himself. This is *not* a suicide."

Kurt slammed down the phone harder than he meant to and turned scowling at the two troopers standing there like a pair of oafs in the towering entryway.

"Thank you, Officers," he said curtly. His face was set, his emotions contained. "This isn't— Thank you."

He looked over his shoulder at the rumpled form of his sister where she'd thrown herself down on the couch in the living room. Jill was sitting beside her, gently rubbing her back and occasionally leaning over to mutter some heartfelt consolation. Kurt saw the troopers out the door and went back to Gracie's side. Kneeling down next to her, he put his arms around her and held her tightly. Gently, he stroked the back of her head while she shook and sobbed.

"It'll be all right," he murmured. "It'll be all right."

Inside, Kurt Ford felt empty. The agony, he knew, was there—sealed off like a big cat, rumbling furiously behind the door of its cage. When it got out, it would tear him apart. It would maul him from the inside out, and he really didn't know if there would be anything left by the time it was done. But for now he knew he had to keep it contained. Before he let it destroy him, he would find out what had happened to his son, and he would avenge his death. That much he knew.

"Can I go with you?"

"With me?" Kurt said quietly. He stood up, his eyes drawing a focus on Jill. Her face, pretty in its distress, reminded him so much of that same day he'd just been thinking about earlier, the day he had gone to rescue her from that other life. But that seemed to him now like a good movie he'd seen years ago. Through his haze of anguish it elicited only disjointed scraps of emotion that seemed not just jumbled, but far away and unimportant.

A lunatic demon in the back of his mind jumped out, screaming that this was what he deserved. Annie hadn't really wanted him to give his life to another woman. It was he, kidding himself, fortifying his own selfishness by pretending to know what she would have wanted. Collin was all that had been left of Annie, and on the day he had defiled her memory by asking another woman to replace her, fate had snatched him away too.

Still, for all that, he couldn't help the way he felt. He looked lovingly at Jill, his only lifeline in a lonely and torrential sea of grief. All he had to do was grab hold of her and he felt certain she could keep him from drowning in the horror. He touched her face gently with the back of his fingers.

"You can't go alone," she said. Her expression was distorted by pity.

Kurt closed his eyes briefly. "I'll be all right. I'm more worried about Gracie." He reached down and gently rubbed Gracie's back.

"Do you want me to stay with her, Kurt?" Jill asked. "Would that be the best thing?"

"I think it would," he told her quietly in a strangled voice. "I really think it would."

Kurt's plane touched down in the bright moonlight. He hopped into a rented Suburban that was waiting for him on the tarmac and drove himself straight to the morgue. The detective, whose name was Olander, met him at the door with a mousy-looking partner, a young woman with a drab head of long hair and thick glasses. Olander introduced her without fanfare as Detective Carol Dipper. Dipper looked apologetically at the floor, and the three of them went into a small office where a television with a VCR rested on a battered gray metal desk.

"What's this?" Kurt asked as Olander removed a VCR tape from a shelf over the desk and began to insert it into the machine.

"You can identify the body on videotape," Olander said as he fiddled with the buttons.

"It's easier that way, Mr. Ford," Carol Dipper whispered.

"No," Kurt said. "Take me to— I want to see him."

Olander regarded him blandly with a frown. Dipper looked pained. "Okay," Olander said. "If that's what you want. We can do that."

Olander picked up the phone and talked briefly to an assistant M.E.; then the three of them descended a wide set of stairs to where the bodies were kept. The piercing smell of formaldehyde filled their nostrils, growing

stronger until they were standing in front of a stainless
steel cart burdened with a sheet-covered body.

Kurt Ford looked without emotion. He felt strangely
cold as the assistant M.E. drew the sheet down over
Collin's face, exposing his bare shoulders.

"Is that your son, Mr. Ford?" Olander asked
solemnly.

Collin's face was badly discolored. It looked like his
son. Could it be someone else? Could the whole thing
be a bizarre trick? No, it was Collin.

"That's my son," Kurt said in a hoarse whisper. He
was outside himself. He was spinning. When Annie had
died, he thought nothing could ever wound him so
deeply or cast his mind so near to the boundaries of insanity. But now this.

The assistant M.E. mercifully pulled the sheet right
back up over Collin's face. Kurt looked away. He returned to his truck and followed the two detectives back
to headquarters.

It didn't take more than a few minutes for Kurt to peg
Marshal Olander. He was a hardened cop who'd been
on the job too long, a miserable bastard, potbellied,
stooped. He was still on the good side of fifty, but even
so, his scalp had retained only a few patches of wispy
blond hair around his ears. His eyes were narrow and
dark, set amid the prodigious circles of an insomniac.
His nose, also narrow, also prodigious, gave his whole
face the aspect of a starved ferret. To provide some visual point of demarcation between his sunken chin and
his strangely thick neck, he wore a close-cut dirty blond
beard.

His partner, the woman named Dipper, was apparently inconsequential. Olander tolerated her the way a rhino tolerates one of the birds that picks the bugs off its leathery back.

While they waited for the captain, Kurt sat patiently and answered what to him was a meaningless set of questions about his son. No, Collin didn't suffer from any mental illnesses; he hadn't been depressed; there was no reason for him to have been that way.

Kurt felt as if he were walking a razor's edge. He wanted Olander to know that he could come down on him like an avalanche. A few well-placed calls to the dozen or so senators and congressmen he knew—not to mention some old friends within the Service who might even be able to get the old man himself to pick up the phone—could make everyone's life miserable. But the more he observed the detective, the more he had the discouraging sense that Olander was beyond caring. He was a man comfortably locked into his civil service position, with one eye on his pension, impervious to pressure from above.

When the captain, whose name was Jim Todd, came in, Kurt tried not to show his irritation. The captain was Kurt's age, but looked ten years older with his thinning gray hair and the frumpy look of a cop who has spent most of his time behind a desk. The two of them shook hands while Todd nervously turned a pink Canadian Mint over and over between his two smoke-stained front teeth. Kurt then explained as calmly as he could that he hoped they didn't think he was overreacting, but he knew Collin better than anyone did and he knew his son wouldn't commit suicide.

The police listened patiently, but Kurt knew damn well what they were thinking. He was simply a distraught parent. They knew a suicide when they saw one. The kid ate his gun. They wanted to close it out and go on. Real murders remained unsolved. The police were busy people, only giving him the courtesy of their time because he was someone who might be important.

"Why don't you tell him what we've got, Marshal," the captain said politely after a pause. He too seemed to overlook the young woman who sat with her head slightly inclined toward the floor but whose eyes Kurt noticed darted quickly from one man to another.

Olander sighed and went through what they knew. Collin had gone out for drinks with some friends. He met a girl at the bar called Harpoon Alley and left with her not long after. It wasn't anything unusual. Where the two of them went, no one knew, but at some point in the night he returned home. They had no idea how much time he'd spent with the girl, but there was nothing in his town house to indicate that she had returned with him. There was an empty bottle of beer on the coffee table. After finishing the bottle, Collin had presumably gone upstairs, taken off his clothes, and "inflicted the gunshot wound to his head," as Olander put it.

"We got the call at around three-thirty this afternoon," Olander continued. "The one friend, Lou Myslinski, was supposed to pick up your son and go to a baseball game. The door was unlocked, and he found him upstairs."

"What about this girl?" Kurt said suddenly, excitedly. "We've got to find her!"

Olander looked at him with a blank face, then at his captain.

"Mr. Ford," the captain said patiently, "I can't imagine how you must feel. I know you were in the Secret Service at one time, but I have to level with you. Detective Olander is one of the best homicide detectives in the capital area. This is his bailiwick. If this were a homicide, we'd be all over it."

"It is a homicide!" Kurt erupted, half rising out of his chair. "Can't you see? We have to find that woman!"

The small room was uncomfortably silent for a few moments.

"Mr. Ford," Olander said in a flat tone, "there was nothing to suggest that this wasn't a suicide. There was no sign of forced entry. There was no sign that anyone else was even there. There was no sign of resistance at all, no bruise or cut marks to suggest an altercation of any kind, nothing to make anyone think that it was anything but what we've determined it to be."

Kurt looked at the man's uncaring face and he knew that nothing would change Olander's mind. Kurt Ford's genius wasn't in designing the encryption systems that had made Safe Tech a player in the field of technology. He left the esoteric part of his business to a bunch of MIT Ph.D.s. Kurt's gift was with people. He could read them. He knew what he couldn't get and what he could. And he knew how to ask for what he could get. He was rarely emotional about it. It was as objective to him as the moves on a chessboard.

He turned his eyes to the captain. "Captain," he said, subduing a quaver in his voice, "I'm not some rummy who calls you every Tuesday night to complain about the kids in the back alley. I'm a former cop, even if it wasn't what you guys do. Look, I'm no crackpot. I'm telling you I know my son wouldn't have done this. Would you at least dust the house to see if anyone else was there? Could you do that for me and try to find this woman at least to talk to her?"

The captain pursed his lips and considered Kurt. "Okay, Mr. Ford," he said. "I want to help you as much as I can. I really do. But I have to be realistic too. I'll send the lab over there tomorrow to dust it up, and Marshal will do what he can to find out about that woman. If we can find her, we'll certainly interview her, but I'm not making any guarantees. It might not be possible . . ."

"I appreciate that, Captain," Kurt said. "I really do." He turned to Olander. "Should I just stay in touch with you, Detective?"

Olander looked blandly at Kurt and then again to his captain.

"I think," the captain said, "it would be better if I was the one who acted as your point of contact, Mr. Ford. I can keep track of the big picture and let you know."

"Tomorrow?"

The captain looked at his watch and with a heavy sigh said, "I'll see if I can get the lab out there, but it might not be until Monday morning. I can give you a call at home—"

"I'll be at the Ritz-Carlton in Pentagon City," Kurt interrupted.

"There's no need for that," Captain Todd said affably. "We'll do everything we can. I'm sure you'll want to get back to make arrangements . . ."

"Nothing is more important than this, Captain," Kurt said as he stood.

He was opening the door to his rented Suburban when he heard a call from behind.

"Mr. Ford!" It was the woman, Carol Dipper. She was hurrying toward him with an awkward gait somewhere between a walk and a jog. Under her arm was a large three-ring binder. She stopped in front of him, and, before she could catch her breath, blurted out, "I have something you should see."

CHAPTER 3

Kurt waited. Carol Dipper stood before him, breathing hard. Her eyes flickered between his face and the binder while she pushed her glasses back up on her nose and tucked a few stray strands of hair behind her ears. Then her eyes lit on just him and said, "I think you might be right about your son."

Kurt observed her with a fresh perspective. Her owlish eyes looked enormous through the thick curve of her lenses in the bright halogen light of the parking lot. There was intelligence there and, once she was free from her superiors, even a hint of determination.

"I want you to see this," she said. She opened the binder and paged through a set of glossy photos. They were crime scene shots from Collin's bedroom, gruesome and bloody. The boy lay face up, naked, his hand loosely encircling the gun that was stuck up inside his mouth.

Dipper looked up at Kurt and blinked nervously. "Are you all right to look at these?"

Kurt nodded grimly.

"You see the blood?" she asked.

"Yes."

"There was no exit wound," Dipper said. Then, in an academic tone, she continued: "An exit wound from a self-inflicted gunshot wound to the head with a nine-millimeter actually occurs in only sixty-nine percent of the cases, so it's not unusual at all that there isn't one here. Also, as you know, the Secret Service uses a special load—"

"A super-vel," Kurt said, scowling. It was a soft slug, meant to enter and do maximum damage while also minimizing the danger of exiting the body and harming innocent bystanders. It was the standard load for an agent's gun. "What's your point?"

"You see the blood?" she asked again.

"Yes." There was blood all over the bed, from one side to the other.

"My dad was a funeral director," Dipper explained, "and I was an investigator for the M.E.'s office in Richmond before I came here. So I know about these things. What happens with a wound like this is if the bullet strikes the brain stem, the person dies instantly. Sometimes, and— Are you okay with this?"

"I am," he said. His mouth was pressed tightly closed.

"Sometimes, if the bullet enters the posterior region of the brain, the person can— It takes some time. They don't die right away. I'm sorry, but that's what I think happened with your son."

"How does that help me?" Kurt said, icy and irritated.

Dipper looked at him strangely. "The gun is in his

mouth and his fingers are wrapped around it," she said gently. "If he shot himself and lived long enough to convulse and spread that blood all over the bed, then the gun shouldn't still have been in his mouth."

Kurt looked at her incredulously. It was like the simple solution to a mind-bending riddle, impossible at first, obvious once revealed. Of course she was right.

"Didn't you tell this to them?" he asked.

Carol Dipper looked around nervously. "I said something at the scene but . . . well, Detective Olander has been doing this a long time. I'm really new here; I'm sure you guessed that. He told me it was a grounder and that was that." Then she added, "I think that's what he really believes."

"A grounder?"

"Something easy," she explained. "A case that you don't have to work very hard to solve. He thought it was clearly a suicide. It's possible. I've seen lots of strange things with dead bodies. Almost anything is possible. It's just that I don't know if that's what this was. And now the way you described him . . . Most people can't accept suicide, but most times there's also something there, some kind of depression, some sign to someone that this kind of thing might be going to happen. Please don't say I said any of this to you . . .

"I don't know . . ." she continued, shaking her head dubiously. "The blood all over the sheets . . . and that gun, they bother me. I have to go."

The young woman turned abruptly and headed for the building.

"Thank you," Kurt called after her, feeling a sudden

and overwhelming sense of gratitude. What she said made perfect sense, and while he had insisted that Collin didn't commit suicide, there had been a horrible sliver of doubt in his own mind. That was now gone.

The nausea came upon him unexpectedly like a rogue wave. His mind abruptly regurgitated the images he'd just seen and his body followed suit. Kurt bent over and vomited on the pavement, splattering his shoes with flecks of what remained from dinner. When there was nothing left, his stomach gave three final wrenching heaves before he began to cough and spit his mouth clean. He closed his eyes and leaned against the truck door to catch his breath. There was nothing more to do than drive himself to the Ritz-Carlton in Pentagon City.

There would be plenty to do in the morning.

Because they dealt with these kinds of investigations all the time, the best chance of finding a killer was with the local homicide detectives. Kurt knew that while different government agencies had their strong points, none of them could investigate a murder as effectively as a good homicide cop. The problem was that Olander and Todd weren't really handling it like a murder.

Kurt knew from the look on Olander's face that any effort he expended trying to find the woman Collin was last seen with would be perfunctory at best. He also knew that that woman was the key. Any investigation of this sort began with a time line, and there was a lot of time missing right now. The mysterious woman was the only one who could complete the picture. And if the cops weren't going to find her, he'd do it himself. He wondered if the young detective, Dipper, could be any help. Probably not; she wasn't going to do anything to buck her superiors.

At least he'd gotten them to dust the house. Anything they did would be a plus, and if he found something that supported his theory, he'd go back to the captain and get them to do more. But a murder trail went cold fast, and he knew that if something valuable didn't turn up within a week, the likelihood of ever knowing the truth was remote.

When he checked into his hotel, the desk clerk told Kurt he had two messages. She slid a white envelope across the granite desktop before proceeding with his registration. He tore it open. One message was from Jill. She wanted him to know that she loved him and she was there if he needed her. Kurt allowed the warmth of her words to comfort him, but only for a moment before he folded the paper and slipped it into his pocket.

The next message astonished him. It was from David Claiborne. Claiborne was slightly younger than Kurt, but years ago the two of them had served together as rookie agents in Dallas.

While most people had considered Claiborne's brazen style slightly obnoxious, Kurt always called him a friend. Occasionally the two of them had gone down to the Cayman Islands on dive trips. Then Kurt was selected from the field to serve on the Secret Service's CAT team. CAT, the Counter Assassination Team, was the Secret Service's covert strike force within the Uniformed Division. As a group, the team was almost unseen by the public except for the agents who rode in the vehicle that preceded the president in a motorcade. To be selected for such duty was a high honor for the agents who aspired to it. They were the physical elite of the service, and while Claiborne too had attempted to become a CAT team member, he had been passed over.

Besides the CAT team, the Uniformed Division provided the armed guards at the White House as well as the snipers who covered the tops of buildings wherever the president went. Protection agents wore plain clothes and formed the perimeters to provide security for the chief executive. In varying numbers, they were with him at all times, and when he traveled, their numbers were supplemented with investigation agents from the field.

After a few years on the CAT team, where he quickly rose in the ranks, Kurt was offered an ASAIC position—Assistant to the Special Agent in Charge in the Presidential Protection Division. After Dallas, the two friends had drifted apart. Even when Claiborne was rotated in on protection detail for the president, he and Kurt didn't come into contact with each other. The CAT team, as part of the Uniformed Division, was in a different section of the Service from the Protection and Investigation Divisions, and while there was no animosity between the groups, they were very distinct entities with divergent duties.

When Kurt left the Service to form Safe Tech, he had received a call from Claiborne. His friend had heard rumor of his venture and offered up his services to assist in the formation of the new business. "The Service," Claiborne had told Kurt, "isn't the place where someone of my abilities can maximize his potential."

Kurt politely declined his friend's offer, not thinking Claiborne could offer anything to his nascent company that he didn't already have. Not long after, he heard that Claiborne had finally made it out of the field and into protection, and that had assuaged his guilt at not having hired him.

When Collin joined the Service, Kurt learned that his old friend had advanced even further. He was occupying the job Kurt had held when he left: one of only three ASAICs who worked under the Special Agent in Charge of the Presidential Protection Division. It had taken Claiborne almost twenty years to reach the position Kurt held as a young man. That must have bothered Claiborne, who had always had grand aspirations. Nevertheless, even with Collin working underneath him, neither Claiborne nor Kurt had gotten around to contacting the other.

Kurt wondered how his former colleague knew that he was even in the capital. Possibly after he heard about Collin's death, he'd called the house and spoken with Gracie. She'd remember him. That was certain. Kurt smiled to himself. Claiborne was a small man, but good-looking to the point of being almost pretty. Every woman Kurt ever knew remembered David Claiborne. It was too bad that so much time had gone by during which neither of them had bothered to call the other, and that it took a tragedy to precipitate a reunion.

The message was simple. Call David Claiborne on his cell phone. It was important.

Kurt looked at the round brass clock behind the desk. It was two-thirty, but important meant call anytime, day or night, and he knew it had something to do with Collin. He took the elevator up to his room. When he got there, the phone was ringing. Kurt hurried to pick it up. It was Claiborne.

"David," Kurt said, feeling that old familiarity immediately, "I was just going to call you. I got your message."

"Listen, Kurt," Claiborne said in a hushed tone, "I'm sorry about Collin. I'm incredibly sorry."

Kurt said nothing.

"I need to talk to you, but I'm supervising a shift right now. Can you meet me tomorrow?"

"Of course," Kurt said. "But why?"

"I can't talk," Claiborne said. "I have to see you. It's about Collin. Meet me at the Thomas Cole rotunda at the National Gallery tomorrow at noon. Make sure no one follows you. Kurt, make sure!" Then he hung up.

CHAPTER 4

Kurt stood looking at the phone. His mind was sprinting in circles. After a while, he unpacked his things and went to the window. He drew back the heavy golden drapes and stared for a while out at the stars and the light-polluted horizon beyond the Pentagon. He reminded himself again that there was nothing he could do at this hour and if David Claiborne was on duty, he certainly couldn't be expected to break away. Part of him wanted to head for the White House and pound on the gates.

The best thing for Kurt would be some sleep, but he knew his body wouldn't rest. The alternative was simple. He dug into his shaving kit and found a small bottle of Halcyon, a powerful sleeping pill. He took two, removed his clothes, and lay down in the bed staring up at the ceiling. Naked, flat on his back in bed, a sudden and gruesome image sprang to life in his head: his son's dead body in the police photos. Kurt's mind tumbled recklessly from one possibility to another, tormented, until at last, mercifully, the drug overcame him.

* * *

The rotunda that contained Thomas Cole's four-part allegorical depiction of the life of man was one of Kurt's favorite museum exhibits in the world. He didn't care that it wasn't impressionist or done by one of the more famous European painters. He cared about its meaning. He cared about the room, the building, and the capital city that was its home. For all his worldliness, Kurt believed in America and he held a special place in his heart for her greatest artists, authors, statesmen, and scientists. It was, he told those who knew him best, the greatest society in the short history of mankind.

The museum was busy, and after a few minutes of searching for Claiborne in the milling crowd of visitors, he decided that he had been the first to arrive. For over an hour, he had conducted a series of evasive maneuvers in and around the Mall, including quick trips in three different cabs. He had taken his old friend's warning quite seriously.

As his eyes wandered from one painting to the next, he tried to recall whether David Claiborne knew about his affinity for this place or if it was merely a coincidence that he'd asked to meet there. He couldn't remember when he'd first discovered the rotunda. Events from the distant past seemed to run together, and although he was fairly certain he hadn't spent much time with David since he left Dallas, he couldn't be sure. On the other hand, Secret Service agents, even former ones, didn't typically believe in coincidence. They were highly trained, as they joked among themselves, in the art of paranoia.

Kurt wondered how much of that paranoia he had retained, how much it had helped him to succeed in the business of computer encryption and security—and how much of it had returned in the sixteen hours since he learned of his son's unusual death. His eyes came to rest on Cole's painting of Youth, a young man not unlike Collin with his hand firmly fixed on the rudder of his baroque canoe. In the distance, an immense and incredible palace arose from the clouds—the hopes and dreams of youth. The eyes of the boy were fixed there in the sky, and only the viewer could see the impending bend in the stream of life that soon promised disaster.

Kurt moved clockwise in the decorative rotunda to the scene of adulthood. Three demons emerged from the tumultuous, inky sky above the boy who had become a man, who struggled amid the angry tempest in the now rudderless craft. Although murder lingered nearby, the most pernicious demon—and Kurt had always felt this way—was suicide. Again, he wondered if there was a reason for his old friend's choice of this particular place.

"You're sure no one followed you?"

Kurt glanced to his right. A grayer and somehow wilted version of the small, handsome man he had once known stood beside him, apparently contemplating the painting. He'd spoken softly, but his words still had that same imperious ring to them that had always made Kurt smile while others grew irritated.

"I'm sure," he said, turning back to the painting himself, his attention focused on the periphery of his vision where Claiborne now stood. It was a strange reintroduction after so many years.

"Then follow me," Claiborne said flatly. He turned and left the rotunda.

Kurt followed at a moderate distance through the crowded gallery that separated the American painters from the Europeans. When Claiborne reached the immense dome in the center of the building, he looked back to make sure Kurt hadn't lost him. Then he turned to his right until he reached the stairs. He descended slowly, looking over his shoulder before turning off down a long empty hall and darting through an unmarked wooden door.

Kurt followed, glancing around before letting himself in and closing the door gently behind him. Claiborne had already physically separated himself from Kurt by sitting behind a small desk littered with knickknacks, among them a little statue of a golfer made from copper wire. It was the cramped office of a maintenance supervisor.

"Lock the door," Claiborne said. "Have a seat."

Kurt threw the bolt. In the instant before he turned around, he worried that David might harbor some bitterness at his refusal to hire him years ago. The men Kurt had hired on were now multimillionaires. But the thought was fleeting, and when he did turn around, Claiborne seemed to have relaxed somewhat.

The two of them grasped hands across the desk like old friends. Claiborne said, "I'm sorry, Kurt. I don't know what to say."

"I'm sorry I didn't bring you on with Safe Tech, David," Kurt blurted out. "I had no idea it would become what it did. If I'd known the way things were going to work out, I would have taken you with me."

Claiborne's face suddenly broke out in a congenial smile and he swatted the air above his head, saying, "Don't think anything about that, Kurt. That was a long time ago and I forgot all about it . . . I do pretty good for myself. I've got a nice brownstone in Georgetown. I drive a Lexus. Things are good . . .

"No," he continued, his face darkening in consternation, "no, this is so far beyond anything like that . . . I just don't know what to say or how to start . . ."

Kurt eyed him closely. Time and care had worn the edges off his old friend. Claiborne looked to be in good enough shape, but there was something subtly shabby about him. Maybe it was the incongruity of his clothes, or the pungent and expensive cologne he wore. Claiborne was dressed like a much younger man. It was as though his attempt to hide his age only accentuated it. The tight black silk shirt under his stylish olive four-buttoned Country Road jacket contrasted sharply with his faded blond hair and the liver spots that were beginning to populate the backs of his hands. Or maybe it was the once-pretty face that now sagged slightly at the jowls and drooped at the corners of his yellowing eyes. Kurt was reminded of a brilliant bouquet of flowers forgotten in their vase, not yet dried and dusty, but wilted and marred at the edges by the hint of decay.

"I think someone killed your boy," Claiborne said abruptly.

Kurt felt his mouth sag open.

"I think it's possible they might try to do the same to me," the agent added curtly.

"Who are they?" Kurt asked incredulously. "Why? What the hell is going on, David?"

Claiborne drew a deep breath and held it. He let his gaze drift past the metal blinds and through the small window that looked out over the sculpture garden across the street. "Four weeks ago," he began, exhaling, "the old man made an off-the-record move at three A.M. I was running the shift."

Kurt gave him a puzzled look. An off-the-record move meant the president just suddenly announced that he was going somewhere. It didn't happen often, but when it did, it created a special sort of anxiety for the agents on duty.

"Mack Taylor was with him," Claiborne said.

"The SAIC?" Kurt said. It was strange that the Special Agent in Charge would be on duty at such an hour.

Claiborne nodded. "Yes. The two of them got into the limo with a driver, and I got into the chase car with three other agents . . .

"One of them was your son," he added somberly.

After a deliberate pause, he continued. "There were two others. One was killed two weeks ago in a carjacking, and the other disappeared five days after the . . . the incident. No one's heard from her, including her parents."

"What the hell happened?" Kurt asked for the second time. "How come no one knows about this?"

"Oh, people know," Claiborne said flatly. "But no one is saying anything inside the Service. You know how that is. Of course the public doesn't know. The families know about their own kids, but they don't know that other agents have . . . have been killed."

Kurt was flabbergasted. A conspiracy within the Secret Service itself was unthinkable. "What the hell happened out there?" he demanded.

Claiborne pursed his lips, nodded, and said, "We drove out to Maryland to some old farmhouse in the middle of nowhere. To be honest with you, at the time I was thinking some CIA safe house. I still don't know for sure." Again, his gaze drifted out the window, and he continued as if in a trance. "Anyway, we got off the main road and went up a long drive through some trees and the old man hops out with Mack Taylor and heads for the front door. Taylor tells me he'll take care of everything on the inside and for me to take the perimeter. These kids were all nervous about it. I don't think any of them had been on an off-the-record move before, but I sent two out back to watch the door, your son and the girl. I stayed in front with the other kid.

"Nothing happened. We stood around for an hour or so and then Mack Taylor calls me and says to go check out the cars, that they're coming out. I leave the kid in front, tell your son and the girl to come back around, and I walk over to the cars to look them over. They were still in the drive, hidden from the house by a row of trees. Then all of a sudden, I hear someone yelling."

Claiborne looked directly at Kurt now, as if to gauge his level of comprehension. "So I start to run for the house and I see some pushing and shoving. Someone's going ballistic on the old man, but they get whoever it was back into the house before I get there and then they all start coming toward me.

"No one said anything, but I could see from the faces on these kids that something weird happened. They looked like they saw a ghost. The old man was ruffled a little and his face was flushed, but he seemed fine, and when I looked at Mack Taylor, I could tell by his face not to ask any questions. So we get the old man and Taylor loaded into the limo and we all pile into our car and drive back to the White House. No one said boo and I wasn't going to ask."

Claiborne raised his hand and briefly rubbed his eyes. "But the way I figure it, whoever the old man went to see came out of the house after him, pissed off. And whoever it was, nobody wanted to talk about the fact that they saw him."

"But who?" Kurt asked.

Claiborne shrugged. "I don't know, Kurt. I don't want to know. I just hope they don't think I saw more than I did. It had to be someone that the president wasn't supposed to be with. More than that, I figure it was someone he couldn't be with and it had to be someone those kids would recognize. Otherwise, why would he have them taken out?"

Kurt looked intently into Claiborne's eyes to see if he was for real. "Do you realize what you're saying?" he hissed, his own face awash with disbelief.

Claiborne looked down at the backs of his hands, then rubbed his eyes again before he looked up and returned Kurt's stare with matching intensity. "Yes," he said, jutting out his chin. "I do. I think the president had three of his own agents killed. I think they saw something they shouldn't have, and he had them taken out. What else can I think?"

"But they'd know that you would put the whole thing together," Kurt argued. "They'd have to know that you'd see what was happening!"

Claiborne nodded slowly and quietly said, "That's why I probably shouldn't be talking to you, Kurt. I'm hoping that they think I know better than to say anything. Besides, whoever it was, and whatever they said, I didn't see or hear it. I can't implicate the old man, so I'm no real threat unless I start asking questions.

"Hey, you know how things can be. Think about when Hoover was running the FBI. If the right people have their hands on the controls, they can do what they want. They can take out almost anyone, even if it raises eyebrows. It still comes down to proof, and after some initial whispering at happy hour, even the people inside the Service will just write off what happened as three unlucky agents. One disappears, so that's not even a murder. One's killed during a robbery, which happens from time to time around here. It's not unheard of. And one . . . one commits suicide, maybe because he's depressed over what's happened to his friends. The point is, it can all be explained . . . The whole thing could be just a coincidence."

Kurt looked at him sharply at mention of the word. "What about Mack Taylor?" he asked.

Claiborne narrowed his eyes, and Kurt thought he saw the first flicker of emotion since their interview began. It was hatred. He spewed out his words. "Mack

Taylor would gun down his mother if the old man told him to."

"We're talking about the Secret Service, David!" Kurt said testily. "Not a street gang."

Kurt still held the Service and its agents in high regard. When he was a boy, he had been with his sister in a diner in their small town outside Albany, New York, when Eisenhower came in and ate a grilled cheese and tomato sandwich. Kurt never forgot the men who surrounded him, serious-looking, authoritative, and strong, the men who protected the most powerful man on earth. After that, while other boys pretended to be Dick Tracy or the Lone Ranger in the woods that bordered the village, Kurt played the role of a Secret Service agent protecting the president.

Collin had adopted his father's respect for the Service. Despite being well-off, Kurt had raised the boy with a focus on personal integrity. Unlike a lot of people with money, Kurt didn't keep score based on the size of a person's bank account. And he had taught his son from an early age that integrity was the most important thing about anyone. He also told his son that the men in the Service were somehow a cut above other men.

"You're talking insane," he protested to Claiborne. "A SAIC would never gun someone down!"

"I didn't say he did," Claiborne retorted severely. "I'm just saying he would. Or he'd get someone else to. And you say it's not like a street gang, but I say it's like whoever's running it. You know what it's like. It's like the military. You follow orders. We all presume the orders come from the good guys, but sometimes that's not reality. Sometimes the man who lives in the White House is one of the bad guys, and you damn well know it."

"Yeah," Kurt said, knotting his fists, remembering the shameful exploits of some presidents. His voice rose with emotion. "Immoral people, dishonest people, that's one thing—but this?"

Claiborne got up from behind the desk and exhaled impatiently. "I'm not here to argue with you, Kurt. I know what happened. I thought you'd want to know too. I know we don't really know each other anymore, but the Kurt Ford I knew would have wanted to know what happened. I know how much you loved that boy . . .

"Hell," he said bitterly, his eyes boring into Kurt's, his voice thick with emotion, "I remember him when he was riding around on your shoulders in the backyard. I remember you getting drunk down in Grand Cayman and calling to hear his voice and having tears in your eyes when you got done and telling me how much he was like his mother . . ."

The words were like scalding water. Somehow, they were worse than Collin's body or even the horrible police photos. Those things were lifeless, detachable. Memories, though—memories were alive. For a moment, they melted the icy layer that had frozen the inside of Kurt's mind. He shut his eyes and forced back the tears. He wouldn't lose control. He couldn't. He had come to find out what happened to his boy and to do something about it. If he let go now, he might not be able to regain his composure. He might be swept away. He might put a gun in his own mouth . . .

"Shit," his old friend continued gently, rubbing his eyes. "I don't care what you do. Believe me, I know there's nothing I can do. Things like this have happened before. Sometimes people find out about them. Most times, they don't.

"I'm a survivor, Kurt. I know what I can and can't do. I can't stop the old man from whatever it is he's doing and I can't change what he's done. I can only save my ass and hope the next guy in that office is better."

He got up and walked to the door. Kurt continued to sit there, his hands now slowly massaging his temples. Suddenly and unexpectedly, he felt Claiborne's hand on his shoulder. His iron grip was surprising.

"I'm sorry, Kurt," he said.

Kurt just sat.

Somewhere in the back of his mind, he heard the door quietly close. The register by the window began to rattle, emitting a gentle flow of cool air into the room. The second hand on a plastic clock on the desk ticked loudly. The sun outside broke through the clouds and blasted through the slats in the blinds, striping the floor with hot light. Kurt went over in his mind again and again everything he'd heard, ending with the echo of Claiborne's words—*I thought you'd want to know. I know how much you loved that boy.*

It was still almost impossible to believe. But if what Claiborne had said was true—and there was no reason for him to lie—then there *was* something Kurt could do. There was something he would do. He didn't care who the man was, if he was president of the United States or the emperor of China. The man who killed his son was going to die, up close and personal. If what Claiborne said was true, Kurt Ford knew from the bottom of his soul that he was going to kill the president.

CHAPTER 5

An hour's research through periodicals at the nearby Library of Congress confirmed much of what Claiborne had said, at least about what had happened to the other two young agents. It wasn't that Kurt mistrusted Claiborne, but if there was a conspiracy afoot, he wasn't taking anything at face value. Claiborne's story was extraordinary and he wasn't going to act unless he was certain. Strangely, neither of the other deaths got much newspaper coverage, and only an astute reader would have recalled either one of them, let alone connected the two. Including his son's murder, they had each fallen approximately two weeks apart.

Everything so far supported what Claiborne had told him. Still, Kurt was determined to find an actual link between his son, the other dead agents, and the president. If the police wouldn't or couldn't find the girl who was with Collin on the night of his death, he would find her himself. At least he would have to try. He didn't believe that she was a coincidence.

On his way back to the hotel, he called Collin's friend Lou. He asked him to meet him at Harpoon Alley and bring his other friend as well. He could tell the young man wasn't thrilled with the idea, but neither could he say no to the father of his dead friend.

Kurt believed that being in the place they'd last seen Collin might jar their memories and dislodge some detail, no matter how small, that might give him the edge he needed to find the girl. He had already seen the statements each of the friends had given the police, but he also knew that the police interview wasn't thorough. They had been working under the presumption that Collin killed himself.

When he got to the bar, the two young men were already waiting for him. He knew Lou by sight, having taken him with Collin on a dive trip to Antigua when they graduated from Princeton, and also from seeing him occasionally when he was in D.C. on business. Kurt always tried to have dinner with Collin on those occasions, and his son usually brought one or two friends along. Kurt had always kept an open-door policy toward Collin's friends. He believed that if he welcomed his son's friends, he'd see more of his son.

Kurt could tell that Lou and Allen were uneasy. The sweaty pint glasses on the table were nearly empty. Kurt signaled the cocktail waitress for two more, then sat down. Golden afternoon sunlight from the street spilled in through the window and the throngs of Sunday afternoon tourists whose shopping bags cluttered the wooden floor gave the place a festive air, a dire contrast to the crestfallen faces of the three men.

"Mr. Ford," Lou began.

Kurt held up his hand. "Kurt, I always tell you. Call me Kurt."

Instead of complying, Lou simply continued: "We just . . . We're sorry. I'm sorry. I don't know what to say . . ." His lip began to quiver. Allen cleared his throat and muttered something that sounded like, "Me too."

"Listen," Kurt said, looking hard at them. "I appreciate what you're saying. I know this is hard. It's hard for all of us, but I don't want to think about it right now. I don't want you two to think about how you can say the right things to me to make me feel better. I feel the way I feel and I don't want sympathy. I want your help."

He let that sink in.

"Whatever you want," Lou finally said.

"Yes," Allen echoed.

"I want you to remember Friday night," Kurt told them sternly. "That's why I wanted to see you here. I want you to think hard about what you saw. That girl, I think she's the key. Collin didn't kill himself."

The two of them looked embarrassed.

"Hey, listen to me," Kurt said, demanding eye contact. "I'm not some crazy father who can't stomach that his kid committed suicide. Collin was murdered!

"I know what the police are saying," he continued, as if reading their minds, "but there's at least one detective who thinks like I think. The clues aren't what they look like. Look, I don't want to have to go through it. You guys just trust me. I need your help. I need to find this girl. She was probably the last person to see Collin before he was killed. She may have even had something to do with it."

The waitress came with two new pints. Lou finished his old one and looked up at Kurt. "So how can we help?"

Kurt could see that his son's friends didn't fully believe him, but he could also see that they were willing to go along with him and help him as best they could for his sake.

"Tell me what she looked like. Tell me what happened."

"She was very pretty," Lou said.

Allen nodded and added, "She pretty much got everyone's attention. We all saw her when she came in."

"She had this dark hair," Lou continued, "long and straight, and she was pretty with these eyes that were like cat eyes or something. You know, like yellow. I mean really yellow, not like anything you usually see. And she had dark skin like she was Italian or Latino or something."

"And a body," Allen said, "she had a killer body."

"Was she tall?" Kurt asked.

"Yeah," Lou said, "she was."

"His height?"

"About," Lou said. "Yeah, just under six feet."

"And did Collin know her? Had you guys ever seen her before?"

"He did," Lou said. "He said she was the girl he'd been telling me about that he'd seen in his coffee shop. There's a Starbucks a couple blocks from his place that he stops at most mornings before work and he told me that he kept seeing this girl. I guess he spoke to her a few times, but didn't get her name. It was pretty casual, but he definitely recognized her from there."

"So how did Collin end up leaving with her?"

"I don't know how, but he went to talk to her and before too long they got up and left. He didn't say why. We were giving him a hard time," Lou explained with a touch of unnecessary guilt. "You know, three buddies and one gets the eyes from this nice-looking woman so we were just looking on, giving commentary, you know."

Kurt nodded.

"So she said something to him and they got up and left," Lou said.

"He gave us the evil eye," Allen added.

"Wasn't there anything she did or said that you heard?" Kurt asked. "Did Collin say where they were going?"

"He didn't say," Lou said uncomfortably, "but I figured he'd just take her down the street to another place, someplace a little, I don't know, quieter, I guess."

"Why do you say you figured?" Kurt asked.

"Well, I saw them go out and start down toward the water, but then they turned around and went up the street."

"What does that mean?"

Lou shrugged. "I don't know for sure, Mr. Ford, but there isn't much besides shops and town houses if you go up King Street from here. I really thought maybe she lived there and that's where they were going, either that or to her car, but it didn't make sense."

"Why not?"

Lou shrugged again and looked at Allen. "I don't know, just too quick I guess. I mean he pretty much just said hello and they took off. I doubt she's asking him back to her place. Two almost total strangers, you know? I've just never seen it outside the movies or something."

"They could have gone to the Brew Cellar," Allen pointed out quietly.

"She didn't strike me as that kind of girl," Lou said. "That's kind of a rough place. But I guess they could have gone there.

"It's a little dive around the corner," he explained to Kurt. "I just didn't think that was her scene. She looked real nice, you know?"

Allen nodded. "She did, but that's where I thought they were going."

"We kind of got into an argument about it," Lou explained. "We put a bet on it. We bet . . . we bet on what was going to happen." Collin's friend looked down at the table and sipped at his beer.

"And you never heard her name?" Kurt asked.

Neither had.

Kurt grilled them for another fifteen minutes, but learned nothing new. They were able to identify the bartender who had been working that night by describing her to their present cocktail waitress. Kurt wasn't able to convince the waitress to give out the bartender's phone number, but she did say that the same girl would be coming on at six. Kurt would have to come back. It was a slim chance that the bartender would remember anything even if she'd heard it, but slim chances had to be exhausted.

Kurt gave the waitress his credit card and told her to keep the tab open for Collin's friends. When they protested, he said, "No, that's okay. I appreciate your help."

"I feel like we couldn't really help," Lou said.

"Maybe not," Kurt told him. "But maybe you did. If you think of anything, call me. I'm staying at the Ritz-Carlton in Pentagon City and I might call you if I have more questions. Thanks."

"Thank you, Mr. Ford," Lou said as both he and Allen stood to shake Kurt's hand.

Allen told him how to get to the Brew Cellar and then he left them. In his mind, Kurt now had an image of the woman who had lured his son away from his friends. That was what must have happened. It couldn't be coincidence. An alluring woman who had been seen in Collin's favorite coffee shop shows up in a bar, targets Collin, takes him almost immediately away, and later the boy is killed. Each incident in itself is possible. Things like that happen, but not all at the same time. It was more than a coincidence, and Kurt felt his blood start to pump fast. He knew they were somehow connected.

He walked up King Street and rounded the corner, intensely scanning the street as if some clue might appear in front of him. When he entered the Brew Cellar, he paused inside the door until his eyes adjusted to the gloom. He was surprised when he realized that at the back of the bar, Carol Dipper was sitting at a small table with a tall, lean, dark-bearded man. When Kurt got close, he saw the man also wore a silver hoop in each ear.

"Mr. Ford, I . . . I'm," Carol Dipper stammered, "I'm working on your case."

"Can I sit down?" Kurt asked.

"What if she said no?" the man interjected rudely.

Kurt eyed him critically. He was probably in his mid-twenties, but the beard and the long black hair that was pulled into a ponytail made him look older. His eyes had the sarcastic twinkle of a brazen smartass.

Kurt sat without waiting for Carol to answer.

"Mr. Ford," she said uneasily, "this is Henry Minter. He was the bartender on Friday night and he remembers Collin."

"Who's Collin?" Minter demanded. "I didn't say anything about any Collin. You asked me if I remembered a dark-haired chick, a looker. That, I told you about, not any Collin."

"He was the man with her," Dipper explained, blinking with uncertainty at the bartender.

"The sap?" Minter said with a chuckle.

Kurt felt his stomach curdle. Blood surged hot through the veins in his head and neck.

"The woman who was with Collin came into the bar earlier in the night and asked him," Dipper quickly explained, nodding toward Minter, "to fill her glass with water every time she ordered a double shot of vodka for her date."

"Hey!" Minter exclaimed as he pushed his chair back

from the table. "I don't like the way this guy is looking at me. If I'm not under arrest, I gotta get back to work."

"Sit down," Kurt commanded in a low, seething voice.

"Excuse me, mister?" Minter said, leaning his face across the table with the hint of a smile on his face. "The last guy that told me to do that was my father when I was twelve, but on my thirteenth birthday I flattened the side of his head with a brick."

Kurt looked into the young man's dark eyes. They were unafraid and challenging, the eyes of a man who was used to other people backing down.

Like lightning, Kurt reached across the table with both hands and grabbed him by the back of the head, slamming his face down onto the hard surface. Minter's nose popped on the first blow, but Kurt slammed his face down three more times before heaving him up by the throat and pinning him to the brick wall behind the table with his toes dancing wildly on the dirty floor.

Carol Dipper emitted a shrill cry and fumbled with her badge, which she proceeded to stick into Kurt's face. "I'm a police officer, damn it!" she cried.

So absurd were her words that Kurt might have laughed aloud if he weren't focused so intently on the bartender.

"That was my boy you're talking about," he hissed, tightening his grip. Blood from Minter's nose ran freely down Kurt's arm, tickling his elbow where it dripped to the floor. "Now you tell me who that black-haired bitch was and you tell me quick."

Minter shook his head from side to side as earnestly as he could and croaked pitifully that he didn't know.

Kurt dropped him to his feet and brought his free hand up with a twisting vise-grip on Minter's groin. "You tell me what you know about her or I'll ruin you for life," he said through clenched teeth.

"She never said her name," Minter whined, his face scrunching up in pain. "She asked me to do it. She said it was a joke and she gave me a hundred dollars. I never saw her before. I don't know anything else!"

Kurt looked hard into his eyes. He wasn't lying. He was shaken and humiliated, but he wasn't lying.

"Mr. Ford!" Dipper shrieked. "Let him go!"

Kurt did and turned to go. Dipper stomped along beside him through the small crowd of gaping patrons and Minter's coworker behind the bar.

"I'll sue your ass, man!" a recovered Minter howled as they reached the door.

Kurt turned and stared hard at him before allowing the young detective to pull him by the arm out through the open door. "A real tough guy," he muttered.

"Mr. Ford," Carol Dipper exclaimed when they were on the sidewalk. "You cannot do that! I am trying to help you and you . . . you . . . you just can't do that! My authority as an officer will be . . . I could get into trouble when this gets reported."

"This isn't going to get reported," Kurt said, absently flicking his arm and spattering the brick paving stones with Minter's blood. He looked at his trembling hand with disgust. There was a day when a nose-to-nose, knockdown confrontation in a bar wouldn't have unsettled him quite so much.

"How can you say that?" Dipper asked, still aghast.

"Because a guy like that doesn't want to have to tell anyone what happened again and again. He won't call the police."

"I am the police!" she protested.

"I know. I didn't mean it like that. I meant that he won't call anyone else," Kurt said. He sounded calmer than he felt. "Now listen, what that guy said proves something was going on. This woman got Collin drunk, brought him back to his place, and, either alone or with someone else's help, she shot him with his own gun and made it look like a suicide. Even Olander has to see that now."

Dipper looked skeptical at the mention of Olander, but Kurt continued emphatically: "This is what we need to do. We need to get a composite drawing of this woman and find out who she is. Collin's two friends are right around the corner and between them we should be able to get a decent idea of what this woman looked like.

"How'd you get to that guy before me anyway?" he asked, stopping to stare at the flustered detective.

Dipper's cheeks flushed and she avoided Kurt's stare. "I started at noon asking at every place up and down King Street if anyone saw a man and a woman that fit their description. I am a detective, Mr. Ford," she said, looking up at him defiantly with her owlish eyes. "And I know we'll need a lot more than a composite drawing to find out who this woman is."

"No," Kurt said. "We won't. You get me the artist to do the drawing. That's all I want. If you get that for me, I won't ask you for anything else. Not now, anyway. In fact, I don't want you to say anything to Olander or your captain. I may not need their help."

Dipper looked at him and blinked. They had reached Harpoon Alley now, and after glancing in through the window to make sure Collin's friends were still there, Kurt had stopped to talk.

"Why is that?" Carol Dipper asked.

"Because I have a friend who might be able to find this woman with nothing more than an accurate sketch."

Dipper looked at him quizzically, but Kurt wasn't going to say anything. He wasn't going to tell her that a man in David Claiborne's position could access the National Security Agency's comprehensive computer files for women who looked like the one who had been with Collin. He wasn't going to tell Carol Dipper that he'd start with the ID badges of the operatives in the CIA and the other intelligence agencies and work his way through the military and then to the public in general and their driver's licenses if he had to. But if what Claiborne had suggested were true, then most likely the woman would have some connection with the government that would make her accessible to the president and his people. And if she did, then Kurt would not only find her, he'd find her fast.

CHAPTER 6

Carol Dipper knew a competent police artist in D.C. But when Dipper contacted her she said she had no intention of coming in to work on a Sunday evening to do a sketch based on the recollections of two half-drunk young men. Kurt overcame her reluctance when he told Dipper to offer the artist a thousand dollars in cash to meet them at her precinct station. Two hours later, both of Collin's friends were nodding with admiration at the composite the artist had come up with.

With a computer disk of the sketch in hand, and Dipper's agreement not to report their activities to Olander or the captain, Kurt said good-bye to his son's friends and went to his Suburban, which was parked on a dark street adjacent to the police station. It was a short walk, but the night had cooled off with a breeze. Kurt took his blazer off the passenger seat and pulled it on before hopping in and dialing David Claiborne's cell phone.

"Hello." Claiborne's voice was flat and hard like slate.

"David, it's me," Kurt said.

"Call me at two-o-two, five five five, seven eight two three," Claiborne said and promptly hung up.

Kurt dialed the number.

"Kurt?" Claiborne said after one ring.

"Yes."

"Are you calling me from a digital phone or an analog?"

"Digital." Kurt knew as well as anyone that an analog phone could be overheard by any ordinary person with an emergency scanner. Digital, however, was relatively safe.

"Good. Do you need to talk?"

"Yes," Kurt said.

Claiborne gave him directions to a seafood restaurant in Georgetown that overlooked the river. "I'll be there in thirty minutes. Watch your back," he said and hung up.

Kurt couldn't help feeling slightly annoyed at his old friend's mysterious behavior. It had been so long since he himself had to think in terms of security protocols. Even in the world of computer security, where industrial spies and hackers weren't unknown, he'd grown used to talking freely on the telephone. And despite what he knew, he was having a hard time altering his behavior to match the magnitude of the situation. The notion that the chief executive of the United States was embroiled in a conspiracy like this was almost unthinkable. But when he considered the possibilities, he knew that Claiborne's conduct was exactly correct. If the president and the people around him had plotted the deaths of three Secret Service agents, then they would be at the height of vigilance, especially when it came to Claiborne, the only man left alive who could possibly put all the pieces together.

Kurt took one hand off the wheel and felt instinctively under his arm where an agent's gun would be; for the first time in a long while he felt naked without it. Maybe David could help him with that. If things got dicey, he didn't want to be the only guy at the party without a weapon. The momentum of the entire situation seemed to be carrying him along like a riptide. He was perfectly willing to go with it, but he didn't want to flounder like a novice.

He knew how to play this game. He'd played it well, in theory, anyway. The truth was, for all the training of his body and mind—and that was twenty years ago—his experiences with live fire had been limited to one incident when they had run a counterfeiting ring to ground in Seattle. But the countless hours of training had served him then, reinforcing his reactions so that they became instinctual under fire. The question now was how much of those instincts had remained with him. He hoped most of them, because something told him he was going to need them.

It was after ten when Kurt walked through the large glass doors and into the spacious dining room, where the few remaining patrons were mostly having their dessert. Claiborne was already there, sitting at a lonesome table by one of the many broad windows overlooking the water. A tired-looking young waitress with white hair brought Claiborne a club soda with lemon and glanced nervously between the two to see if they wanted to eat. The kitchen was about to close.

Kurt suddenly realized he was ravenous. He ordered a New York strip and a glass of merlot.

"Steak in a seafood place," Claiborne said blandly. "You always were different." It was his first allusion to their past fraternity, and it somehow comforted Kurt.

"And you don't eat anything but"—Kurt hesitated, remembering his old friend's crude mantra with a constrained smile—"anything but food after nine at night, right?"

Claiborne smirked and nodded. Kurt looked at his hand to see if he wore a wedding band. In the last days before he'd left Dallas, he remembered David getting engaged to a blonde bombshell, a young finance major and cheerleader from SMU. He searched his mind for her name but came up empty.

"Did you ever marry . . ." he began.

"Sheila?" Claiborne said. "Nope. She's still around, but I dodged that bullet."

"Still around?"

Claiborne grinned smugly. "Still engaged as a matter of fact."

"All this time?" Kurt exclaimed, searching his friend's face to see if he was teasing.

Claiborne nodded. "I kept putting it off. Then about ten years ago, we set a date, invitations out, place booked, honeymoon, everything set. But the night before I just figured, why? I had everything I wanted and the way I wanted it."

"How did that go over with her?"

"Not great, but she got over it. She gets over things . . . What about you? You ever get married again?"

"No," Kurt said solemnly.

"Why doesn't that surprise me?" Claiborne said with a hint of what might have been sarcasm.

Kurt said nothing, but smiled. The two of them then talked about the old days in Dallas, the good things they remembered. After a while, their conversation turned to the Service. At first, the discussion was amiable enough, but it soon took a disastrous turn that left them face-to-face with Claiborne's disappointments and Kurt's unparalleled success.

Kurt couldn't help feeling uncomfortable again at the thought of how different things could have been if only he'd given his old friend the job that he asked for. While Kurt didn't care about the clothes he wore or the car he drove for that matter, he knew such things meant something to David. He surreptitiously examined the Presidential Rolex on his old friend's wrist. By the way the second hand moved, he knew it was a fake, and he wondered what would prompt a man David's age to wear a fake Rolex.

But then Claiborne completely diffused his apprehension by suddenly saying, "I'm proud of you, Kurt. You did real well for yourself and I'm damn proud of you."

"I appreciate that," Kurt said, and he did. It was comforting to know that his old friendship with David had overcome the time, distance, and circumstances that had arisen between them.

An uneasy silence ensued. Kurt had never learned to navigate the subtleties of an intimate conversation. He was more used to going straight at things, and whenever he was confounded, he simply remained quiet.

"So where are we now?" Claiborne finally said in a more serious tone before taking a sip of his drink.

Kurt finished off his glass of wine. He removed the disk from his pocket and held it in the air. "I have an artist's sketch of what she looked like, the woman who was with Collin before he disappeared. I know her approximate height and age, and her eyes were an unusual color. They were yellow, like a cat's."

Claiborne eyed the disk. His face remained impassive, but Kurt could see the nervous excitement in his eyes and it puzzled him briefly.

"I was hoping," Kurt continued, "that you could help me access the NSA files. I want to cross-check this rendering for a match."

"That's going to give you thousands of matches," Claiborne pointed out, "and you can't be certain of the accuracy of a drawing."

"I know," Kurt said. "But I don't want to search for a match against all their files. I want to start narrow, with CIA operatives. Then I'll check the other agencies and the military, special operations units first, if I can confine the search, which I think should be possible. My presumption is that whoever this woman was, she knew what she was doing. In an operation like this, even if she were a pawn, they wouldn't use someone outside the community, I don't think. Besides, when you see the picture of this woman, you'll see. There aren't going to be too many matches. She's unusually beautiful."

Claiborne pinched a wedge of lemon between his fingers and worked his mouth as if he could somehow taste it before letting it fall back into his drink. "I admire your work," he said. "You've obviously taken what I said to heart."

Kurt's food came. He cut big pieces of the steak and wolfed them down with a second glass of wine, realizing that he hadn't eaten since the morning. After savoring the blood from several mouthfuls of the hot meat, he said, "I want to find out who this girl is. I want to find out who sent her and who killed Collin."

"You know who sent her," Claiborne said with a scowl.

"I have to know for sure."

"Then what?" Claiborne looked expectantly at Kurt.

Kurt stared into his old friend's face for a moment before answering. Certainly, Claiborne didn't really want to know what he would do. "I just want to know," he said evasively. "I want to know the truth."

"I doubt you'll find any direct link to the president," Claiborne said. "The police won't be able to help you, if that's what you're thinking. Neither will the press."

"I know that," Kurt said flatly. He began to work on the last half of his steak, chewing those pieces more thoroughly than he had the earlier ones.

Claiborne nodded and watched him impassively while he finished. "I've got a guy who can get into the NSA's computer system," he said quietly.

"Can you do it now?" Kurt asked.

"You want to do it right now?" Claiborne said with a raised eyebrow. "It's after eleven on a Sunday night."

"Yes. Now."

"I could call him and maybe have him tell me how," Claiborne mused. "He's not going to meet us. He's got a family . . .

"But I'm not going to be able to do it," he continued. "I'm not big with computers."

"If you have a password and the site and the name of the search program," Kurt said, "I can get in and figure out how it works. I'd rather do it myself anyway."

"I'll make the call," Claiborne said without emotion, "but we still need a computer. We can't go back to my place. We shouldn't."

"They'll have a high-speed access computer at the business center in my hotel," Kurt said.

Claiborne shrugged. "I'll call him."

"Let's go," Kurt said. He surreptitiously took a clip full of cash from his pocket, peeled off a couple hundred-dollar bills, and slid them under the edge of his plate.

"I'll get that," Claiborne said, reaching into his jacket.

"Please, David," Kurt said quietly, holding up his hand. "I can't tell you how grateful I am for what you're doing. At the very least, let me buy you dinner."

Claiborne smiled and nodded in agreement, and the pair headed for the door. Claiborne stopped at the pay phone near the bathrooms and got his NSA contact out of bed. After speaking with him for a few moments, he rejoined Kurt outside the restaurant.

"He wasn't happy," he told Kurt as they left the restaurant, "but I got it."

"David," Kurt said after a quick glance around, "I need a gun."

"Why do you need a gun?" Claiborne asked, surprised.

"I don't know what's going on, but if it's what it looks like, I don't want to get into a situation where I can't fend for myself. Can you get me anything?"

Claiborne's answer was as casual as if Kurt had asked to borrow a flashlight. He said, "I've got a three fifty-seven in my trunk you can have."

"Clean?" Kurt asked. He preferred to have a reliable gun that wasn't traceable to anyone or anything. He looked sideways at his friend as they walked past a large, raging fountain that dominated the center of the empty courtyard outside the restaurant. The steady hiss of water swallowed the sound of their footsteps.

"Yeah," Claiborne said. "It's clean."

"You keep a gun like that in your trunk?"

"You never know, right?"

"True."

They walked to the garage where Claiborne had left his Lexus coupe. Claiborne removed the gun and its shoulder holster from the hatch and handed it to Kurt, who strapped it under his arm before covering it with his blazer. The two agreed to take separate vehicles and meet at the Ritz-Carlton. It was just across the bridge.

The hotel's business center was closed. The night concierge apologized, but he didn't have a key. Only the manager would have that at this time of night and the concierge didn't even know if she would have one. Kurt asked for the manager and brought out his thick clip of money. A thousand dollars later, they were ensconced in a dark, vacant room on the second floor, sitting in front of a desktop computer that had high-speed cable access to the Internet and all the capacity Kurt needed to conduct his search.

To be safe, Kurt hacked his way into the interactive Web site of one of his larger clients. From there, he could access the NSA system without leaving any trace back to himself. With Claiborne's information and a working password, he was soon inside the NSA system. He fed his disk into the A drive and brought the sketch up on the screen.

Claiborne inhaled sharply through his teeth. "That's the woman?" he said incredulously. "That's who Collin's friends saw him with on Friday night?"

"Yes," Kurt said, turning from the picture of the exotic-looking woman to his old friend. "Why?"

"You don't have to do a search," Claiborne said grimly. "I know who she is."

CHAPTER 7

She's one of us," Claiborne said. The empty expression on his face was illuminated only by the blue glow of the computer screen. The rest of the room was cast in a gloom that emanated from a single dull hooded lamp on a low end table by the window. One of the shaggy faded locks of Claiborne's hair had fallen from its place and drooped across his forehead, giving him the appearance of a disheveled corpse.

"What do you mean?" Kurt asked.

"She's an agent," he said quietly. "Or she used to be. Leena Ventone. She was a sergeant in the Uniformed Division, a group leader on the CAT team. She got jammed up about six months ago when she got drunk and wrecked a police car on her way home. The cop in the police car was the nephew of some congressman and the kid lost his leg."

"The CAT team?" Kurt exclaimed. "She's a woman."

"They have them now," Claiborne said with a patronizing smile. "You know better than anyone the politics involved in government service. It's politically correct to have women agents."

"I know that," Kurt said. "But the CAT team?"

The CAT team was more like a military special ops unit than a bureaucratic government agency. Even the ranking within the group took its lead from the military, as opposed to most of the Secret Service's governmental grade levels. The team was essentially a combat unit, an elite strike force trained in weapons and tactical assault, but camouflaged under the more passive CAT acronym, which suggested a "counter" strike force, a defensive unit rather than an offensive one. But the acronym was only a political convenience, to avoid giving the general public the perception that the president of the United States traveled around the world with a deadly assault team at his fingertips.

"How well do you know her?" Kurt asked.

"Not well," Claiborne answered. "But when she came to Washington, obviously people around the White House were talking. She's a striking woman. The word was that she came from the military, the air force, I think. But that was a few years ago, and by the time she made the CAT team I think people were used to seeing her around, but she had a habit of going out and drinking too much and taking home strange men."

"But why wouldn't Collin have recognized her from the Service? His friends said he knew her from a coffee shop in Alexandria."

Claiborne said, "She became part of the CAT team before Collin came to Washington. You know the Uniformed Division and protection people don't mix, and it's even more that way with the CAT team. They're off to themselves, so no one sees her walking around like a million bucks like you did when she was in protection. And the times you did see her, you couldn't really tell who she was with all the gear they wear and the sunglasses and the cap."

Kurt nodded. Wearing the cargo pants, heavy boots, and bulletproof vest of a CAT team member, even a lovely woman would look inanimate.

"Is she capable of doing something like this?" he wondered aloud.

Claiborne shrugged. "You'd know better than I the capabilities of someone on the CAT team."

"I didn't mean could she," Kurt said. "I meant would she."

"I didn't know her that well, Kurt," Claiborne said. "But she was a capable agent, disgruntled at being bounced. If Mack Taylor and the president sat down with her in a back room, telling her she was somehow back in the loop, and if they targeted someone, telling her they were a threat to national security or something like that, who knows? Crazier things have happened."

"But a woman," Kurt mused in disbelief. "You just wouldn't think that of a woman. Especially a woman in the Secret Service . . ."

"What's the difference?" Claiborne asked, sounding slightly annoyed.

Kurt only looked at him.

"Well," Claiborne grumbled, "now you've got your proof. It's exactly what I thought. The old man was behind it."

Kurt pondered the computer screen for a minute then said, "I want to talk to her."

"Why would you do that? That's only going to tip them off," Claiborne argued. "If you talk to her, you're going to be a target. Don't you see that?"

Kurt's mouth turned down in a mean-looking frown and he looked fiercely at Claiborne. "I don't care. I want to hear it from her. I want to know exactly what happened and why. I want to know why, David!"

Claiborne coolly assessed him. His eyes shifted in quick little jerks that seemed to be outward signs of his internal calculations.

"What's the access code?" Kurt asked. He was going to find out as much as he could about the enemy before an encounter.

Claiborne read it off the scrap of paper without resistance. But as Kurt hammered away at the keyboard, he said, "Now, you're covering our tracks, right? No one's going to know it was you and me going into these files?"

"No," Kurt said. "I'm accessing them from someone else's Web site. It's kind of like using a stolen car to commit a robbery. I get in and out and the only traces I leave belong to someone else, in this case a huge corporate entity."

Claiborne watched enviously as Kurt worked his way through the confounding labyrinth of programs and systems until they were staring at a comprehensive file on Leena Ventone. After examining her history, Kurt felt he had some understanding of her.

She was driven by something. She had worked her way through college on an ROTC scholarship, then done military service, with abnormally brisk advancement, then entered the Service, two years in the field, a year in protection, then straight to the CAT team. She was obviously a smart, adaptable, physically superior human being with an internal drive most people could only dream of.

But now, everything she'd ever worked for was gone. And, if she believed somehow that she could regain it . . . Kurt imagined that a meeting such as Claiborne described with the president could have that effect. Still, he couldn't think of anything that would cause an agent, even a disgruntled ex-agent, to become involved in the murder of another agent. It was inconceivable.

Kurt's mind clicked and churned like the hard drive of the computer in front of him. Wasn't it also possible that the girl was simply a pawn in a much larger game? She might have been the lure to get Collin isolated and off guard.

No, he thought, she was directly involved. She had plied Collin with vodka, drinking water herself to maintain her own sobriety. Then, most likely, she took him home and kept the drinking going until he was completely inebriated and too helpless to defend himself. Then she, or someone with her, killed his son. They stuck the barrel of his boy's own gun into his mouth and pumped one of the vicious soft-tipped slugs into his brain.

Against his will, Kurt's mind turned to Collin, flailing in his bed, spurting blood from his mouth, tossing from side to side like a dying fish, alone, horrified, and helpless. A sickness twisted his insides and the hot flames of anger burned his face. He punched the keys that got him back to the beginning of Leena's file. For a moment, he stared into her yellow catlike eyes, their perfect almond form, and the majestic bone structure of her cheeks, forehead, and nose. She was exquisite, but Kurt saw the devil, a cloying demon that had shattered his own carefully constructed world with one fell deed.

Talk to her? Yes, he wanted to talk to her. He wanted to learn as much of the truth as was possible. But sitting there staring at her visage, he knew with a vicious certainty that unless there was some very unusual answer for what had happened, he was going to execute her as well. He took the address from her record, copied it, exited the NSA network, and went quickly across the Net to Maps.com. In seconds, directions from the nearby Pentagon to the girl's home in Maryland were being expelled from the chattering mouth of the printer.

"What are you doing?" Claiborne asked.

Kurt ripped the page off the printer and said, "I'm going there."

CHAPTER 8

"To where she lives?" Claiborne exclaimed. He looked at his watch. It was two-thirty. "Now?"

Kurt snatched up the directions and stood. In the last thirty hours, he'd lost all sense of time, but even if he hadn't, he couldn't think of a better opportunity to find Leena Ventone at home, unawares, and hopefully alone.

"Yes," he said. "Thank you. You saved me a lot of time, David. I won't forget what you've done, and don't worry, no one will ever know about your help."

"I can't go with you," Claiborne replied defensively. "What you do from here on in, you'll have to do on your own. You understand that?"

"Of course," Kurt said. He held out his hand and took his old friend's grasp with equal force. "Good-bye, David. Thank you. Thank you so much." He left Claiborne standing there, staring thoughtfully at him. He pushed the button for an elevator up to his room, but thought better of it and decided to go straight down. There was nothing he needed in the room.

Kurt went south on the George Washington Memorial Parkway, and as he drove, he began to feel the weight of Collin's death pressing down on him. He wondered how he could ever have worried about anything else in life but the well-being of his son.

It wasn't that he hadn't been concerned with Collin. It was just that over the past twenty-some-odd years there had been so many other things he'd worried about as well—the everyday worries that came with running a business. But what did his business matter? It was true that one of his largest divisions linked doctors all across the globe to share medical knowledge, in the hopes of saving lives. It was also true that he had used millions of dollars of his profits to fund an anonymous foundation for sick children and their families. But the people whose lives Kurt had affected were nameless and faceless to him.

Compared to Collin, everything else paled. Maybe it was selfish, but he knew with certainty that there wasn't a thing, including his own life, that he wouldn't give up without hesitation if it would bring his boy back to life. He tried to think about that objectively and after a time concluded that it was a universal human curse. People worried about things that, when put to a true measure, were insignificant.

He soon crossed the Potomac at the Woodrow Wilson Bridge and lost himself in a thinly populated area not too far south of Andrews Air Force Base. He wondered if the girl's past connection with the air force was the reason why she lived in such an out-of-the-way place. With the directions pinned to the wheel with his right hand, Kurt navigated his way through a labyrinth of back roads until he came to a silver mailbox that gleamed in his headlights. The number belonged to Leena Ventone, and the box marked a gravel drive that dipped down into a wood bordering Tinkers Creek.

Kurt went past the drive and up the twisting road a short way until he found a shoulder big enough where he could tuck his Suburban under the eaves of the trees. He climbed out into the warm night air that was alive with crickets. Overhead, the bright moon drowned out all but the brightest of stars and cast deep purple shadows from the trees onto the winding road. When he reached the gravel drive, he was painfully aware of the loud crunch of stones under his feet. Small white clouds of dust marked every step he took, and he could clearly see the vehicle tracks leading in and out of the drive. He stepped off the crushed stone and into the ferns that grew in the damp loam lining the way. Down the slope he moved more quietly, but the dew soon began soaking into his socks.

It was nearly two-tenths of a mile down the drive, and a bevy of frogs had joined in to accompany the chorus of crickets before the narrow way opened onto a grassy swatch bordering the creek. The fresh gravel dipped down again and made a bright gray loop in front of a sand-colored double-wide trailer. Near one corner of the dwelling was a telephone pole mounted with a brilliant halogen streetlamp. Amid a blizzard of insects, the harsh white light illuminated the trailer, the weedy bank of the pitch-black creek, and the entire lawn as brightly as the parking lot of a shopping mall. On the far side of the trailer, a narrow chain-link kennel surrounded a large doghouse. The homestead was a sterile abode, bereft of flowers or painted shutters or ornaments of any kind. It might have been a small industrial shop instead of a place someone called home.

The only sign of a human presence was a shiny black Jeep Cherokee that stood guarding the front entrance. Kurt remained motionless well within the shadows of the woods on the edge of the light, studying the setup and wondering what other kind of security measures were in place, if any.

He knew the first and often best deterrent to intrusion was bright lights. Well, she had that covered. He circled the perimeter carefully, away from the doghouse, crouching down from time to time to look for posts or any hardware attached to the trees that might house a detection device. Halfway to the creek he found an infrared eye on a small black metal post. His eyes went instantly to the trailer, wondering if he hadn't already broken a beam during his search.

There was no sign of life, but that didn't mean anything. A perimeter of infrared beams wasn't something a person did to discourage burglars. It was a much more sophisticated method of protection and one that would probably trigger a silent alarm, enough to wake the girl inside but not enough to startle an intruder. If that was the case, then she could be searching the woods right now with the nightscope of a high-powered rifle from the darkened window of her bedroom.

Quickly, Kurt found the next eye in the circuit and established in his mind just where the beam was: two and a half feet from the ground. He jumped it and went straight for the house, zigzagging wildly as he crossed the grass with Claiborne's .357 clasped tightly in both hands. His face was pulled tight with the expectant grimace of a man who suspects he might be shot. When he got to the corner of the trailer, he flattened himself against the siding and gasped for air amid the ringing in his ears and the tumultuous pounding of his heart.

Finally, his body quieted and he dabbed the sweat from his forehead with his sleeve. He was in, inside the perimeter, anyway. The next step was not to find a way inside the trailer, but to get the girl to come out. The Jeep was his first thought, then the dog. If the car had an alarm, that would get her up and out. If not, the dog would be the next best bet.

He started slowly around toward the front of the house, ducking under a window and stopping to listen as he went. The chorus of frogs and bugs was a sweet steady hum; otherwise all was quiet. He was at the front of the trailer, under the shaded picture window and halfway to the Jeep when a dark figure slipped out the back door and moved silently around the trailer behind him. Kurt never suspected that he was being outmaneuvered until his body jumped involuntarily at the sound of the harsh voice behind him shattering the night.

"Drop the gun or I'll put a fucking bullet in your head!"

Immediately, a dog shot out from its house to throw itself repeatedly against the fence, while barking manically.

Kurt stood up slowly from his crouch with the gun held high up over his head.

"I said drop it!" she screamed. Kurt could hear her

rage and something told him that she would kill him if he even hesitated. He dropped the gun.

"Now turn around, slow!" she ordered. Then she screamed at the dog, "Kay! Quiet!"

To Kurt's surprise, the big dog instantly went silent. By this time, the frogs and insects were quiet too, scared into stillness by the German shepherd's frenzy. He turned to face her. It was Leena Ventone, and even in the harsh halogen light in the middle of the night, wearing no makeup, a ponytail, and a loose-fitting black T-shirt and shorts, she was stunning. Kurt knew everything Collin's friends said was true, and he could see how the girl had enticed his son.

"Now you tell me who you are and who sent you!" she commanded. She held her big Glock steady, aimed directly at the center of his face. She gave the gun a subtle jerk and Kurt involuntarily winced as he started to speak.

"I'm Collin Ford's father," he said. He saw that this shocked her, but only for a second. Then her eyes narrowed and she seemed to gather herself, settling into her stance just a fraction, taking careful aim the way any professional would. Kurt felt the heavy truncheon of fear strike his midsection.

Before he could react, the silence of the night was suddenly blasted by a crack so loud that it sounded like the splitting of a stone. At the same instant, crimson tissue and blood spattered the side of the trailer in a pattern four feet high. A trickle of blood sped down the side of Leena's face and her mouth opened and closed without making a sound. She dropped where she stood.

Kurt, too, dropped to the ground and rolled instinctively toward the cover of the Jeep, grabbing his gun as he went. He heard the call of his name as he spun across the gravel and came to rest beneath the front wheel.

"Kurt!"

He heard it again. It came from the edge of the woods. The dog's whine now matched the pitch and intensity of a dying rabbit's squeal. Kurt remained silent, but peered from beneath the Jeep at the form of a man jogging toward him, crunching down the gravel drive. In his hand was a long rifle mounted with a tremendous scope and a muzzle that was silenced by a baffle the size of an aerosol spray can.

"David?" Kurt shouted, as his friend's features materialized in the light. He stood warily, still queasy from the shock of seeing the woman slaughtered at close range. Claiborne jogged all the way to Leena's crumpled form and bent down over her briefly before rising with a grim face.

"Let's go," he said, taking Kurt by the arm and ushering him around the Jeep and up the drive. Their feet crunched noisily, but Claiborne seemed to care nothing for stealth. He was in a hurry to get away. When he noticed Kurt staring at his weapon, he said, "Nightscope. Don't worry. I wasn't going to miss."

Kurt looked at his old friend's face, now lit only by the moon. He felt awash with gratitude. Claiborne had just saved his life.

"She was going to kill me, wasn't she?" he heard himself mutter quietly.

"Yes."

A long silence followed between them as they strode up the path. Finally Kurt said, "What made you follow me?"

Claiborne smiled warmly at him. "I knew you might need a backup. You were good, Kurt, one of the best. But so is she and she's twenty years younger than you, or she was, anyway."

"But now what are you going to do?" Kurt said, his mind beginning to clear. There was a dead woman lying there in the grass behind them, a dead woman that people would find, and not just some anonymous young woman. She was a former Secret Service agent.

"I'm not going to do anything else but get you back to your hotel and get you out of D.C.," Claiborne said. "The people behind this whole thing are going to be looking hard to find out what happened and I don't want you anywhere near it all."

"What about you, David?" Kurt asked. They had reached the main road now. The moon had dropped below the trees and it was eerily dark. Claiborne's dark shadow patted his rifle.

"This goes in the Potomac. That," he said, pointing toward the .357 Kurt still clung to, "can go with you, and no one will ever know either of us was here except the other. It's our secret, Kurt."

"My God," Kurt muttered. But what else was there to do?

As if he was reading Kurt's thoughts, Claiborne said, "She was going to kill you, my friend."

"I know it," Kurt replied. "David . . ." He didn't know how to properly express his gratitude and his regret for not having made Claiborne a part of his team years ago.

Before he could speak, Claiborne grasped his shoulder. "Get back to where you belong. Go home. And if you do decide to do anything else, you'd better think it through pretty goddamn well, not like this. The next time I guarantee I won't be there to bail you out."

Kurt was silent. His mind was turning, end over end. It wasn't over. The woman who might have killed his son was dead. But she might not have killed him, and even if she did, there were those behind the scenes who had arranged it. They weren't going to go unpunished.

"Good-bye old friend," Claiborne said, then suddenly turned and started off down the road in the opposite direction from Kurt's car. Kurt went too, jogging down the shoulder of the dark road until he could make out the dark form of his Suburban.

At five-fifteen, he arrived back at the Ritz. Bleary-eyed, he let himself into his room. It was dark, but he closed the door behind him without finding the light. Too exhausted to care, he stumbled through the entry-way fumbling for the switch. Then he froze. His surrender to exhaustion was suddenly reversed by a fresh burst of awareness from some unknown reserve. The black space of the hotel room seemed to have shrunk. He couldn't see, but some sense that was just as convincing caused the hair to rise on the back of his neck. He wasn't alone.

CHAPTER 9

Kurt drew the .357 from its holster and crouched low, flattening himself against the wall. His eyes ached from the strain of trying to pierce the darkness and find the form of what he knew was another human being. Nothing moved. His breathing seemed louder than a city bus opening and closing its doors.

Trembling, he groped for the light switch somewhere on the wall above him. When he found it, he flipped it on and rolled across the floor, coming up from the roll with his gun ready to fire. A form shot out of his bed in a swirl of sheets and blankets. Kurt hesitated.

"Jill!" he cried angrily. "What the hell!"

She blinked at him, confused and still half asleep. "What?" she exclaimed, bleary-eyed. "What happened?"

"I almost killed you," Kurt growled with a mixture of horror and relief. "What are you doing here? How did you get in my room?"

"Why do you have a gun? What's wrong?" she asked.

Kurt looked at the .357. "I'm sorry," he said, and set

it on the desk before explaining. "Nothing's wrong. I just . . . I didn't expect you."

She took her eyes from the gun and gave him a sad and tentative look. Quietly she said, "I thought you needed someone, Kurt . . .

"Gracie thought it was a good idea too," she quickly added. "I've been worried about you. You didn't call."

Jill held her chin high. Kurt knew she was too proud to cry, but her eyes were moist and he felt certain that that was exactly what she wanted to do. The thought that he could hurt her amid all this wounded him. As if she sensed his self-recrimination, Jill got out of the bed and took a tentative step toward him. Kurt crossed the room and hugged her. He breathed deep, absorbing the familiar scent of her hair. The feel of her body was firm and comforting. He dipped his head to meet her lips.

Their kiss ignited a passion that went up like kindling in the center of a great bonfire. Soon the flames consumed Kurt's entire frame, and gently but urgently, he began to undress her and she him. And when they finally lay quiet in the bed with Jill's head tucked snugly under his arm and her arms circling his waist like a child's, Kurt felt the blessed tranquillity of emptiness. In that moment, there was nothing inside him to twist and gnaw. His mind felt suspended as if inside an enormous airplane hangar, dark, empty, silent, and expanding rapidly. The emptiness somehow took on a weight. It pushed him down in a slow steady spiral, down into deep sleep.

*   *   *

Sunlight, hot and bright, burned through the heavy drapes of the tall windows and fell in musty columns across the soft bed. Kurt awoke with a film of sweat on his brow and a scorched dryness in his mouth. Jill put down a book and rose from the high-backed chair in the corner of the room where she'd been sitting with her shapely legs curled up underneath her. She crossed the room to sit beside him. Gently she brought her lips to rest against his before kissing his eyelids and smiling at him in an almost maternal way.

"What time is it?" he croaked, then cleared his throat.

"Ten-thirty," she told him.

Kurt lay still. He reached for her hand and gave it a squeeze, then smiled back weakly. Her presence was like a shady porch on a hot summer day, a comfortable reprieve. But now, with his body refreshed from sleep, the nightmare of what was happening to him came spilling back, flooding his mind with the realization that things were just as sinister as they had been the day before. His son was dead and so now was the woman who had probably killed him. The same horrid monster of grief and insanity clamored from the recesses of his mind, threatening to undo him.

Kurt closed his eyes.

"What?" Jill whispered. "What's happening?"

The question bumped up against him, threatening his equilibrium. "I love you," he said abruptly, opening his eyes and looking into hers with a nearly maniacal intensity.

"I know," she said in a somewhat unsettled tone. "I love you too. That's why I came."

Kurt sat up and stared at the hypnotic pattern on the bedcover for a while before saying, "How much? How much do you love me?"

"As much as anything in my life," she whispered urgently. "Ever."

"What about your career?" he said.

Jill emitted a scornful laugh. "My work? I love my work, but Kurt, I said I'd marry you. That's everything to me now, everything . . ."

Kurt considered her, how she had magically taken away all his pain, even if it was just for the night.

"And you're everything to me, love," he said, kissing her gently.

They were both quiet for a moment before he said, "I think I may need to start my whole life over, our life . . ."

Jill wore a puzzled expression. "I don't understand," she said.

Kurt pressed his lips together, choosing his words carefully. "I've worked a long time now, long and hard. Now this . . . I just want to get away, Jill. I want to disappear, to leave this world behind. I thought maybe we could be married and just go someplace, maybe an island in Greece or the South Pacific, just the two of us and start a life away from everything . . ."

"Oh my God, Kurt," she said quietly. "I would love that."

"What about your work?" he asked. "Really."

Jill thought for a moment, then said slowly, "I enjoy my work, yes. I like to think it's important."

"It is."

"But I hope the center of my life isn't about programmable chips and more effective encryption systems," she said. "Kurt, I love you. My life with you is what matters more than any of that by far."

"What about friends?" Kurt asked.

Jill frowned. "The people that I work with . . . and my friends, well, I care about them, but again, you are what matters most. And I'm sure Talia could come visit us wherever we are," she added. "You know she and Henry travel all over the world half the time anyway."

Talia was Jill's best friend and the one person Kurt expected might be a hindrance to her leaving New York.

"But," Kurt said hesitantly, "what if she can't?"

"Oh," Jill said, waving off the idea. "She can always come. Even if it's only once in a great while."

"But, really," Kurt insisted. "Just suppose she couldn't for some reason. Would you still go with me?"

Jill smiled strangely at him and said, "Why are you saying this?"

In his mind, Kurt knew that they would be hunted and their disappearance under those circumstances might not then sound as romantic as he was making it out to be. Of course, he couldn't tell her what he was planning. He would have to tell her something, though. Then he'd just have to hope that when the time came and she knew what he'd really done, she would understand why and forgive him. If she didn't, well, then, she didn't love him as much as he hoped.

"Is this why you have a gun?" she asked quietly, breaking his trance. "What's happening?"

"Collin didn't kill himself," Kurt said softly. His face cringed as if in pain. "He was killed. Some people had him killed . . . because of something he saw . . .

"No, don't worry," he said, watching her eyes dart from the desk where the gun still lay and then back to him. "I'm not in any danger, and neither are you. I just . . . didn't know. They're bad people and I didn't know if I was going to come face-to-face with them or not."

"You're not going to do anything crazy, are you, Kurt?" she asked. Kurt said nothing.

She shifted uncomfortably and after a while, she asked, "What are you thinking about?"

Quietly, but forcefully, he said, "If I have the chance to bring them to justice, I won't lie to you, I'll do it. I'll expose them—and truthfully, it's part of the reason I want us to go away. It's possible they might try to find me when it's over. But I can take care of everything. You have to trust me, Jill. It's the right thing."

"You're going to expose them?"

"Yes."

"But it's dangerous?"

"I won't lie to you," he said with a grim smile. "It could be dangerous, but nothing I can't handle."

"And that's why you asked about Talia?" she said. "Because we might have to hide?"

"Yes," he said solemnly, "we might. There's a very real chance you might not be able to see her or anyone—ever."

Jill was silent. After a time she reached out and brought his hand to her mouth, kissing his fingers lightly. "I don't want that, Kurt," she said softly, "I really don't. But if you're asking me will I still go away with you, even with all that, the answer is still yes. Yes, I will."

His mind began to spin now, but in an ordered, balanced way, like a gyroscope. There were a million things he had to do; a million things he had to consider. Each one had to be thought out and executed to perfection. The simplest error, like the brush of a sleeve against a house of cards, could ruin everything.

First, he had to avenge his son. At the same time, he had to plan an effective escape, not just for himself, but for Jill. He had to do it in secret. If things went wrong, he didn't want her to be culpable. If his plan worked, he wanted to be able to whisk her away and disappear without a trace. He'd have to find a place for them to go. He'd have to create new identities. He'd have to move his money out of the country so they could live out their lives in hidden comfort. It was a daunting task, but Kurt knew if he could build a billion-dollar company from nothing, he could do this too.

"Thank you, my love," he whispered, repeatedly kissing her face and hugging her tight. When he finally felt her relax, he gave her one last gentle squeeze and got up to take a shower.

"Call the pilots, will you?" he said with a disarming smile. "Tell them we'll be heading back in two hours."

"Are we going home?" she asked excitedly.

"Yeah," he said as he disappeared into the bathroom. "We'll go to the lake. I need some time to think about how I'm going to do all this."

Kurt came out of the shower refreshed and steadier than when he'd gone in. But the undercurrent of sadness that hung about him was palpable. Only the arrival of Jill had bolstered his spirits enough to give him even the outward appearance of calm. The image of the dead girl from the night before had been relegated to the same dark corner as the photos of Collin. But the troubling emotions from everything that had happened lurked just beneath the surface. He needed to get out of Washington, back to a place where he could consider the situation from afar. Then he would act.

Jill had everything packed and had arranged for the plane to be ready by twelve-thirty. They had a late breakfast in the hotel restaurant and then stopped briefly at the Starbucks across the street for cappuccino before heading out to the airport. Their conversation was limited to fluffy banter, each of them apparently keeping it afloat for the sake of the other.

At thirty thousand feet, however, their talk ebbed. In the pocket on the side of Kurt's leather recliner were stuffed several newspapers from that morning. On page three of the *Washington Post* was a story about the president's campaign schedule for the coming months. Kurt eyed Jill warily before digging into the article. She was oblivious. She had already taken his cue and was reading her book.

A third of the way down the page, Kurt nearly gasped aloud. His eyes were locked on the words "Skaneateles Lake." The article said the president was coming to Skaneateles, his town, the town where he kept his summer home, in less than six weeks. An appearance at the nearby New York State Fair would give the president the opportunity to glad-hand the swing voters of upstate New York that could carry the state in what people were predicting would be a close race. Kurt's mind went back into high gear. It was serendipity, the events of the earth and the stars lining up to serve the implacable forces of justice. Kurt had the intoxicating thrill of a man about to commit an act of almost religious significance, a man about to eradicate a scourge from humanity.

Killing the president was something that required fearlessness and luck. Getting away with it would require even more of both. Inside knowledge—that he had—but also serendipity. Now he had that too. It was as if it had been written down long ago. It was meant to be.

The president and his wife were to be the guests of a federal judge whose turn-of-the-century mansion was almost directly across the lake from Kurt's. Six weeks gave him plenty of time to reconnoiter the house and the grounds before the advance team for the Secret Service even began their work. Kurt could get in and around the house and devise his plan without arousing the slightest suspicion. It was an opportunity so perfect that his heart raced in his chest and a merciless grin broke out on his lips.

CHAPTER 10

In the Oval Office of the White House, the president of the United States, Calvin Parkes, sat behind his desk facing the high-living, obese secretary of state and the ramrod-straight chairman of the Joint Chiefs of Staff. Behind them, by the door, Mack Taylor stood impassively as he always did, less obtrusive than a floor lamp to those who spent any time at all around the president. The president measured his words carefully before he spoke.

"Let's try to talk to the Iranians," he said. He was a large man, and although his shoulders were rounded he liked to keep them pulled back straight. His blustery red face, thick white hair, and deep, sonorous voice made him an imposing figure.

What he wanted to say was: "Let's launch some missiles." But that wouldn't do. It was one of the most painful things to him about being president. Calvin Parkes had grown up accustomed to saying anything he thought. As a boy in Pittsburgh, he was the son of Jonathan Parkes, the third-generation owner of the Pennsylvania and Ohio Railroad. From an early age, the president had grown used to flinging his opinion care-lessly about, whether it was asked for or not. Now, with the entire world hanging on his every inclination, he had learned to bury his more caustic sentiments beneath the guarded mumbo-jumbo that he'd come to acquire in public life.

He hadn't chosen politics out of need but desire. It was a desire, however, born from a vanity that super-seded most men's needs. His father had successfully sold the family railroad in the seventies and just as successfully invested the proceeds in the stock market. So people thought things came easy to the Parkeses.

While being the scion of a long line of millionaires had its advantages, it also incited jealousy, and only among the vulgar did it garner real admiration. Men of accomplishment tended to view a young man who came from old money with skepticism, linking every achieve-ment back to his inheritance. Calvin Parkes had wanted to be admired for himself by people who counted, not pandered to because of his wealth. The difficulty was that any success he ever had in business would be inex-orably linked to his family money and connections. What he had wanted was a medium in which he could excel that transcended his birth.

The answer came to him at a political fund-raiser that his father hosted for the governor of Pennsylvania at the Duquesne Club one late spring evening. Calvin was just home from college. It was a chilly evening and a steady rain had spoiled all the joy of the coming summer. Calvin came in from the raw weather stamping his feet and tapping the rain from his umbrella on the oriental rug covering the entry floor. He was straightening his black tie as he entered the main room with its heavy and intricately carved wood when he was struck by an image that he could recall to this day by simply closing his eyes. It was his father, white-haired and red-faced, with his imposing walrus mustache, his tall frame bent over, actually stooping to the floor to pick up a cuff link that had popped loose from the governor's sleeve.

Calvin had never seen his father stoop for anyone or anything. He watched with fascination as the others, prominent men of his father's station, also fawned over the one man who appeared so much less substantial than the rest. The governor at that time was a sickly looking fellow with pink, watery eyes. His skin was pale, his teeth gray, and he spoke in the lilting voice of a clothier. Calvin had expected much more from the man who held the state's highest office and who people claimed had real potential for a run at the White House.

It was that moment, and the courage he gained from comparing himself to the then governor of Pennsylvania, that had led him to his calling. The governor had grown up on a farm and studied law. The battlefield of politics didn't belong exclusively to the rich. If Calvin Parkes succeeded in that arena, no one would doubt his own personal prowess.

Calvin quickly discovered that he was a born politician. He was able to honestly assess his own strengths and use them with a ruthlessness that impressed even the patriarchs of the party. He took advantage of his money and family connections without a hint of shame.

He broke into the game as a congressional representative. Then, after a four-year hiatus from the legislature at a high-level job within the Reagan administration, he ran for U.S. Senate and won. After two terms of doling out pork on the Ways and Means Committee, Calvin was ready for his run at the White House. It was an upset victory, really. He had been a dark horse in the primaries, but it came down to the thing his opponents reviled him for most: that old money. He outspent them all at a staggering rate, using the media with a deft ruthlessness that set a new standard in American politics.

But being president, he learned in his first three and a half years in office, wasn't as liberating as he thought. The zenith of any American politician's career was as much a burden as it was a reward, and it seemed to him now that the most important thing he could do was to leave a legacy. He wanted to do something that people would look back on and say, "It all began under the Parkes administration."

While the temptation to launch some kind of military action against another nation was great, it no longer held the same allure it had in days gone by. The luster had faded from military engagements. It was true that the Gulf War had been a dynamic national experience that resulted in great admiration. But it had faded as quickly as a peculiar fashion in women's clothes. Military aggression was no longer a fertile prospect for presidential exaltation.

Still, that primal tug like a boy feels when he regards his father's gleaming gun mounted above the fireplace left Parkes feeling slightly remorseful at the sound of the carefully chosen words that dropped from his lips.

But whimsical statements belonged to Calvin Parkes's past. As president, everything he said or did was heard. Most of it was scrutinized. He was almost a prisoner of his own power. The Secret Service, the men who had sworn to give their lives to protect him, couldn't do their job if they weren't with him always. When he broke wind in his sleep, they heard it. The things he said in his office were preserved on tape, all of them. So he knew better than to suggest they bomb the Iranians, even though he could hear the words in his own mind ringing out clearly.

Of course, there were times when the Secret Service men and the recording machines weren't around. It was during those times that the president did his best work. Sitting around as he was now and pontificating with advisers was all well and good. He had to do it. It was expected and it was necessary. But the really important things, the things that kept him in a position of power—those things were done when there weren't any microphones, or cameras, or even agents around to hear or see.

His thoughts returned to the mark he planned to leave, and that led his mind to wander. He stared at the lamp on a side table that was his own personal mark on this office. Would it stay? There above it hung a painting from the Lincoln administration. The table itself was Andrew Jackson's. But evidence of many of the men who had held this office had been removed over time. The chattel that remained in the Oval Office from administration to administration was the measure of a president's true greatness. Calvin Parkes wanted his lamp to still be there right on top of Andrew Jackson's table two hundred, even four hundred years hence. And what, he wondered, about a coin?

He remained impervious to the incessant droning of the chairman of the Joint Chiefs of Staff and thought about the Internet. If they could spin it right, he just might sell the world on the notion that his tax would serve to preserve the world's greatest experiment, its most powerful democracy. The bill he planned to sign into law that taxed the Internet—that would be his legacy. It would revolutionize the entire system of taxation and absolutely guarantee the preservation of the United States federal government. In the future, all commerce would be electronically transacted. By taxing each individual transaction, the new law would equitably spread the tax burden among people and businesses and would lock down the government's revenues forever.

It was a controversial bill, one that had been spawned outside his own administration. But he saw the powerful brilliance of the idea and took it for his own. Despite a virulent opposition, he had been able, with the same kind of behind-the-scenes bullying that got him into the Oval Office, to rally the votes it needed to get through Congress. Soon he would turn it into law. It was a use tax, really. Ultimately, it would result in less tax on the individual and more on the corporate entities who currently avoided much of their tax obligation through loopholes. High-tech companies were dead against it. But they were the robber barons of the twenty-first century and they were fighting hard to go on squeezing

American society without restraint. His own family fortune had come in a similar manner, but he felt the loathing old money always had for new.

Special interests of all kinds were lined up against him. But if he played things right, he could keep them guessing just long enough to win the next election, and then it would be too late. He would sign the bill and crush their efforts without having to worry about the repercussions. He could only serve one more term and he would be remembered as the president who had made a bold move when necessity demanded it. Historians would say that he, Calvin Parkes, not only strengthened but saved the nation. One day, he suspected, his face would adorn some form of American currency. He would be remembered forever, and that was what he really wanted.

"So talk to them, Lonnie," he said impatiently after picking up on the tail end of the discussion that had erupted between the two men, "and if you need me to make a call, let me know. Other than that, I've got a campaign meeting and then a speech to give at that Girl Scouts' convention at the Hilton . . ."

In response to the sour look on the face of his secretary of state he said sharply, "Give me a break, goddamn it, will you, Lonnie? Does it really bother you that much when I do something that wasn't your idea?

"We both know what's going to happen anyway," he added impetuously. "Sam will get the navy to move some ships around, the army shuffles some troops to get their attention, and it all works out before the weekend."

With that, the president rose to his feet, signaling an

end to the meeting. The two men left and as they did five more scurried in and surrounded Parkes as he sauntered out the side door and into the Rose Garden where there weren't any tape recorders.

"Where are we at, Marty?" he said impatiently. He had taken a chocolate mint from a jar on his desk and now he popped it into his mouth as he glared up at the sky.

Marty Mulligan was his campaign chairman, a gaunt, chain-smoking Irishman from Yonkers with dark eyes and a shadowy face. He skulked along beside the president like a willful cur.

"We're about ten million dollars short of where I want to be," he said in the raspy voice of a man who looked down on the rest of the world.

"So give me the bad news," the president said with a deadpan face before breaking into a snarl. "Dammit! I'm so tired of people wanting me to use my own money for all this. Bush never used his own money! Clinton didn't!"

"Clinton didn't have any," Mulligan's assistant innocently pointed out from the fringe of the group.

Calvin Parkes stopped and glared. "What's Reynolds doing?" he railed. "Why isn't the party more worried about raising the money? I'll tell you why! They want me to use my own! Damn, I'm sick of it!"

"We need ten million more," Mulligan said, apparently oblivious to the president's moods. "I'm not saying we need it right away, but we need it. I want to up the advertising budget for later this summer when we go into New England and New York."

"Yeah, I want to talk about that New York trip," the president said as he rolled the green foil from the mint into a little ball with his fingers. "People can't even say this Skinny-annie-whatever-it-is. Where the hell are you sending me, Marty? People are asking me and I don't like not knowing why."

Mulligan worked his fingers in anticipation of the cigarette he'd have the moment he walked away from this meeting. He replied in an indignant tone, "We talked about this three times, Cal."

Mulligan was the only man anyone knew who could speak to the president in such a way. To everyone else, Calvin Parkes was "Mr. President." Even though they all knew it was Mulligan's strategizing that had gotten the president to where he was, and that he would be integral in keeping him there, his casual manner still made them uncomfortable. Part of the reason for other people's discomfort may have been that whenever Mulligan did call him Cal, the president glared around the group as if in silent warning to the rest of them.

The other men shifted awkwardly. Their eyes couldn't help roving to Mack Taylor's chiseled, soulless face. The SAIC stood behind the president staring straight ahead, his pale gray eyes as lifeless as those of an obedient attack dog. Despite the agent's sharply tailored dark suit and his short, clean-cut gray hair, each of the president's aides was acutely conscious of the primal threat emanating from him like an odor.

He was the usual sort, a thick-necked former special ops officer who had joined the Secret Service after Vietnam. During a combat tour, Taylor was rumored to have specialized in field interrogations. The only one Taylor didn't faze was Mulligan. In a strange way, they seemed to be cut from the same cloth. Each was the kind of man you never wanted to turn your back on.

"You'll be staying with Max Shapiro, the federal judge," Mulligan continued, "which is important in and of itself. We'll hit the State Fair, where you can press some flesh and get some good photo ops with a bunch of babies, and the press corps will love this. This place is beautiful. The water looks like the Caribbean or something. It's an old New England–type town with brick sidewalks and cast-iron lampposts. It's a place where you can look like you're relaxing, like you're a normal American taking his summer vacation enjoying this country's beautiful natural resources. And we'll unveil our plans for more stringent EPA water standards on one of the cleanest lakes in the world. The greens will love it. We'll have you drinking some water right out of the lake and saying it should be every American's right to have clean water or something."

"What about their businesspeople," the president complained, throwing his hands in the air and beginning to stroll again. "They're already all over me for not vetoing that emissions legislation. You're sounding more and more like a Democrat, Marty."

"We have to win New York, period," Mulligan said. "Hey, can I get a coffee or something?"

The campaign chairman's assistant tore away from the group and made for the Oval Office, whispering to someone inside that Mr. Mulligan needed a coffee with milk, no cream.

"So," Mulligan continued, "you want the election, you gotta get New York. You want New York, you gotta sound a little green. Don't worry, it's just talk."

Mulligan looked at the president with his unblinking reptilian eyes. The president looked back. Both knew the other well. They were men who did what they had to do to get where they wanted to go. Anyone who had closely followed their actions knew that it didn't bother either of them to circumvent scruples. Scruples were for fools.

"Good," said the president, as if the idea were his all along. "We'll go to Skinny-whatever and drink clean water and hopefully somewhere along the line we can get in a round of golf and pick up an extra ten million."

CHAPTER 11

Rain fell in sheets on the lake. Kurt felt his way across the water's fractured surface in a small skiff whose engine couldn't be heard above the teeming downpour. It was two-thirty in the morning on Tuesday. He was alert, and would look down at the compass on his GPS from time to time, but the steady sound of rain and the dull vibration of the engine under his grip on the throttle lulled him into contemplation.

He had spent the day holed up in his library, breaking only for a subdued dinner with Jill and Gracie on the veranda overlooking the lake. Afterward, Jill had suggested that they take a walk. Kurt had declined, saying he still had more to do. He had gotten up from the table and given her a perfunctory kiss and an apologetic smile.

"You've been working all day," she had pointed out. "Don't you think you should take a break?"

"No," he'd said. "I can't do that. You know what I'm up against, Jill." He had glanced quickly at Gracie, signaling that it wasn't the time or place for her to start quizzing him.

Jill had followed him into the library, into the drift of books and papers covering his desk and the reading table.

"Stay with me, love," he had pleaded. "Trust me. I have to do this my way, but it will all work out."

He knew her nature demanded more—she had the archetypal mind of a scientist, acute and probing. But he also knew he couldn't give her more. She would have to trust him, to stand by patiently while he sought a resolution for what had happened and a plan for moving on. He had kissed her again, warmly and deeply this time, then told her good night. With one last longing look at his work, she had forced a smile and left for their bed.

That's where he had found her sometime well past midnight, sleeping soundly. Her wild hair radiated from her face, its golden streaks shining like beams of sunlight even in the dim yellow glow of the reading lamp next to the bed. He had slipped into his closet and pulled on some dark clothes and a black baseball cap. On his way out, he had checked his instinct to gently lay his hand along the pretty curve of her cheek.

In the blind darkness of the wet night, Kurt was jarred from his reverie. The aluminum skiff had bumped suddenly and loudly against the judge's pier. He strained his eyes as he lashed his boat to a metal cleat, but nothing stirred. The house sat amid a cluster of towering oaks, and only a handful of the high old windows were lit from within at random spots throughout the large mansion. Still, they cast enough of a glow for him to vaguely make out the shape of the building if he looked indirectly at it, using his peripheral vision.

But the house wasn't his only concern. He wanted to locate and assess what he knew would be the first perimeter of security. What he found confirmed his recollections of the property that he had previously only seen from the water. The judge's mansion was a point of interest for out-of-town summer guests during leisurely boat tours around the lake. So he had already seen the cobblestone wall that ran down to the lake and suspected that it completely encircled the property. As he walked its length, he knew that the first perimeter would be a ring of men just outside the wall, with another handful patrolling the water's edge. Besides the front gate, there were two other walk-through gates, one to the north and one to the south, decorative wrought-iron doors guarding the arched openings in the eight-foot stone wall.

The second perimeter would be inside the wall and just outside the rough ring of trees surrounding the house. As Kurt circled the mansion, he imagined the concentration of men who would be stationed in the front where the driveway curved its way through the trees from the immense wrought-iron gates that led to the road. His own experience as an advance agent in protection was so intense that it all came back to him as if he'd done the job only last week. He knew where the men would go, he saw the inherent weaknesses in the layout, and he knew exactly how they would communicate to their counterparts if something or someone breached their perimeter.

The third perimeter would be just outside the house itself, with agents covering every possible point of entry—a difficult cordon to penetrate, but not out of the question. The conundrum, of course, was the fourth perimeter. That would be inside the house. The fourth perimeter would be comprised of the agents immediately surrounding the president. They were the true bodyguards. In time of need, they were expected to give up their lives to protect him, and they hovered constantly about the rooms where the president sat, or ate, or slept.

Kurt bit down on his lip at the thought of his own son, who at times had been a part of that fourth perimeter. The boy who only wanted to be honorable and do good things for his fellow man and had sworn to give his life for the president. And in the end, he had given it, but not for the reasons he was supposed to. His life had been snatched away by the very man he would have died to protect. Kurt flushed the bitterness in his mind. But this was no time for painful contemplation. This was a time for objective assessment. He let the thought go and focused his attention on the house.

He wanted to get a feel for the layout. Later he would discreetly obtain the plans from the town hall and peruse them in detail. He'd seen the renovation work going on last summer at the judge's mansion and he knew that it required a filing of updated plans of the house's interior with the building inspector: public documents. He circled the house in the rain-soaked gloom of the light that oozed from the handful of glowing yellow windows.

Moving with feline caution, he scanned his path for the kind of security that the dead woman from the Secret Service had installed around her Maryland trailer. Kurt doubted a paranoid system like that was in place to protect the judge. People came to Skaneateles to get away from security systems. It was a town where people left the keys in their cars and gave out their phone numbers freely, needing to recite only the last four digits.

Kurt stopped beside one of the monstrous oaks, his wet palm against its dripping hoary bark. He shut his eyes and squeezed them gently with his free hand. The idea of penetrating the four perimeters of security that surrounded the president was an overwhelming puzzle. Most people would say it was unsolvable.

But Kurt knew from his business experience that often what appeared to be impossible could be attained with perseverance and intellect. He reminded himself of the story one of his first scientists in the early days of Safe Tech had told him about a group of German engineers during World War Two. The men had been ordered to attain an extra thirty thousand miles' use from the fan belts in the German army's personnel carriers without using any more precious and increasingly scarce raw materials. On its face, it was an impossible problem: getting twice the wear out of the same amount of rubber. But the engineers took the time to think about it and brainstorm among themselves until they actually found a solution. By twisting one end of the belt one hundred and eighty degrees before attaching it at the other end they created a Mobius strip. Both sides of the belt would incur the debilitating friction rather than just one, and the life span of the belt would be doubled.

That was what Kurt hoped he could find, some kind of Mobius strip, a brilliant and logical solution to an apparently impossible problem. In the back of his mind, he suspected that a large part of the answer would come from commandeering the Secret Service's communications. He was fairly confident that was something he could do. He had access to the kind of technology that would enable him to monitor and decipher the interactions between the agents protecting the judge's home. Sitting innocuously in his fishing boat on the lake, he could easily listen in. Those communications would typically be encrypted and then decrypted as they traveled across the airwaves. But encryption was one of Safe Tech's businesses. He could solve that with the right box.

A plan began to form in his mind. By eavesdropping on the Secret Service's internal communications, Kurt could obtain the passwords necessary to override the protocols set up on the perimeters. He could record the various voices coming out of the command post and create a data bank that would enable him to electronically re-create those voices. He also knew that within his own company there existed the technology to override an individual agent's radio. Kurt could approach a lone agent outside the wall, for instance, override his communication with the command post, and literally clear his way through one of the walk-through gates. The procedure was purely technical and could be resolved with mathematical equations by a trustworthy friend and employee of Kurt's named Cheng.

What Kurt couldn't figure out was how he could do what he had to do and get out. Getting in, with his knowledge and the technology available to him, was quite possible. But the fourth perimeter was so tight that it was impossible to penetrate it unnoticed. He could confuse the agents and get into the president's presence. That he felt confident about. But once he pulled the trigger and the president was dead, he would almost certainly be killed or captured himself. That was the impossible puzzle.

Kurt didn't want to kill the president at the cost of his own life. He had a strong desire to live, and not just to exist in a jail somewhere. Kurt wanted the life he had described to Jill. Right now, he was thinking about someplace in the Italian hills on the Amalfi coast, maybe in a beautiful villa overlooking the Mediterranean. But unless he came up with a solution, he wouldn't make it out of the judge's house alive.

A high-powered rifle came to mind. That was certainly possible. But Kurt knew what he was and what he wasn't. He was no marksman and he didn't have time to become one. The chance of a miss was too great. Explosives were unwieldy and subject to discovery, by no means as sure as a point-blank pistol shot. Beyond that, this was an act of revenge so personal that Kurt felt a driving need to look into the president's eyes at the moment he cast him into hell.

He purposefully wandered the grounds, making mental notes, familiarizing himself with every possible detail—the trees, the gravel paths, the gardens, and the shrubbery where he could best melt into the night. The more comfortable he got, the closer he went to the house, until finally he was crossing the porch, darting in and out of its shadows like a burglar. In one window, he was startled by a black cat staring intelligently out at him from her perch on the back of a sofa. He quickly melted back into the trees, adrenaline coursing through his body like a torrent.

When he caught his breath, disgust set in. He shouldn't have been so close to the house. Any advance warning that something was amiss could jeopardize the entire presidential visit. If the Service had a hint that even the trace of a conspiracy was afoot, they would change the president's itinerary altogether.

On the north side of the house was a freestanding garage that Kurt knew would serve as the command post. He entered it through an unlocked side door and looked around, imagining how in just a few short weeks it would be empty of cars and bustling with men and equipment. This would be the brain that he would somehow have to anesthetize.

An hour after he'd arrived, Kurt made his way back down to the water's edge. The rain was beginning to thin. His mind moved restlessly over the idea of coming in from the lakeside. But as sexy as it might sound to emerge from the water like some eerie frogman, he knew that getting through the random patrols would not only be a gamble, but would demand the kind of dark commando clothes that wouldn't serve him when he got closer to the house. To get into the third and fourth perimeters, he would have to walk through disguised as an active agent.

He cast his boat off and let himself drift downwind a way before starting up the little outboard. By the time he chugged into his own boathouse, the rain had stopped. The moon suddenly appeared low in the sky among a bank of tattered clouds, signaling a definite end to the dampness. But his hands were already numb. He puffed into them and tied up the skiff. A shiver escaped from his core and shook his entire frame. He'd been wet for more than two hours, soaked through like a drowned cat, but only now, with the adrenaline gone, did he feel the chill. He walked stiffly in his wet clothes up toward the house and entered through the back of the garage. In the laundry room, he stripped to nothing and was startled when he turned to find a wide-awake Jill standing there, staring at him with her arms crossed.

"Where have you been, Kurt?" she asked. Her tone was calm but insistent and her face was lined with worry.

"Geez, Jill!" he exclaimed, one hand moving instinctively to cover his privates. "You scared the hell out of me. I was— I took a walk. Actually, I took the skiff out on the water."

"On the water?" she exclaimed, peering out through the rain-tarnished window at the night.

"I— I was thinking," he said evasively. He felt as foolish as he looked, standing there with nothing on. "I just needed to think."

"Kurt," she said patiently, "it's four in the morning. I know this is hard for you. I can't imagine. But please, tell me if you go like that. I woke up and I didn't know what was going on. I don't care what you do, but could you just tell me?"

Kurt pulled a towel out of the laundry basket and

wrapped it around his waist. He closed the gap between them and hugged her warm body to his nearly naked frame. Her long hair spilled across his arms, warming them.

"I'm sorry," he said, closing his eyes.

And then, without warning, a low guttural moan rose up out of his throat.

"Kurt?" Jill said anxiously. "Are you all right?"

"I have to tell you something," he whispered hoarsely, his eyes still shut. "You have to know that this is all my fault . . ."

"Kurt?" she said dubiously.

"Listen," he hissed through gritted teeth. He reached up and grabbed two handfuls of his own hair. "It was me who had him go into the Service. It was me! Don't you see?" His voice was laden with anguish and nearly hysterical. "When he graduated from college, he came to me for advice. To me!

"He said he wanted to follow my footsteps. He said he wanted to come to Safe Tech and learn the business and one day earn the right to take over.

"To earn it." Kurt laughed bitterly, his eyes flashed at her to see if she understood. "That was Collin. He meant it. He didn't want anything given to him. He wanted to work and deserve everything he got. He wasn't a spoiled rich kid. And I took advantage of that! I killed him! Don't you see? It was me who suggested he join the Service! It was me all along, and now—now he's dead!"

He made the same strange noise again, an agonizing moan that instead of growing louder was somehow strangled into a low gurgle, until finally he was silent. Kurt drew long deep breaths of air, as if he'd just finished a run.

"I'm sorry," he said in a hushed voice, holding her close to him again.

Jill held him back. After a time, she whispered, "I'm scared Kurt. I don't know what's happening, but I'm scared."

CHAPTER 12

Jill never went back to sleep. Kurt passed out in her arms, his body's temperature finally climbing to equal her own. When his breathing was deep and comfortable, she slipped out of bed and dressed for a workout. She'd always been an early riser. As a young girl she was on a swim team, and their practices started before school in the dark hours of the day. But even on weekends, even after a long night, she typically rose before the sun. And, maybe because of her swimming past, she liked to get her workout in then as well.

One of the great pleasures Jill had when they came to Skaneateles was to ride her bike. She liked to ride around the lake even though it took nearly three hours. With Kurt sleeping soundly and having just dropped off, she knew she didn't even have to hurry. She stretched for ten minutes in the darkness of the broad circular driveway. When she was limber, she laced up her shoes, strapped on her helmet, and set off up the long drive to begin her journey. By the time she made the climb through the woods and reached Route 41A, her legs were burning. She turned south in the dark and set off at a breakneck pace.

After the burning had subsided and her endorphins had kicked in, she began to think. In addition to trying to maintain a permanent size six, this was why she loved to ride or run or swim as much as she did. During a long workout, her mind achieved total clarity.

And so she couldn't keep from analyzing what had happened over the past seventy-two hours, turning the events over unhurriedly in her mind. She thought about Collin. It was hard to believe he was really gone. She couldn't even imagine the pain Kurt and Gracie must feel. She knew how badly she herself felt, and she hadn't even known him that long. But in that short time, Jill knew he was special. In fact, he had made her feel welcome from the beginning.

To introduce Jill to his son, Kurt had planned a weekend at Skaneateles. He had flown Collin and his girlfriend up from Washington. The four of them took a tour of the nearby wine country in the middle of the day on Saturday and then returned to the house for a late afternoon swim. When Kurt swam out to the diving raft, Collin's girlfriend had excused herself to use the bathroom and Jill found herself alone for the first time with Collin.

"You're different," Collin had told her without warning.

Jill had looked at Kurt's son, then out to Kurt who was swimming steadily toward the raft. A half-finished bottle of wine stood on the small wrought-iron table between them and a large umbrella protected them from the glaring sun.

"Thank you, I guess," she'd said. Up to that point she had been uneasy with Collin, not because of anything he said or did, but simply because his eyes were the same eyes as the woman whose picture was everywhere throughout Kurt's home and office.

"You're welcome," Collin had said with an easy smile. "It's a compliment. He's never acted this way before. You should know that, and I want you to know that I'm glad. I'm really glad . . ."

Jill could remember clearly the endearing congenial look on his face at that moment and she felt tears well in her eyes. A minivan raced by her and distracted her until it disappeared over the next ridge. Then her mind returned to Collin.

When someone like him died young, the sense of injustice was wrenching. But as much as she had loved Collin for himself, she cared for him even more because of how much he meant to Kurt. And now the pain of his death was exacerbated by her empathy for Kurt and even for Gracie. The mask of anguish that had affixed itself on the older woman's face was so pitiful it made Jill wince just to think about it.

But, while she thought she understood the intensity of emotions Kurt was feeling, she meant what she'd said. She was scared. Kurt had always been a rational person. That was one of the things she loved about him. You always knew what you had with Kurt. He was strong, and sometimes stubborn, but never mercurial, never unpredictable. That had somehow changed in the last three days, and she was afraid that it went beyond just mourning for his dead son. There was a deadly glint in his eye that Jill feared went beyond simply bringing his son's killers to justice.

Her attention was suddenly drawn to the opposite side of the lake. She had emerged from a deep dip in the road and mounted a high hill that provided a view that actually made her forget her contemplation. The eastern sky had begun to glow in a crimson wash that extended from one end of the lake to the other. The low ceiling of purple clouds hovered just above the fiery horizon in a dramatic, brooding mass.

The angry blood-red sky somehow filled Jill with foreboding. Kurt had told her he wanted to expose Collin's killers. But was it possible that he was going to do more than that? Yes, it was possible. She had never seen him respond in a violent way to anything. Kurt always kept his composure. Even in the most contentious meetings, he simply stared at his opponents with an enviable serenity. But that meant nothing. He was a deeply passionate man, and if he believed that someone had killed the only child he had, it wasn't hard to imagine him wanting them dead.

Jill checked herself. She was thinking too much.

"You're too smart for your own good," her father used to complain. "Sometimes a person can be so smart, they're stupid."

Her father hadn't meant what he said to sound as scathing as it might to someone who didn't know him. But he was a relatively simple man, not in his intellect, but in his way of life. He ran a bakery in Merrick on

Long Island. Jill's parents had a tiny house near the train tracks not far from the town's center. Her father was an immigrant from Hungary, and despite having come to America when he was a young boy, he revered many of the old country's chauvinistic ways. Jill knew other girls whose fathers were also first-generation Americans, but who encouraged their daughters to excel in school.

"The boys don't want a girl to be smarter than they are," her father would grumble. His life's ambition had been to have her brother grow up to run the bakery, and her to marry a rich Jewish boy like Ivan Mendelson, a regular customer whose parents owned a large kosher chicken-processing plant.

The more her father said it, though, the more Jill had been determined to be the smartest woman any of them had ever seen. She studied and she read and she worked in school with a grim determination that sometimes left her alienated. The normal distractions for a young woman didn't seem to apply to Jill, maybe in part because she had been a gawky thing with a rail of a body, glasses, wild hair, and teeth slightly big for her face. She had won an academic scholarship to Cornell, where she earned degrees in both math and physics before getting her master's and then her doctorate in computer science. At the same time, she bloomed. Her body filled out. Her face caught up to her teeth. She shed her glasses for contact lenses, and for the first time her unruly hair became an alluring asset rather than a liability.

That was when she met her young husband, a point guard for the basketball team who would graduate from the school of hotel management. Suddenly, she was vindicated for all the hard work her father had chastised her for. She was where she wanted to be in life, married to a popular, handsome man, but still a thinking woman with both hands on the wheel. That was until her marriage fell apart and she became haunted by the imaginary vision of her father's derisive smirk. She didn't look so smart then.

Still, it was her position at Safe Tech and her prodigious intellect that had ultimately led her to Kurt, so she was vindicated again. But now, really for the first time, she felt she understood the adage that linked ignorance with bliss.

The sun, now golden, boiled up over the far hill in a blinding haze. As it cleared the distant treetops, it illuminated the placid deep green lake below and the rich dark carpet of trees on the steep-sloping hills. She marveled at each of the earth's elements: earth, water, fire, and air, and how they flaunted themselves around this lake in a vivid pageant that was never the same from one day to the next.

Without warning, the summer heat bit into the cool morning air. Jill had one brief glimpse of a meadow teeming with insects brought to life by the warmth before she plunged down into another shadowy ravine cooled by a thick wood of towering pines on either side of the road. With the majestic view gone from sight, her mind returned to its musings. She huffed at the notion, but she was thwarted by the sense that somehow her father had been right. She was so smart, she was stupid.

She began her climb out of the ravine, breathing hard, her legs on fire again. The incredible whining vacuum of a tractor-trailer suddenly jolted her from her meditation. The truck, a big white behemoth with New Jersey plates, had come up behind her doing seventy. Jill's surge of fear was doubled when the truck took the rise and veered to the left, gobbling up half of the other lane. A pickup truck coming the other way hit the rise at the same time and swerved off the road toward the deep ditch on the opposite side. When the pickup's driver spun the wheel back to regain the road, he overcompensated, crossed the yellow line, and headed straight for Jill.

It all happened in the space of a second, but the moment was inexplicably sluggish and Jill was actually able to mourn the man she loved for the second death he would have to endure in just three days. And in her mind, she could actually hear his reproach. It was the same long slow monologue he recited to her regularly about the insanity of riding her bike along that lonely rural highway.

Then came the impact.

CHAPTER 13

Jill swerved and hit the guardrail just as the pickup smashed into her bike and careened back out onto the road before screeching to a stop a hundred feet away. While country music drifted indifferently from the truck, a big man escaped from the cab and raced back to where the broken bike lay mangled about the rail. A low moan escaped his throat when he saw the inert figure of a woman lying fifteen feet off the road on the gloomy needle-covered ground at the base of an immense tree. The plastic shell of her lime green helmet had been shattered and marred by the tree's bole.

The man leaped the rail and lumbered down the slope to her side. His chin, like the rest of him, was big and square, and tears streamed silently down his swarthy face. His yellow hair was thin and receding. He wore the faded greasy jeans and grungy salmon-colored T-shirt of a farmer, and his boots, like his clothes, were covered with dust and cow dung. He felt her neck for a pulse and uttered a sharp report that sounded something like laughter when he found it, strong and steady. He wanted to make sure she was breathing as well. Carefully, he rolled her onto her back and inhaled sharply. She was like an angel with her beautiful face resting peacefully amid a tangle of golden brown hair.

The farmer, Jeremiah Mann, was also a state trooper. He knew how slow the emergency response was at the south end of the lake, but he was afraid to move the woman any more than he already had in case her neck was broken. He ran back to his truck and dialed the dispatch on his cell phone. By the time he got an answer, he was climbing back over the guardrail huffing unintelligibly. At the same time, he noticed the girl was sitting groggily, rubbing her temples.

Jeremiah snapped his phone shut and knelt down beside her. "Are you all right?"

Jill looked at him dazedly. "I think so."

"My God, I'm sorry," he said. His voice was incongruously soft for a man so large. "That truck came right at me. I had to swerve and I lost control. I didn't see you until it was too late. Are you all right?"

"I think I'm fine," she said. She started to rise. Jeremiah took her arm and hoisted her to her feet like an overturned chair. He began nervously to dust her off until he realized with horror that he was pawing the Spandex that covered her compact rump.

"I . . ." he muttered. "I didn't mean— Can you walk?"

Stiffly Jill started up the slope toward the road. "Yes, I'm fine," she said shakily.

Jeremiah walked beside her, helping her with one hand on her upper arm and another resting gently in the middle of her back.

"My God," she said when she saw her twisted bike.

"I'm sorry," he said again feebly. "I feel terrible. Let me take you to the hospital."

"No," she said firmly. "No, I'm fine."

When she looked into his pale blue eyes, however, her stern look seemed to falter. People would regularly confess to Jeremiah that he was one of the biggest human beings they ever met. But they would also just as likely swear that the effect was only temporary and completely offset by the way his twinkling eyes would practically disappear into his chubby red cheeks when he broke out into his easy smile.

"I'm a police officer," he blurted out.

That didn't look as if it surprised her at all. She merely nodded.

"A state trooper," he continued. "I have a farm up the road a piece . . ." He floundered with his words. She was looking at him now and her long-lashed eyes were the deep blue of a bluebird's wing. A handful of freckles were cast about her straight, small nose. Instead of looking angry, she gave him an uncertain smile, and that planted an irrational thrill in Jeremiah's heart.

"I'm Jeremiah Mann," he muttered uncertainly.

"I'm Jill. Jill Eisner." Jill cleared her throat and said, "Would you mind taking me home?"

Jeremiah looked behind him as if he'd forgotten that he was the only person there she could speak to and said, "Do you want to wait and file a report? I'll have to call my supervisor anyway to report the accident. You didn't get a license number or anything on that truck, did you?"

"No. I didn't see anything, just a big white truck. Can't you just do it without me?" she asked, rubbing her elbow where she'd hit the ground. "I'd like to just get home."

She was shaking and it pierced his heart. "Yeah, I can do that," he said. "I'll call it in after I drop you off, sure. You wait here, I'll get the truck."

He jogged to his pickup and whipped it around. Pulling past the mangled bike, he hopped out again. While he tugged at the bike to free it from the guardrail an old man in a faded green cap driving a brown Plymouth Duster came up the road and stopped beside them, his engine spewing pungent blue smoke into the air.

"Everything okay, Jeremiah?" the old man said in a kindly rattle.

"Everything's fine, Mr. McGurdy, thank you," Jeremiah said without pausing in his effort. Without looking up, he asked, "How's Mrs. McGurdy?"

"She's healing up fine, son," came the answer, "and we appreciate the eggs you brought by."

"My pleasure, Mr. McGurdy," Jeremiah said. "I'm glad I could oblige you folks."

"You see this, Jeremiah?" the old man said archly, holding up the morning's newspaper as if the two of them were having coffee at the counter of a diner rather than stopped beside the road at the site of an accident. "The president is coming to our lake!"

Jeremiah nodded, still without looking, and said, "I saw that this morning, Mr. McGurdy. It's something."

"And you'll probably be guarding him, won't you?

You being a trooper and all. You'll probably get to shake his hand, son. You'll be a hero around New Hope."

Jeremiah blushed and looked with embarrassment at Jill. New Hope was a crossroads made up of about thirteen farms, two dozen houses, and a firehouse in the middle of nowhere—a place that no more than seventy-five people called home.

"Nothing like that, sir," he said and turned back to the bike.

"Anything I can do to help?" Mr. McGurdy said, curiously eyeing the pretty young woman in her foolish-looking getup.

"No, thank you, Mr. McGurdy," Jeremiah said, freeing the bike with a horrible screech. "There was a slight accident. One of those damn interstate trucks."

Mr. McGurdy shook his head in disgust. "There was a day . . ." he began, but then thought better of it and simply said, "All right then. Good day, miss."

Jill nodded to him as he rattled off.

"You want to get in?" Jeremiah said quietly, holding the door open as if he were picking her up for the prom. She unsnapped the battered helmet and removed it from her head. With the expression of someone who realizes they're lucky to be alive, she gave the bike one final glance where it lay destroyed in the pickup's bed. When she looked up and saw Jeremiah's painfully embarrassed face, however, she offered him half a smile and climbed up into the truck.

"Your truck looks pretty bad," she casually observed

as they pulled away. The front corner was crumpled back.

Jeremiah only nodded. He was more worried about what it looked like on the inside. It was his work truck and it was unkempt enough to provide a habitat for spiders. At that moment, one was scurrying past on the dashboard. He took a furtive swipe at it, then said, "I hope you wouldn't mind if I just swung by the house real quick." He cast a nervous glance her way before saying, "It's on the way and you see, I was on my way back from picking up a lightbulb from a neighbor's."

Jill wrinkled her brow and stared at him dubiously.

"It's a kind of special bulb," he explained in his soft voice. "It's for my niece. Well, not for her really, but for these eggs I've got for her. It's an incubator. My sister-in-law won't let her have any pets of her own. She's a lawyer over in Auburn. She doesn't like pets and it wouldn't surprise you, to know her. But my niece comes out to the farm whenever she can and she just loves animals. And, well, this morning I noticed the incubator light was out and she'd have her heart broken if anything happened to those chicks. We marked them special just for her, with a pencil of course. You don't want to use a pen. They're eggs now, but they're gonna hatch real soon. So . . ."

Jeremiah's cheeks reddened. He knew he must sound foolish prattling on about an eight-year-old girl's chicken eggs. He wasn't much of a talker most of the time. But for some reason, he felt compelled to fill the silence.

"Do you mind?" he asked tentatively. "Her name is

Sara. Oh, you'd love her. She's cute as anything you've ever seen. I really like kids. There's something about a farm too, you know. It's a place for kids, I think. It's right up this way, do you mind? I'd hate to have those chicks die. It'd break her heart."

"I don't mind," Jill said after a slight hesitation.

Jeremiah smiled shyly at her and swung the truck down a side road that dipped slightly then wound its way gradually up until they turned off onto a gravel drive that went straight uphill to a white farmhouse with black shutters. The house and its three giant maple trees stood atop the highest point for miles around. From the cab of the truck, Jill could see ten miles all the way to the end of the lake where the town rested like the painted scenery on a game board.

"This is a beautiful view," Jill said placidly.

The old white farmhouse was immaculate. On the porch an old collie rested beside a rocking chair without bothering to get up. The grass was close cut and the gravel drive looped down behind the house to where two old barns stood bright red with fresh coats of paint. Birdhouses on thin posts dotted the grass everywhere and iridescent tree swallows swooped about them in the morning sun chirping shrilly with their liquid calls.

Jeremiah looked at her nervously and flushed again. "I'm glad you like it. Back in the late seventeen hundreds, my great-great-great-grandfather made a trade with the Greenfields. You see Mandana? The little cove where the marina is? Well all the farm fields you can see between there and town used to be the Mann farm. But my great-great-great-grandfather was going to marry a girl from New Hope and their great-great-great-grand-father who lived in New Hope was going to marry a girl from town and the two of them just decided to trade farms.

"It was a bad deal for us Manns as it turned out. When the rich people from New York City started to come here the property values down near town went through the roof. The Greenfields are millionaires now, but they still farm. The Manns, well, we just farm. I do, anyway. There really aren't any more Manns but me. Like I said, my brother married a lawyer and well . . ."

Jeremiah blushed even harder. "I'm sorry," he said, and after grabbing a small dusty box containing the lightbulb from the seat between them, he hopped down out of the truck and jogged awkwardly up to the house. While he was gone, Jill continued to stare at the breath-taking view.

Soon Jeremiah came striding back out of the house. He stopped to pat the old dog's head before bounding down the steps. When she caught him looking at her furtively, Jill smiled back.

"I'm sorry," he said as he climbed back into the truck. The cab shifted beneath Jill as Jeremiah settled in with his three-hundred-plus-pound frame. His meaty hands engulfed the steering wheel like it was a toy. "But my niece, she'll be awful happy."

He drove past the house and started down toward a large barn where there was room to turn around.

Suddenly, Jill said, "My God! Cows!"

Jeremiah regarded three black-and-white heifers staring blandly at them from the small pasture fenced off behind the barn and looked back at Jill in surprise. "Yeah," he said slowly. "Those are cows."

"These are my favorite, the black and white," she said in a somewhat embarrassed tone. "What kind are they?"

"Gateways," Jeremiah said blankly.

Jill began to nod, then looked at him sharply and said, "No, really, what are they?"

"They're Holsteins," Jeremiah said with an impish grin. "The brown ones you see around are Jerseys," he continued pleasantly as he swung the truck around and back up past the house. "Now, where is it I'm taking you? I imagine someplace close to town?"

"We're off West Lake Road," she said contritely as they bounced down the gravel drive. "Fire lane fifteen."

Jeremiah looked at her sharply. "The old Randal place?"

"Randal?"

"Sure," he said, swinging out onto the country road. "Fire lane fifteen. Old man Randal made his fortune building the Thruway, paved it from Buffalo all the way to Albany, they say. The big white house down the hill right on the lake? Yeah, that's the Randal place, or it was."

"Oh," was all Jill could apparently think to say.

As much as Jeremiah had talked before he delivered his incubator bulb was as little as he talked on the way back. His smile, however, remained indefatigable so as not to make Jill more uncomfortable than he suspected she already was.

"The Randal place," he said quietly as they pulled in.

"You folks sure fixed it up nice," he added as the house came into view through the trees.

"Thank you," Jill said. "And thank you for the ride home."

Jeremiah got out and hoisted her mangled bike out of the back. "Um," he said, "you want me to put this somewhere?" He held the bike out as if it were nothing more than a Christmas tree ornament, his huge arms bulging like five-pound bags of flour. Jill shook her head.

"I can drop it at the dump for you if you like," he said, examining the twisted metal. "I didn't know if you wanted your insurance company, or my insurance company to look at it."

"No, that's fine," she quickly replied. "I'm just glad to be breathing. I'm not worried about the bike. If you could just junk it that would be great. I'll get a new one."

"Um, I've got your name and now I know your address. I'll take care of the accident report and everything and I'll try not to bother you with anything if you're okay."

"I'm fine," Jill said warmly. "It was an accident, so please don't worry about it."

"Do you do that a lot?" he asked, tossing it back into the bed of his truck. "Ride around the lake, I mean?"

"I'd like to do it every day if I could," she said. "Normally, we're only here on weekends, but I have the feeling we're going to be around a lot more this summer, so I'll be out there all the time. It's really beautiful, you know. But I don't have to tell you, not with the view you've got from your farm."

Jeremiah smiled sheepishly at the compliment and nervously touched his hand to the bristles that marked his receding hairline. "Well," he said, looking around at the imposing old home that had been restored to its original grandeur. Through the carefully manicured trees, he could see the brilliant aqua green water of the lake. "I'm real sorry about your bike. I better be going now, if there's nothing else I can do for you."

"No," she said, "there's nothing else. Unless . . ."

Jeremiah looked expectantly at her.

"If you stop me for speeding sometime, you can let me off with a warning."

He smiled broadly at her and Jill smiled back.

"You got it," he said, then climbed back into his truck. With a wave, he whipped the vehicle around and started up the drive. Jill never did see him as he strained his neck for one final glimpse of her figure in his rearview mirror. And even after, when he could no longer look at her with his eyes, her image filled his mind so that he knew he would have to somehow see her again.

CHAPTER 14

Collin's funeral was surreal, nightmarish. Like a minimalist drama played out on a modern stage, there were no extras. The service was held in an old funeral home in the village of Skaneateles. Kurt told Jill that he didn't believe in the significance of funerals and grave sites and he said Skaneateles was as good a place as any. He wanted to conclude the matter with businesslike efficiency. He made no accommodations for his friends in the city or Collin's friends from Washington. Besides Jill, Kurt, and Grace, there was only the funeral director and the pastor from the local Presbyterian church.

Against the advisement of the funeral director, Kurt didn't give enough notice to any of the rest of his family to attend. Jill watched the director, a man obviously adept in these types of situations, try to sway Kurt into undertaking a grand affair. He pointed out quite clearly that conventional wisdom suggested that a funeral service was really for the living and not the dead. Kurt politely let him finish, then without emotion told him how it was going to take place and that if he uttered one more word to the contrary he'd go down the road and purchase his son's twenty-five-thousand-dollar mahogany casket there.

There were no tears at the funeral either, and both the funeral director and the pastor eyed the family nervously. Jill felt sad, but she tried her best to model her outward demeanor after Gracie, who had subdued herself over the past several days with doctor-prescribed Valium, and Kurt, who was as frozen as if the veins that had been filled with formaldehyde were his. The times that Jill felt she was about to cry, she bit her cheek hard and sniffled quietly into a handkerchief. Kurt seemed not to notice.

When it was over, he shed his suit coat without comment and holed up in his library. He was on the phone a lot now too. Jill could see one and sometimes even two or three lines lit up together for hours on end. Their meals were filled with silence or sparse conversation about nothing important. Jill knew that some families dealt with death in this way, with stoic silence. She had to keep telling herself that it was important for her just to be there. The only consolation she had in her loneliness was at night when Kurt would crawl into bed and hold her tight.

In the darkness, they would whisper together, talking wistfully about the new life they would share very soon. Jill didn't know whether it was healthy or not for him to not openly confront his boy's death. She suspected that eventually she would have to raise the issue with him, to dredge up the dangerous emotions of anger and grief so they could run their natural course. But the loving moments in their bed at night were so powerful that she was afraid to taint them with talk of the tragedy. Each night she would put it off. Instead, she would scratch Kurt's scalp as they lay there, and as they talked about the things they would have in their unknown, faraway villa by the sea, he would drift off to sleep.

On Thursday, after a long bike ride, she knocked on his office door and let herself in. Kurt rose from a morass of papers with a scowl on his face that faded slowly. He removed his reading glasses and left them on the desk. The lines around his eyes were more pronounced, and for the first time since she'd known him, Jill was conscious of the difference in their ages.

"I'm really busy, Jill," he said, pinching the corners of his bloodshot eyes, "but come in."

He motioned her to the couch and came out from behind his desk. They sat down together and Kurt gently touched her face. She averted her eyes from his to the lovely view from the grand picture window that looked out over the shady green lawn and onto the lake. Somehow, looking at him made her emotional. Softly, he turned her face back toward his until their eyes met once again. She fought back her hysteria, but couldn't help from suddenly bursting into tears.

"What? What's wrong?" he said. He spoke as though he had no clue as to why she would be crying.

"I just—" she said, quelling a sob, "I just want to know that you still love me, Kurt. Because I still love you. I know this is hard. I know you must be suffering inside, but I just want something to do. The only time we talk is at night, in the dark. I want to live a life with you. I'm hanging around here walking on pins and needles!

"Gracie, she's practically comatose. You, you're shut up in here day and night. You said you wanted me to stay here, and I am. But now I just want to know what you want me to do . . . I feel like I'm losing my mind . . ."

Kurt looked at her as though he only that moment realized she had been so distressed during the preceding days. "I'm sorry," he said gently. He pulled her head next to his and stroked the back of her hair while she calmed herself.

Then she pulled away and, shaking her head, she said, "I'm sorry too. You're the one hurting in all this and here I am bawling like a baby . . . I'm sorry. I just want to talk to you, Kurt. I want us to talk about what's going on in the daylight when you're not exhausted from a day of whatever it is that you're doing."

"I'm doing just what I said I was going to do," he said quietly. "I'm putting things into motion that are going to expose the people who killed Collin.

"It's not dangerous," he said after reading the expression on her face. "Not yet. When it happens, and they're exposed, it will be time for us to go. I'm planning for that too. I'm also divesting myself of everything to do with Safe Tech . . ."

"Kurt?" she said. Safe Tech had been so much a part of his life. Of course, he would have to leave his company if he was really going to carry out whatever plan it was he had been talking about, but to hear him say it was shocking. It highlighted just how determined he really was.

"That's why I'm holed up in here. Do you understand now?" he said urgently. "There are a lot of things to do, as you can imagine. I want to disengage myself from the company without crippling it. Once I do that, we'll take a long trip, just the two of us, and start a new life—together."

"Kurt, you built Safe Tech from nothing," Jill said in a soft, almost mystified tone. "Think about the things you've been able to do—the medical links, the data protection division . . ."

"None of that means anything," he said calmly.

Jill simply stared.

"Just stick by me, Jill," he pleaded. "The next month and a half aren't going to be easy. I need to free myself from everything at Safe Tech and work my way through Collin's death at the same time . . .

"And," he said, his eyes afire with anger, "I want these people to be punished!

"I guess," he continued more gently, "sometimes . . . I guess sometimes I'll need to be alone. Just bear with me. There will be times, I know, that this will be hard. But I love you and I know I can count on you. That's why I asked you to marry me. That's why I want to share the whole rest of my life with you."

Jill felt a pang of guilt. Wasn't marriage supposed to be for better or for worse, in sickness and in health anyway? Kurt wasn't himself right now, but that was no reason for her not to stand by him and believe that he would work his way through this difficult time.

After all, the only child he ever had had suddenly been killed.

"I want to help you," she whispered.

"Thank you," he said earnestly. "You can help. You can wrap up everything you've got going at Safe Tech. Don't talk about why, though. I don't want to create an internal panic. Why don't you just tell the people that really have to know that you and I are going to go away on a quiet trip. You can turn all your projects over to your team.

"I'd like you to tie up any loose ends in your private affairs as well," he continued gently. "Terminate your lease, whatever you need to do. Send anything that's really important up here and I'll have it taken care of."

"I'll need to go back to the city," she began with a worried expression.

"Yes," he said. "I was hoping you could go down and get it done in a day or so. I know I'm distracted with everything during the day and you might think I'm not as attentive as I should be, but I need you. I need to have you near, please . . ."

Jill looked from Kurt's face to the massive ring on her finger and back to his face. She could see the anguish lurking beneath his surface. She knew he needed her.

"I can get Gus to arrange almost everything and maybe just go down for the day," she said hopefully. Gus was her assistant.

Kurt looked at her fondly. "Thank you.

"Everything will work out," he assured her. "Just give me a few weeks. Give me time and you and I will be off to have a life of our own. It'll be just us, love. No meetings, no phones ringing, just you and me. Trust me, it will be— It will be everything we've dreamed of."

His smile was warm and winning. She could see the pain in his eyes, a symptom of the grief she knew he felt. Jill knew she couldn't do anything but smile back at him.

"Thank you for understanding," he said. "By the way, if you're out this week, shopping or anything, stop by the Wal-Mart and get two sets of passport photos."

"My passport is good for a while."

"Well . . . I want to make sure everything is in perfect order."

"You don't have to worry about mine," she said. "I just had it renewed not three years ago."

He looked at her painfully. "Honey, can you just do what I ask? I need them, that's all." His voice rose slightly and he spoke in a constrained tone. "Is it that big of a deal, or can you just do it?"

"I can do it," she said calmly.

"Thank you," he said, back to the Kurt she knew. "Now, if you don't mind, I've got so much to do . . ."

CHAPTER 15

Kurt worked until his back was sore from sitting and his ears ached from the constant pressure of the telephone headset. He set his glasses down and rubbed the sides of his nose as he got up to stretch. The shadows cast by the trees on the back lawn had grown long and he recalled now that it was several hours ago that Clara had knocked on the door and asked whether or not he wanted lunch. He was hungry, so he went to the kitchen and found a ham and cheese sandwich that Clara had evidently made for him before going off to her other duties. Kurt poured himself a glass of milk and wolfed the sandwich down without bothering to sit or to taste his food. As he mechanically ground down his meal, he gazed out at the lake, enviously pondering the people going by in their boats, oblivious to his acute world of pain and torment.

In such moments, the grief pressed down on him with infinite weight. He thought of Gracie. He knew she was bearing up, aided by the sedatives Kurt's doctor back in New York had prescribed. Whether it was because of that or because of his own preoccupations,

Kurt really hadn't reached out to her the way he knew he should. At the very least, he owed her an explanation of what he was planning to do. He would also have to be sure that he extricated her from the upcoming events so that there would be no criminal culpability. But to do justice to her required more than just shipping her back to Greenwich. Gracie had been a part of his life for too long.

He wondered briefly if there was a way to bring her. That notion was enough to amuse him. He was old enough to be able to judiciously weigh sentiment against practicality. It was hard to imagine Gracie anywhere but home. The house in Greenwich was essentially hers. She had fussed over it through the years, conducting an endless cycle of decorating and remodeling. She had friends there. It was a beautiful and comfortable place with its rolling grassy lawns and its labyrinth of flower gardens, fountains, and greenhouses. Kurt made a mental note to have the deed transferred into her name as well as establish a comfortable trust fund.

While he knew Gracie would miss him, his real connection to her over the last twenty years had been Collin. After Collin had gone away to school, Gracie and Kurt spent less and less time together. It wasn't that either of them had stopped loving the other, it was just that their lives had begun to follow different paths.

Kurt set down his milk glass and went up the back stairs to Gracie's room. He knocked quietly on the open door before going in. The room was expansive enough to allow for her bedroom furniture on one side and a sitting area on the other. Everything was as neat as if no one lived there. Gracie was between the two areas, sitting in the large window seat in a black dress with her long gray hair pulled back into a tight, austere bun. She was staring blankly out into the front yard. Tear tracks ran from her eyes under her gold-framed glasses all the way to her pointed chin, and her face drooped with anguish. Beside her on the seat lay an open scrapbook. Kurt looked down at the half dozen pictures taken at a birthday party they'd had for Collin when he was only six.

The sight of his boy, so young, his face beneath the conical silver hat and afire with delight, gripped Kurt's throat like a chokehold. He closed the book gently and sat down noiselessly beside his sister.

"Hello, Gracie," he said quietly.

"Hello, Kurtis," she said, choking on her words without averting her eyes from the window. In her hand was a string of rosary beads, and Kurt saw now that as she fingered them, her lips moved silently. Kurt knew that for the first time since he'd come back from the capital, Gracie wasn't under sedation. Her eyes were sharp and her words had an edge of pain that was unmitigated by the drugs.

He watched her without speaking. The idea of telling her what he planned to do sounded easy enough. He just didn't know how to start.

"It's a mortal sin, Kurtis," she softly wailed. "It's a mortal sin and I can't get it out of my mind the way that little boy was so afraid of hell. Remember that old Bible I had? He was so afraid of the picture of hell. He was no more than a baby. He made me get rid of it . . ."

Kurt was confused for a moment, but then his Catholic confirmation lessons came back to him. "Suicide," he whispered. A Catholic who committed suicide was doomed to hell.

"He didn't commit suicide, Gracie," he told her.

Gracie's eyes darted his way and she glared accusingly at him. "Don't say that," she said. "Don't say that to make me feel better, Kurtis. God knows and it's his will, not mine!"

"No, Gracie. He didn't. He really didn't do it," Kurt said urgently. "He was . . . He was murdered . . ."

A strange light filled his sister's faded blue eyes as she whispered, "How can you say that?"

Kurt told her in solemn tones what he now believed had happened on the night Collin was killed. He omitted, however, the details of who the girl was, who sent her, or why. When Gracie asked who would do such a thing, Kurt chose to be evasive. He said he was looking into it.

"I'm going to find them, Gracie," he assured her. "I'll find them and . . ."

"And you'll kill them," she said flatly.

Kurt stared at her, not knowing what to say.

"I know you," Gracie said, looking away from him and back out the window. "And I'm not going to try and stop you."

After a few moments she said, "The Lord tells us to turn the other cheek, but the Bible also says that for an eye an eye shall be taken . . ."

A tall, dark walnut grandfather clock that stood on the opposite wall clicked. Its gears churned audibly and five deep gongs filled the room before the silence returned.

"I want you to stay with me for a few weeks," Kurt said quietly. "Stay here with us, me and Jill. But then you'll have to go back home, Gracie, to Greenwich. I'm giving you that house, and enough money so that you won't have to worry about anything."

Gracie nodded and Kurt knew from a lifetime together that he didn't need to say anything more. She understood completely.

"Is she going with you?" she asked without a hint of bitterness or envy. It was simply a question.

"Yes," Kurt said, then added, "I think so."

"You think?" Gracie said, looking back at him. "You'll need her, you know."

"Yes," Kurt said, "I know."

Gracie looked back out the window. "She'll go with you. She loves you very much, Kurtis. You would have been very happy together."

"Maybe we still will."

Gracie sighed heavily and bit into her lower lip, wincing in pain before nodding violently. Fresh tears coursed down her cheeks. Without looking, she reached over and gave his hand a quick and forceful squeeze before taking up her beads once again.

As Kurt stood to go, he saw her lips take up their silent dance of prayer. This time he knew the prayers weren't for Collin's soul, but his own.

CHAPTER 16

Jill looked around at the things that made up what for several years had been her home: the worn beige leather couch with its carved wooden oriental coffee table, the Modigliani prints, the stain on the hardwood floor next to the rug where she and Kurt had knocked over a bottle of red wine the first time they ever . . .

A mischievous smile crossed her lips. Still, for all the pleasant and comfortable memories, the homey feeling of the place had gone stale. Most of her time lately had been spent with Kurt, in his grand flat on Central Park West, or in Greenwich, or at the lake. More than anything, her apartment had become a reminder that they weren't a married couple, and a place she might occasionally spend the night if he were out of town and she found herself for some reason on the east side of Manhattan. So it was with nothing more than a vague sense of nostalgia that she taped up the last of the boxes she had marked to be shipped up to Skaneateles, descended the elevator, and waved a pleasant good-bye to the liveried doorman. His bluff good humor proved that he had no idea it was the last time that he would ever see her, and that made Jill feel somewhat deceitful.

It was a pleasant day and Talia's office was no more than six blocks up Madison Avenue and halfway down 72nd Street in the direction of Central Park. The shop windows along the way were filled with extravagance: jewels, gold, rare ornate wood, and small women's clothes cut from rainbows of silk. Even the grating smell of the rancid subway below that would waft up occasionally from beneath the street couldn't seem to taint the brilliant scene. Jill enjoyed the walk despite being profoundly aware of all the little things she would miss about New York. She passed her favorite patisserie, an Italian restaurant that had the best take-out veal in the city, and a coffee shop where they still knew what she wanted without her having to ask. She still wore a short Donna Karan business suit from the office that morning, and as she walked, male shopkeepers and pedestrians stole surreptitious glances at her figure.

It wasn't long before she left the brilliant sunshine and turned into the shade of 72nd Street, where she came to the heavy bronze door of Talia's office. She mounted the steps and rang the bell. The prim receptionist let her in and offered her a glass of Evian while she waited in the cool opulence of the marble-walled sitting room. Soon, a man in his mid-fifties dressed in a dark suit and brilliant cobalt blue tie walked quietly out of the office and in low tones made another appointment for the same time next week. When he'd gone, Talia appeared in an elegant short-sleeved cashmere sweater and tailored slacks, topped off with a heavy necklace of black pearls. She was a tall woman with short hair, heavy features, and thick bones that would have given her a nearly androgynous appearance but for her masterful work with her hair, makeup, and clothes.

"Jill!" she exclaimed, hugging her friend closely and leading her into the office. She asked the receptionist to bring them tea, then shut the tall doors. Jill sat down in an arrangement of thick overstuffed furniture opposite the space where Talia worked.

"I feel like I should be sitting over there," Jill said, nodding toward the comfortable leather chaise that was still warm from the man with the cobalt tie.

"You're welcome to," Talia said, eyeing her carefully. "What's wrong?"

Talia had been away to Europe with her husband or else she would certainly have known about everything that had happened. Jill sighed heavily and paused while the receptionist placed a tray of tea and delicate cookies down on the low table between them. When she was gone, Jill related everything, pausing only to allow Talia a brief look at her diamond ring and accept joyous congratulations. As her story grew more and more grim, Jill's voice sank lower and lower.

When she was finished, Talia's face was a mixture of pity and disbelief. "Oh, that sweet boy . . . You should have called me," she said with concern.

"You were away," Jill replied. "I didn't want to bother you and Henry."

"Nonsense," Talia said with an emphatic wave of her hand.

"Do you think he really means it? To sell Safe Tech? To leave?" Jill asked.

Talia's dark eyes narrowed and she seemed to consider the pattern on the oriental rug before looking up and saying gently, "Grief is like a pocket of magma that has to erupt. The resulting volcano can take on many forms, all of which are based on the geology that already exists at the earth's surface. Sometimes an eruption will smoke for years and that's it. Others disgorge lava and ash like fireworks, and no one can predict either one . . .

"You're doing the right thing," she went on after a pause. "Your instincts were correct. Let him say and do what he will. Be there for him."

Talia rose and crossed the room. After briefly searching the bookshelf on the opposite wall, she removed a book and brought it to Jill.

"Read this," she said. "There are some very good ideas in here and it will give you a more complete idea of what you're dealing with."

"Thank you, Talia. What about . . . revenge?" Jill asked after she flipped through the book's table of contents and placed it down on the floor beside her purse.

"Revenge?" Talia said, raising a single eyebrow. "Yes, sometimes. Sometimes very strong. Although I've seen people who've lost a child that you might think would be murderous turn docile. Others . . . One time I had to call the police to intervene. It could be worse," she continued. "People in his situation are often suicidal, sometimes irrationally violent. That's the lava. Under normal circumstances, it will pass. It's almost never easy though. In a case like this, he will probably find a way to blame himself. He might even blame you . . ."

Jill frowned. He had certainly blamed himself already. She wondered if the second part might be true as well. If he blamed her somehow, it might explain some of the tension between them.

"I'm just telling you this so you can be prepared," Talia said, reaching across the table and taking Jill's hand in her own. "My point is, we can't sit here and predict all the forms his grief might take. Everyone is different. All we can be sure of is that most likely the worst of it will be temporary. It's not that it won't change him. Grief like that changes a person like a volcanic eruption changes a landscape, but that doesn't mean when it's over that things can't go back to normal."

Jill's eyes softened and she said, "I'm glad you think I'm doing the right thing."

"You make it sound like . . . I don't know . . ." Talia said.

"You know you always said I was brilliant in everything but men," Jill reminded her.

Talia smiled wryly and said, "Please, dear. Do you remember Michael Stokes?"

"Michael Stokes was nice," Jill protested.

"Michael Stokes was nice," Talia conceded with a nod. "He was brilliant too. But he wasn't for you. He was a skinny, tousle-headed genius who couldn't match his socks or talk about anything that didn't have to do with physical chemistry. Even Henry had a hard time understanding him."

"Do you remember when we went to Treeman

Park?" Jill giggled, referring to the state park near Cornell.

"Oh my God! Remember that?" Talia howled.

The four of them—Talia, Henry, Jill, and Michael Stokes—had taken a picnic to the waterfalls in the park. It was a torrid day and Michael Stokes wore the oddest hat any of them had ever seen. It was a baseball-like cap, only the crown was high and round, and off the back hung a swatch of cloth reminiscent of the French Foreign Legion. Unable to laugh at himself, Michael Stokes had given them all a stern lecture on the principles of kinetic energy and aerodynamics. It seemed everyone else in the park was a fool and only he, Michael Stokes, was properly prepared to enjoy the day.

Out of sheer loyalty, Jill had valiantly agreed with her nominal boyfriend. Some frat brothers at the adjacent picnic table, however, didn't agree. And as the hot afternoon depleted their keg of beer, the ribald comments grew louder and more obnoxious. Finally, the muscle-bound ringleader of the group staggered over, toe-to-toe, to a quivering Michael Stokes. When Michael balled his hopeless fists to defend himself, Jill intervened, pushing the shirtless frat guy with a shove powerful enough for him to break his arm against the seat of the picnic table on his way down.

The two women howled with delight reminiscing about the ensuing ambulance and the park cop who didn't arrest anyone, but tried desperately for the next several weeks to get Jill to go on a date.

"My God," Talia exclaimed, wiping the corners of

her eyes, "then you went to the opposite extreme! A basketball player."

"Oh, yes," Jill said, and suddenly both of them were sober.

"I'm sorry," said Talia, who knew better than anyone what a disaster that turned out to be. "But I guess what I want to say is that, in Michael Stokes's terms, you always exhibited magnetic polarity. You gravitated to the extremes. A genius, but a nerd. A handsome jock, but a self-centered brute. Kurt, though, he's different."

"Do you really think?" Jill said brightly.

"Of course," Talia responded tersely. "I've said so before."

"I know, but I didn't know if you really meant it," Jill said. She had seen Talia so regularly during her divorce that she might as well have been a patient, and she suspected that Talia's praise for Kurt was born from sympathy.

"Have I ever said what I didn't mean?" Talia said, raising both eyebrows. "He's smart but not odd, successful but not conceited, strong but gentle, handsome but not obnoxious. He's perfect for you, Jill. I really think that—"

"And I need to give him time," Jill muttered.

"Time, and space, and love," Talia added.

Jill nodded. She couldn't have been more pleased by what she was hearing. Then her brow grew dark and she said, "Do you think he really means to leave the country and never come back?"

"Maybe not," Talia said. "But if he did, what would

be so bad? You've already told me that nothing in your life is as important as him."

"I was thinking about us," Jill said quietly.

Talia burst out in mirthful laughter. "Nothing can separate us, my dear. You should know that. Even if you're off someplace on the other side of the world, you'll get ahold of me and I'll come to you. You and I? No . . . Only death could separate us. Only death."

CHAPTER 17

The riddle remained unsolved. Kurt still had no idea how he could penetrate the fourth perimeter and get out alive. Nevertheless, he was proceeding with every other aspect of his personal mission as if the problem were already well under control. He knew he could extricate himself from Safe Tech; it was only a matter of time and money, money spent on lawyers. Kurt had some of the best, and because of the magnitude of the transaction, they were working overtime for him. Funneling his fortune into an offshore account in the Cayman Islands was a separate matter and something that required discretion. That was another benefit of having the biggest and the best lawyers in New York City. They'd seen this kind of thing before and they knew how it was done.

Kurt wanted to remove any possible link between him and the money. After he did what he was about to do, only an impenetrable legal veil would protect him from being hunted down by anyone simply tracing the path of his funds. But Kurt was being assured that that was exactly how the Cayman banks did business. They had surpassed even the Swiss when it came to discretion.

Between the conference calls and meetings with lawyers who flew in from New York at his insistence, Kurt was pressed for time to plan out and orchestrate not only an assassination but also his escape. Things were made more difficult because he didn't want to rely on anyone but himself. However, there were some things he needed that he couldn't easily get. False identities for him and Jill, for example. He also needed the appropriate equipment programmed to enable him to commandeer the Secret Service's communications.

If he could get his hands on that, then he would have the passwords he needed to infiltrate the president's protection. Only a former agent would have the knowledge to pull it off. With the ability to intercept and interrupt the Service's communications, Kurt, knowing the protocols, the jargon, and the typical behavior of an agent, could penetrate the first three perimeters of protection almost with ease. But, while he had a working knowledge that the technology for such equipment existed, there were only a few men in the world with the capability to actually bring all the different elements together to create a simple working machine.

Fortunately, there was a man whom Kurt trusted that he could go to for both. Cheng Yu had been with Kurt since the inception of Safe Tech. Kurt had hired him as a Ph.D. student out of MIT. A Chinese national, Cheng had come to the States with his family when he was just four. While Cheng had great affinity for the country that had provided his family with a safe haven and himself with a fortune, he had an even greater love and devotion toward Kurt. Kurt was the man who not only had made him a multimillionaire, but had repeatedly used his political contacts and influence to help to bring many of Cheng's family and friends over from China through the years. All of them, including Cheng himself, who could afford to live anywhere he wanted, resided in Chinatown in lower Manhattan. Cheng was Safe Tech's chief scientist, Jill's boss, and a man of unparalleled genius. He was also streetwise, the perfect person to help Kurt with discreet issues like fake passports and classified electronic equipment.

Kurt flew Cheng up from New York on his own jet so the two of them could spend the day together in Kurt's office, going over the details of everything Kurt needed. By three in the afternoon, neither of them had yet mentioned the reason for Kurt's requests. But Kurt knew that was Cheng's way. In fact, he counted on it. Part of that characteristic came from Cheng's upbringing, but part of it Kurt also knew was simply his friend's nature. Cheng wasn't one to ask questions, especially of his patron.

Cheng was the only person in the entire world whom Kurt knew he could trust so completely. He could put his life in Cheng's hands. In fact, he was doing exactly that. After he and Jill disappeared, he presumed that Cheng Yu would be the only man on earth who could possibly find them.

Kurt supposed he trusted Cheng even more than he did Jill. It wasn't that he questioned her love. He didn't. He truly believed deep down that after he'd done what he had to do, Jill would still willingly go away with him and spend the rest of her life with him. He felt he knew that much about her. But he couldn't help also being afraid that if she knew what he was planning she might try to stop him. She might even do something foolish. Cheng, on the other hand, would never do that. Cheng would fully understand avenging the death of an only and beloved son.

This was why the two of them were poring over Kurt's plans in the cool leather aroma of the library one afternoon not long after Collin's funeral. Kurt was explaining the importance of having passports that would be completely untraceable. He also wanted an additional set, preferably Canadian, with indistinct photos of both him and Jill that could be used to establish new identities in a foreign land.

Cheng nodded and, looking through the thick lenses of his plastic-rimmed glasses, said, "I know the people that can do this. There are some bad people in Chinatown. Very bad, but very good for this kind of thing. But I don't trust any of them. No. I only trust myself. My idea is this. I'll get them to fix these passports, two sets. They do wonderful things, these people. They can get into Customs computers and not just make a phony passport. They create the backup data. They create a person, Social Security number, everything."

Cheng blinked his large dark eyes before going on. "But this is what I plan to do: I will be the one to insert the photos and stamp them and laminate the passports. To these people, they've just made one more fake ID.

That way, they'll never see your photo—then no one will make a connection to you."

After a satisfied nod, he continued in a low voice, "I don't know what it is you're planning, Kurt. I don't want to know. But I think maybe your picture is going to be all over the TV and the news after you do it . . ."

Kurt gave his old friend an intelligent look. The seamless skin of Cheng's face topped by his dark thatch of straight hair made him look as young as the day Kurt had first met him. He certainly still dressed the same: slacks and a short-sleeved, awkward-fitting dress shirt with no tie, his pocket overburdened with pens. He was thin to the point of emaciation, but Kurt had witnessed his training at a martial arts dojo in the city so he knew not to be deceived by the mild appearance. Cheng was a deadly character with the quickness and sting of a whip. Kurt was smiling at him fondly when the door to the library suddenly burst open and Jill strode in with her arms open wide.

"Cheng!" she cried with delight, clasping his hands in her own. "I didn't know you were here! Cheng, it's so good to see you. Kurt, you didn't tell me Cheng was here. I had to hear it from the driver," she said, scolding them both. "Cheng, you look wonderful—what would you like for dinner?"

Cheng had stood to greet her with a subtle bow and now he shifted uncomfortably from foot to foot, blinking at Kurt.

"I'm so glad to see you," Jill continued excitedly. "You're just what Kurt needs. They say there's nothing like an old friend to pick you up! Don't they say that, Kurt?"

In her excitement, Jill failed to notice that Kurt's expression was nothing but somber. "Cheng can't stay for dinner, honey," he said quietly.

She looked at him as if anticipating some kind of punch line. Cheng always stayed for dinner. "No?" she asked. "Why not?"

Cheng looked down at his feet in obvious embarrassment. It was a rather awkward moment. As a rule, Cheng never refused an invitation. It was one of their shared pleasures in life, sitting together over a meal, splitting their conversation between business and a myriad of other topics.

"Well," Kurt said, "we just have a lot of work to do and then he's got to get back to the city."

"You're kidding," Jill said, still holding on to a scrap of good humor. "What are you two doing?"

An embarrassing silence ensued.

"Cheng is just . . ." Kurt began. "He's just helping me with some things on the transfer of the company. We're working out my succession plan, that's all."

"That's no reason not to stay for dinner," Jill said lightly.

"Jill," Kurt snapped suddenly, "you can't just burst in here—" He stopped, realizing how boorish he sounded, and said more gently, "I'm sorry. He just can't stay, that's all."

Jill appeared to ignore him. "Well, Cheng, it was very nice to see you anyway," she said demurely, her chin held high. "Have a safe trip back." Then she turned and stormed out of the room.

The warm feelings Kurt had begun to have throughout the day working with Cheng were suddenly chilled. The realization of what he was planning to do had been brought painfully home by Jill's entrance. How could he be sure she'd go with him when it was all over? The clandestine nature of his movements between now and when the president came wasn't going to change. If anything, need would require him to become even more secretive in the ensuing weeks; he wondered if Jill and he would even make it that far.

"I think if you don't need anything else, my friend, then I'd better go," Cheng said quietly.

Kurt realized that he was simply standing there in the middle of the room transfixed in thought. He looked up abruptly. "Yes, Cheng," he said with a quickly constructed smile. "When do you think you can get me the equipment that I need?"

"I have everything you need. The only problem is that they're in different pieces in different plants," Cheng explained. "I'm going to put this together myself, Kurt. But it will take time. Everything has to be shipped to my laboratory. That could take one week, maybe less. Once I get everything I need? Maybe I can have it for you in one week if I don't do anything else."

"Two weeks, then?" Kurt said.

"Yes," Cheng replied after careful consideration. "And the passports I'll get this week."

"Good. I want to ask you something else, my friend."

"Of course."

"Obviously I'm leaving the country, for good." With visible discomfort he said, "I won't come back."

Cheng blinked but said nothing.

After a slight bow from his friend and employee, Kurt said, "And . . . I meant what I said about a succession plan . . . I was thinking of having Johnson take over as CEO, but I won't do that if you don't think it's best, Cheng."

Cheng looked at him slyly and said, "You think I wouldn't like to have another man as my boss?" Then he smiled broadly. "No, Johnson is the right man. I know what I am and I know what I'm not. I'm a scientist, not a businessman. If you're not going to be here, the only thing I care about is Safe Tech's stock, and if you say Johnson is the man to keep it up, then Johnson is the man for the job."

"That's what I think," Kurt said slowly, measuring Cheng's reaction. "But I wouldn't do it without your consent."

"I thank you for asking," Cheng said, bowing low.

"And I'll let Johnson know it too," Kurt said.

Cheng bowed again, slightly this time, and said, "Thank you. Now if that's all, I have work to do for a very good friend, a friend that to me has been like a brother . . ."

As the two of them embraced, neither had the slightest idea that they were being watched. Nor did they know that everything they had just said and everything they planned to do had been heard.

CHAPTER 18

Along the southern edge of Kurt's property, a thick hedge of lilacs, now a naked green without their brilliant purple blossoms, mobbed the spaces between a lofty row of blue spruce. In the midst of that wild tangle lay a man dressed from head to toe in leafy camouflage. The sight of him, even the idea, would have been ridiculous except for the nasty 9mm Glock that was strapped to his hip, complete with a gleaming black silencer.

Under his leafy hood the man wore a pair of earphones. In front of him on a small tripod lay a directional microphone sensitive enough to pick up the voices from within Kurt's library by the faint vibrations they made on the large picture window. When he wasn't listening to that, he had his headset switched over to a receiver that picked up a transmitter tapped into the phone lines on the pole that ran up the side of Kurt's long driveway. And still, no matter what he listened to, the snatch of a Bruce Springsteen song he'd heard that morning on the car radio spun around and around in the back of his mind so that often he caught himself humming its tune.

The man's name was Mitchell Reeves. He was a special agent within the Secret Service. A short, compact man with dark hair and olive skin, he was a former officer in Military Intelligence, and had once been an aggressive soldier and a devotee of discipline. He was secretive by nature and uniquely qualified for this type of work. He had no recording devices. He reported to one man and one man alone. He asked no questions. He took no action that he wasn't first authorized to take.

This job was Reeves's chance at redemption. After leaving the military more than a decade ago, he'd spent time training insurgents in South America for the CIA until that whole thing went sour. Since then, he had drifted further and further from the legitimacy that he once enjoyed as an officer in the army. His most recent job before this one had been so squalid that he hated to think about it. But now there was no cause to recall the dark cellars and the shocking human moans—he was back in the real world, with a real assignment. The first meeting with his new boss was still fresh in his mind. After a glossy black Seville had delivered him from National Airport in Washington, he was treated to an elegant lunch at the Four Seasons and offered the job before coffee.

But while Reeves didn't ask questions aloud, even to his partner with whom he shared connecting rooms at the Holiday Inn in Auburn, he did wonder to himself. He wondered how long this man, Kurt Ford, was going to be allowed to proceed. He wondered why he wasn't recording what was being said. If the Service was going to grab him—and he knew they would—wouldn't they want the things he was saying and doing preserved for a jury to convict him?

Deep in his mind, Reeves was convinced that people much higher than he within the Service intended to let this whole thing reach critical mass. Then—and only then—would they insert themselves between Ford and the president. Reeves had to admit it would be a spectacular public relations coup for the Service, whose morale had suffered since the Clinton scandal with Monica Lewinsky, when agents were asked to testify against the man they protected.

Whatever the reason for the inaction, Reeves was convinced that he wasn't the only one who knew Ford was going to make a run at the president. How, he wasn't yet certain. The fact that he'd seen Ford through his night binoculars chug all the way across the lake in the middle of the night to visit the judge's mansion by boat suggested a surgical-type assault. But that certainly didn't make any sense when one considered the lengths to which Ford was going to ensure his escape. Reeves knew Ford was a former agent. While that experience, along with some very advanced technology, might allow him to penetrate the fourth perimeter, he also must know escape would be impossible. And Ford was obviously very bent on escape. As far as Reeves could see, most of his time was devoted to that end.

The only other possible rationale for what was happening was that the entire thing was a sham, a kind of training mission, a test for Reeves and Art Vanecroft, his partner. That wouldn't surprise him. At this level, the government was always up to some kind of shenanigans, one agency testing the effectiveness of another, or testing the viability of itself to justify more money. At the end of the day, that was what everything was about—more money. Reeves didn't have to ponder that for very long.

He looked at his watch and shifted his position ever so slightly. He had several hours to go. A fat mosquito landed on his nose; Reeves could just make it out if he shut one eye and looked hard. It bit him, but he didn't move to swat it away. That would be careless. It wasn't easy, working twelve-hour shifts, holding almost perfectly still until dark. But that was part of the deal. Being involved in anything covert included more drudgery than it did excitement. But when it was exciting, it was really exciting. That was what kept Reeves going. He liked being in the eye of the storm.

If this whole thing was for real, Reeves was pretty certain of one thing: There would be a good chance somewhere along the way for someone, probably Kurt Ford, to be killed, and that was the ultimate high, really. Life-and-death stakes—that was excitement. That was living on the edge. And if someone did have to be killed, odds were that Reeves would be the one who got to do the killing. It was the kind of killing you didn't go to jail for, either. It was like in the movies, like James Bond, 007—licensed to kill. The idea made him smile.

CHAPTER 19

The next morning, Jill rolled out of bed at five, changed, and crept quietly downstairs. She was going to take a long ride. The rubber from the tires of her new bike filled the garage with their pungent aroma. Jill sniffed the air with faint disgust and wheeled the bike out of the garage with her cycling shoes and socks in hand.

On a whim, she set the bike down in the driveway and walked barefoot back around the house toward the water. She followed the meandering path, over an old stone bridge that spanned a small creek, and across the expansive lawn that stretched for more than a thousand feet from side to side beneath the ancient trees. Soon she was standing on the stony beach with a warm south wind in her face and the waves lapping gently at her feet. In the glow of the coming dawn, only Jupiter blinked overhead. She could see nearly fifteen miles to the end of the lake where the magnificent glacial hills plummeted into the deep narrow corridor of water. It was an exhilarating place to be: Skaneateles. Over the last several summers, she had grown not only fond of it, but also attached to its placid beauty; she wondered if Kurt's plans would ever bring them back.

Sighing heavily, she made her way back up the path toward the house amid the now noisy revelry of the waking birds. On her bike, she pumped her way to the top of the drive and set out as usual, eager for the endorphin high she knew was waiting for her only a few miles down the road.

The lush woods and streams and fields brimming with nascent sprouts of corn and wheat and alfalfa rushed by and her mind wandered to weddings. Over the last two years, she'd been to a few with Kurt. Two had taken place at the Pierre in Manhattan. They were fresh in her mind, memorable for their opulence, with flowers cascading from columns that rose all the way to the ornate ceiling. That wouldn't bother her, to do it right like that. Especially after her failed first marriage. She'd like people to know that this time things were going to be different.

Her first wedding had taken place in a small church in Binghamton. The reception was in the nearby VFW hall. The only member of her family willing to attend was her brother, and part of her wished he hadn't. She could still remember the shame she felt seeing him sit there in the sweltering heat with his overweight wife, drinking iced tea and smiling politely at the dregs flopping drunkenly about on the dance floor in ill-fitting rented tuxedos and frumpy pastel-colored dresses. It had been a nightmare.

But now, would she even have the opportunity to invite people to a wedding? Kurt hadn't said anything about it, but the way he talked made her suspect they were simply going to elope. And although she felt a pang of shame, with the way Kurt had been acting she didn't want to even ask. There were moments when she felt the eerie sensation that she was playing out the role she'd taken on with her first husband, the same role her own mother had played with her father. But Jill was sure, as sure as she'd ever been of anything, that any irritability or restraint on Kurt's part was temporary and born only from grief. Talia's words came back to assuage her anxiety.

As she rounded a bend in the road and began to climb the last big hill before the ravine where she'd been run off the road, Jill became aware of a person up ahead. By now the sky was ready to burst into day and the imminent morning sun was quickly burning the last orange haze in the east away. As the first ray pierced the sky, it shone full on the figure, an enormous man wearing red shorts and a white T-shirt with a biking helmet that reminded her of a fruit bowl. Beside him was a racing bike, as new as her own.

Even with his hand buttoned to his forehead to block the bright sun, the figure was recognizable as Jeremiah. Jill tittered bashfully to herself as she pulled right up to him and stopped. He had obviously been waiting for her. She could see his house perched above them away to the west.

"Hi," she said cheerfully. "I didn't know you had a bike."

"I don't. I mean, I do now," he responded. "I just thought it looked like fun."

"You look like you mean business," she said, eyeing his brand-new biking shoes.

"Is this the right stuff?" he asked, looking down at the rigid-soled shoes. "I just got what they told me."

"You did good," she told him. "The shoes alone will save you half an hour around this lake."

He gave her a puzzled look and said, "Really?"

Jill nodded. "Think about when you ride a bike in regular shoes. When you push down on the pedal, half the force is used up by the bend in your foot. With these, every ounce of push goes into the bike."

"I hope you don't mind," he said after a pause in which he continued to contemplate the shoes, "but you said you ride almost every day and I got this bike yesterday and I just thought I'd watch the sun come up and see if you came by. Do you mind if I join you?"

"No," she said. "I think it would be great. I'll feel safer just knowing you're not out driving around in your pickup truck."

Jeremiah's face drooped pitifully until Jill laughed cheerfully and said, "I'm kidding."

At that, he brightened and climbed up onto the bike whose seat sprouted ridiculously high from the frame on its chrome stem. Jill couldn't help herself from thinking of a bear she'd seen in the Big Apple Circus riding a tiny scooter. But she checked her remark and, thankful for a companion, said, "Let's go."

Later that morning, after breakfast by herself and a lonely swim in the lake, Jill found Kurt in his library. He was busy and he looked up impatiently at her as he replaced the phone on its receiver. She suddenly felt an unwarranted pang of guilt.

"Remember the man I told you who almost hit me, the farmer who gave me a ride back here after my bike was ruined?" she asked. "He was really so nice about it and it wasn't his fault at all."

"Yeah," he said somewhat testily, sliding some papers off his desktop and into the drawer. "I remember."

"Well, I saw him today," she said tentatively. "He was out riding a bike too and we ended up riding around the lake together. He's a very nice person, Kurt. I like him. I told him I'd ride with him again, but I wanted to say something to you before I did. I don't want you to think—"

"The farmer? Of course not," he scoffed, dismissing any notion of jealousy with a wave of his hand. "Listen, I appreciate your saying something to me about it, but you go ahead and ride your bike. I'm glad you've got someone to ride with. Don't worry about that at all."

Despite Kurt's hastily spoken permission, Jill felt ill at ease. And whenever she felt that way, there was only one person she could call. She dialed Talia's home number in part to reinforce her spirit and in part to gain further approval for her actions.

"He said that?" Talia exclaimed.

After a moment of consideration, Talia continued in her typically spirited manner, "Then you go right on ahead and do it. You need some human contact."

"Talia," Jill moaned, "it's not like Kurt and I don't talk at all."

"No, I didn't mean it like that," her friend said ardently. "I already told you how I feel about Kurt and I still want you to support him. But I'm talking about you now. It won't do him any good when he comes out of this thing to have you falling apart. You need some company, a friend!"

"Well," Jill said, "I don't know why I feel guilty about it, but I do. But if you think it's all right . . . then I'll do it."

"I think it's a wonderful idea," Talia said. "And Jill . . . I admire what you're doing. I respect it. It's right to stick by Kurt, but let's not forget about you, Jill. You can't do that. You may think you're doing everyone else a favor, but for those of us who really love you— and I'm sure that includes Kurt—we want you to be happy too."

"Thank you, Talia. Thank you."

CHAPTER 20

It wasn't long before Jill began to round that same bend in the road with great anticipation and a clear conscience. Every morning it was like a new pleasure to see Jeremiah standing there beaming foolishly at her with his boyish grin. They never talked about the fact that they would meet the next day—they just did. Then one particularly hot morning, after nearly two weeks of circling the entire lake together, Jeremiah apprehensively asked if she would like to take a swim.

"We could double back," he suggested. "I've got a lane down to the lake and a swinging rope . . ."

They were riding along the east side of the lake, directly across from his farm, which he had pointed out to her with pride on their first ride together and every day since. With the heat already waffling up from the pavement, the idea of a swim was too great a temptation to say no to. Of course, she could swim by herself when she got back home, but it would be nice to take a dip with someone who'd shared the same grueling ride in the heat. It was like going to a movie. Jill never went to movies alone. She liked to share the experience or not have it at all.

"Okay," she said, "let's do it."

By the time they were coasting down the gravel lane, Jill had sweat dripping from her nose, and Jeremiah looked as if he'd already taken a swim. The sun was yellow in the sky, burning angrily behind a thick humid haze. Even the shade of the enormous old willow that had thrust itself into the side of the stony bank brought no relief from the heat.

The water looked invitingly cool. Many years ago, the Manns had used a bulldozer to cut the lane down into the steep embankment, pushing the earth into the lake to form a little grassy picnic area and a small beach. An old wooden retaining wall kept it mostly intact, but beyond that, the water plunged to an unfathomable depth. Jill left her bike on the gravel lane, hung her helmet from the handlebars, and walked awkwardly in her biking shoes to the water's edge. The lake's depth gave its aqua green color an intensity that was mesmerizing. It seemed almost man-made, a rich luminescent fantasy color fabricated from a mixture of neon blues and greens.

Suddenly, right in front of Jill, swam two enormous dark shapes. She jumped back with a gasp. Jeremiah sprang to her side and broke out in his easy laughter.

"Scared you?" he said. "They're just water dogs."

Jill looked from his mirthful face back to the two dark, ponderous shapes moving eerily away. "What?" she asked.

"Just carp," he told her.

"Carp!" she exclaimed. "In this lake? I thought this was one of the cleanest lakes in the world!"

"It is," he said. "Carp don't mean a lake is dirty. They're just bottom feeders. The dirtier a lake is, the better it is for them, but they can live in almost any lake. There aren't many here, but the ones we do have are so damn big we call 'em water dogs."

"They're about as big as a dog," she said.

"See?" he said. "Come on, don't worry about them. They're long gone and they wouldn't hurt you anyway. Look at this rope."

Shedding his shoes, socks, and finally his T-shirt, Jeremiah began to climb the rocky bank wearing only his red mesh shorts until he reached a ledge about ten feet above the water's surface. His prodigious torso was shockingly white next to the deep farmer's tan that colored his face, neck, and arms. From a twisted branch, he unwound a thick old rope that shed its furry fibers like an aging dog. Without warning, he grabbed hold and launched his enormous frame from the ledge, swinging well out over the lake before letting go and plunging into the green water in a boil of pure white bubbles. He came up with a loud whoop.

"Come on!" he yelled. "Grab the rope and climb up."

The knotted rope was swaying from its limb just within reach of the break wall's edge. Jill took off her shoes and socks, got hold of it, and began her ascent. From up on the ledge, the whole thing looked a lot scarier.

"It's okay!" Jeremiah hollered, his massive limbs pumping like a steady machine to keep him afloat out in the deep water. "Come on! Just swing out and let go just before you start to swing back."

Jill grasped the rope tightly and musical laughter bubbled up out of her throat. She let herself fall from the ledge and swung down toward the break wall, then past it and up into the air like a swallow. At the peak, her eyes grew wide looking down at what seemed to be the tiny shape of Jeremiah grinning up at her from the pure green water. She let go and her laughter became a scream. She dropped through the air and plunged deep into the water, cooled instantly by its brisk temperature. With several strong kicks, she thrust herself upward, shrieking with delight as she burst through the surface.

The two of them laughed together, all the way to the break wall and down its length to the open end on the north where the gravel beach spilled out into some shallower water and they could easily climb back out.

Together they walked back toward the rope. While Jill excitedly told him the story of how she and her brother used to swim in a cloudy pond in the Catskills, Jeremiah stared into her eyes. Their color had somehow changed in the unusual reflection of the green water. They were striking. Jeremiah never looked down from those eyes, though. It was as if he were afraid to let his vision wander down the front of her athletic frame for even a brief glance at the places where her dark T-shirt now clung tight to her shapely torso.

"Want to do it again?" he asked.

"Of course," she said with a laugh, and they swung and jumped over and over until they were cool and breathless, lying on their backs in a lush patch of grass that grew beneath the willow's shade.

"This is so beautiful," Jill whispered after a while, looking up through the softly rattling leaves of the tree at the wispy sky.

"You're beautiful," Jeremiah blurted out.

"Jeremiah!" Jill said, turning her head toward him with a tolerant frown. "Why did you say that?"

"I'm sorry," he said bashfully. His cheeks were burning cherry red and he kept his eyes focused straight up in the air. "It just came out."

After a pause, Jill smiled and said quietly, "You're a sweet person, Jeremiah. You're a friend."

He sighed heavily.

Jill took comfort that she had been very clear about Kurt. It was on the very first day they rode around the lake together that she told Jeremiah she was very much in love and engaged to be married. She didn't want to confuse him.

"I'm glad I'm your friend," he said. "And I know that's all it is, but I'm glad anyway. Your fiancé, he's the luckiest person on earth, you know. I don't think there are many women who are as beautiful on the outside and still that beautiful on the inside. I'm just saying it. I don't mean anything by it . . ."

"Thank you, Jeremiah," Jill said softly. "I appreciate it."

They lay there quietly for a time, each of them thinking about the other. Jill's Spandex pants began to dry and grow uncomfortable. She sighed, sat up, and began to put on her socks and shoes. Jeremiah continued to lie there covertly watching her with his hands under his head, his broad pale chest rising and falling peacefully.

"Don't be mad," he said to her.

She looked at him fondly and replied, "I'm not, but I have to go."

"I know," he said. "Will I see you tomorrow?"

"It's supposed to rain," she said, "finally."

"Rain doesn't bother me," he said. "I'm a farmer."

"All right," she said with a smile. "I'll see you tomorrow."

As she pedaled leisurely home, her mind was preoccupied with her new friend. She was devoted to Kurt, but there was a small voice inside her that cried out in admiration for Jeremiah. Their conversations over the past two weeks hadn't been limited to their bike rides. It wasn't uncommon for them to stop in town at the Skaneateles Bakery, where he would eat half a dozen egg sandwiches and they would both have coffee. Jill knew most of his story by now, about how he had attended the state university in Albany, become a state trooper, and lived in a small house on the edge of their farm.

"My parents moved to Florida and my older brother got the farm," he had told her frankly. "Then my parents died and my brother became a Jehovah's Witness."

The brother, ten years Jeremiah's senior, sounded to Jill like he had been a bit of a slacker to begin with. When the parents went south he abandoned the family farm and moved with his lawyer wife and kids into a two-family home in Auburn to be closer to their church. When that happened, Jeremiah moved back into the main house and took over the farm. He refused to give up his job with the state police and instead switched to working mostly nights. "They might want to come back," he had simply explained.

So he had fixed up the property to the way it had been when his father was young and strong, and he worked diligently at both jobs, long hard night shifts with the troopers, then as a steward to the family farm during the day until his brother decided to come back.

"What if he never comes back?" Jill had asked.

Jeremiah had simply tossed down the rest of his egg sandwich, shrugged, and said, "Then he never comes back. I don't know. I don't think about it. It doesn't matter if he comes back. The farm belongs to him. The house on Mead Hill is still mine and I've got a good job. If he came back, it'd be good. I'd get to see my niece more and I wouldn't have to work the farm."

After that comment, Jill had shaken her head and suggested mildly that Jeremiah might want to wrest control of the property from his brother.

"That's city thinking," Jeremiah had said benevolently, leaving her to feel slightly ashamed.

But that was part of why she couldn't get him out of her mind. He was so foreign to her. He was like a friendly giant from a children's storybook, kind and passive and affectionate. But she knew he was more than that too. Occasionally she had seen glimpses of his sterner side, and she imagined that he cut an intimidating figure in his trooper's uniform. Jill wished she had a sister or a close friend that she could fix him up with. She thought Talia was probably the only woman she knew open-minded enough to appreciate someone like Jeremiah, but of course Talia was already married. Jill racked her brain for someone.

In truth, Talia aside, Jill didn't have many real friends. Acquaintances from her first marriage were mostly limited to the wives of her husband's friends, almost all of whom had faded into oblivion after their break. There were a handful of women at Safe Tech whom she considered to be nominal friends, but not even the best of them would consider the notion of marrying a farmer from New Hope, New York.

Well, who could find fault with that? She certainly couldn't imagine leading that kind of life. At least she couldn't bring the image quickly to mind in a favorable light. He had cows, for God's sake. She supposed, though, if she took some time to think about it there were some good things . . .

Her ruminations were so intense that she passed her own driveway. When she realized it, she backtracked and coasted down through the trees, parking her bike in the garage. Kurt was awake and sitting on the flagstone veranda in back of the kitchen. He was having his breakfast and reading the newspaper. By now her clothes and her hair were dry so she sat right down, hopeful and somehow optimistic that this would be the moment when she broke through to the Kurt she knew before that fateful phone call three weeks ago.

"Hi," he said, looking up only briefly before dipping his head back down into the paper.

Jill poured herself a glass of juice. Clara, the local woman who cooked and cleaned the house for them, appeared in the doorway and silently mouthed the question as to whether she wanted anything to eat. Jill shook her head no and waited to see if Kurt would come up from his paper for air. She tapped her foot impatiently. Here they sat under the shade of the massive trees hissing in the breeze, with a spectacular view, financially free from the cares of the rest of the world, recently engaged, and about to start a whole new life together. But none of it was as sweet as Jill had dreamed it would be. Over the last few weeks, Kurt had subtly and gradually grown distant. Something was happening, something that made her question whether the two of them would ever be the same again.

After a time she gathered her emotions and softly said, "Kurt, could I talk to you?"

She got no response. He only continued to read.

"Kurt?" she said patiently.

"What, Jill, what?" he said somewhat peevishly, snapping the paper shut as if she were some kind of pestering teenager.

Part of her burned with anger. She felt the urge to toss her juice in his face, but she won the struggle to remain calm by remembering the state he had a right to be in. She had read Talia's book on grief and she knew better now the multiplicity of effects that it had on those who had lost an important loved one. Oftentimes, she had read, grief hid behind the mask of anger. Maybe she contained herself because of the irrational pang of guilt for secretly enjoying her friendship with Jeremiah.

"I just . . . wanted to talk," she said.

Kurt looked confused, as if she were speaking Chinese. "What do you want to talk about?"

Jill nodded, biting down on her lip to keep from becoming emotional. "I'm having a hard time," she said in a whisper, "with everything . . ."

"What's that supposed to mean?" he asked irritably.

The dark circles under his eyes accentuated the red in them. Jill knew he wasn't sleeping much, and when he did, it wasn't uncommon for him to rise up out of bed in the middle of the night shrieking in horror. While at first she had been able to soothe him to sleep by stroking his hair, it seemed now the only way he could sleep was when he collapsed from sheer exhaustion. She wondered to herself now if she'd woken him when she left the house for her ride.

"It's just . . ." Jill's hands were trembling slightly now. The complaints that had seemed so cogent were now stuck in her throat. During her ride home, they seemed justified, but somehow saying them out loud to a man who was suffering from the grief of a lost child suddenly seemed selfish. What concerned her most was that Kurt's moods didn't seem to be getting any better. On the contrary, he seemed to be growing worse, drifting farther and farther away from her. It all seemed so unfair, as if she were cursed never to find happiness in a relationship.

"I know how much you loved him," she said abruptly, breaking through the barrier of shame. She was bolstered by the words she had read; there was truth in them. To begin to heal, the book said, an aggrieved parent had to confront the reality of their child's death. "But he's gone, Kurt."

"I know he's gone." Kurt glared, his voice turning instantly bitter. "I don't need to be told that he's gone. I feel it every second of every day. I'm afraid to sleep, you know. I see him in my dreams and he's real! Then I wake up and I have to feel the sting of his death all over again from the beginning. I have no peace! I can't stop feeling it.

"Do you know what it's like?" he exclaimed in a voice pitched with pain.

Then his words faded almost to a whisper, and as he spoke, Jill thought that for the first time the tears of despair were pooling in the rims of his eyes. "Do you know what I can't stop thinking about?"

He looked at her now with his face contorted in agony. "When Collin was in high school, they played in the county lacrosse championship game. I knew it was important to him, and I planned to be there. But I was also in the midst of closing the financing on the Edison Lab that was going to get Safe Tech the navy contract. Well, we almost lost the deal at the last minute because the credit manager at Bank of New York felt the deal was undersecured, so I had to stay in the city. I convinced him to let the deal go through—but I missed the game.

"They won," he continued quietly, his eyes drifting down to the backs of his hands, "and Collin scored the last three goals to win it. It was probably the highlight of his life, and I wasn't there . . .

"But what happens with someone you love is that you

just assume that they're always going to be there. It's like your health. You don't really realize how good you had it until it's gone. And I just can't stop thinking about that game and all the other moments in my life that I wasn't with him when I could have been, when it was important to be with him. But I wasn't there because I never imagined that I couldn't just make it up to him the next day . . .

"Now . . ." Kurt's brow wrinkled, and Jill was certain he was about to cry, but she could see the immense struggle going on inside him. His body twisted and he held his head in the awkward position of a lifeless puppet.

Jill reached across the table and grasped his hand. "It's all right to cry, Kurt," she said desperately.

"No it's not!" Kurt was standing now and he slapped the paper down on the table to emphasize his words. Anger seemed to burn inside him like a live ember. His glare was filled with hatred, and Jill looked away from him, tears running down her face.

"I know what I've become!" he howled at her as he burst into tears. "Do you think I like it? Do you think I like brooding and tearing myself apart from the inside out? Someone killed my boy!

"I asked you," he said. He was panting, fighting back the flow of tears. "I asked you for help. I asked you to be patient with me. Is this being patient? Is it?"

"No," she sobbed, shaking her head.

"I will get through this!" he said intently, wiping his eyes clean and hiding his face in his hands. In a muffled voice he continued: "I told you I would. Now please, give me time. This will all work out, but you've got to give me time!"

CHAPTER 21

The moon rose over the ridge on the east side of the lake like an enormous luminescent melon. Oblong and orange, its glow cast a parade of sparkling light across the rippling water. With weary, bloodshot eyes Kurt set off in his skiff and eased his way across the lake to the judge's property. He wasn't able to sleep anyway and he felt that if the solution were going to come to him, it would come to him there. In recent days, he had found that the more he thought about it, the more impossible it all seemed.

Part of his mind seemed to be carried away by insanity. He caught himself wistfully considering other options—taking the president out on the street with a high-powered rifle, or wild things like obtaining a missile on the black market and launching it from his boat, blowing up the president's bedroom in the middle of the night. There were even moments of despair when he found himself pondering a simple suicidal rush. These, he knew, were the most effective means of assassination. They were the darkest fears of the Secret Service.

But besides his own will to live, there were two reasons why Kurt continued to strive for a solution to his puzzle. First, he wanted to be certain of success. He wanted to personally put the bullet into the president's brain at close range. Second, he wanted Calvin Parkes to know why he was going to die. He wanted to see the anguish on his face when he realized the mistake he'd made when he ordered Collin's death. He wanted the president to know that he was going to die at the hands of a vengeful father. He wanted him to think about it, to see the terrible black hole in the end of a gun barrel and know that death was imminent. He wanted the president to experience the same horror that his own son obviously had. Somehow that was as important to Kurt as the act itself.

If anyone could kill the president and then escape, Kurt believed it had to be him. He had spent the first part of his professional life focusing on protecting the president. He knew the weaknesses in the system, the things agents most feared and why. He had then spent the second part of his adult life building a company part of whose mission was to provide sophisticated technological security. That business operated in a perpetual cycle. Every time one group conceived a new protection, another group would work to engineer their way around it. And the people most suited for that circumvention were always the ones who knew most about the construction of the impediment. Kurt knew the obstacles the Secret Service raised to prevent people from getting to the president, and because of his experiences over the years with his team of Safe Tech scientists, his mind was uniquely attuned to getting past them.

He was jolted from his reverie by a sharp crack. He had ground his teeth so hard that he snapped off the corner of a molar. He rolled the sharp little chip around the inside of his mouth so he could get at it with his fingers. The thought came to him—an eye for an eye, a tooth for a tooth, a life for a life—straight from Gracie's Bible. The boat bumped gently up against the judge's pier. Kurt cast the piece of tooth away. With his tongue, he toyed with the remaining jagged edge for a moment before hopping from the boat. Quietly he tied up his skiff, then crept past the boathouse and up the gently sloping back lawn.

He flitted from tree to tree, less comfortable than he had been a few weeks ago in the dark rain. The moonlight now cast clear shadows beneath the trees and Kurt darted about, his heart racing, reinforcing his mental model of the layout. After noticing a few extra cars in the front drive, he made for the walk-through gate to the north. There was a cluster of camps on that side of the property that would make his initial approach less obvious, and he figured while he was here he should scope it out one more time.

As he reached for the cold handle of the decorative iron gate, he heard the voices of two men on the other side of the wall. He froze and panic crept down his spine. They were coming toward him. Frantically, he scanned the immediate area. He silently chastised himself for taking the chance on coming back.

Twenty feet back down the path was a large sycamore tree with one branch that was low enough for him to reach. He dashed for the tree and took a running leap at the branch. In midair, he heard the screech of the gate as it was opened from the other side of the wall.

After scrambling up four more branches, Kurt stopped. The hammering in his chest forced him to suck in air like a deep-sea diver breaking the water's surface. As the two men made their way up the path, he fought to quiet his gasping breath. He could hear the murmur of their voices, but could see next to nothing in the shadows of the trees. Then they stepped into a swatch of moonlight and Kurt stopped breathing altogether.

He was nearly certain that the shorter of the two was David Claiborne. Then his old friend lit a cigarette, casting a brief but vivid patch of orange light against his face and confirming his identity. Kurt's stomach turned sour. Why was Claiborne here? The president wasn't due for two more weeks. It was early for an advance agent to be surveying a property. It was also unusual for an ASAIC to be that agent. It did happen on occasion: Sometimes, an agent with some seniority would request a rotation that took him near to home. But Claiborne was from Seattle. It concerned and puzzled Kurt that his old friend had put himself in charge of the advance work for the visit to Skaneateles.

The last words Claiborne had spoken to him rang out in his mind. "The next time I guarantee I won't be there to bail you out."

But here he was.

"Wall makes it easy, doesn't it?" Claiborne said through a cloud of smoke to the other man. "All we're missing is a moat. You couldn't get into this place with a Trojan horse."

"I just think you might want to let some of the locals on the inside," the taller man said. He was Sean Fullingmore, the agent in charge from the nearby Syracuse office. His role in the visit was to act as liaison between the Washington agents and the local officials. "If they get a little close it keeps the whole bunch on their toes."

Claiborne looked at him blandly for a moment before muttering something into a handheld radio.

White light pierced the night suddenly with the shock of an explosion. Kurt started and almost lost his grip on the tree's branches. He hugged the trunk tightly and saw with horror that the two men below him were scanning the area, now flooded by a brilliant spotlight that had been mounted somewhere on the roof of the house.

"That's good," Claiborne said sharply into his radio, and the night was instantly dark again.

Kurt could see nothing until his eyes readjusted to the blackness. By the time he could discern one shadow from another, he realized the two men had proceeded up the path. With his heart racing wildly, he quickly scrambled down the tree and followed the inside of the stone wall all the way to the water's edge. After carefully scanning up and down the shore, he eased into the water and swam straight out. There were several swim buoys about a hundred feet out, and he swam underwater from one to the other until he was back by the dock, clinging tightly to the nearest buoy and searching the shore for movement.

His cautiousness was rewarded when he saw the dark figures of Claiborne and Fullingmore approaching the boathouse from the lawn. Kurt sank as far as he could down into the water and watched in horror as they proceeded out onto the pier. They would see his boat.

But instead of pausing to investigate, the two men went right on past, stopping only when they had reached the very end of the dock. The night breeze prevented him from hearing exactly what they were saying, but he could tell by the way they pointed that they were discussing the security arrangements for the waterfront. Then Claiborne pointed to the roof of the boathouse, where Kurt imagined the agents would post more lights, plus a counter-sniper team from the Uniformed Division. If someone were to come up out of the water in a diving suit late at night, they would very likely be greeted with a bullet.

Again Claiborne spoke into his radio, and again the night was shattered by a burning bank of white lights from the roof of the main house. Less startled, but still shaken by the intensity of the brightness, Kurt dove to the bottom and waited desperately for the lights to be switched off. If he stayed on the surface and they were looking, the piercing glare would enable the two men to clearly see him clinging to the buoy. After what seemed like a lifetime, the lake went black again. Kurt raced for the surface and did his best not to make noise, but his intake of air was so sharp that it cut dangerously through the sound of the water's gentle lapping. Fortunately, the two men were already at the boathouse and heading for the lawn.

Kurt shut his eyes and tried in vain to quell his gasping breaths. His body shook from nerves and he wondered for the first time if what he was doing had any foundation in sanity. The beast in the corner of his mind stirred restlessly, threatening to undo him completely. Against his will, images of Collin and then Annie filled his consciousness. Tears streamed down his face and he heard a sob escape his throat. He felt an uncontrollable urge to shriek Annie's name and then his son's as well, but he fought it back.

He focused on taking long slow breaths and concentrating on his plan. He knew if he broke down now, it would be over. He had to maintain his composure. He had to stay sharp. This would be the best chance he'd ever have to avenge Collin's death and he needed to take it.

Rest, that's what he needed. It had been a foolish thing for him to come back to the judge's. He had nearly compromised everything tonight, and for what? He was no closer now to a solution than he'd have been if he had pondered it from his study. The president's visit was only two weeks away, and what had Claiborne said? The place was like a fortress, impenetrable even to a Trojan horse.

The men were gone from sight now. After several minutes of deep breathing Kurt swam quietly toward his skiff. He untied it quickly and wrapped its bowline around his chest before slipping back into the water and towing it well out into the lake. By the time he was far enough out to where he felt comfortable starting the motor, he had drifted downwind to the north so far that the judge's house wasn't even in sight. Wearily, he climbed into the skiff, fired up the little outboard, and headed for home.

When he arrived back at his own mansion, he fell into bed exhausted, his hair still wet. When he woke, his head was dry, Jill was gone, and the image of a Trojan horse again sprang into his mind. A giddy smile broke out across his face as he considered the false gift. He sprang from his bed and began to pace the room, heedless of the beautiful summer day spilling in through the French doors that led out onto the balcony. His trip across the lake hadn't been for nothing. It had given him his own Mobius strip. Like the German engineers with their fan belt, all he had to do was give the problem half a turn and it would work.

All along, he'd been trying to solve the wrong puzzle. For weeks now he had tormented himself over how to penetrate the fourth perimeter in the middle of the night, how to commandeer the Service's communications, break into the president's bedroom, kill him, and escape unscathed in the confusion. Now the answer was so clear to him that he felt foolish. He should have known all along. Kurt Ford didn't have to go to the president. Bearing the appropriate gift, he could bring the president to him.

CHAPTER 22

During the first week of his presidency, Calvin Parkes had only to mention the idea that it would be a fine thing to have a putting green on the patch of grass in the trees behind the Oval Office. In early March the White House staff exultantly led him around the corner and back into that very cluster of trees to present to him a beautiful seamless green. That moment—the moment he realized that even his wishes were commands—had filled the president with great pride.

So, like Huck Finn sneaking off to his favorite fishing hole, the president would slip out back to chip and putt whenever the slightest opportunity presented itself. And it was quite typical for him, when his secretary, Margie, finally told him his schedule was clean, to whip off his coat and head straight across to the green with plenty of time before his wife expected him in the mansion for dinner at seven. This was also the only time that those who knew him well could be certain he would be relaxed, in a relatively good mood, and at the same time willing to talk extemporaneously.

When Butch Reynolds, the chairman of the Republican National Committee, entered the trees along the trim gravel path with Marty Mulligan, he was delighted to see the president sink a chip from fifty feet away. Parkes howled and pumped his fist into the air amid the polite clapping of two young staffers and Mack Taylor as well as the Secret Service agents who were dispersed throughout the circumference of trees. The president's sleeves were rolled up to his elbows and his red face was flushed nearly purple from the heat of the late afternoon sun that filtered through the canopy of trees.

"Ah!" he cried on seeing Mulligan and Reynolds. "Marty! Did you see that! Butch, what are you doing? I don't need a mulligan after a shot like that!"

The president's light blue eyes twinkled mirthfully at his own wit and his large frame shook with delight. His wrinkled white shirt bore liberal sweat stains under his arms and his upper lip was beaded as well. He chortled.

Reynolds broke out in his own toothy grin. He too was sweating like only a fat man can in the summer heat of the South. The lenses of his silver-framed glasses were fogged over from the humidity, but he shook the president's hand with enthusiasm. Even the SAIC had allowed himself a crooked smile at the president's jest. Only Mulligan's face remained impassive. He sniffed noncommittally at the rich smell of cut grass that wafted up from the carefully manicured turf and took the president's hand in his own iron grip.

"Cal," he said, acknowledging the president's grin by inclining his head.

The president turned excitedly and began chipping away at the cluster of balls at his feet, talking as he played. "What brings you two out?" he asked. "Oh! Did you see that! I almost did it again!"

"You play a pretty game, Mr. President," Reynolds said in his heavy southern drawl as his eyes followed the ball's loop around the edge of the cup. He was from an old family in the great state of North Carolina, and to prove it he strode around Washington in seersucker suits.

"We found some of that ten million dollars we talked about a few weeks ago," Mulligan said bluntly.

This brought the president to a standstill. He stood up straight and rested the head of his club on top of his shoe, eyeing the two men warily. "You got the money, Butch?"

"I'm going to get it, Mr. President." Reynolds beamed. "All you have to do is fish for it."

The president puckered his mouth and sourly said, "So I'm the one who has to get it. You have the idea, but I'm the one that has to pull the bull out of the barn. Well, that's great. That's just what I need."

"No," Reynolds said pleasantly, waving off the idea. "I meant what I said in the literal sense. All you have to do is go fishing, on a fishing trip—not even a trip, just for an afternoon—and we've got ourselves a five-million-dollar contribution!"

"Five million?" the president said softly and whistled. His eyes narrowed. "Not the Chinese . . ."

"No," Mulligan said with a sneer. "His name is Kurt Ford. He's the founder of a company called Safe Tech. He's about as American as you can get. He's worth about a billion dollars."

"And," the president said in disgust, "he wants to talk to me about the Internet initiative, wants to give me five million to talk me out of it."

"He did say he wants to jaw at you about it some," Reynolds broke in, "but I made it right clear, Mr. President, there'll be no quid pro quo, none a' tall. He understood. Told me he didn't expect to change your mind, but that he supported your other ideas and would like to have the chance to at least give you some ideas on the limitations you might want to think about before signing the bill."

The president eyed the chairman skeptically. "How about a game of golf? Why can't I play golf with this guy? Why do I have to ruin an afternoon when I'm supposedly on vacation?"

Reynolds shrugged. "I don't know. He was pretty ornery on that point though, I can tell you that for sure. I mentioned a game of golf, but he said he thought it would be a shame for you to be right there where they have some of the finest fishing in the United States and not get out on a boat. Besides, he apparently doesn't golf."

"You'll be there anyway, Cal," Mulligan said in a surly tone. "He lives right there in Skaneateles, for Christ's sake. You're the one who wants us to figure ways to help raise the money we need and now we've got it. If the guy wanted to sit around and do needlepoint, it would be worth it. Just think about how many speeches you'd have to make and dinners you'd have to eat to take in five million dollars. This will be the biggest single contribution in the history of politics and all you have to do is reel in some damn halibut or something."

"Halibut is an ocean fish," Reynolds said confusedly as he took a handkerchief out of his breast pocket to wipe the fat on his neck.

"You know what I mean," Mulligan growled. "Fish to me comes inside breadsticks you take out of the freezer. Anyway, it'll be good for the upstate vote. Those people are nuts about fishing. You should see the money the state spends raising fish just so they can let them go and people can catch them again. It's fucking ridiculous. Someone told me they do the same thing with pheasants, for Christ's sake. But I wouldn't mind seeing a nice shot of you reeling in a goddamn fish on the front page of the *New York Times* . . .

"And fishing is okay with the greens too," he continued in a low mutter. "They don't mind fishing."

"So I go out on this guy's boat for an hour or two, catch some fish, and he dumps five million into the party and then you put it right into my campaign, Butch?" asked the president.

"Of course," Reynolds said.

"Yeah, every cent of it too," the president said a little more harshly than was necessary.

"Of course, Mr. President," Reynolds said defensively. "You know the party's priority this fall is your reelection."

"I didn't see the money flooding in when Marty said we needed another ten million to spend in the Northeast," Parkes said bitterly.

"Mr. President," Reynolds explained, "it wouldn't

help your administration if we lost the Senate. We've got some tough battles out west that need funding."

"Yeah," the president said, turning his back on the chairman and taking a whack at one of the remaining golf balls, "and they don't have my kind of money. I know—well, what the hell. We've been through this enough. Fine, I'll play golf with this guy—"

"You mean go fishing," Mulligan interjected.

"Yes, that's what I meant," the president said sourly. "It was a Freudian slip or whatever you call it. Yeah, I'll fish with this guy, but just don't make it an all-day thing, will you, Marty? Can you do that, anyway?"

"I'm sure Mr. Ford will understand that despite his generous contribution to the party," Mulligan said, "the president of the United States only has so much time—"

"Because I do want to golf while I'm up there," the president snapped as he took another shot.

Mulligan turned to Mack Taylor and said, "Any trouble for your people to clear this guy?"

It was short notice and they all knew it. The president's trip was less than two weeks away. Normally, the people he would be interacting with on a trip like this would have had background checks already completed.

"It shouldn't be a problem at all," Taylor said. To the apparent surprise of everyone, he added, "He used to be one of us."

"What's that supposed to mean?" the president said sharply.

"Kurt Ford used to be a Secret Service agent during Reagan," Taylor replied. "And his son was with us . . ."

The president stood up straight and his grip on the club went slack. "His son?" he said, his face aghast.

"Yes," Taylor said quickly, "the one who killed himself."

The president turned his head away and said nothing.

"That makes it even better," Mulligan exclaimed. "We can get mileage out of that. The president commiserates with the father of a fallen agent. People will like that. The women will like it."

Parkes was silent for a few moments more before he looked at Taylor as if to ask for his advice. "I don't know . . . Isn't he apt to be . . . distraught?"

The SAIC shrugged and said indifferently, "From a security standpoint it shouldn't be a problem."

"It's a triple play," Mulligan interjected. "We get the money, the fishing plays to the yokels without pissing off the greens, and we tug the heartstrings for the women. You've got to do this one, Cal."

The president glowered at Mulligan. He was the president. He didn't have to do anything.

CHAPTER 23

When Jill walked into the house, the workers were packing up their tools outside the library. Fresh wood shavings littered the marble floor in the hall and a fine yellow dust tainted the dark wooden threshold. The doors were closed, and Jill noticed right away the gleaming brass lock that had been installed just below the ornate knobs. She'd also seen the sign on the workers' van—Fradon Locks. One of the men, a skinny youth with long blond hair and a full beard and mustache, smiled nervously at her and touched his dirty fingers to the bill of his hat as he passed her with his case full of tools.

Under normal circumstances, Jill would have rapped on the door and demanded an answer. But the circumstances weren't normal. Not only was she growing used to Kurt's reclusive ways, she was feeling somewhat guilty. She had been on her way back from some pointless antique shopping in Geneva when Jeremiah pulled up behind her in his cruiser and briefly flashed his lights. Jill had pulled over with a smile and waited patiently as her gigantic friend got out of the car and adjusted the tall hat that made him loom even larger.

"In a hurry, ma'am?" Jeremiah had said politely.

"No, Officer," she'd responded, suppressing a grin. "I think I was going the speed limit."

"That's what I thought. So I figured if you weren't in a hurry, you'd have time for a cup of coffee."

And so she did. But now, back at home, she felt it was somehow wrong. She turned around and went upstairs to change into her swimsuit. In the long hall, she stopped in front of Gracie's room and knocked softly on the door. While Kurt's sister was still mostly silent, Jill thought that over the past several days Gracie had begun to show signs of healing. Just yesterday, Jill had seen her venture out of the house for a short walk into one of the flower gardens.

"Gracie?" she said quietly. "Are you in there? I'm going down to the lake. Do you want to come?"

"Come in," Gracie said in a muffled voice.

Encouraged, Jill pushed open the door and went in.

"Asking an old lady like me to go for a swim?" Gracie said archly. She was sitting, straight-backed, at a writing desk against the wall next to the towering grandfather clock. While her spirits seemed more animated, she was still dressed exclusively in black and she wore the weary expression of an earthquake survivor.

"You looked like you were swimming pretty well early this summer," Jill said. She could recall several occasions when she had watched with admiration as Gracie swam back and forth between the dock and the diving raft for thirty minutes at a time. "I know Kurt likes to refer to you as his older sister, but you're in pretty good shape if you ask me."

Gracie rose from her desk and opened her arms toward Jill. "Come here, my dear," she said. Jill crossed the room uncertainly. Gracie embraced her gently and softly said, "This must all be so hard for you, being cooped up in this house with two bereaved siblings."

"That's all right, I—"

"Ah!" Gracie said, holding up her hand. "Don't. You don't have to say anything. I know you're just doing what you think is right. I know you're that kind of person. I knew that from the start."

She held Jill out at arm's length and it surprised Jill to realize how much taller she was than Gracie—Kurt's sister was one of those people who seemed bigger by the sheer force of their personality.

"There aren't a lot of women with the self-confidence to live in the same house with a ghost."

Jill looked at her quizzically.

"I'm talking about Annie," Gracie said, smiling weakly. "Not a literal ghost, but she's everywhere, really. The pictures Kurt has out, and . . . and Collin, when he was with us. I'm sure you saw the resemblance. But you've carried on without a word of discontent. I should have told you that I admired that about you long ago, but . . . well . . . ."

"I feel like lately I haven't been as equable as you're making me out," Jill said, blushing at the thought, having only just had coffee with another man.

"None of us has been ourselves," Gracie continued

pensively. "I know I haven't. But these things take time to pass. If they're to pass . . .

"Well," she continued brusquely, "you've caught me in a contemplative, fairly buoyant mood. I'll be overcome by the blue devils by lunchtime and I might even have to take one of my damn pills, but I'm glad you came to see me."

She then said somewhat enigmatically, "I'm leaving tomorrow, and I don't know if— when I'll see you again. I respect you, Jill, and I know you're going to make Kurt hap— I know you'll make him as happy as he can be."

She brought her hand gently to Jill's cheek. It was cool and soft and Jill briefly shut her eyes. She wanted to ask Gracie a million questions, but of course she couldn't. Gracie was older than Jill's own mother would have been if she were alive. And, while the two of them had always gotten along, their difference in age and demeanor was an obstruction that neither of them had been able or willing to overcome.

Still, she was grateful for the reprieve from formality between them. She even wished fleetingly that their relationship had been different. But it wasn't, and now it was too late. Jill pressed her own hand against Gracie's, but instead of confiding, she thanked the older woman, kissed her on the cheek, and quietly left the room.

With a heavy sigh, she continued on down to their bedroom at the end of the long hall, where she changed into her swimsuit. The windows were open and a wonderful breeze, cooled by the towering trees, wafted past the white lacy curtains and into the room. Jill grabbed a large white towel from the bathroom and her book from the bedside stand, then went down the back stairs and straight outside. On the path, she stopped only to look fleetingly up at the big picture window into Kurt's library. He wasn't at his desk, but she could make out his form in a black polo shirt, poring over a bank of papers at the library table while his head wagged emotionally back and forth. He was talking into the headset connected to his phone. She sighed again and turned toward the lake.

After a dip in the water to cool off, Jill coated her face and limbs with sunblock and lay back in a comfortable lounge chair on the pebble beach. A jet ski droned by in the middle of the lake and spun around like an angry hornet. Jill looked up, shading her eyes, and silently cursing its rider for disrupting her tranquillity. She opened her book, *Memoirs of a Geisha,* and submerged herself in the world of a woman whose problems far exceeded her own. After a few chapters, she moved her chair into the shade of a large red maple whose branches encroached on the water's edge. Soon she was asleep.

When she woke, she picked the book up from where it lay on the small, smooth stones, brushed it off, and stood to go. She had no idea how long she'd slept, but when she got back to the house she could hear Kurt's voice, coming not from the library but from the large great room that dominated the center of the old home on the main floor. She walked through the kitchen, past the breakfast room, and into the great room. Her face flushed as three men in suits rose from one of the large couches centered on the fireplace. They greeted her simultaneously and with uneasy politeness.

"This is my girl— My fiancée, Jill, Jill Eisner," Kurt said stiffly. His smile was forced, but he rose from the couch opposite the three men with the appropriate decorum. "Jill, these gentlemen are from the Secret Service."

Jill looked at Kurt with alarm and forgot for a moment that she was standing in front of three strange men in her bathing suit. When she realized, she quickly wrapped the towel around her waist, crossed her arms in front of her chest, and said hello.

"Ms. Eisner . . . I didn't see that she was going to be going on the trip with you and the president, will she?" mulled the oldest of the three men, Agent Morris, a tall, homely man with a blond crew cut and a bulbous nose.

"No," Kurt replied.

"Then that's about all we have, Mr. Ford," Morris said after a reflective pause. "Thank you for your time. As I said, we'll be back on the day of the trip and pretty much take over the whole property, but like you already know, we'll do our best not to inconvenience you."

"Of course not," Kurt said, leading them out into the spacious entryway whose richly paneled walls were adorned with old oil paintings.

Jill caught one of the younger agents, a square-jawed redhead who also wore his hair cropped close, peeking back over his shoulder at her on his way out. She frowned at him and waited for Kurt to return.

"What's going on, Kurt?" she asked when he came back into the room.

Kurt used the same false smile that he'd worn for the

agents. It made her shift uncomfortably. "I'll be taking the president out on a little fishing trip when he comes for his visit," he said. "You might as well get ready for the publicity. It'll probably be all over the news."

"That's exciting," she said somberly. "What made you think to do that?"

"I want to talk with him about this Internet tax that they're talking about putting into law," Kurt explained. His words sounded prepared and his eyes wandered to some vague spot in the air beside her. "We both know I'm leaving Safe Tech, but you know how I feel about the company and the people in it, and this is an opportunity to help it continue to thrive. This will be my last act as CEO. I'd be negligent if I didn't take the opportunity to help. Besides, he's the president of the United States. It's not often he's staying in the neighborhood. It'll be an experience . . ."

This was the first time since Collin's death that Jill felt she had the moral advantage to say what she really felt. Her words came without forethought—she just spoke. "Kurt, are you absolutely sure you want to leave Safe Tech? I mean, I know you've talked about going away, starting a life together, and I want that. But can't we do that right here? Can't you still do what you have to do, expose whoever it is that has to be exposed, and keep living your life like it is? I don't care who they are, Kurt. You can hire protection. We don't have to really go anywhere. Do we?"

Kurt sighed long and heavy. He pinched the corners of his eyes before looking up at her with a weary expression. "Honey, please," he said, "I told you what I have to do . . ."

There was a pause between them. They both knew that he really hadn't told her what it was he had to do. And then Kurt seemed almost angry.

"No," he said, "I can't stay. You have to trust me. Neither of us would be able to stay after this is over, not in peace . . . You're not having second thoughts?"

His eyes bore down on her and Jill remembered her own promise that she would follow him to the ends of the earth if she had to. She was having second thoughts about her blind faith, but to say so somehow felt traitorous. She did love him, very much, and she did want a life with him. Her father's words came into her mind and she dropped her eyes. She was overthinking this.

"No," she whispered vehemently, shaking her head. "Of course I'm not having second thoughts."

"Good," he said, and the dark cloud passed. The grateful smile that lit his face was almost reward enough for her self-containment. He closed the space between them and hugged her close.

"I've been thinking," he said casually. "There's this beautiful chapel in the woods outside on the other side of the river from Montreal. It's on a hilltop and you can see everything for miles and miles around. It's called St. Olaf's and I was able to reserve it for a small ceremony. I don't think there could be a more romantic place in the world to be married . . . I was hoping we could do that. I've always said that if I ever were to get married . . . again, that I'd do it there. I know you'll love it.

"And if it's all right, I thought you could go up there

a few days early and make some preparations. I've already booked you a room at the Ritz-Carlton in Montreal under the company name. It'll be a zoo when the president arrives here anyway and I thought you could take care of everything and then we could leave from there on our honeymoon."

"Honeymoon?" she said, unable to keep the excitement out of her voice. "How long are we going for?"

"How long?" Kurt said, raising his eyebrows. "I was hoping the honeymoon was going to last for the rest of our lives . . ."

"Kurt," Jill said, squeezing him tight. "That's so nice."

Kurt kept his chin on her head as he spoke so that she couldn't see into his eyes. "And I'd like you to make sure that, when you're making the arrangements, you put everything under your name. This presidential visit will draw a lot of attention to my name, even over the border, and I just think it's better if we have a private ceremony. We'll get married the day after my trip and be off to a place that I know you're going to love . . . But don't ask, it's a surprise.

"Now listen," he continued, taking her shoulders in his hands and looking now into her eyes. "Don't overthink all this."

She nearly winced at his words. It was strange, him saying what she'd just been thinking.

"You and I are going to be happy once I get everything settled here," he said earnestly. Then his voice dropped and his eyes began to mist as he choked out the words. "I'm not going to be in mourning forever, Jill . . .

Just help me get past these next seven days and I promise, I promise things will be different."

Without giving her a chance to respond, Kurt planted one more kiss on her forehead and disappeared behind the doors of his library. For a moment, Jill felt an equanimity that had eluded her since the day Collin died. She did have to trust him and stop overthinking things, and this one time she really believed she could.

But then a quiet grating sound ravaged the silence of the room, the sound of the bolt on the library door sliding home. It was an obscene note that pierced her to the core. It was the sound of deception and it punctuated the fact that she had just been played for a fool.

Jill turned and angrily wrung her hands as she went upstairs to change. A small voice from inside her heart whispered that despite her anger, the right thing was to do what he asked. But her mind, the one thing she'd always coveted with pride, cried out. Something was happening, something very dangerous. She huffed at herself disgustedly under her breath. The voice of her father echoed in her mind once again and she wanted to spit.

"Well, maybe I am too smart for my own good," she said aloud with a scowl. But she wasn't her mother. She had never believed in blind subservience and she couldn't start now. It wasn't her. Yes, she wanted to marry Kurt and she would even go away with him. But something was going on, something strange, something very wrong. She was going to find out what it was before things went any further.

She stood still and listened. Over her own breathing

she could just make out the rumble of Kurt's voice in the room directly below her, talking animatedly on the phone. She pulled a shirt over her head and pressed her lips tightly together. He could lock the door, but he couldn't keep her out.

CHAPTER 24

The next day Kurt watched a delivery truck rumble up the drive and disappear into the trees. The vehicle shifted gears with a clank that echoed through the woods. Kurt looked up at the flurry of tree swallows swooping through the sunshine and chattering loudly at each other in their liquid melody. The birds reminded him of Collin. Collin had been the one to encourage him to have nesting boxes put out for them in the spring.

One evening several years ago, the two of them had been sharing a bottle of wine over dinner at Rosalie's Cucina, their favorite restaurant right here in the village of Skaneateles. Collin had pulled a rumpled, folded-up article out of his jacket pocket and pushed it across the table. It was about the birds and the thousands of insects they ate. He'd torn it out of an airline magazine on his flight up from D.C. The two of them went out the next day to a little shop just past Auburn called the Bird House, purchased two dozen box kits and poles, and put them up together all over the lawn. It was a small thing, but a good one, the two of them working and sweating together out on the lawn to help propagate the musical little birds.

Kurt stood there for several minutes, his mind wafting slowly among images from the past. Tears began to spill over the rims of his eyes. He didn't seem to notice until the flow was steady and he could actually taste the salt on his lips. In his daydream, he seemed to be lifted out and away from his own body, and he was faintly reminded of the stories of what happened to people when they died.

He could see himself standing in the same spot, in the sunshine, only he wasn't alone. His arms were wrapped around a full-grown Collin and Annie as she was before she died. So real was the fantasy that Kurt could almost feel their bodies. A long low sob escaped from his throat and he shook his head violently to clear his mind. Breathing deeply, he wiped the tears roughly from his face and turned to the ample stack of freshly delivered boxes.

With a razor, he slashed them open one by one to reveal an ensemble of underwater equipment, all of which was midnight blue and smelling of fresh paint. He had known exactly what he needed and ordered everything over the Internet in a matter of a few hours. Even though he could have had any number of people who worked for him around the house unpack the gear, Kurt had given every one of them including Clara the day off. He carried each piece down to the boathouse himself and loaded it carefully into his twenty-five-foot fishing boat. In the other slip was the boat Kurt used more often than not for pleasure cruising or waterskiing, a twenty-three-foot open-bow that was practically new. The cream-colored fishing boat was in good shape too, but older. It had come with the property when Kurt bought the house seven years earlier. It was equipped with the appropriate down riggers for deep trolling as well as pole-holders for surface lures.

Kurt had already gone through the boat's equipment, and the new fishing gear he'd ordered had arrived the day before. The boat was outfitted as if Kurt was a professional guide. He'd carefully familiarized himself with all of it so that on his trip with the president it would look like this was a regular pastime for him, which it wasn't. In one corner of the stern was a toolbox, built into the hull of the boat. Using the tools from a workbench right there in the boathouse, Kurt had constructed a false bottom in the toolbox with a spring-loaded release. By pushing down on both sides simultaneously, he could cause the bottom of the box to pop up, revealing a three-inch well underneath. Made from sheet metal and covered over with the appropriate greasy set of tools, the bottom would look just like the real thing.

Beneath it was a 9mm Browning loaded with ten hollow-point slugs. On top of the haphazard mess of tools, he had placed two brand-new flare guns that looked alarmingly like snub-nosed pistols. They would create a false alarm that would distract the agents searching the boat from the real threat underneath the chest. It was an arrangement that Kurt fussed over like a nesting hen, checking it every time he came on the boat to see if it was just right, often deciding that it wasn't and stopping to poke around.

Once the dive equipment was fueled up and on board, Kurt looked at his watch. Jill had taken Gracie to the airport and wouldn't be back for another hour and a half. Kurt had finally convinced his older sister to go back to their house in Greenwich. She had a small group of friends there, and he had also arranged for his other older sister, Colleen, who lived in Boston, to stay with her for a while. Kurt still regretted leaving Gracie behind, but he knew for certain that it was best for everyone.

Their conversation last night had unsettled him. Over the past several weeks, Gracie had undergone a change that Kurt hadn't fully noticed until then. She seemed to have somehow found a level of peace that was foreign to him. It was possible that intense mourning had worn down the edges of her pain.

Maybe that was why she tried to stop him. Perhaps she no longer felt the acute agony that plagued him every time he thought of his son.

"I don't think you should kill them, Kurtis," she had said. "Whoever they are, I don't think it will help you."

Kurt had stared at her in disbelief.

"I know what you're thinking," Gracie had said, "but you and I are at different points in all this. I have had the luxury of grieving these last few weeks. You haven't.

"I know what you're doing," she'd said. "You're using it to spur you on, to motivate you. You're keeping your hate alive. I felt the same hate, Kurtis. But I see now that it can't help. You need to mourn Collin's death to heal yourself. Killing his killers won't help you, Kurtis. It can only hurt. It can't bring him back . . ."

Kurt had glowered at his sister. That wasn't what he needed to hear, and he told her so.

"I know I can't change you, Kurtis," she had wearily replied. "I know you too well. I know you'll do what you have to do, and I don't know . . . Maybe for you it's the right thing. I just want to help you. You know I love you and you know I'll always be here for you, no matter what you decide to do."

It was those words that made Kurt certain she would forgive him, not only for killing the president but for leaving her to live by herself.

It wasn't that Gracie hadn't been attached to him through the years, but Kurt knew that it was Collin she really lived for. And he wasn't leaving her without any means. The house in Greenwich had been transferred into her name, as well as a fifty-million-dollar trust fund. Gracie would live in comfort, if alone.

Kurt backed the boat out of its slip and onto the lake. It was Tuesday, a slow day on the water, especially during midmorning. Kurt headed out to the middle and then north toward the village. The closer he got, the more the little village reminded him of the eclectic tangle of colorful homes and shops that was characteristic of the hamlets along the waterways of Europe. The stunning water and the multiplicity of flower boxes gave the unkempt row of buildings a charm that was decidedly un-American. A mile out, almost directly in front of the country club, he eased up on the throttle and began to

search the depths over the side for the enormous intake
pipe for the nearby city of Syracuse's water supply.

The pipe itself, fifty inches in diameter, could still be
seen at a depth of around thirty feet. It terminated, he
knew, at about forty feet, and that wasn't very far from
where it disappeared from sight. Following the line of
the pipe, Kurt spotted an orange ball floating twelve feet
below the surface that was chained as a marker to the intake valve. He dropped his anchor at that spot and
looked around. Two jet skis were noisily tearing up the
water down closer to the village, and another fishing
boat half a mile away to the south trolled steadily. There
was no wind, so the sailboats were idle. Kurt felt confident that this part of the lake belonged to him alone.

Ten minutes later, he was in his scuba gear. After a
quick nervous look around, he hoisted one of the five
AV-1 underwater scooters from the boat's deck and
carefully dumped it over the side. Next he tossed over a
black net bag that contained a second set of scuba gear
with a dry suit that was fitted for him, as well as a
weight belt, regulator, some chemical hot packs, and an
air tank, all of which sank quickly to the bottom. He adjusted his mask and went over backward and into the
lake. The water was thick with smallmouth bass hovering around the intake. The fish scattered quickly to the
edge of Kurt's vision; he knew this would be a spot
where the president would want to stay anchored.

The AV-1 was barely buoyant. Kurt started it up easily and used it to shoot through the water this way and
that, familiarizing himself with its operation before pro-
pelling himself down to the bottom. He found his gear

without a problem and dragged it twenty feet to the north of the intake cage, an eight-foot cube that prevented curious divers from being sucked up by the steady influx of water.

He tucked his gear under the edge of the pipe, even though there was no reason to believe anyone would be down there who could find it. The divers who cleaned the intake did so twice a summer, once in late July and not again until September. And, while Kurt was aware that divers would scour the area around the judge's mansion, he also knew that the Service protocols called for no kind of underwater inspection for a presidential boating excursion. They would check the boat, they would flank Kurt's craft with boats of their own, they would even have a helicopter standing by on shore, but his gear would fall outside their predetermined area of consideration. Using the drawstring that held the net closed, he tied the AV-1 down and wedged that too under the edge of the pipe.

Halfway to the surface and looking down to inspect his work, Kurt changed his mind and swam back to pile some rocks around his gear. His life would depend on having that equipment there, and he didn't want to take the chance of having some teenage kid inadvertently discover it while he was impressing his girlfriend by showing her he could dive down to the cage. Kurt knew it would be unusual for someone to free-dive forty feet to get at it in the first place, but it wasn't unheard of.

Finally satisfied with his work, he hung suspended in the brilliant aqua green water between the pipe and his boat above. He snapped an underwater GPS unit the size of a pack of cigarettes from his vest and logged in his position. Back on board the boat, he toweled off his face, hoisted the anchor, and headed south. Using his depth finder as well as the GPS, he located a spot three miles away where the lake's bottom was only fifty feet deep. He looped a nylon strap through a twenty-five-pound weight, then clipped it to a second AV-1 and another air tank. To the handle of the AV-1 he attached a mesh bag full of chemical hot packs. Then he put his diving gear back on, heaved the machine, the tank, and the weight overboard, and followed them in. When the flurry of bubbles from his plunge cleared, Kurt let the air out of his vest and slowly swam down into the depths after his equipment. At thirty feet he could see the unit resting placidly on the gravel bottom. He looked around. There was nothing to see but the luminescent water and the rocky lake bottom. Hovering above the equipment, he set his position on the GPS.

Because the underwater propulsion units ran on batteries, each one had a range of just over three miles. After three more stops, Kurt had five units at the bottom of the lake and thus the capacity to traverse almost its entire length underwater. That was how he intended to assassinate the president at close range and get away. He would wait until the fishing trip was well under way and the agents flanking his craft on either side in boats of their own were lulled into complacency by what he hoped would be the heat of the afternoon sun as well as the tranquillity of the setting. He could spring the gun from its hiding place, put a bullet in the president's brain, and be over the side before the Secret Service knew what had happened.

The AV-1s were essential because Kurt knew it would only be a matter of minutes before divers were dispatched from nearby helicopters to seek him out. But he was quite confident that he would have enough time to get his tank on and zip well away from the scene of the crime before the divers could arrive. He also knew that while the infrared images taken from NSA satellites could locate almost anything on the face of the earth, they wouldn't be able to penetrate even thirty feet of the relatively cold lake water. A deep underwater retreat like Kurt's was probably the only way a single person could escape after killing a U.S. president.

The auxiliary air tanks that he was staging on the lake bottom were filled with a special mix called Nitrox 32 that would also help enable him to remain below the surface until dark. By then, the area of search would include the entire Skaneateles Lake region, which would yield more than forty-three miles of shoreline to cover. That was if they knew to cover it at all. First, they would have to figure out what had happened. After shooting the president, Kurt would simply disappear over the side. His gear was deep enough down so that no one would be able to see him from the surface. The agents on board the boats who weren't racing to the president's aid would be scouring the water's surface, expecting him to come up. There was a good chance that one or more of them would get off a shot in Kurt's direction, and that might lead them to believe he was lying dead somewhere on the bottom.

The ensuing confusion, the coming night, and the extensive shoreline would give him ample opportunity to break through any dragnet the Service could establish, drive to northern New York, slip across the back roads into Canada, and take off on an already scheduled corporate flight on his GV to Switzerland. Kurt had handled the paperwork himself. In the small town of Bedford just outside of Montreal was a little airport that accommodated numerous private international jets. One of the things Kurt had done in the past several weeks was to create a Canadian corporation operating out of Montreal, sell his plane to that shell company, and have it delivered to a hangar at the Bedford airport.

The plane was one of the easiest aircraft in the world to fly. Kurt, a licensed pilot since his early days in business, had taken the time when he first bought the GV to have his pilot, Bob Brown, instruct him on its use. Since everything was completely automated, the only time a pilot ever had to handle the controls was while taxiing and occasionally during the initial takeoff. Otherwise, Kurt simply had to program his long-range navigation units and handle the communications with the various air traffic control centers about every forty-five minutes.

Kurt scanned the shoreline. He was less familiar with the south end of the lake. It was deeper and narrower than the northern end, in some places almost four hundred feet to the bottom and only half a mile from shore to shore. The sides of the rich green hills on the south end were steep and forbidding, and substantially fewer and much farther between were the camps and homes that crowded the north end. It was as if Skaneateles were two entirely different lakes: the north flanked by rolling hills and dairy farms, the south more like one of the secluded Adirondack mountain lakes in the far northern reaches of the state.

To the west an unmarred blanket of trees stretched to the distant height of the towering ridge and Bear Swamp, an uninhabited state park just south of the tiny hamlet of New Hope. That was where Kurt planned to hide the black BMW R 1150 GS motorcycle that he kept in the last bay of his four-car garage. It was a big, fast machine that could go on or off road. He had purchased the bike on a whim, and only rode it as a novelty when he felt like taking in the countryside. Jill refused to get on the back. Now it would be the perfect vehicle to help him escape. He could dump it in the woods, deep in a thick clump of evergreens not far from where they would sometimes park to cross-country ski on the rare occasions they came upstate during the winter.

He wasn't going to ride the bike all the way to Canada, but it was easy to hide, and he would only use it to get to the Suburban he would leave loaded up with supplies and ready to go at the Wal-Mart parking lot in Auburn. The bike would also allow him to ride the unmarked farm roads through woods and fields and avoid an inevitable dragnet. The only remaining question was how best to ascend the precipitous mountainside in the dark.

It wasn't too long before Kurt came upon the Mann lakefront property. He remembered vaguely noticing it before, only because the gravel roadway that had been cut into the bluff was so dramatic and at the same time so remote. Most people who took the time and energy to accomplish a project of that magnitude did so to develop their lakefront. But the Mann property was bereft of any sign of life except an old retaining wall and a thick rope swing hanging from a massive old willow. It reminded Kurt of an undeveloped office park with meticulously paved and lighted streets but lacking a single building.

This was the perfect place for Kurt's ascent to Bear Swamp. Tomorrow morning, while Jill was out for her bike ride, he too would be out before most people were up. That would allow him to find his way up to the swamp in the light of day before he tried it again in the dark of night. After two trial runs, and with the help of his GPS, he knew he could make it. He knew he could kill the president—and get away with it.

CHAPTER 25

The next day on Skaneateles Lake, the sun rose ghost-like behind a sky that was already boiling with clouds and awash in a thick orange haze.

Three times since their first morning swim, Jill and Jeremiah had doubled back halfway across the lake instead of completing the loop. While the sense of fulfillment wasn't as great, the distance wasn't much different, and it allowed them to take an early morning swim together. The decision was predicated entirely on the weather. A particularly hot spell had taken hold of the Northeast, and the thought of plunging into the cool clear water from the apex of the rope swing was just too much to turn down when the pavement was already bleeding tar by six-thirty in the morning.

At the old blue farm silo that marked the halfway point of their ride, Jill didn't even have to ask. She simply looked at Jeremiah. He nodded and immediately began to slow down. Jill did likewise, and after checking for traffic circled her bike around and headed back the other way. Sweat drenched them both, but it looked to Jill as if steam from the heat was building up beneath Jeremiah's red face. She was reminded of a hot dog on the grill ready to split open without warning.

"Are you still losing weight from all this riding?" she asked. Jeremiah had told her a week ago that he'd dropped ten pounds from the added activity.

"No," he huffed at her as they began to build up speed. "I gained it back."

"Really?" Jill replied. "Well, it's not unusual for exercise to increase your appetite."

He shook his head and said, "No, I eat more, but not from appetite. I eat from nerves."

"Nerves?" she said. "What are you nervous about?"

They rode for a minute before Jeremiah pulled up alongside her and said, "You."

"Why are you nervous about me?" she asked.

He glanced her way and shrugged. If it were possible, his face became even redder. "I don't know. I think about you a lot."

He paused to catch his breath before continuing. "You've been a lot more quiet. You used to . . . to talk a lot. Lately it seems like something's wrong. It makes me nervous, I guess . . . Just not knowing . . ."

"Well," she said, "it's nothing bad about you."

"No," he told her, "I didn't suspect it was . . ."

"What did you suspect?" she said curtly.

"That it's . . . about him," he replied slowly. "I guess, honestly, I'm thinking you might be having second thoughts."

"Well, you're wrong," she said flatly.

Jeremiah shrugged. "Sorry."

"I didn't mean that to come out the way it did, Jeremiah," she said kindly.

They rode in silence for a time before he said, "You want me to lead?"

"All right."

Jeremiah pulled ahead and Jill edged right up behind him to catch his draft.

She was glad he hadn't taken her harsh tone to heart. He was right anyway—she had been acutely preoccupied with Kurt. She was suspicious as to why she had to go to Montreal two days before the president's visit. Well, she thought smugly, she'd soon know the answer to that and a lot of other things. On her way home from the airport the day before, she had stopped at Fradon Locks in Syracuse. The same skinny blond kid who'd tipped his hat to her at the house was behind the counter. Three smiles later, Jill had her own copy of the key to Kurt's office. It was resting at the bottom of her makeup bag waiting only for the right time to be used.

They rode the rest of the way in pleasant silence, taking turns in the lead in order to share the draft. When they finally turned into the gravel drive that meandered steeply down to the lakeshore, it was almost seven-thirty. After a long stretch through a wide-open wheat field, the path finally dipped down into a cluster of pine trees that bordered the last bend before the lake came into view.

There Jill skidded to a stop. Gravel and dust spun up from beneath her wheels and the bike slid sideways. Jeremiah was a good twenty feet behind her and he braked too at her frantic signal. She hopped off her own bike and quickly ran it back up the hill and around the bend.

"We've got to hide!" she whispered frantically at Jeremiah. Her eyes were lit with panic.

"Why?" he asked in total confusion.

"It's Kurt!" she hissed. "He's here!"

The shocking image when she'd rounded the bend was hot in her mind. It was Kurt's fishing boat, anchored not far from the shore, and him swimming steadily through the water, headed unmistakably for the retaining wall and Jeremiah's beach. She was sure he hadn't seen her—yet.

"Come on," Jeremiah said. He took his bike and awkwardly walked it straight into the pines. Jill followed. No sooner had they lain their bikes behind a fallen tree and dropped down side by side to their knees than they heard the distinct crunch of feet steadily climbing the drive.

From the gloomy wood, Jill peeked around the trunk of a tree. Through the trees, she was able to make out a picture of Kurt as he walked uphill. His face was grim. He was dripping wet, and as he strode by he was concentrating intently on something in his hand.

Jill was trembling. "What's he doing?" she moaned to herself. She was irrationally awash with guilt. She looked over at Jeremiah, who was unlacing his bike shoes.

"I'll find out," he whispered, rising from the thick bed of pine needles.

Jill grabbed his massive arm with both hands and in a near panic gasped, "Where are you going? He'll see you!"

"Even if he sees me," Jeremiah said calmly, "which he won't, what's he going to say? He doesn't know me. This is my land . . ."

Jeremiah moved nimbly off through the trees, leaving Jill to herself. Alone, she reflected uneasily on her penitent reaction to seeing Kurt. She'd told him about Jeremiah from the start. He had told her to go right ahead and ride with him, and that's what she'd done, nothing wrong. So why had she panicked? Maybe it was because riding and taking a swim off a remote dock were two different things. Or maybe it was because, deep down, her feelings weren't completely innocent.

No, that wasn't it. She loved Kurt, really loved him. Yes, she thought highly of Jeremiah: anyone who knew him would. But it was completely platonic. She fully intended to stick by Kurt. Now was a difficult time for him. His mysterious actions frustrated her, but she certainly wasn't going to abandon him. At her core, Jill was loyal, and she believed things between Kurt and her would ultimately work out. Of course, Jeremiah was a wonderful person too. He was the kind of man who deserved to have someone special. Someone, but not her. The debate went back and forth in her mind until she realized she was chewing up the inside of her cheek.

Impatient, she moved slowly through the gloom in the direction Jeremiah had gone. Halfway to the edge of the trees, she saw him coming back into the woods and she stopped.

"He went straight up the hill through the field and into the trees," Jeremiah said breathlessly. "It looks like he's headed for Bear Swamp. If you want to get back, you should just go now. I'm going to go back and follow him. Don't worry. He won't know I'm there. These are my woods. I know I look like a big bear to you, but if I can sneak up on an old ten-point buck, you better believe I can sneak up on some rich guy from New York City."

Jill looked at him sadly.

"I didn't mean anything by that," he said kindly. "Just you go. Don't worry. I'm just going to see what he's doing. I don't think he saw us."

"Not now," she fretted as they moved back to where the bikes lay. "But he must have seen us sometime before—otherwise, why is he here?"

"I don't know," Jeremiah said, knitting his massive brow. "But you go and I'll find out what I can."

"I'll call you later," Jill told him, tipping her bike up off the ground. "Will you be home?"

"I've got to combine a field, but I'll keep my cell phone with me," he said. Then he lowered himself down on his haunches and with narrowed eyes stared hard up through the trees and across the field at the spot where Kurt had disappeared.

"You get out on the drive, and watch me go into the woods on the other side of the wheat field. If he's a good way up in there, I'll give you a wave and you go. If there's any chance he'll come back out, I'll cross my arms like this and you just tuck up back in these pines. Okay?"

Jill nodded and said, "I feel like I'm doing something wrong. I shouldn't feel that way, should I?"

"Of course not," Jeremiah scoffed. "Now go."

Jill watched him lope across the field in his big bare feet without wincing. She recalled the thick yellow sole of calluses she'd seen when he took off his shoes to swim. Taking her bike out onto the drive, she waited at the corner of the trees. She couldn't shake the nagging sense of shame. Jeremiah darted into the woods for a moment, then came back out and waved his arms frantically before disappearing again. Jill got up on her bike and took off for home.

Although it had already been a long, hot ride, she didn't lack for energy. One clear beacon of certainty shone amid the storm of questions in her mind about what Kurt was doing and why. She was going to resolve the doubts and suspicions that had been nagging her now for weeks. She was going to use the key she had and unearth the secrets she knew were hidden in Kurt's office.

CHAPTER 26

A tangle of brambles tore into Kurt's leg with its needle-sharp thorns and he cursed out loud. On the night of the assassination, he'd be sure to wear his wet suit all the way up the hill. But for now, he was dressed only in his bathing suit, a damp T-shirt, and a pair of black nylon water shoes. He glanced down at his GPS. It showed not only his position in the woods, but also where the roads were that marked the park's entrance, and the spot where he would hide the motorcycle. Without it, he wouldn't stand a chance. Several times the terrain forced him to double back until he finally came across a cool, mossy stream that took him in the right direction. He entered the spot into his GPS, marking it for later reference.

At one point he had to skirt around a small hunting camp, but once past that, the stream took him almost directly to a cross-country skiing trail. The trail was overgrown now with grass that reached up to Kurt's belt line and showered his legs and feet with ripe seeds. Still, it was an easy path to follow and he had to take only one turn before he found the cluster of pines in which he planned to hide his BMW. The job was longer, hotter, and harder than he had imagined. But when it was done, he was quite satisfied that with the electronic trail he'd marked on his GPS, he'd find the spot again without too much trouble.

He logged the final spot and turned immediately downhill. Getting back to the boat was much easier, and the trip reinforced his familiarity with the rough terrain. He stopped at the edge of the run-down break wall and scanned the lake. Out near the middle, boats now careened back and forth at regular intervals. Kurt was bedraggled, dusty, sweaty, and covered with grass seed. He plunged into the cool water and was instantly revived. With a strong, steady breaststroke he swam back to where he had anchored his boat. Before climbing up onto the swim platform next to the out drive, he submerged himself completely in order to more easily slip out of his T-shirt.

As he wrestled himself free, Kurt peered down into the luminescent green depths of the water. It was eerie to think of himself down there, fifty feet deep, in water that was less than sixty degrees, in the dark, with all the force the world could bring to bear scouring the landscape in search of him. It would be a difficult mission, and for the first time, his mind was disrupted by doubt.

He climbed aboard his boat, toweled off, and put on some dry clothes. As he dressed, he reminded himself what was at stake. If he didn't carry out his plan, then Collin's death would not be avenged. That was enough to make him proceed, even if in the end he didn't escape. The urgency to survive had been born from his love for Jill and the hope of their life together. And while he still did love her, the feeling, despite his will, seemed to have grown indistinct over the past several weeks. The energy that he had expended devising and implementing his plan for revenge seemed to have left nothing for anything else, anything at all.

Weary and depressed, he started the engine and opened the throttle, cruising quickly back to the north end of the lake, oblivious to the brilliant sunshine and the pleasant breeze on the water that brought some relief from the heat. With the boat back in its slip, he strode up the path. By the time he reached the house, he was sweating again. Even the towering shade trees couldn't fend off the sticky heat. A locust buzzed loudly overhead as he let himself in through the French doors that led to the kitchen. He went inside and found no one there. He presumed Jill was still out riding and Clara was grocery shopping.

He was about to go up the back stairs and change when he thought he heard a noise come from his library. Tiptoeing into the living room, he made for the library with his heart dancing nervously. He froze outside the door, listening. The Secret Service agents who had visited him only a few days ago came immediately to mind. He tried to dredge up any error he might have made, any conversation they might have heard on a phone tap since the fishing trip had been arranged. Anything before that wouldn't make sense. They wouldn't have been watching him until the last few days, if at all.

He was suddenly jolted by the image of David Claiborne. But if Claiborne were going to take any action against him, wouldn't it only be to warn him off? After everything that had happened at the National Gallery and Leena Ventone's trailer, only a warning from his old friend would make sense. It was quite possible, given Claiborne's almost seditious overtones, that even if he suspected Kurt, he wouldn't intervene. Maybe, however, Claiborne had had second thoughts about the sanctity of his job. Maybe he had put himself on this detail for just the purpose of keeping a special eye on Kurt and foiling any attempt he might make on the president's life.

In the library, Kurt could hear the distinct sound of someone rifling through his papers. He thought of the gun he had down in the boat. He thought of escape. Then, without thinking at all, he peered cautiously through the narrow gap between the open door's hinges.

"Hey!" His angry shout rang out like a shot. He thrust himself into the room, outraged at what he saw. "What the hell are you doing?"

Jill looked up, ashen-faced, her lips trembling. But a darkening brow quickly replaced her shocked and frightened look and she glared at him through furious narrowed eyes. "That's not the question," she shot back. "The question is, what the hell are *you* doing?"

"You . . ." Kurt snarled, looking down at the sensitive information she had uprooted from the files in his desk.

"Yes," she said defiantly. "I know, Kurt. I know now why you want me to go to Montreal. I know why we have to leave . . . I know the answer to a lot of things after seeing this."

She held up a manila file bursting with papers. There wasn't one specific thing in them that spelled it out, but Kurt knew she was smart enough and instinctive enough to know exactly what he was planning.

He stepped uncertainly toward her and stopped in the face of her crazed expression. Conflicting emotions churned madly inside his head. But beneath them all, anger still boiled. She couldn't stop him. She wouldn't. He would either kill Calvin Parkes or die trying. And if she had him put in jail? That would be the same as death.

"What are you going to do now?" he demanded.

"I'm going to stop you," she said emotionally. "You can't do this."

"I can," he told her somberly. "I can and I will."

"I won't let you, Kurt," she said, with tears beginning to spill down her cheeks and her lips quavering. "I can't let you destroy yourself this way. Do you realize what you're planning? It's mad."

"If you stop me, that's the only thing that will destroy me," he said flatly. His eyes were wild and there was an edge to his voice that bordered on insane. "Can't you see that? Can't you see what's happened to me?" He lifted his hands out and up. "If I don't do this, I can't live! I can't rest, I can't think, I can't even feel . . . not with this thing inside me! I have to kill that man, Jill. That man killed my boy.

"He killed Annie's boy!" he suddenly bellowed. "My God, can't you see that? Don't you know me at all?"

Kurt felt the beast stirring within him, choking him, filling his eyes with tears. He felt it straining, as if on the end of a leash, to tear him apart and consume him. He fought hard and the internal struggle caused him to tremble.

"I won't go with you, Kurt," Jill was saying defiantly, and that got through. He forgot about everything else for a moment. He knew from the sound of her voice that she meant what she said, and for the first time he realized how much it meant for him to have her.

"Don't say that," he said desperately. "Don't say you won't go with me, Jill. I need you. I love you. I just have to do this. I have to."

She stared at him.

"I know you don't know, but try to imagine," he continued, pleading. "Try to imagine if you had a boy and that boy was killed—killed for no reason, murdered! Think of Collin! Think of what he was!"

"And if you kill someone," she said passionately, "you think that will make things better? You think that will bring him back? Kurt, you need to let it go. You need to tell people what happened. There are laws. He'll be punished. But if you try to do this, your life will be over. Our life together will be over. You'll go to jail, Kurt. That's if they don't kill you first. How could you even think like this? You, of all people! Don't you realize how absolutely crazy this is? You're talking about assassinating the president!"

"There are no laws for him," he said bitterly. "You're being naive. This is the president of the United States. My God! Do you really believe that he would ever be punished for what he did? You just don't know. You forget that I know how all this works. He can do almost anything he wants.

"And they won't get me," he added defiantly. "They won't. This is my game. I helped make up the rules."

Jill just stared for a moment before she said in an empty voice, "My God, you really believe what you're saying, don't you?"

The room was heavy with silence.

Finally, Jill shook her head sadly and said, "No, Kurt. I won't do it. I won't be a part of it. I don't care about Calvin Parkes, even if he's the president. I'm not that patriotic. But you're wrong. I know you, Kurt. I know you better than you think.

"You'll be in jail, Kurt," she continued. "Even if you can kill him, that's where you'll be. You can't get away with this. No one ever has. And as much as I love you, I don't want to be there too . . . I'm sorry."

She set the papers gently down on the desktop and walked quietly from the room. Kurt stood without moving, his mind whirling in crazy gyrations. In the stillness, he listened. He listened to the sound of her feet moving across the floor above him. As her steps descended the stairs, he opened his mouth to yell something, but nothing came out. He listened to her open the front door and leave in the noisy little refurbished MG convertible that he'd given to her as a birthday present nearly a year ago.

The sound faded up the drive until it was gone. Kurt felt as though all the insides had been violently sucked out of his body. Yet the emptiness was so complete that the pain was less than he would have imagined. At the same time, in a strange way, he felt relief. A huge burden was now gone. He no longer had to worry about Jill. It was just him now, a lethal killing machine with the knowledge and the access to take out the most important man in the world. He wasn't going to worry about her turning him in either. She wouldn't do that. And even if she did, there was nothing he could do about it anyway. He would proceed as planned. And when he didn't have to account for Jill in his plan, everything just became that much easier, that much more certain. Nothing could stop him.

CHAPTER 27

Reeves drove bleary-eyed down Route 20 to the town of Auburn in the early evening heat. Once a thriving port along the Erie Canal, the small town's biggest claim to fame now was a maximum-security prison. Many of the once-proud edifices from grander days had devolved into tenements for the devoted families of inmates from downstate. Reeves never saw the nicer parts of the town, the homes by the lake, the grand history of the place. He only knew about the traffic lights, the mini-marts, the inside of his musty room at the Holiday Inn, and a little Mexican restaurant just down the street from the prison.

Reeves had no idea why his partner hadn't relieved him in the field last night. Odds had it that something was wrong, and the feeling was exacerbated by the fact that Kurt Ford's girlfriend, a pretty little dish, had busted loose. Reeves knew that meant trouble somehow, some way. He got out of his car and took a moment to stick the gum he'd been chewing onto the door handle of the car next to him. Smiling mildly to himself as he mounted the stairs, he hummed his tune and thought of the handful of goo someone was going to get. He was puzzled when he opened the door that joined his room to the next and saw Vanecroft's burly form daintily packing underwear into a faded old plastic Samsonite.

"What happened?" Reeves asked.

"We're shutting down," Vanecroft answered sullenly. He was dressed uncharacteristically in shorts and a polo shirt. His calves bulged from below the hem of the shorts like small watermelons.

"Because?" Reeves said, surprised.

Vanecroft shrugged. The thick muscles surrounding his neck heaved like plow blades. "Boss said it's over. Something about the regulars being involved now. Everything will be handled at the right place in the right time. This whole thing never happened."

Vanecroft looked at him maliciously and added, "He wanted me to tell you that."

His dark little eyes, dangerous and unfeeling, were set close to the bridge of his nose, and it wasn't hard for people to take offense at the expression that typically graced his face. But Reeves knew that his partner was just angry, period. He was angry with his government and angry at the world. On a much smaller scale, he was angry at having drawn the night shift on this assignment. He bitched about it openly. But someone had to have rank, and Reeves, being almost twenty years senior, got the nod.

It wasn't that he thought he was superior to Vanecroft. Reeves was too cautious for that. He respected his counterpart, his training as a Ranger and his record in combat, even after the way he'd been discharged from the army. Reeves was familiar with the difficulties of adhering to rules written by scholars behind a desk when you were faced with live action out in the field. Vanecroft's only crime was that he got caught. Gunning down Iraqi prisoners wasn't all that unusual during the Gulf War. The problem Vanecroft had was that his platoon had done it too far behind American lines. Reeves understood how these things happened. Vanecroft's dishonorable discharge had nothing to do with the reason why he found the man at times too much to bear.

Now he pursed his lips irritably at the subtle affront, but said nothing. The comment about the whole thing never happening didn't deserve a response.

Reeves was a professional. He knew that everything they did never happened. He'd spent the better part of his life doing things that never happened, and this topped the list. He could imagine the fallout if this Ford character really did get away with killing the president. He shook his head and chuckled at the lunacy of it, remembering the stories some of the old-timers in Military Intelligence used to tell about how the FBI knew Kennedy was going to get it. Vanecroft looked at him quizzically, but Reeves wasn't saying anything. He'd show the big buffalo how quiet he could be. He'd just enjoy this little private joke to himself.

Black humor: That's what it was. There was something about Ford, about the way he talked, the way he was handling his affairs, that told Reeves the guy was for real. If anyone could pull off an assassination of the president, it was hard to imagine a better candidate than

Ford. What had he said to his girlfriend? This was his game.

Reeves hoped that for the sake of the people in charge they knew what they were doing. If anyone had bothered to ask him, he would tell them the guy should be taken out right away. A late-night visit, a tiny needle inserted into the hairy part on the back of his neck, and a simple heart attack. That was the easiest way to take care of something like this, and everyone knew it. But Reeves liked his job and he knew he wouldn't keep it by telling the people upstairs how to do things. What success he had enjoyed in his career had come by keeping his mouth shut and achieving his objectives as they were given to him.

He thought of saying something along those lines to Vanecroft and slipping in another jab about his seniority. But bitterness oozed out of his partner, and he knew even a small comment could incite something that he hadn't the energy for. Instead, he nodded cheerfully and returned to his own room. On his way out the door he turned and said mysteriously, "You may not want to pack so fast. Something happened and they may not want us out of here so fast."

Vanecroft looked at him angrily, searching his face for some clue. But Reeves said nothing more. He closed the door tight and threw the bolt before opening up his digital phone. He dialed his own special number and then punched in a security access code.

"It's me," he said.

"I ordered no further contact," came the emotionless voice from the other end. "Haven't you seen Vanecroft?"

"The girl knows," Reeves said, cutting right to the chase. "She went through the stuff in his office. He caught her and she told him she knew what he was planning. They had a tiff and she left."

"Where the hell did she go?" the voice demanded. It was fraught with emotion, something that nearly made Reeves wonder if he was speaking with the right person. Until now, emotion had never been a part of the equation.

"I have no idea," he responded calmly. He was used to the kind of crap that was about to come, but he knew how to play the game. He had his orders and he stuck to them. The higher-ups would always chide you for failing to use initiative, but Reeves knew that initiative could also get you eliminated.

"You should have followed her." The complaint came as if on cue. "Didn't you think of following her?"

"Of course not," Reeves said. "I was told to stay right there and listen to everything that was said and watch everything that was done. If I left, I wouldn't have been following my orders."

There was substantial huffing on the other end of the line and then pensive silence. Finally, "Can you find her?"

Reeves bunched up his face doubtfully. "I don't know," he said. "I hadn't thought about it. It won't be easy. I have no idea where she could be."

"Now, how the hell is that possible after weeks of surveillance?" snapped his boss.

"Because I haven't put one ounce of thought into what she's doing and why. That wasn't what we were ordered to do. We were ordered to stay on top of *him*, to listen in to what happened around the house. I've seen her go places, but I never even thought to find out where. She never spoke to anyone on the phone except her one friend and her office in New York. To be honest with you"—Reeves thought of the salacious moments he'd spent training his spotting scope on her nearly naked figure as she lounged by the water's edge—"she's kind of a loner."

"What did she say before she left?"

"Not much," Reeves replied, digging deep in his brain. "She said he would go to jail. She didn't say by her, though. She said she wasn't no patriot, but she wasn't going to be a part of what he was planning to do. I presume she's just going to drop out of sight until it's all over."

"You aren't in the position to make presumptions, really, are you?"

Reeves didn't respond. The silence lingered.

"Find her," his boss said finally. "Do whatever you have to do, but find her. We've got him taken care of at this point, but that's where you should start. He'll probably try to contact her or she might even contact him."

"And when we do find her?" Reeves asked.

"Then," said his boss, softly again and without emotion, "in a very quiet way, you'll do what you do best."

That was how the order always came. Reeves was simply told to do what he did best. The association was so strong that his reaction was as physiological as it was emotional. His heart pumped true and his scalp tingled. He'd just been given the order to kill.

CHAPTER 28

Jeremiah had never seen anything like it. Jill simply showed up in her little MG Spider convertible, without the big diamond ring on her finger, and asked if she could stay with him. He knew right away from her body language that he wasn't to presume that it was anything more than one friend helping another.

Still, he held out hope that whatever she was going through would pass, and then there he'd be, nothing flashy, nothing sophisticated, but a good solid man that she could count on. He was her age and he wanted a family too. The idea had been building in his mind for some time now. He loved her passionately, and despite his sense of decency, he couldn't say he felt bad that her engagement had been shattered.

He wanted to make her happy; he thought that he could. There weren't any fancy high-tech companies nearby, but he knew several intellectual types in the area who worked at Welch Allyn, a big medical instrument manufacturer in Skaneateles. He was sure someone with her background could find work there. Maybe he could even work out a deal with his brother to buy the farm.

Over the next several days, Jeremiah's hopes never failed. He was busier than normal anyway with preparations for the president's visit. His troop was taking an active role in augmenting the protection detail as well as blocking off roads for the president's travel, and between that and getting his hay cut and baled, he had little time to fret about Jill. But when he did stop to consider her, he worried. She had asked him to show her where Kurt went on the day he journeyed into Bear Swamp. When they found a motorcycle hidden there, she told him to leave it. But it was obvious their discovery affected her deeply.

It was as though she were in mourning. She said very little, and sometimes he would walk out on the back porch to find her crying there in the swing, just rocking by herself with her feet curled up underneath her and her book lying open on the pillow by her side.

When that happened he would simply nod his head toward her and continue on into the backyard and down to the barn as if he'd been going there all along. Not once did he feel she had afforded him the opportunity to really talk to her. One morning she asked if he would show her where Kurt had gone on the morning they'd seen him by the tire swing, but other than that her questions were simple and limited to subjects like where did he keep the pancake mix. She took up the preparation of food as if it was an agreement they'd come to together.

When they did share a meal, Jill would quietly ask him about his farm work, or what the latest news was on the president's visit. Never did she invite him to ask anything even remotely intimate, and in a strange way,

Jeremiah was quite content to leave things that way. It was dreamlike really, just having her there, moving softly around his farmhouse like a beautiful forgotten ghost, and he simply preferred not to wake up.

He even went so far as to call his brother's wife and say it would probably be best if his niece didn't come for her typical Sunday afternoon visit. That tore into Jeremiah, because part of him wanted the little girl, and his brother and sister-in-law, to see Jill. And he wanted Jill to see his niece. But his better sense won the day. He knew that the sight of his brother and sister-in-law would do anything but cheer Jill up. He knew them too well. Ten minutes wouldn't go by before they began to browbeat her and assail whatever religious convictions she had. Instead of dealing with that situation, Jeremiah opted for solitude.

But as Monday became Tuesday, and Tuesday turned into Wednesday, Jeremiah had the distinct feeling that something was changing inside her. She seemed to cry less, and more often than not he would catch her on the back porch staring pensively northward at the magnificent vista that stretched from his farmhouse across the long majestic lake and beyond its encompassing hills. Even when he told her excitedly how he had had the opportunity to shake the president's hand as the great man strolled past his station on the main street in the middle of town, she had only responded with a vacant stare. So when she told him Wednesday morning at breakfast that she needed his help with something very important, he wasn't surprised at all. He'd already been stricken by the sight of the big diamond ring back on her finger.

Jeremiah wiped his lips with a paper napkin and pushed back the chipped china plate that held the scant remains of half a dozen fried eggs and a hunk of grilled ham. "I'll help you in any way I can," he told her solemnly.

"What if I asked you to do something illegal?"

Jeremiah's eyebrows shot up instinctively. He'd seen a lot of questionable bending of rules during his years as a trooper, but not enough so that he was completely callous to the workings of the law. There was still enough of the old Boy Scout in him to leave him shocked at even the suggestion of something illicit.

"I don't know about that," he heard himself slowly saying. Inside, his heart was thumping madly and his mind was skittering. Despite his words, he knew deep down there weren't many things he wouldn't do if she asked him.

"It's not something bad, Jeremiah," she said, smiling indulgently. "It's something good."

"Oh," he said with obvious and ingenuous relief. "What is it?"

Jill leaned across the red checkered tablecloth. The old kitchen chair creaked beneath her. Her wild hair spilled freely about her shoulders but her face was entirely composed.

"I want you to arrest Kurt," she said deliberately.

"What?"

"I don't want you to really arrest him," she said quickly. "Listen, Jeremiah, if I tell you something, will you swear to keep it secret?"

"Of course I will," he said, nearly offended.

Jill looked at him for a long moment, her eyes flickering as she stared into his until they narrowed painfully and she said, "Kurt is . . . is planning to kill the president."

A dumb smile broke out on Jeremiah's face and he snorted humorously.

"He is," Jill said in a desperate voice. "I mean he really is. He thinks the president had his son killed. His boy was a Secret Service agent in Washington and about a month and a half ago they found him dead. It looked like suicide, but Kurt found out that it wasn't really. He was murdered and they made it out to look like a suicide. Oh, Jeremiah, I don't know if the president really was behind it or not. I just don't know. He probably was. You have to know Kurt, but he's just not wrong about things like that. He used to be in the Secret Service. He knows . . ."

Jeremiah looked down and thought about all the intricacies of the president's protection. Only someone who knew about it from the inside could sanely hope to do what she said Kurt was planning, but even so . . . Then the fishing trip he'd read about in the newspaper jumped into the forefront of his mind.

"My God," he said. It was clever, ingenious really. He looked up from the tablecloth. "What do you want me to do?"

"Tonight I want you to go to the house and arrest him," Jill said. "I've been thinking about how I can stop him. I don't want to go to the police or the Secret Service. They'd arrest him and his life would be ruined. He has plans in his office that spell out pretty clearly what he's going to try to do. He'd go to jail, Jeremiah—for the rest of his life.

"I want to stop him," she continued, "without anyone knowing. I've been thinking, if you can take him and bring him back here, if you can keep him here for just a day, he'll miss the fishing trip. The president is leaving the next day. Kurt won't get another chance like this and I think over time he'll realize how crazy it all is."

"A cooling-off period," Jeremiah said, nodding, then feeling foolish for trying to sound smart.

"Yes," Jill said patiently. "That's what I'm hoping."

"But I can't just arrest him and bring him here," Jeremiah said. "That's . . . that's the illegal part, huh? It's kidnapping."

"Do you trust me, Jeremiah?" she said, her eyes shining with emotion. She reached across the table and grasped the edge of his enormous hand.

"Of course," he whispered.

"He won't press charges," she said. "He won't do it. No one will know except you and him and me. But no one else can go with you. You'll have to be careful. He might not come easily. I think you'll need to surprise him."

"Oh, I can get him," Jeremiah said, confident after a lifetime of overpowering other men. "I can just go up to the door and before he knows what's happening I'll have the cuffs on him."

"You can do it tonight," Jill said. "Everyone who works at the house goes home in the evening. He'll be alone."

"What if he doesn't answer the door when he sees my cruiser?" Jeremiah asked.

"He will," she said. "He's used to all this. He knows how involved a presidential visit is, that it wouldn't be unusual to have someone from the state police stop and talk to him. He'll come to the door. That's Kurt. He's not going to try to run and hide. He's betting on the fact that everything will work out through the proper channels and he'll get on that boat with the president."

Jeremiah shifted nervously in his chair and it screeched loudly on the tiled floor. Still she held his hand.

"I don't want you here though," he said, shaking his head. "I just don't think that it would be good for you to be here. He's going to be mad as a hornet anyway and I can only imagine if he sees that you're here, that you were staying here . . . I don't think anything will go wrong, but if it does, I don't want anyone to get hurt. I'll just get him in cuffs, put him in the back of my cruiser, and get him out in the hay barn. He'll be okay. But if you want me to do this, that's my one condition."

Churning through Jeremiah's mind was every domestic call he'd ever been on as a cop. Those were the ones that got you killed. When you had to respond to a domestic call you got the two people as far apart as quickly as possible. Emotions, including hatred and rage, flowed hottest within the circle of a man and woman bound by intimacy.

"You go stay at the Sherwood Inn for the night," he told her. "Then you can come get him Thursday night. When I take those cuffs off to let him loose, it'll be over.

He'll know he's not going to get to that meeting with the president. Then I definitely want you here to explain to him why we did what we did. If he doesn't go along with us, then I'm the one who could end up in jail."

He didn't really believe that. What was Kurt Ford going to say? That a trooper illegally prevented him from killing the president? Jeremiah said it anyway because he wanted to make clear to Jill that although he didn't want any trouble of any kind, he'd take the chance because of her.

"All right," Jill said after a moment, "but you'll have to call me and let me know when he's all right."

"Fine."

"So you'll really do it, Jeremiah?"

"Yes," he told her solemnly. "For you, I'll do it. Tonight."

CHAPTER 29

Kurt came out of the boathouse in the early evening and looked anxiously up at the muggy brown sky. Its hue was as unnatural as the smoggy afternoon sky that hung over a big city. The leaves hung limply from the trees and only on occasion would a feeble waft of air mar the flat surface of the lake. On his way to the house, Kurt thought he heard, from far away, the low murmur of thunder.

In the living room, he opened the cabinet and turned on the TV to find the Weather Channel. A screeching bright red screen suddenly replaced the radar image of the local forecast. A flashing bulletin scrolled down the screen to warn people in the region of severe thunderstorms. As recent as that morning, the ugly weather was predicted to pass to the north. Now it appeared that the Finger Lakes were going to take a direct hit from a front that had already savaged the Midwest with tornadoes, high winds, and golf ball–sized hail.

How bad it would be and when it would pass were the questions that pulled Kurt's face into a tight mask of anxiety. After the storm warning and during a commercial break he went to the refrigerator and took out a tall can of Ruddles, an English pub ale. With the creamy brown liquid nearly foaming over the edge of his glass, he sat down on the edge of the coffee table and tapped his foot until the weatherman returned to the screen. It was with great relief that he saw the forecast now predicted that the storm would move through the region shortly after midnight. Tomorrow should be a bright, blue day.

Kurt stood and raised his glass to the unknowing weatherman before taking a sip that left him with a frothy beige mustache. This forecast would open the door for history to be made. He flipped the TV off and paced the length of the cavernous living room a few times before wandering into his library. This was the hard part. Everything was ready, right down to the fresh bait he'd purchased that afternoon for fishing. He had spent much of the past several days tooling across the quiet countryside, perfecting the escape route on his motorcycle, but even with the myriad choices he was satisfied that he had the best combination of back roads and farm fields to avoid detection. All he had to do now was wait and somehow remain within the bounds of sanity.

The storm came with the suddenness of an accidental death. One minute the strange calm was loitering about like an unemployed teenager, the next a deluge of ice, water, and wind was blasting the side of the house and ripping down tree limbs. The lights flickered and went out. Kurt found a flashlight in the kitchen. He was alone in the house, but his only concern was that the storm not impede his plans in any way. He was suddenly struck by the horrifying thought that the president might somehow be killed before the morning. It was a ludicrous notion, but it crawled into his brain.

Still, it made Kurt acutely aware of how important it was for him to be the one to look the man in the eye and pull the trigger that would blast him from this world. He was empty now of everything but that. He hadn't spoken to Jill and he had worked hard not to let himself think of her. It was just him, and the ugly thing in the back of his mind that he was certain would tear him apart the moment all this was over, the moment he stopped to think. It didn't seem to matter as much to him now whether or not he got away. He wanted to escape, and would do his best, but without Jill . . .

He found another can of beer in the icebox and poured it into his tall glass. He sat down at the kitchen table to look out over the lake and the distant hills. Malevolent blue-and-white cords of electricity pounded the earth. The power came on for an instant and then went out again. Kurt sat in the darkness, watching the brilliant light show as the storm flashed up and down the lake. Water raged from the sky and hail clattered against the roof. Thunder fractured the night with the frequency of a horrifying battle. After a time, the torrent of rain abruptly diminished into a thin drizzle. The lightning, however, continued to illuminate the sky like a flickering lamp. A few seconds later, Kurt thought he heard someone pounding on his front door.

Mystified, he groped his way through the blackened house until he stood staring up through the open door at one of the biggest men he'd ever seen. The visitor was dressed sharply in the uniform of a state trooper, and Kurt could only think that the man, whose long, powerful flashlight illuminated everything within twenty-five feet of its beam, had for some reason come to inquire if he was okay.

"Mr. Ford?" the trooper said brusquely. "I have to ask you to come with me, sir."

Kurt's heart skipped a beat. He looked at the man in disbelief, and then scanned the flickering gloom outside beyond the police cruiser. If this had anything to do with the president, he wouldn't be standing there alone with just a single New York state trooper. He'd be facing down a pair of agents backed up by a platoon of snipers.

"I have to ask you to turn around and put your hands up against the wall, sir," said Jeremiah, his voice quavering ever so slightly.

"Obviously there's been some kind of mistake," Kurt told him calmly. "Do you know who I am?"

Nevertheless, Kurt stepped out of the house and turned to put his hands up against the wall outside the door. Before he knew what was happening, the trooper, with speed that belied his size, had his hands cuffed snugly together behind his back.

"Hey!" he cried out in surprise. "What the hell?"

The trooper, whose name Kurt still didn't know, grabbed him firmly and led him across the blacktop before tucking him into the backseat of the car. The trooper's hand practically swallowed Kurt's head as he guided it in under the lip of the car's roof. Kurt sat bewildered without bothering to struggle. The size and strength of the man who was arresting him would be tough to overcome, if he could overcome it at all, and Kurt still held the image of tomorrow's fishing trip like a bright clear beacon in the forefront of his mind. He knew there must be a mistake somewhere, and there was no sense at all in exacerbating the situation by tangling with a cop.

Again he reminded himself frantically that if the president's security were involved, it certainly wouldn't be a lone trooper they sent to secure or interrogate him. He laughed quietly out loud, but broke off suddenly as they turned left onto West Lake Road, heading south instead of north toward town. Kurt searched his memory, but couldn't remember ever seeing the location of the nearest state police barracks, so he presumed they were headed down toward Cortland, the next real city of any kind to the south.

"This is a ridiculous mistake," he said after a mile or two of wet road in the flickering light. "Do you mind giving me some idea why it is you've put me in handcuffs and where you're taking me? Do you realize I'm taking the president of the United States out on a fishing trip tomorrow afternoon?"

The enormous man said nothing. He merely checked Kurt out in the rearview mirror before turning his eyes back to the road. Kurt thought he saw a nervousness that he didn't like. Why would the trooper be nervous? Kurt's stomach sank. He searched the inside of the vehicle for some sign of a ruse, but everything he saw said this was a real police cruiser.

Kurt decided to say nothing more. There was no

need. The cop wasn't talking. He wasn't the brains behind this. That was obvious. Kurt would save his breath
until he met whoever was in charge. But when the car
slowed and turned into some rural road, he sat up
straight and couldn't help from asking again, "Where
are you taking me?"

His eyes darted about in alarm when the cruiser took
another turn and began a slow climb up a gravel drive.
The breath left his body as if he'd been socked in the
stomach. Suddenly he took a deep breath and his panic
was replaced by a total calm. It was a reaction he'd experienced before. In critical situations, Kurt suddenly
became calm. He knew police didn't arrest people and
take them to rural locations to see a judge. He was being
taken to this remote place to die. But when the realization was fully formed in his mind, instead of being
blinded by horror, he was able to somehow coolly assess the situation.

The people responsible for killing Collin had found
him. This man wasn't a trooper at all. The car was the
real thing and must have been stolen. It was still almost
unthinkable that the president of the United States could
be connected with such diabolical lawlessness. But the
image of Collin, lying dead in the morgue, filled his
mind and Kurt knew that if that could happen, anything
was possible.

Objectively, he looked around the inside of the
cruiser. There was nothing at hand he could use as a
weapon. If he were going to have any chance at all, it
would come outside the car. If an opportunity came, he
would have to see it and seize it instantly. He presumed

they weren't going to waste much time. He would be taken out and killed within minutes, possibly seconds. There was nothing anyone could learn from him. Kurt looked outside his window, taking in the terrain. If he could somehow disable the big man and flee, he needed to know as best he could where to run.

As the tail end of the storm passed to the east, a flicker of lightning allowed him to examine the farm fields bordering either side of the driveway. To his right was corn, tall and thick, bordered by a patch of old timber that seemed to trail off down the hill into a lowland. On the other side was nothing more than field after field of wheat and beans. If Kurt could get away, east was the direction he would take, into the corn and hopefully the woods beyond.

He didn't have time to think much more about it before they crested the hill and followed the drive around one side of a very stately old farmhouse that rose up out of the gloom. In a flicker of lightning, Kurt could make out the neatly trimmed lawn and a handful of towering old hardwood trees that surrounded the white clapboard house. Even in his desperate condition, he was aware of the panoramic view that flashed into view before them as they rounded the corner. It was as if the house straddled the top of the world. It was an altar.

An altar of death.

CHAPTER 30

Instead of stopping at the house, Jeremiah drove down the grade in back and pulled out of the thin rain into the main barn. At one time the building had held dairy cows, but now it was used for little more than storing hay until the stables from Florida came for it with their tractor-trailers during the winter months. The odor of fresh-cut hay was heavy and thicker than the dust that danced in the broad beams of the cruiser's headlights.

Jeremiah got out of the car and walked past his glowering prisoner, out of the barn, and back up to the house. There was still no power, but the phone lines were working and he dialed the Sherwood Inn. The town had its own electric company, so while most of the lake rested in prehistoric darkness, Skaneateles twinkled brightly. Jeremiah gazed down at it through the clearing sky from his kitchen window and asked to be connected to Jill's room. She answered on the first ring in a tone that bordered on hysterical.

"I've got him," Jeremiah told her.

"Is he all right?" She fretted. "Are you?"

"He's fine," Jeremiah said, exhaling with relief.

"Everything's fine. He's in my barn and there's no way for him to get out until tomorrow night when the president takes off and we let him go."

"Do you think I should come there and see him?" Jill asked.

"No," he said, "definitely not. He needs to cool off. Tomorrow night will be fine. You'll come then."

"Jeremiah?"

"Yes?"

"Thank you so much," she said emotionally.

"Like I said," he told her, "there's not much I wouldn't do if you asked."

Jeremiah returned to the barn and eyed his prisoner warily in the darkened back of the cruiser. In the gloomy light, he could make out Kurt's face staring back at him with cold intensity. He took a length of heavy chain off a nail on the wall and looped it around one of the thick square beams that supported the hayloft before clasping it shut with a heavy padlock he removed from his pocket. He returned to the front seat and opened the rear window just enough so that Kurt could reach outside with both hands. Then he got back out of the cruiser and picked up the other end of the chain.

"Now," he said addressing Kurt in his best trooper's voice, "you can do one of two things. You can put your hands outside that window so I can undo one of those cuffs and hook you up to this chain so you can move around a bit and take a leak or whatever, or you can stay right there in the back of this car. I don't really care which, although on second thought, I guess I'd rather not have to hose out the back of my cruiser if you pee in your pants . . ."

Kurt looked out through the open space above the window, his eyes boring hatefully into Jeremiah. Nevertheless, he nodded and turned his back to the window so that he could stick both hands outside the car. Jeremiah wasn't taking chances. He had planned to be careful anyway, but there was something about Kurt that reminded him of a coon in a trap. They'd sit there looking sadly at you like a little girl's stuffed animal. Then you'd get within striking distance and they'd explode like a wet cat straight out of hell.

Well, the way Jeremiah was handling things wasn't going to give Kurt that chance. He'd take one cuff off and hook it to the chain, then get in the car himself, safely protected by the barrier between the front and back seats, and then open the window to let Kurt climb out. After that, Jeremiah would simply back the car out of the barn, close the big heavy door, and try to forget about his prisoner until the president was on his way out of town and Jill was here to calm him down.

Carefully, Jeremiah unlocked the cuff on Kurt's left wrist. With Kurt's right hand in his left, he reached down and picked up the heavy chain.

CHAPTER 31

Kurt tried not to shake, but a wild torrent of adrenaline flowed through his body. When his hand came free, he knew it would be his only chance. As Jeremiah straightened his back, rising from the floor with the big chain in his fist, Kurt spun his body around and grabbed the big man with both hands by the wrist. With all his might, he braced his feet against the car door and yanked the trooper toward the car. Jeremiah's head hit the doorframe with a resounding thud.

Without letting go of the trooper, Kurt kicked viciously at the open window. It shattered into a net of glass cubes that dropped to the ground like broken candy. Yanking the stunned cop halfway into the car, he grabbed the big Smith & Wesson .45 from Jeremiah's holster and brought the handle of the gun down viciously on the base of his skull. Then he cocked the hammer of the gun and crouched down, ready to fire at whoever else might be coming. He waited. The sound of his own breathing was heavy and audible even with the continuous rumble of the passing thunder.

When the eternal minute had passed, Kurt began to

wonder if the two of them might be alone. That made no sense at all.

The confusion was unsettling, and he felt a sudden bolt of panic return. He scrambled up from the floor of the car and wormed his arm outside the window, groping for the handle. Jeremiah filled the space almost entirely, and Kurt was unable to get his arm at the right angle to open it. There were no handles on the inside. Frantic, he began to stuff the cop back out the window. His frenzied efforts soon left the big man lying unconscious, maybe even dead, on the barn floor.

Kurt stood over the body, his chest heaving from the struggle, and tried to think. He pressed the big .45 down against the enormous trooper's temple. He hesitated, then let the hammer down gently with his thumb.

He wasn't certain what stayed his finger. It was a feeling more than a thought. It just didn't make sense. Nothing did. Without thinking, he fished the key out of the trooper's pocket. He freed himself and cuffed Jeremiah to the chain, then instinctively turned and ran into the darkness for the cover of the woods.

CHAPTER 32

Reeves had all but given up hope. Nothing either he or Vanecroft had tried turned up anything on the girl. Reeves had pumped a contact he had at the NYPD down in the city, and Vanecroft had talked to a guy he knew at the FBI. It was as if Jill Eisner had disappeared from the face of the earth. His boss was frantic, edgy, and hyper-critical of his and his partner's failed efforts. Reeves had the sense that other people were searching hard for the girl as well.

Still, he watched and waited. It was all he could do and it was what he'd been ordered to do. It was the night before the president's visit, when the storm hit, that he finally decided enough was enough. He was trudging up through the woods in the midst of the horrendous wind, rain, and hail when he saw a pair of headlights flashing through the trees.

Despite his skepticism, Reeves was professional enough to jog back through the trees just to see who it was. As the car wound down past him, he thought he'd seen a rack of lights on the roof during a particularly sustained flash of lightning. By the time he got back to where the trees opened onto the lawn, the cop—it was a cop car—had gotten out of the cruiser and was headed for the front door. As suddenly as it had started, the torrential downpour stopped. In its wake was a pesky drizzle.

Reeves yanked the microphone out of his dripping pack and fumbled with the headset. All the while his mind was chewing on the scene. The best thing he could come up with was that the girl had been found. Maybe she was even dead. That would explain why no one—her friends, family, or work associates—had seen her for days. Reeves felt like a candle inside him had been doused. Sanctioned kills didn't come along every day, so when he got one, he cherished it.

He got his equipment set up just in time to hear and see Kurt answer the door. The cop said nothing about the girl, and when he flipped a set of cuffs on Kurt Ford, a faint sigh of relief escaped Reeves's throat. She was still out there, waiting to be taken out, but now he was more puzzled than ever. The cop was arresting Ford without any apparent reason. Reeves knew that if it had anything to do with what Ford was planning for the president, there would be a lot more than one cop at the scene.

Intuitively, Reeves turned and began to run. He didn't bother going for the woods. He ran straight out into the driveway and started up the hill. He was nearly to the top when the lights of the police cruiser lit the trees off to his left. He dashed into the woods and behind a large tree. As soon as the car passed, he bolted back out to the driveway and continued his sprint up the hill. He saw the cruiser turn left. His own vehicle was across the road and up a gravel drive that led to a small rural airstrip. Fumbling with his keys as he ran, Reeves jumped into the car, fired up the engine, and tore out onto West Lake Road in hot pursuit of the cop car.

Three miles later, he crested a big hill and could see the gleaming taillights of the cop car on the next ridge. He stepped on the gas and dug the phone out of his pack to speed-dial his boss.

"It's me, Reeves," he said at the sound of the abrasive voice on the other end.

"Hang on," his boss said curtly. There was a fumbling noise and Reeves thought he heard the voices of other people before he heard the rude demand, "What?"

"I need instructions," he said. He was rewarded with an impatient huff.

"A cop came and took Ford away," he continued. "I thought maybe it was about the girl, but—"

"What?" his boss cried. "What the hell are you talking about? What cop?"

"I think it was a state trooper," Reeves said. "I don't know. It's dark here and there's a storm."

"Go get him! Did you lose him?"

Reeves smiled broadly to himself. That's why he made the big bucks. His instincts were the best. "I'm right behind them," he said, smirking.

"Follow them," his boss said, pausing to consider the situation before continuing. His voice was on edge. "Follow them and keep me informed. Let me know everything and don't let anything happen to Ford! I mean it. Don't let *anything* happen to him. Do whatever it takes, but stay with him and let me know the minute you figure out what the hell's going on. Where's Vanecroft?"

"At the hotel."

"Well, get him out there with you. I don't want this going bad. I need Ford! You get him back. Do whatever you have to do, but keep everything quiet."

Reeves hung up. He dialed Vanecroft and filled him in. His partner said he could be there in twenty minutes. Going ninety, Reeves was gaining quickly on the police cruiser.

At the top of the next hill, Reeves had closed the gap considerably. In case the cop was alert, he put his signal light on and began to slow down. As soon as the cop car disappeared over the next ridge, he flicked off his headlights as well as the turn signal and raced ahead in the dark, using the flickering sky and the cruiser's taillights as his guides. The brief flashes of lightning were the only things that illuminated the car enough to be spotted. But with a wet rear window, he was confident the cop wouldn't see him.

When the police car left the main road and turned again onto a gravel drive, Reeves stopped to dial his boss.

"He's not taking Ford to a police station," he reported. "It's got to be a house or a farm or something. There's nothing out here and they turned off the road."

There was silence for a moment and then, "Go get him. Go get Ford. And Reeves—don't leave any witnesses behind. Do what you do best and clean up any mess you make."

Reeves's hand crept involuntarily to the Glock under his arm. The thrill washed over him like heavy surf. He turned carefully into the gravel drive. Without the cruiser's taillights to guide him up the narrow lane, the going was much slower. The lightning helped, but the intervals of pitch-black seemed to be lengthening, and twice he was forced to stop completely. It was painfully slow, but he was determined not to give away his approach or to drive his car off the road. As he worked his way slowly along, he called Vanecroft again to give him directions.

When he came to the house, Reeves pulled his car off on the grass and got out. Now he thought he had an idea of what was happening. He recalled a conversation the girl Jill had had with Ford nearly a month ago. She'd been hit by a car, and a few days later the farmer who'd hit her rode his bike around the lake with her. Reeves remembered it because he'd expected Ford to have trouble with the girl. He personally wouldn't have allowed her to keep hanging around with the guy. The trooper must have some connection to the farmer. Could he *be* the farmer? Reeves could only guess that the girl had somehow convinced her new friends or friend to kidnap Ford to keep him from carrying out his plan.

If the cop had taken Ford inside, it was quite likely the girl would be there as well. Reeves looked at his watch. If he moved fast, he might get a double kill before Vanecroft even arrived. Already decked out in camouflage, he moved confidently in the dark, across the front of the house, and around back where the drive led to a group of barns. There was a dim light coming from one of them and he sprinted toward it. When he got there, he pulled up abruptly outside the big door and peered carefully inside. The cruiser sat there in the middle of the barn with its headlights burning bright, the driver's door open, and the dome light spilling a weak yellow glow around the radius of the car. Reeves gritted his teeth when he realized the great gray hump on the dirt floor beside the car was the inert body of the cop.

He walked cautiously inside, his eyes suspiciously roving the darkened corners. "Ford!" he cried out. "It's okay. I'm here to help you."

The oppressive, dank air and the heavy stacks of damp hay quickly swallowed up the sound of his voice. The last thing he needed was a panicked man shooting at him from the shadows.

"Ford?" he bellowed uncertainly.

When he reached the body, Reeves quickly read the signs of the struggle and knew that Kurt Ford had escaped. He went to the opening in the barn door and peered out into the flickering night. He almost jumped out of his shoes when he turned around to the sight of the big cop sitting up and staring bleary-eyed at him while he rubbed the back of his great pumpkin head. There was a bleeding lump on his temple that had already swollen to the size of a plum.

Reeves smiled and walked toward the cop. "He really lambasted you, didn't he?" he said with an evil grin. "A real headache?"

The cop nodded painfully but scowled at Reeves, obviously wondering who he was and what had happened.

"I got something for it," Reeves said. His voice had

a giddy edge that sounded bizarre in the eerie light of the muffled hay barn.

In one quick motion he drew the silenced Glock from under his jacket and clanked off a heavy round right into the big trooper's forehead. Jeremiah jerked backward with a puzzled look, then dropped flat on his back and flopped about for nearly a minute, spouting blood like a wild twisting garden hose. Finally, after a violent shudder, he exhaled peacefully and lay still.

CHAPTER 33

Kurt was miles from his home, but he found the main road after less than an hour and started back. Every time a car came from either direction, he ducked off the road, either behind some trees or into the ditch if there was no other cover. The passing storm had brought with it some relief from the heat, and he began to shiver in his wet clothes. His feet sloshed uncomfortably in the pair of leather moccasins he wore, but he pushed it out of his mind and tried to figure out what had just happened.

It wasn't too long before he began to believe that the trooper just couldn't be connected with the people who had killed Collin. He and the trooper had been alone, but they shouldn't have been. Or, if they were alone, and this cop was one of the lethal killers used by the president, then he shouldn't have tried to take Kurt out of the car the way he did. The people who killed Collin were better than that. They wouldn't have blundered. Kurt would now be dead.

"Jill," he muttered—and then he knew.

Kurt felt a glow of joy rise up inside him. It could all still work. The trooper was somehow connected to Jill.

Like Reeves, Kurt too remembered the conversation he had had with Jill a month earlier. She had talked about a farmer whom she rode bikes with and said that if it was all right with him she was going to do it again. Could the giant trooper be the same man? He supposed a man could run a farm and be a cop too. Either the man was the farmer or a very close friend of the farmer's. Whatever the case, Kurt was convinced that the farm he'd just escaped belonged to the man Jill had befriended.

If that were true, then he had a lot less to worry about. The president and his men still didn't know about Kurt's plan. Neither were Collin's killers hot on his trail. Only Jill could stop him. She and her friend who was now chained inside the barn had failed. Kurt loosened his grip on the trooper's pistol and picked up his pace.

It was more than three hours before he turned down his own drive. His feet were in bad shape, chafed and sore, when he hobbled into the house. The power was back on and he immediately began shutting off what few lights were on in the house. He went to the fridge and gulped some skim milk straight from the carton. It was well past midnight. He needed to sleep because if he didn't he wouldn't be sharp for tomorrow. Tomorrow was everything.

Upstairs, Kurt took a shower. Clean and exhausted, but still wired, he gulped down two sleeping pills. As a precaution, he pushed the bed right up against the door. With the trooper's .45 in hand, he climbed into bed and waited for sleep to come.

The alarm went off at seven-thirty, and Kurt flew from his bed quickly, trying to comprehend everything that had happened. It was a minute or so before he separated his dreams from what had really happened during the night. He took several deep breaths and blinked at the bright sunlight spilling in through the window. He crossed the bedroom with the gun still in his hand and turned on the TV for the local news.

He didn't expect to learn that the police were out looking for a man who'd thumped a state trooper on the head, but it felt good to watch the news and not see anything unusual. Of course, the biggest news of all was the president's visit. What local restaurant or store people thought he was going to visit next had become a surprisingly popular sport. Two of the more popular spots, Johnny Angyl's Heavenly Hamburgers and Doug's Fish Fry, had a highly publicized contest to see who could bring the president through their doors. The whole town was thrilled when he visited both. There was also no shortage of grinning Jane and John Does to fill the screen with smarmy anecdotes about how far they'd come just to get a glimpse of the president, let alone shake his hand.

"And," the morning newscaster continued with a toothy grin, "after a round of golf today at Bellvue Country Club with Governor George Pataki, DEC commissioner John Cahill, and the national GOP chairman, Butch Reynolds, President Parkes will be 'gone fishin'.' The final stop on the president's upstate New York vacation itinerary calls for a three-hour angling excursion on Skaneateles Lake with high-tech billionaire Kurt

CHAPTER 34

The president was in a wonderful mood. He'd just taken five hundred dollars from the unwilling governor in a game of skins. So jovial was Parkes that he told Mack Taylor to have the car stop in town. He wanted to walk around a little. His wife was at a local elementary school and he thought he might like strolling the pretty brick sidewalks of the village by himself. He and the first lady had taken just such a stroll only two days ago for the media's sake, but somehow the prospect seemed so much more enjoyable without her.

"There," he said spontaneously, pointing to a little coffee shop in the center of town. "I want a cappuccino."

Traffic going either way on Route 20, which ran straight through the town, had already been stopped. The motorcade pulled to a stop in front of the Vermont Green Mountain Specialty Company. Agents piled out of their Suburbans and hovered alongside the street. The CAT team stayed in their vehicle up ahead, their faces belying none of the internal anxiety the president created whenever he made an off-the-record move. A handful of agents that included Mack Taylor quickly formed a makeshift fourth perimeter around the president as he walked into the shop, waving to everyone on the street. Inside, the high school girls who worked behind the counter tittered and grew flushed with excitement and the owner hurried out from the back, wiping her hands nervously on an apron to personally make the president his cappuccino.

To the chagrin of the agents around him, coffee in hand, the president began a stroll down the main street, waving cheerfully and shaking hands as he went. Mack Taylor was right there beside him, as was Butch Reynolds with a decaf French vanilla. Taylor's face was devoid of any emotion—only his eyes shifted quickly from one point to another as he talked furtively down into the microphone in his lapel, moving agents like pieces in a speedy game of checkers. The motorcade moved slowly down the street alongside the president and his protectors. When they came to the end of the buildings, the sidewalk crossed a small bridge and opened onto a little park beside the water. The president was struck again by the sheer beauty of the lake. He nodded to himself, understanding why they called it the jewel of the Finger Lakes.

The water stretched peacefully into the distance between the rolling hills quilted with farmland and hardwoods. The sky, cobalt blue after the previous night's storm, was marred only by a few random puffs of pure white cloud. Next to the long pier that jutted out from the center of town into the lake were public docks. Vacationing families dressed in shorts, polo shirts, and Docksiders stopped what they were doing to point and

sometimes wave at the imposing figure of their president. Parkes waved back heartily.

"If you've got to go fishing," he said placidly, turning to Reynolds, "this is sure the time and the place to
do it."

Reynolds's face, flushed from a day in the sun, broke
out in a broad grin. It was nice to hear that the event he
had agreed to was no longer irksome to the president. It
had to be done. The money was too much to pass up.

"Maybe I'll even catch something," Parkes muttered.

"I'm sure you will, Mr. President," Reynolds said in
his heavy southern drawl.

"Okay," Parkes said, "let's go."

During the ride to Kurt Ford's estate, the president
fretted to Reynolds about whether or not Ford would
have the beer he liked on the boat. Michelob Light was
his favorite, and that's what he expected to get. Reynolds,
apparently unfazed by his boss's frivolous concerns, assured him all that had been taken care of. He also went
over the arrangements the press secretary had made with
the media. There was an area on the grounds where they
could shoot him arriving, as well as a spot on the dock
where they could get him leaving on the fishing boat.

"Are we doing anything special for him, you know,"
the president said uneasily, "regarding his son?"

"No," Reynolds said somberly. "We were advised
that it was best just to offer your condolences rather
than make a big thing about it. You know how it is with
a suicide . . ."

The president looked outside his window and nodded
without comment.

As they rolled past the state troopers who were posted on the first perimeter at the entrance to the drive, Parkes peered curiously down the hill for a glimpse of the billionaire's home. But the drive was curved and he wasn't able to see anything except trees until they were nearly at the bottom of the hill, as the thick woods opened onto a spacious lawn with beautiful gardens, towering trees, and a magnificent old home that had obviously been refurbished. At intervals around the yard was the second perimeter, a mixture of agents wearing fishing vests and khaki pants and state troopers in their gray uniforms, purple ties, and tall hats.

The press area snapped to life and cameras began to roll. Kurt Ford stood waiting on the front steps with Agent Morris and Marty Mulligan. They were inside the third perimeter of agents who surrounded the house and the boathouse beyond. When the president stepped out of the car to shake hands, photos began to flash. The CAT team got out of their black Suburban and casually dispersed. The fourth perimeter was made up of the agents in the follow-up car, and Kurt Ford stood inside them all with the president of the United States.

"I was so sorry to hear about your son," Parkes blurted out the moment he grasped Ford's hand.

A shadow of pain crossed Kurt's face, but he regained his composure so quickly that few people, including the president, who was looking at Mulligan, even noticed it. Kurt took them through the house and out onto the back veranda, asking the president if he wanted a drink there or if he preferred to get right out on the boat. The president was ready to fish.

CHAPTER 35

As a group, the president and his entourage meandered down the walkway that led to the stony beach and the large old boathouse. Kurt, who had prepared a list of topics in his mind to keep conversation fluid throughout the afternoon, was relieved that his guest turned out to be quite voluble. The idea of perpetuating the facade of a pleasant admirer had troubled Kurt all day. But Parkes was as charming as he was imposing and Kurt didn't have to worry about his deep-seated hatred boiling to the surface. The president talked so much that Kurt was able to mold his face into a permanent smile and actually take time to assess his odds of success.

At the beginning of the day, he had undergone a strange experience with David Claiborne. It was the first time Kurt had spoken to his old friend since the night Claiborne saved his life in Maryland. That was almost two months ago and it seemed like another lifetime. As the lead advance agent, Claiborne was busy supervising the setup of the Service's temporary command post in Kurt's garage. Claiborne seemed distracted, and Kurt could understand why, with two new sites to secure—his home as well as a golf course—in a single day. When Agent Morris introduced them at the front door, Claiborne was pleasant but distant. Kurt followed suit. And although Kurt searched his old friend's face carefully for some insight into his thoughts, Claiborne wore a mask of stone.

What Claiborne knew obviously disturbed Kurt a great deal, but as with everything else that had taken place, he was determined to proceed no matter what the cost. Anyway, for Kurt there was a clearly defined sense of destiny to everything that was happening. Even the way he had been able to escape his captor the night before suggested that his plan was somehow predestined to succeed. So he forgot about what Claiborne was or wasn't thinking and got back to his own mission.

An even more disturbing moment had come shortly after Kurt showed Morris and Claiborne to the garage. He immediately repaired to the veranda with a cup of coffee and the paper where he could carefully watch the Service's activities. He was unmoved by their invasive swarm until he saw two agents make their way toward the boathouse. He knew they would search the boat, mainly for explosive devices, and he figured that unless someone was unusually suspicious, they wouldn't be looking for false compartments under a tool chest. Still, he hurried down after them and casually walked inside just as they were about to go over the boat with a magnetometer.

"I've got to check my rigging," he explained. "I'll just wait until you guys are done."

When the agents came to the tool chest, Kurt

watched with a placid face that belied his anxiety. The wand emitted a shrill yelp. The cover was lifted, and an extremely embarrassing moment ensued as the agents extracted the two pistols. With shocked faces, they turned to Kurt, who smiled sheepishly.

"They're flare guns, guys," he said with a foolish grin. "Don't worry. If they bother you, take 'em out. I imagine if we need help today we won't have to signal for it."

The agents smiled inanely. "Maybe I'll just keep them at the command post until later," the senior of the two said, looking the pistols over curiously. "Not for me, but you know how the supervisors can be, sir. I don't want them coming down on me."

"It's been a while," Kurt said, "but don't worry about me. It's not a problem. I understand completely."

And then, to Kurt's relief, after a cursory glance back in the chest at the remaining tools, the lid was shut. The boat was sanctioned clean. Kurt exhaled long and slow. Despite his calm exterior, that moment had been a difficult one.

Now, unless Claiborne had some kind of bizarre resurrection of loyalties, the way was completely clear. All that changed in an instant, however.

The entourage arrived at the dock, where the president posed briefly with Kurt. But when Kurt opened the boathouse door, his entire plan was put into peril as Mack Taylor announced he was going to accompany them in the fishing boat.

CHAPTER 36

There were dozens of people around Kurt and the president, all of them awash in the summer sun. The media was bunched up behind a roped-off area on the grass. Agents scurried over the docks, loading themselves onto the two large chase boats, thirty-two-foot scarabs requisitioned from the New York State Police. Despite all that, Kurt felt like he was on a stage, in the glare of a spotlight with the entire world looking on in total silence. The players were himself, dressed in water shoes, a black knee-length swimsuit, and a beige polo shirt; the president, in golf slacks, shirt, and loafers; and Mack Taylor, standing rigid in a pair of khakis and a loose-fitting navy windbreaker that covered his own personal armament. The president was silent. The unspoken conflict was between Kurt and the vicious-looking agent.

From his years of experience as a sophisticated businessman, Kurt quelled his instinctive urge to squash Taylor. The man had no right to insert himself into Kurt's tête-à-tête with the president. It had all been pre-arranged. Kurt had already slipped his check for five million dollars into Butch Reynolds's greedy hands, and in exchange the president had committed to take a three-hour fishing trip with just him. Kurt had been explicit with Reynolds about his requirements. Reynolds had consulted with Marty Mulligan, who had in turn spoken directly to the president. They had assured him that it would be just the two of them on Kurt's boat.

But Kurt knew there was no sense in looking to the nearby Reynolds. Taylor was savvy and his instincts were correct. A boating trip was the one situation in the Service's protocol that substantially loosened the fourth perimeter by stretching it all the way onto the flanking chase boats. Taylor was a part of the fourth perimeter, and he wanted it tightened down, right there at the president's side. There was only one man who could alter the agent's intended course of action, and that man couldn't be challenged on the terms of the deal that had been struck between Kurt and Reynolds. That man had to be subtly manipulated.

"Mr. President," Kurt said in a low but pleasant tone, "I understand Agent Taylor's desire to get in on some of the best fishing in the world, but I have some things I need to talk to you about that are highly sensitive."

The president gave Kurt a practiced look of confusion, as if he couldn't imagine that anyone, let alone Kurt, would have anything to say that needed to be kept private.

"There are some technical aspects to my business, Mr. President," Kurt softly explained, "that I had planned to reveal to you based on a purely confidential meeting. Of course, I know that a Secret Service agent is nothing if not completely trustworthy. The problem isn't with Agent Taylor at all. It's with me, with my own discomfort. I hope you don't mind, sir."

The president looked at Taylor, who seemed to be staring back at him with unusual intensity.

During the pause, Kurt put his hand gently on the president's shoulder and said, "Thank you, Mr. President. I appreciate your tolerance."

The president balked. Taylor began to speak.

"Mr. President, I—"

"No, that's quite all right, Mack," Parkes said, holding up his hand and cutting Taylor off. "I'll be fine."

That was it. There was no arguing with the president. Kurt knew it, and Taylor knew it. The SAIC gave Kurt a malignant look, but did as he was told.

"This way, Mr. President," Kurt said, leading Parkes into the boathouse.

Kurt helped the president on board and showed him to the high bench seat, which was even with the captain's chair but on the port side of the boat.

"How about a beer, Mr. President?" Kurt said.

"That would be fine," the president said. He was still a little stiff, but Kurt presumed that after a few drinks and some time out on the water, he would loosen up. Although it wasn't always possible for a president to relax in the company of a major donor who he presumed was going to try to influence him on some legislative issue, Kurt was confident the uniqueness of the setting would prevail.

Kurt served the president his cold Michelob Light and opened one for himself that was mainly for show.

He backed the boat out of the boathouse and eased it around. As he opened the throttle, the two scarabs joined him on either flank like dogs on a leash. Soon they were out in the middle of the lake.

"I thought we might troll for a bit, Mr. President," Kurt said, eyeing his old friend Claiborne, who stood next to the scarab's driver, sunglasses on, staring straight ahead like a robot. Kurt, wearing sunglasses of his own, was able to examine the president's reaction without appearing to stare. Parkes wore the bland look of a man who wished he were somewhere else.

Kurt felt the nasty hatred well up inside him and he fantasized about running right that moment to the stern of the boat, pulling out his pistol, and wiping the expression off the man's face with a 9mm hollow-point slug. But he was too prudent to allow even the capricious vision to distract him from his carefully laid plan, and he pushed it from his thoughts.

He left the wheel, and while the boat idled slowly forward, he tossed a pair of flame-orange planing boards off either side. After reeling out enough line for the boards to drift a good fifty feet from the boat, Kurt attached a line with a lure to a wire hoop and clipped it onto another hoop that drifted all the way down and out to the board. After repeating the process on the other side and setting the poles in tubelike holders that extended out away from the boat, he set up two more rods on either corner of the stern that would drag lures directly behind them. In this way, they were able to troll four lures across a space of more than a hundred feet.

The president watched, apparently without interest.

"When the pole snaps up," Kurt said as he retook the wheel, "that means we've got a strike and you just grab the pole, set the hook, and start reeling."

The president grunted and asked about another beer. Kurt got him one from the cooler and, after handing it to him, launched into his prepared pitch on the Internet tax. His argument was watered down substantially compared to what it would have been if he knew it really mattered, and his low-key approach seemed to be a relief to the president.

Kurt finished by holding up his hand and saying, "Mr. President, I want you to know that I realize what your position is and I appreciate your willingness to take this opportunity to listen to me."

"I think it always makes sense to listen to industry leaders whenever new legislation is at hand," the president said diplomatically. "Of course, my job is a difficult one. With every move I make as president, some people are happy, while others are concerned. But my job is to lead—that's what the people elected me to do."

Here, Parkes looked pointedly at Kurt, his pale blue eyes blazing, and said, "People will look back for generations to come and understand that this moment in our country's history was a crossroads. And they'll understand that the difficult task of imposing a tax on the Internet is what will have preserved the government of this great country for the future. They'll remember that Calvin Parkes, struggling against powerful interests in the technology industry, was able to assert his leadership and make a difference, preserving the very democracy that made the technological revolution possible in the first place.

"This tax, Mr. Ford, will take the huge rewards from that revolution out of the hands of a few and redistribute it, through the federal government, to the many."

Kurt had no intention of going any further, but he was struck by the president's vehemence, and he, like all billionaires, was quite accustomed to voicing his own opinions.

"You sound very much like a Democrat, Mr. President," he heard himself say.

Instead of boiling, the president's swarthy red face broke out in a broad white smile. "And therein, Mr. Ford, lies the greatness," he said quietly. "Therein is the achievement. I will have gone beyond the restraints of traditional party-driven issues. Like any great leader who wishes to make a mark, my move is a bold one . . ."

Kurt smiled grimly at the man's prodigious ego. Clearly such a man wouldn't hesitate to take the life of a young boy who somehow stood in the way of his own grand plan for permanent and personal glorification. Kurt was also suddenly aware that Collin's death was somehow related to this issue. It was the kind of event that tilted the balance of fortune and power, and anytime you had that, you also had people who were willing to kill for it. Only something so monumental, Kurt believed, could so thoroughly corrupt the office of the president.

"Not many fish in this lake, are there?" the president said, snapping Kurt from his reverie.

"Would you like another beer?" Kurt asked in response. As he got it, he said, "I'll try changing the lures, sometimes that works . . . I wish those scarabs weren't so close."

The president eyed his men standing on post in the big white rumbling boats on either side of them. "Do they matter?"

Kurt shrugged and said, "Probably. They've been drifting up and back pretty close to those lures on the planing boards. They spook the fish."

Kurt smiled to himself as the president popped out of his seat and shouted out across the water for Mack Taylor to give them some more space. Kurt had rigged the lines with lures that typically didn't attract the lake trout that populated Skaneateles Lake. He knew that any person on a fishing boat, experienced or not, grew weary of not having a single sign of action after a while, and he bet on the president's frustration to help him back the Secret Service boats off a ways. He knew that after a time the agents would grow comfortable with the space and probably maintain it throughout the afternoon. And for Kurt, even ten feet could mean the difference between success and failure, life and death.

After two more beers for the president and some limited action on the new lures Kurt put out, he took a deep breath and flipped on his GPS. He wasn't far from the city water intake. As he reeled in the lines, he apologized to the president and guaranteed him lots of action at their next spot. With the lines on board, Kurt moved slowly forward until he came to a stop over the intake. He idled ever so slightly upwind, looked hard over his stern, saw the underwater buoy, and dropped his anchor.

The positioning of the boat would allow the president to simply drop his line over the port side and reel in fish.

Kurt rerigged a pole with a bobber, baited the hook, and handed it to Parkes.

"Just cast it out, Mr. President," Kurt said, "and watch that bobber. You'll get some action quick."

Parkes tossed his line inexpertly off the port rail, and within seconds, the bobber was popping in and out of the water.

"Set the line," Kurt cried, "and reel it in."

A minute later, Kurt used his net to scoop a two-pound bass out of the lake and into the boat.

"A good one!" the president said excitedly.

Kurt took the bass off the hook and held it up for the president to see. Parkes beamed at his fish, glad for some activity after what had started out to be three of the most boring hours of his life.

The two of them kept fishing, and as they did Kurt noticed from behind his sunglasses the subtle shift in body posture that meant the Secret Service agents on the scarabs were growing more and more relaxed in the waning afternoon sun. The only men on the scarabs who appeared to be on the alert were Mack Taylor off the port bow and David Claiborne off the starboard stern. Each of them stood straight and stared steadily at Kurt's fishing boat. A cool breeze rippled the water ever so slightly; that pleased Kurt because it would make it harder for anyone to see him once he went down over the side.

Kurt took off his bobber and cast his line over the top of the intake valve. The president was sitting on the high padded seat directly behind the passenger seat. He was protected from the sun by the canopy, but was still able to have his pole jutting right out over the side of the boat. Kurt reeled in his own line. He caught the hook on what he knew was the cage, and snapped the line with a jerk.

"Broke my line and lost my sinker," he said, showing the president the straggling end of his empty line. "I think I need to take this reel apart. I've got a pair of pliers here somewhere . . ."

Kurt felt like he was talking in an empty tunnel. His heart seemed to expand and the blood roared through his body. Time took on a new dimension and he felt as if he were moving in an atmosphere of molasses. He bent down and took the lid off the tool chest. The president pulled a fish right up into the boat with a pleasant yelp and watched it flop on the deck, waiting for Kurt to take the hook from its mouth as if he were a common boat hand.

Kurt pressed down on both sides of the bottom of the chest. It clicked and sprang gently back up at him. He tilted it, removed the big Browning 9mm, and spun around, sitting firmly on the lowest step in the stern.

When the president saw the gun, his eyes grew wide and fear stretched his mouth into a perfect circle. He dropped the pole to the deck and uttered a low involuntary moan.

Kurt felt a tremble in his hands. He glanced briefly down at the gun. The shake felt worse than it looked.

"I'm going to kill you, Parkes," he said. His voice

sounded steady and calm, but Kurt could feel his face quivering.

The president's eyes were crazy with fear, and Kurt absorbed it. He relished it.

"These are hollow-point slugs," he hissed. "I'm going to shoot you in the eye. The slug will expand as it passes into your brain and blow out the back of your skull."

Besides a face suffused with horror, the powerful posture that held Calvin Parkes upright was now gone. Confronted with the end of his life and no way to stop it, his big shoulders sagged. He glanced desperately to the boat off the stern.

"No, no," Kurt hissed. "Don't move. Don't say a word. That will just bring the end quicker. You want to live. Everyone wants to live, and as long as you do what I say, you get to live, even if it's just a few seconds. You want that, don't you?"

The president choked and nodded.

"Of course," Kurt said. He was the spider, Parkes the fly. He wanted to watch him twist and turn. He wanted to drink his panic in long slow gulps.

"Now, tell me why you had my boy killed," he said through gritted teeth. "I want to know." His glare bore down on Parkes and he saw the president's shock. It was real. The words had hit the man like a truncheon.

"I didn't," he blurted out. "I didn't have anything to do with your boy. I didn't! You're making a mistake! Please, you're making a mistake!"

"You knew!" Kurt growled. "You killed them all! Every agent that was at that meeting! You made an off-the-record move three months ago. You went to Maryland in the middle of the night. My boy stood outside that house to guard you! To protect you! To give his life for you if he had to! And you, he saw you with someone he shouldn't have. They all did and you had them killed. Now I want to know what— I want to know what it was that cost my boy his life, because now it's going to cost you yours."

Kurt felt the beast inside him stirring. Images of Collin and Annie cascaded into his consciousness against his will. He felt suddenly weary, weary beyond anything he'd ever known. He blinked and shook his head. He ran his hand over his face. They were gone. He had to stop thinking about them. He had to focus. He had to kill this man and he had to get away. If he wavered, he would fail.

"It wasn't me!" the president begged, his eyes wide with terror. "I promise you, whatever you think! I didn't have your son or anyone killed!"

The president spoke fast now, so fast he was nearly incomprehensible. "That meeting was nothing to me! It was with Alan Pimber! Alan Pimber, the vice president, and Brian Yale, the chairman of Global Software! They wanted to meet about the same thing you did. They wanted me to drop the Internet tax! It was nothing to me! If anything, it was them! Yale came out of the house and threatened me. I have nothing to hide from that meeting! You can ask David Claiborne. He set it up. You used to work with Claiborne. Ask him. Ask him. Don't do this! Don't!"

Kurt's face had grown tight as the president spoke,

and when Parkes mentioned Claiborne, he jumped to his feet involuntarily with the gun still leveled at the president's head.

Cries rang out from all directions amid the deafening shots. Kurt dropped his gun as he dove over the side. The president went down hard to the deck of the fishing boat. In midair, Kurt's body was spun by the impact of a bullet. He twisted in pain, splashed down into the water, and began to sink. Bullets rained down on the spot where he'd gone in and the water grew cloudy with blood.

CHAPTER 37

From the front window of Kabuki, a small but chic Japanese restaurant in the middle of town, Jill sat looking across the street at a swatch of grass: a village park alongside the lake. Birds flew in and out of a weathered martin house that sat atop a tall wrought-iron pole. The house, like many of the hundred-year-old homes of the village, was Victorian, painted white, with a high-peaked roof and decorative trim. Mottled chicks barked greedily as their harried parents delivered small insects and an occasional struggling dragonfly. Jill poked disinterestedly at her salad as she watched them, the dark purple males and the charcoal gray females, swooping to and fro over the water, returning like clockwork to the colony of nests and their young.

Human families milled about on the grass below. Some sat on green park benches eating ice cream and gazing out at the water, while others had entire dinners spread out over their faded blankets. A majestic old tour boat, the *Judge Ben Wiles,* bursting with festive tourists, tooted sonorously as it backed free from its moorings for its nightly dinner cruise. The entire community, in fact, was festive. The first real visit by a sitting president somehow created an atmosphere that wasn't unlike an amalgamation of the Fourth of July and Christmas.

But Jill wasn't feeling any of that. The knot in her stomach made eating a strictly mechanical function without taste or pleasure. Her brow was furrowed and the waiter who bubbled up to her table to ask her if everything was all right couldn't help but frown defensively when he saw Jill's face.

"Everything's fine," she said wanly, then spun around in her chair to see the disturbance outside the window.

The entire village suddenly erupted with sirens. Police cars and ambulances soon sped into the center of town, stopping traffic and scattering people in the park with two long lines of yellow tape that stretched from the street to the dock where the *Judge Ben Wiles* had embarked. An ambulance backed up over the curb and across the grass right up to the dock. Village police, sheriffs, and state troopers appeared and stood alongside their parked cars with their doors open and their radios filling the street with a cacophony of strident noise.

Jill stood involuntarily, her napkin dropping to the floor. She rose in confusion, took a twenty from her purse, dropped it on the table next to a half-finished glass of Riesling, and walked out of the restaurant into the street. News that the president had been shot was in the air like the pervasive hum of crickets in an evening meadow. Everyone seemed to know. People on the now silent street spoke in hushed whispers. Jill's attention too was drawn to the police scarab racing straight for town with its lights flashing and sirens wailing.

She stood frozen on the sidewalk, craning her neck along with the older couple next to her to get a glimpse of the body the agents were unloading from the boat and into the ambulance. Men dressed as fishermen but bearing heavy automatic weapons climbed into the back. The doors were slammed shut and the ambulance raced up out of the park and into the street, where it was engulfed in a convoy of Secret Service Suburbans and police cruisers that as a group rocketed off through the middle of town.

A low moan escaped Jill's throat and she felt her feet carrying her steadily down the street toward the Sherwood Inn. Her strides became a lope and her lope a full run.

"No, no, no," she groaned, dashing for her car in the back of the inn.

The tires of her Spider shrieked as she tore out into the side streets of the village. She found West Lake Road and punched the accelerator, pushing the little car until it began to shake. She was forced to slow as she passed the house, since police cruisers still lined either side of the road just outside the driveway. But once she was clear, she floored the little car again, pushing it for all it was worth all the way to Jeremiah's farm.

She turned off the road and rocks careened up into the undercarriage, shooting out from under the car like popcorn. A smoky trail of dust followed her up the hill. When she saw the house, she jammed on her brakes, flipped off the engine, and bounded up the front steps and in through the front door.

"Jeremiah!" she screamed. "Jeremiah!"

She raced through the house, knowing somehow that it was empty, but wanting to make sure. When she went out the back, the big barn gaped obscenely at her, its big doors yawning wide.

"Jeremiah!" she cried, running across the grass and down the hill into the dark opening.

Streamers of sun burst through the seams in the old barnboard walls, and motes of dust gyrated wildly in the stripes of light. In the sudden gloom, Jill saw nothing. Then, slowly, as her eyes adjusted, the dark picture revealed itself to her. The cruiser sat in the middle of the barn, its waning headlights burning faintly yellow. Teeth of glass glinted dully in the broken rear window and Jill's eyes were drawn down to the large body that lay there, branded by pinstripes of light, lifeless on the dirt floor.

She groaned and ran to Jeremiah. Something between a gasp and a scream burst from her mouth. A dark veil of bluebottle flies scattered from his face, revealing a dime-sized purple hole just above his left eye. The sticky crimson mask of blood that had erupted from his mouth and nose now mottled his face and his extinguished eyes stared blankly into space.

The rank smell of death and ripe hay filled Jill's nostrils and she vomited her salad out onto the dusty floor. Sobbing, she staggered back out of the barn, gasping for clean air. Even with her stomach empty, she continued to retch, sick with the sight of death, even sicker with the thought that Kurt could have done such a thing.

CHAPTER 38

David Claiborne was the first to draw and the first to fire. That's because he knew all along what was going to happen. Reeves and Vanecroft belonged to him and they had given him the information that let him know everything was going according to plan—his plan. In the confusion of shots and the boats racing toward the president, he wasn't absolutely sure if he'd hit Ford. He was confident, however, that Ford had done what he was supposed to do. He'd seen the president go down, that was for sure. And he had bet everything on Kurt Ford's effectiveness.

It was the same effectiveness that had never failed his old friend, the same effectiveness that had made Kurt a billionaire while he himself had toiled on as a government employee. Claiborne easily recalled Kurt's irritating competence at every bend in the road. So it seemed quite fitting that the very thing that had goaded Claiborne from the beginning and left him in Kurt's perpetual wake was the thing that would even the score.

Claiborne knew better than anyone that of all the men on the face of the earth, none was better situated to carry out an assassination of the president of the United States. There were other retired Secret Service agents who could also have used their knowledge to penetrate the president's protection. But even if such men were as capable as Ford, none were as rich, and none were as easily manipulated as the one whose own son was so closely connected to the president. It was a perfect plan and it had been executed to the letter.

Claiborne knew well the vice president's ruthlessness. The man was bereft of scruples. Claiborne had spent many hours in close proximity to Alan Pimber and had earned his trust over several years' time by becoming the person the vice president could go to if he wanted things done outside the box. When the Internet tax issue was born, Claiborne saw his opportunity to finally cash in. He knew that billions were at stake and he knew the vice president had alliances with the one man who had the most to lose. Brian Yale was the reason Alan Pimber was in the office of vice president to begin with. With monumental fortunes in the balance, Claiborne knew that if he could come up with a plan to save them, he could extract a heavy price.

Twenty million dollars, that was his take. Like Kurt Ford, Claiborne too had mechanisms in place that would allow him to disappear and spend his money with impunity. Unlike Ford, Claiborne probably wouldn't have the NSA, the Secret Service, the FBI, and the CIA hunting him down for the rest of his life. Claiborne's patron would be ensconced in the White House, the most powerful man in the world. He would veto the Internet tax, preserving the monetary power of Yale and others. The perfect plan would be complete.

The scarab swerved up to the fishing boat and the agent at the helm reversed it hard, coming to a full stop. As the wake heaved the scarab up and down, Claiborne and two other agents jumped into the fishing boat. The president lay prone on the deck and Claiborne fought a wicked grin when he saw the copious puddle of blood pooling underneath his face. The two younger agents looked to him for the next move. None of them had a chance to do anything before there was a terrific thud and a new scramble of men as Mack Taylor launched himself into the boat from the other scarab and went straight for the president.

Taylor scooped the body up as if it were nothing more than a suit bag and immediately made for the stern of the boat. The second scarab had secured itself alongside, and Taylor handed the president over to two waiting agents without a backward glance. When the president's body was on board, he turned on Claiborne with a disdainful glare and said, "Did you get him? I saw blood in the water."

"I think I did," Claiborne said.

Taylor nodded and yelled back to Claiborne again as he hopped on board the scarab. "You stay back and tell the state police what you saw. I'm getting him out of here!"

With that, the second scarab took off like a rocket for the shore, with Taylor barking into his radio, directing the motorcade to meet him in the village. With intense satisfaction, Claiborne looked down at the blood on the deck where the president had lain. He had a strong urge to dial up the vice president. His phone, the one he used to communicate with Reeves and Vanecroft, was secure. Instead, he turned to his men and said, "Tie up our boat."

The earpiece in his left ear was filled with the panicked cries of agents ordering other agents to move quicker, drive faster, and get the appropriate civilian facilities prepped for the president's arrival. He knew they would be taking him to Community General Hospital. He'd done that advance work himself. He also felt confident from what he'd seen that none of that would matter. The president would arrive only to be pronounced dead. The body would be taken immediately to Air Force One and flown back to Washington.

Claiborne dialed up Captain Shultz, his liaison with the New York State Troopers. He knew that while they would have to share this investigation with the FBI, the troopers would take the assassination as a personal failure. They would react fast and furiously.

Shultz was surprisingly calm, but intense. He took all the information Claiborne gave him and paused for a minute to think before he began laying out for Claiborne his plan of action. He would dispatch divers from police helicopters to look for the assailant's body. He would enlist the help of a nearby squadron of army Comanche helicopters to help his own aircraft scour the area in the event of Ford's escape. He would set up a loose ring of roadblocks preliminarily, and then reinforce them if the body wasn't found in the water. Finally, he had three other scarabs in the region as well as at least two sheriff's boats he could borrow to get more men out on the water.

Claiborne assured him that the scarabs the Service was using would be at his disposal as well. "We don't have any jurisdiction over the investigation," he told Shultz. "This thing belongs to you and the Feds."

It was only minutes before Claiborne saw a pair of police helicopters pop up over the horizon. They came screaming across the lake like missiles, then pulled up fast. Together they hovered in the air over either side of the two boats just ten feet above the water's surface, blasting everything with wind and spray. The back doors slid open and divers in full gear appeared. One after another they dropped into the water, plunging down into the clear green depths until they were gone from sight.

Claiborne knew that Kurt's escape plan had something to do with underwater gear, but he had no idea exactly what. Reeves had informed him only that Ford had received a shipment of gear and taken it down to his boat, where he had proceeded out onto the lake. None of that had been Claiborne's concern, but he wondered about it now. He certainly couldn't inform the state police about what he knew.

And even if he could, he wouldn't. If Ford were to be killed during his escape, that would be the best thing. But if he did somehow survive, Claiborne certainly hoped he would get away. Kurt's capture had the potential to complicate his own situation by linking him to Leena Ventone's murder. And even though Claiborne was prepared for a quick disappearance, he preferred to fade out slowly, neat and clean.

The second scarab soon returned from shore with Captain Shultz aboard. Claiborne talked quietly with him on the deck of his own boat before the captain vaulted back over the side and disappeared belowdecks with two of his lieutenants.

Despite his mask of bereaved concern, time passed pleasantly for Claiborne as he stood alone out on the scarab's broad bow taking in the late afternoon sun. He had escaped to the bow to be alone and out of the way of the frantic troopers. A mountainous range of clouds drifted in from the west, scattering the sunshine and bringing with it a breeze. The faintest hint of a farmer fertilizing his field was carried out over the water and the deep green hillsides glowed in patches where broad beams of sun sneaked through the thickening sky.

It was a beautiful summer day, but Claiborne was the only man out there who could truly enjoy it. The rest of them, even the lowest-level agent and cop, were grinding their insides, trying to scrub away the guilt of having failed in their most important mission, and wondering what they could have done to prevent what had just happened. Finally, one of the divers from the police search-and-rescue team swished to the surface and pulled off his mask. Shultz burst up out of the cabin and leaned over the stern.

"There's nothing down here, sir," the diver exclaimed. "We can't find a body. We can't find anything. The water intake valve is down here. I don't know, maybe his body got sucked into it. There's a hole in one side where it's rusted away."

"Keep looking," Shultz commanded sternly, then turned and disappeared back down into the cabin.

Claiborne was tickled by the news. He imagined Kurt's wounded body being sucked up into a giant water intake. That would finish him off neatly if there were anything left to finish.

In his ear, he was surprised to suddenly hear Mack Taylor's voice. "David," the SAIC said gruffly, "the president would like to know if Ford was killed."

Claiborne staggered, slipped, and almost fell overboard. His insides gave a startling wrench and he felt certain he would retch. Dizzy, he told himself that he must have heard Taylor incorrectly.

"The president?" he said weakly into his lapel. "Mack, I thought— Is the president all right?"

"He's fine," Taylor responded curtly. "He got a concussion and broke his nose when he dove to the deck. He's bruised and a little bloody, but he's fine. We're on our way to Air Force One and he'd like to know if Ford was killed."

"Ford?" Claiborne muttered in horror. "We don't know . . ."

CHAPTER 39

Kurt was so cold the insides of his bones ached. For the first couple hours of his desolate journey, the evening sun had filtered faintly down through the glowing green water, but now the night was absolute. Only the dim glow from his GPS and the lighted display of his dive computer kept him from wondering if he hadn't gone blind. The cruel cold and the vast darkness made him think of Collin. The last memory of his boy was his body being slid into the cold and the dark, a drawer in the morgue. But there had been nothing left of Collin, not really. Kurt, however, was very much alive.

For how much longer he didn't know. The bullet that had pierced his side left a wound that now throbbed like a diesel engine straining up a hill. He had no way of knowing what kind of internal damage had been done. He knew the bullet had passed through. When he stripped his shirt off underwater, replacing it with his wet suit, he could see the entry hole halfway down his rib cage on the left side of his body, pumping blood into the water in great clouds. He was also able to just feel the exit wound midway down his back where the slug had punched through the muscle. That was comforting anyway, that he wasn't carrying the bullet around with him.

Kurt watched his GPS carefully. After traveling his first three hours at fifty feet, he was now decompressing, traveling for the last hour in the dark at twenty feet. His last tank and a fresh AV-1 were back down at forty feet, so he wanted to get right over the spot before he dove to that additional depth to change gear.

When he hit the spot, he directed the AV-1 downward and cruised to the bottom. A powerful little lantern that was clipped to his buoyancy vest lit the area around him with an eerie beam. His equipment lay in a heap just twelve feet away. Kurt swapped his used tank and regulator for the new one and tied it off to the spent AV-1, anchoring it to the bottom. In a mesh bag strapped to the fresh AV-1 was also a fresh set of hot packs.

With trembling hands, he popped the plastic packs and exchanged them for the old ones inside his suit. Six he wedged into the torso, wincing from pain as he did so and trying not to let the plume of blood unnerve him. Of the remaining four, one went inside each glove and boot. Soon, he was almost too warm. But while the heat was a relief from the icy depths, he knew that the packs would soon wane and that for at least the final twenty minutes of his dive he would be cold again. He grabbed onto the AV-1 and snapped off the lantern.

With his GPS to guide him, Kurt sped on through the water at his twenty-foot depth, finishing his decompression, his mind returning to the dilemma of what his next step would be. Escape was his first priority, but he wasn't worried right now about getting overseas. He was only concerned now with escaping whatever dragnet the police and the FBI had erected around the immediate area. His jet could remain in Canada. A new flight plan would have to be submitted, but he could do that anytime. Ultimately, he would use the jet to escape from North America and retreat into a rural coastal region of Italy. But that part of his escape was on hold for now.

Right now he had another mission to accomplish. There was no way, despite everything he'd been through, that his determination to avenge his son's death had faltered. If anything, it had been exacerbated. He simply had the wrong target. He grimaced behind his scuba mask. The manipulation that he'd been subjected to was as monumental as it was diabolical. He tried unsuccessfully to prevent his mind from going back to everything Claiborne had said and done, and he chastised himself for not suspecting him, not seeing through his elaborate deception.

There was a moment, he remembered, back in the National Gallery, when just a flicker of suspicion had crossed his mind regarding Claiborne. That had been erased when Claiborne shot and killed Leena Ventone. But now Kurt recalled that Claiborne had tried to dissuade him from finding her in the first place and from seeking absolute proof of the president's connection to Collin's murder. Then, when confronted with the possibility of Kurt's finding the truth, Claiborne had simply taken her out—his own person, sacrificed.

Kurt wondered what was in this deal for Claiborne.

What price could prompt a man to kill an old friend's only son? But then, Claiborne was no friend. Kurt wondered if he ever had been. He knew David had always harbored a certain amount of jealousy over his success. He also realized that not taking him on board when he formed Safe Tech was a bitter pill, but he never imagined that it had hardened him beyond the bounds of human decency. The "why" didn't really matter, though, and that's why Kurt kept trying to push it from his mind and concentrate on his own "how."

How was he going to kill David Claiborne? That was what he needed to keep his mind focused on as he raced along beneath the water's surface. He knew where Claiborne lived, and as simple as that might sound, Kurt believed that was the best place to get him, in his own home. He didn't know how much information Claiborne had, but he suspected that he had watched Kurt carefully. Claiborne would have wanted to make certain that Kurt was going to carry out the plan he had set in motion. That probably meant the people who killed Collin were the same ones who had been watching.

It made Kurt's skin crawl to think that they'd been there, somewhere in his own town, watching him and reporting back to Claiborne. Yes, they could have assured him, Kurt Ford is planning to assassinate the president. They could have seen his shipment of scuba gear. They probably tapped his phones. They might very well know his plan of escape. But none of that information could have been disseminated to anyone else in the Service. How could Claiborne explain it, even now? So Kurt's obstacles wouldn't be a phalanx of Secret Service agents backed up by the FBI and the D.C. police bent on protecting David Claiborne. Claiborne was alone. Except for the men working directly for him, Claiborne was exposed, and Kurt knew the best way to get him was a quick assault right where he felt the safest—his own brownstone in Georgetown.

Even if Claiborne suspected that Kurt had discovered the truth, he would have no way of knowing for sure. He would presume, at least initially, that Kurt would try to flee the country. It would be madness to remain in the U.S. when every citizen across the nation would see his face plastered across the TV for the next several days. But madness or not, Kurt knew it would give him his best chance to get David Claiborne, and he had already made that a promise—to his son, to his wife, and to himself. He would kill Claiborne no matter what the cost.

CHAPTER 40

When Kurt drew near to the Mann family's waterfront, he headed in toward the shore and began his final ascent. He broke the water's surface quietly, removing his mask and breathing the real air deeply. The fresh scent of pine trees was a tonic after so many hours of the sterile Nitrox mixture. The lake had lost its brilliant daytime luminescence, and in the lee of Bear Mountain it had faded into a dark placid pool. The wooded ridges lay like slumbering giants along either shore. The canopy of stars and the faintest sliver of the new moon shining through the tattered clouds were a brilliant mosaic after the blackness. The contrasts were so startling that for a moment Kurt forgot the pain in his side and the hatred contaminating his heart.

His reverie was quickly broken by the staccato chop of a state police helicopter as it cruised down the lake from the north. Monstrous spindly legs of brilliant white light crawled along beneath it, probing the shoreline. From the south, he now detected the buzz of a scarab looping into the lake's last cove before heading north on a sweep of the western shore. Kurt scanned the Mann waterfront carefully. He saw no one and nothing. Quickly, he fixed the mask back onto his face, put the regulator in his mouth, dropped below the water's surface, and accelerated the AV-1 toward the break wall.

Twelve feet down, he wedged the machine blindly into a gap in the ancient cribbing. No sooner had he finished than the water was electrified with white light. Kurt could see clearly the gnarled timbers and old rocks that made up the break wall and he felt as if he were standing on a busy street corner in Manhattan in the middle of the day. He was completely exposed. With the determination of a windblown insect, he clung tight to the cribbing. Overhead, the hovering aircraft rippled the water's surface. The light lingered and panic began to seep into Kurt's blood.

Still the light remained, and the helicopter seemed to be descending with predatory determination. Kurt held tight, but his mind began to work through a series of quick calculations. How far would he have to dive to escape the powerful lights? How much air did he have left? How far would the spent battery of the AV-1 take him? And amid all this, a secret voice began to chastise him for relying solely on one plan. He should have had contingencies, several of them.

And then the light was gone. Kurt could see its broad beam burning up the water as it moved to the south. After a minute, it began to wane. Soon it was nothing more than a distant glow, and finally he was left once more to his perfect darkness. Without waiting, he kicked hard, pushing himself toward the surface.

He tried to lift himself up over the edge of the break

wall, but the weight of his equipment was too much for his cold, injured, and exhausted frame. Impatiently, he began to strip off his dive gear. Even after freeing himself, he was just able to pull his body up over the edge onto the gravelly surface. He rolled to his back gasping in pain. He was afraid of stiffening up if he lay still too long, so he rolled over and grimly rose to his feet. The GPS hung from a clip on his wrist and he consulted it as he made his way steadily up the gravel drive, across the wheat field, and into the woods.

After the pitch-darkness of his dive, even the dull glow from the starlit sky seemed to fully illuminate the wooded terrain. Kurt lurched forward, his wound throbbing. He found the stream and followed it uphill. When he came to the unlit hunting camp, he cut right through the lot and under a little bridge, invisible in his black wet suit. By the time he reached the cross-country ski trail, he was in a full sweat. He stopped to remove his hood and unzip the torso of his suit. A gentle breeze whispered in the tall grass. He ran his hand over his short hair and blinked at the GPS, fighting hard to block out the pain in his side. He was nearly there.

Ten feet from his camouflaged motorcycle, a stick snapped beneath him. The angry beam from a light caught him in its glare and all Kurt could think about was the .357 Claiborne had given him in D.C. He should have had it or the trooper's .45 with him instead of leaving them in the Suburban. Now he realized too late that the greatest need for a gun might be before he got to his truck.

He spun and darted off into the trees, hunching down against the inevitable impact of bullets.

Instead came the desperate cry of "Kurt!"

He stopped and turned, holding forth his hand to block the glare of the light. It bobbed toward him.

"Jill," he said wearily, not knowing what her presence meant. It could mean the end, or it could mean a new beginning. "How . . ."

She was next to him now, and she held the light down at her side. In the glow, he could see her dust-stained face and the tracks of her tears. She was wearing a faded pair of jeans, a white T-shirt, and a jean jacket that he recognized as his own. The love he felt for her flooded over him. Her hair was a wild tangle and her abject sadness somehow heightened her beauty. She was crying still.

"Did you kill him?" she wailed accusingly. Her voice had a hysterical edge that unsettled him. "Did you kill him?"

"No," Kurt said wearily. "It wasn't him. The president didn't kill Collin. It was Claiborne all along. I realized that, and I stopped. They shot at me, but I didn't—"

"Not the president," Jill moaned, cutting him off with a vicious wave of her hand. "I'm talking about Jeremiah. Did you kill Jeremiah?"

"Who is Jeremiah?" Kurt asked, his face suffused with bewilderment.

"The state trooper," she said in anguish. "The one who came to arrest you. I sent him. He's dead."

Kurt's face fell and a wave of nausea rocked his

frame as he recalled the terrible blow he'd dealt to the trooper's head. He was right, the trooper had been Jill's friend.

"Jill," he stammered, "I . . . I, it was . . . I didn't mean to. I thought he was with the men who killed Collin. I had to get away . . ."

"Oh God," she moaned and sank to her knees on the bed of needles. The flashlight fell from her hand and spilled its light across the forest floor. Files of towering pine trees stood straight and still, accusing him like a somber jury.

"Jill," he murmured softly. He knelt down beside her and encircled her shaking form with his arms.

"No!" she cried, tearing free from him. "No, Kurt! You killed him! I loved you and I stayed by you and he tried to help me and now he's dead! You murdered him! You're as bad as they are! You killed him!" She scooped up her light and started out of the woods.

"Jill, wait!" he cried.

"Just go!" she screamed, without turning back or slowing down. "Just go, Kurt! Go to Italy, escape, fine. I don't care. I won't stop you. Go kill whoever you want! Just go from me!"

"Jill!" he screamed. "I didn't mean to! I didn't think I would kill him. I didn't know! Listen to me!"

She spun and stabbed her light at him. "You didn't mean to?" she yelled hysterically. "You shot him! You shot him in the head! Don't tell me—"

"I never did that!" he screamed. "Look at me! I never shot him! I hit him, yes. I hit him with his gun and knocked him out, but I never shot him. I didn't, Jill. Please, you've got to believe me! You've got to!"

Kurt's face was contorted with agony. He had dropped to his knees in the harsh beam of her light. His hands were folded as if in prayer. He was pleading with her.

"Jill," he wailed, his voice cracking, "I love you. I need you. Please . . . Don't leave me. I've been used in this whole thing. I was set up by David Claiborne to kill the president. I don't know why. Everything has gone crazy. I don't want to be alone without you. Don't . . ."

"You didn't shoot him," Jill said flatly. For almost a minute she contemplated him, her mind digesting the possibilities. "You're saying you didn't do it . . . Kurt, if you're lying to me, it won't matter . . .

"I'll find out," she said, her words brimming with vehemence, "and if I do, nothing will matter. I won't stay with you. I won't help you. I'll help them! I'll help them find you and put you in jail. If you're lying to me, tell me now and you can go, but tell me!"

"Jill," he choked, "I am not lying. I never killed him. I promise. Please, I love you. I need you . . ."

Kurt stared into the glare of the light long enough to notice the sound of crickets cascading all around him. He heard clearly the roar of a car engine on the nearby road and the whine of brakes as it slowed to a stop next to Jill's convertible. An instant later, the inky stand of pines was being probed with a powerful spotlight.

CHAPTER 41

The harsh beam of Jill's flashlight wavered and went out.

Kurt found her in the darkness and they embraced. He kissed her deeply, breaking free only when the spotlight flashed just past them and he heard the sound of men's voices coming from the road.

Grasping her by the shoulders, he whispered urgently, "We've got to go. Shh! Don't say a word. Just come. I love you!"

He grabbed her hand and dashed to a nearby clump of ferns. Tearing the camouflage covering free, he yanked the BMW upright and straddled it. With one hand, he pushed his helmet into Jill's hands and then pulled her aboard. With the other, he turned the key, firing up the engine. The whine of the big bike was like a magnet for the searching beam of light that came from the road. Kurt heard the shouts of several men and saw new, smaller beams bobbing as they entered the woods and approached him through the trees.

With the flick of his toe, he slammed the big machine into gear and shot back off into the woods. He hadn't planned to go that way, but it was the fastest way to escape the men who he assumed were police. When he hit the ski trail, he turned north and opened the bike's throttle, tearing through the high grass. Jill clutched him tightly, flooding his injured torso with pain. After half a mile, he came to a road. Without slowing, he leaned the bike, cornered out onto the road, and headed west. Jill buried her head in his back and held on.

Kurt scanned the roadside desperately for a sign of something that would tell him where he was. He had a sense that he was headed in the right direction, but he wanted certainty. If he was going to elude capture, he needed to get back to his planned route.

The narrow, winding road flashed past him like a high-speed video game. Kurt downshifted and leaned into the curves, accelerating out of them with dizzying speed. Before long, he came to a crossroad that he recognized as 41A, West Lake Road. He started one way, then spun around and went back the other when he realized that he'd come out too far down on the main road. A mile later, he saw the dark form of the car that had stopped by the woods where he met Jill. Like a crafty predator, it came suddenly to life. Its high beams blinded him and the bank of flashing lights on its roof made his heart skip a beat.

Instead of slowing, Kurt pressed on directly toward the police car. Then, one hundred yards before he reached it, he leaned the bike into a turn and rocketed up a side road. The police car bolted forward and screeched around the corner with its sirens wailing. Kurt looked over his shoulder and realized that it would only be a matter of minutes before he had the full force of the police, the FBI, and quite likely the military, bearing down on him. He pressed forward, easily bringing the bike's speed up to a hundred and thirty miles per hour and gaining distance on the car. He mounted a hill and took to the air. Jill dug her hands into his ribs and both their screams mingled with the whine of the engine.

When they hit the pavement, Kurt slowed almost to a stop before turning the bike off the road and onto a dirt drive. He braced the bike up on its stand and scrambled down. With a fist-sized stone he scooped from the ditch, he smashed the bike's headlight and then did the same to the taillight. No sooner was it extinguished than the cop car shot up screaming over the hill and smashed down on the road, sending a shower of sparks from its belly. In a rush of noise and frightening speed, the car hurtled past them, whipping up a vortex of dust and grit.

Before kicking the bike back into gear, Kurt took two deep breaths to settle his nerves. It was one too many. Trailing the police car was an Apache helicopter from nearby Fort Drum. Unlike the police helicopters, the army aircraft was nearly silent. But its piercing searchlights blasted either side of the road with white light, and although it sped past Kurt and Jill twice as fast as the police car, it almost immediately swerved off toward the side of the road and doubled back.

Kurt opened the bike's throttle, tearing up the dirt road that separated two vast cornfields. The Apache was soon directly overhead and Kurt was nearly blinded by the intensity of its light mixed with the swirl of dust from the fields. Behind him rose a massive plume that might have been the smoke from a stream of napalm. More than anything, Kurt feared that the gunship would open fire. In the craziness of the flying dust and the motorcycle's maniacal scream, it wasn't himself that he was worried about, but the thought of Jill being torn apart by a hail of bullets almost made him stop and surrender.

But his instincts took over and he raced dead-on for a prodigious stand of hardwoods. He neared the trees and saw clearly the black hole where the forest opened its maw to engulf the road. Instead of taking it, he held out his right foot and leaned hard, spinning even more dust into the air and racing now along the edge of the trees on a small sandy path bordering the cornfield. For a quarter mile he sped along the edge of the field, his path clearly lighted by the intense beam of the searchlight, until he came suddenly to another farm road. Like the first, it bisected two fields and also led straight into the woods.

Kurt jammed on his brakes and spun the bike in a swirling cloud of brightly illuminated dust. But instead of taking the road into the trees, he doubled back straight into the dense cloud that he had kicked up along the path. The plume was a brilliant creamy brown, the color of coffee with milk, until suddenly they were in total darkness. The Apache spotted the road leading into the woods and erroneously presumed that that was where Kurt had gone. The gunship shot up above the trees, stabbing futilely in through the forest's late summer canopy for some sign of the motorcycle.

Kurt slowed somewhat, until his eyes, teary from the

dust, adjusted to the gloom of the starlight. Soon the dust cleared, and by keeping tight to the corn where the stalks smashed past his elbow, he could feel as well as see his way back to the first dirt road. By the time he reached it, the dust had settled enough for him to make out the opening in the trees. This was the thickest wood he had to travel through, and when he'd plotted his escape he had driven through it one afternoon more than a dozen times, familiarizing himself with every dip and turn. Even so, it was slow going, and Kurt's grip on the handlebars was desperate from the tension of trying to go as fast as he could without a wipeout.

Twice the beam of the Apache cut across their path through the trees like a vast column of light from a UFO. Both times, Kurt slowed to a stop and ground his teeth until it passed. Finally, they could see up ahead the dim opening where the dirt path opened onto a gravel country road. Kurt stopped at the edge of the wood and dismounted from the bike.

"Are you all right?" he asked Jill in a whisper.

She nodded that she was, but when Kurt lifted the visor of the helmet to kiss her, he could see that her eyes were wide and her mouth was pulled tightly back in a mask of fear.

He jogged awkwardly up the path and peered cautiously out onto the road. One way, at the bottom of a long descending grade, were the flashing lights of a police car and the hazard lights of a pickup truck. Probably some farmer on his way home who'd been pulled over for questioning. Kurt imagined that everything that moved on these roads would be subject to questioning if not an all-out search. The other way, however, appeared to be clear.

But instead of going that way, Kurt pulled slowly out of the woods and headed for the flashing lights. That was where the next farm road in his escape route lay. The sight of the police car goaded him in the opposite direction. A more rational voice, however, said it was better to stick to his plan and that it was better to drive toward trouble he could see rather than risk the unknown. The police up ahead would be concentrating on whoever they'd pulled over and would not be as apt to see his darkened motorcycle cruising toward them.

With the engine running at nothing more than a purr, Kurt drove halfway to the police car and then turned right onto another road leading up into more cornfields. The road went steadily uphill until he and Jill were high enough so they could look back and see the Apache, which had now been joined by another helicopter, crisscrossing the large thick wood they'd just left. A second police car, lights flashing, raced down the road they'd just taken from the opposite direction on its way to the cruiser that had pulled over the pickup truck. Kurt felt a grateful sense of relief that he'd followed his plan rather than his instinct to just run.

After another hour of careful travel, they turned north onto 38A, the main road that ran up along the eastern shore of Owasco Lake, Skaneateles's sister that lay to the west. Several miles after that they reached Auburn. Kurt took side streets to the Wal-Mart. He wasn't worried about being pulled over arbitrarily this far from where they'd been chased, but he was concerned that his lack of a helmet could draw the attention of a local cop. When they reached the large illuminated parking lot, he eased in among the rest of the traffic and pulled right up next to his Suburban, looking around him as if he hadn't a care in the world.

An overweight woman wearing a ratty pair of furry slippers and a tent-sized house shirt shuffled past under the blue-white light. She gave Kurt's wet suit a funny look. Kurt stared right back at her and she averted her eyes, moving quickly on.

"Will you drive?" he asked Jill.

"Of course," she said, noticing for the first time that he was in pain. "What happened? Are you hurt?"

"I was shot," Kurt said grimly.

"Where?" she gasped. "Let me see. Kurt, we need to get you to a doctor!"

Kurt shook his head, unlocked the Suburban's doors, and handed her the keys.

"We've got to get out of here," he said, rounding the vehicle and getting in. "We'll worry about that later. The bullet went through and I think the bleeding has slowed down."

"Slowed down?" she said incredulously as she started the ignition. "Let me get some bandages at least."

"All right," he said, "but not here. Let's get away from the bike. Let's get out of town and we can stop at a drugstore along the road. We've got to get as far from here as we can. Even though I didn't do anything to the president, they'll put me in jail, Jill. You understand that, don't you?"

Jill bit her lower lip and nodded her head. "Yes," she

said. "And I know I'll be in trouble too, if they catch us."

"No," Kurt said, "you won't. If we're caught, we'll say I forced you to drive me. I'm not letting you take any of the blame. The thing I'm more worried about though is Claiborne and his people. If they find out I'm alive, they'll try to kill me . . . I just don't know how many of them there are. I don't know how deep this thing goes."

"Where are we going now?" she asked. "Do you want me to go to the Thruway?"

"Yes," he said. "Do you know how to get there?"

"I take a right here and then a right on Thirty-four," she said as she drove out of the Wal-Mart parking lot.

"Right."

As she made the turn, she asked, "Are we taking the Thruway to the Northway, and then to Montreal?"

"No," Kurt said. "We'll take the Thruway to Eighty-one. Then go south."

Jill started to speak, but the words got caught in her throat.

"Eighty-one south?" she asked hesitantly. "You mean north?"

"No, south."

"Kurt, why?"

"Because," he said, "we're going to Washington."

CHAPTER 42

Claiborne took a commercial flight back to the capital, leaving the state police and the FBI to their fruitless search for Ford. His fellow passengers and the flight attendants on the airplane saw only a man distraught beyond reason, unresponsive and lost in a fog of great consternation. When he arrived at the airport in D.C., Claiborne got into a cab and sat for nearly a minute before he realized the driver was asking him where he wanted to go.

Once home, he went directly to the second floor of his brownstone and ensconced himself in the spacious leather chair of his small, musty, wood-paneled den. After a moment of consideration, he proceeded to knock down most of a quart of Canadian Club whiskey. Both his cell phones as well as the house phone rang at repeated intervals, but Claiborne ignored them. He was thinking, his mind sprinting desperately along on an endless treadmill, until he was too drunk to care, got off, and climbed the stairs to bed.

In the morning, he staggered to the bathroom and gulped down four aspirins with a mouthful of water straight from the tap. He got back in bed, hoping to pass the next thirty minutes sleeping until the medicine took effect, but his mind was already back up and running. Head pounding, he got up again, shaved, and dressed himself in a pair of tan slacks, a white button-down shirt, and a herringbone jacket.

On the front porch was the paper; Claiborne slapped it down on the kitchen table before pouring himself a glass of juice and preparing a pot of coffee. As the scent of brewing coffee filled the kitchen, his headache began to fade. The paper was full of exactly what he would have suspected, a massive headline about the attempted assassination with pages and pages of little else. Apparently, the police had given chase to two people on a motorcycle late in the night at the south end of the lake, but lost them. Authorities presumed that it was nothing more than drunken teenagers. Claiborne snorted derisively.

With a hot cup of strong coffee in hand, he played back his answering machine. There were several calls of conciliatory concern from some of his peers within the Service. As the lead advance agent, he would endure the brunt of the fallout after the assassination attempt. Someone had to pay for it. Claiborne was unaffected, but when he heard the somber voice of Mack Taylor, he blanched. His boss was requesting that he report to the Secret Service offices first thing in the morning.

"We need to talk," were Taylor's final words before a harsh click.

Something in the SAIC's voice told Claiborne that the meeting was more than just a debriefing after a catastrophic breach in the president's security. Although any connection between Claiborne and Ford would be nothing more than conjecture at this point, it unsettled him nonetheless. Instead of delaying, he called Taylor's office and said that he would be over directly. Before going, he dialed the vice president on his safe cell phone.

"I've been waiting for your call. What happened?" Pimber demanded irately.

"A temporary setback," Claiborne replied. "But I have a solution."

"A solution?"

"I need two million dollars in a suitcase by five o'clock this afternoon and I need to meet you and Mr. Yale somewhere safe. I'll explain my plan. If you like it, you give me the money. If not, then it's over. I go my way, you go yours."

"If this is your way of trying to wheedle money out of Yale, you can forget it," Pimber hissed.

"Two million dollars is nothing to me," Claiborne countered. "I want all twenty and I know I'm not going to get it unless I get the job done. I will get the job done. It won't be as clean for me, but I will get it done. The cash will make an impression on the men I need. That's why I want it. At this point, it's our only chance. You can tell that to Yale."

There was silence on the other end of the line. Finally, Pimber said, "I'll call him. He's in town and if he wants to hear what you have to say then I'll call you back and tell you where."

With that, the vice president hung up.

Claiborne put on a pair of Ray-Bans, walked outside

his brownstone into the sunlight, and pulled away from the curb in his late-model Lexus coupe. It was a short drive to the Service's offices, and Taylor was waiting for him in a conference room with the director of the Secret Service himself as well as two of his deputy directors. Claiborne peered at them from the end of the table through bloodshot eyes. He was properly dejected for an agent intimately involved in a monumental failure.

"I don't know what to say," he began, sighing heavily. "I did everything by the book. You'll see that from my reports, but I know that's no excuse and I would prefer that this not reflect badly on any of the other agents involved in the advance, especially Agent Morris . . ."

Claiborne sat looking at them, one by one. They were annoyingly devoid of emotion and he wondered if it was simply because they had seen right through his subtle attempt to deflect the blame to Morris. It had been Morris's job, after all, to do the interview and background check on Kurt Ford.

"We aren't here to talk about that, David," Taylor said finally. "We want to know about your relationship with Kurt Ford."

Claiborne feigned astonishment as well as indignation. "We were friends a long time ago, Mack," he said defensively. "You know that—everyone who's been around does."

"We want to know about your relationship lately," the director said. He was a wisp of a man with frizzy reddish hair that circled his bald bespectacled head like a clown. Even so, there was nothing comical about him.

His beetle-black eyes bore into Claiborne with characteristic intelligence and intensity.

Claiborne returned the stare, looking hard into his
small dark eyes, then at Mack Taylor. They were bluff-
ing. They didn't have a thing. He could see it. They
were fishing around.

"I haven't spoken a word to him in years," he said
defiantly.

The director's eyes went to Taylor. The SAIC cleared
his throat and said, "The president believes otherwise,
David. Kurt Ford told him about an off-the-record move
that you had arranged between him and Vice President
Pimber."

A smile curled the corner of Claiborne's lips and he
calmly replied, "Kurt Ford is a madman. You must know
that. He tried to kill the president. You must be joking to
take anything he said seriously. Honestly, you can't be
serious."

"How did he know about the meeting?" Taylor demanded.

"His son!" Claiborne said, slapping the words down
like a trump card.

"His son is dead," Taylor pointed out.

"And so, Ford's madness," Claiborne said.

"Mack, this is serious," the director said with a scowl.
"Don't you think we should just leave things as they
are? We've got enough problems as it is."

"The president thinks—" Taylor began.

"Mack," the director said, cutting him off, "with no
disrespect to the president in any way, this is a Secret
Service issue. David is a highly respected member of

the Service, a part of the team, and we have to conduct ourselves accordingly."

"I don't know if Kurt Ford is all that mad," Taylor said grudgingly.

"Anyone who would try to kill—" the director began.

"He didn't try to kill the president," Taylor broke in. The room was silent. All eyes were on Mack Taylor.

"The president said Ford never fired a shot," he continued quietly. His face broke out into a subtly evil grin. "They talked about the meeting with the vice president and Brian Yale. Then Ford just stood up and jumped over the side."

Claiborne's throat grew suddenly tight and he searched Taylor's face for a hint of deceit.

"He's escaped, you know," Taylor continued, with a cunning look at Claiborne. "The papers are reporting that there were two people on a motorcycle that eluded the police last night. The troopers are speculating that it was teenagers, but they know and we know that Ford owns a bike that fits the description of the one they chased. I don't know how he did it, but he's out there somewhere, David. If you have something to tell us, maybe you should do it now . . ."

Claiborne returned Taylor's gaze with equal malevolence and then said to the director, "I resent this, this witch-hunt, and I'm going to file a formal complaint. I have nothing left to say to Agent Taylor, sir. So, unless you have more questions for me yourself, I'm going home." He stood, and so did the director and his two men. Taylor continued to sit and stare.

"I'm sure we can resolve this," the director said. His

stern nasal voice was tinged with anxiety. The last thing he needed now, in light of a nearly successful attempt on the president's life, was an internal scandal. "I don't think any formal complaint will be necessary, David. Think about it. I know both of you have been through a lot. Let's all just take some time to cool off and think about it."

The director turned pointedly to Mack Taylor, who by the look on his face was going to refuse to acquiesce in any way. And really, they all knew that he didn't have to. He was in an unusual position. The director was his superior, but he was the SAIC of the Presidential Protection Division because that's what the president wanted. In reality, if not on paper, Taylor had more influence than any of them.

"Of course," Claiborne said, calmly leaving the room. He didn't mean it, but what he needed now was time. The end of his career was at hand and that might be the least of it. Things were much worse than he had feared.

What had been an emergency plan was now the only hope he had left. It was risky, and with Taylor looking for something already, it would almost certainly connect Claiborne with the president's death. That was why he hadn't tried to do it this way from the start. He knew that even if he succeeded, he would be hunted for the rest of his life. But the look on Taylor's face told him that the life he had now was over.

Taylor might not ever be able to prove anything. But Claiborne's career—that was finished. Taylor's suspicion alone would see to that. But twenty million dollars in offshore bank accounts would enable him to hide in style. That's what he wanted. He wanted to enjoy the wealth he should already have had. The wealth he would have had if Kurt Ford hadn't snubbed him years ago.

But this plan, if it worked, would be even better than sharing in Kurt Ford's wealth. This plan was his doing, and if it worked, he could revel for the rest of his life in his own cleverness. This would be his last chance. He had to act quickly and presume that Yale would come up with the cash. He knew a suitcase with that much money in it would put the deal to bed.

He dialed his phone and when a gruff voice on the other end answered, he said, "Reeves, it's me. Get Vanecroft and meet me at the Tabard Inn on N Street tonight at seven. Ask for Mr. Valance and come to my room. We all have to presume we're being followed, so take every precaution to shake a tail. I've got a critical job for you."

Then he added, "It's the job of a lifetime . . ."

CHAPTER 43

Gentlemen," Claiborne said—he always treated his thugs with great dignity, that was part of the catch—"I am going to disclose to you information that's so classified there are only a handful of people in the entire world who are privy to it . . ."

He paused, looking hard at his men. He already knew it, but even if he didn't he could see clearly from their faces that they liked this kind of talk. Claiborne was behind the desk in the small suite he had taken for the night. Musty books lined the shelves on one wall and a lace-covered bed stood against the wall, neatly made. Behind him was a large bay window that looked out over the quiet tree-lined street. Dusk was nearly at hand, but the tall glass lamp on the corner of the desk lit the men's faces with a clear orange glow. They were grim yet eager.

"The mission we have carried out over the last several months was not what it appeared," Claiborne said somberly. He sighed long and low before continuing. "The president, gentlemen, is on the brink of destroying everything this country has built over its two-hundred-plus-year history. He is on the verge of implementing, along with a few key appointees in the military and intelligence communities, the disclosure of a substantial body of military and intelligence secrets to the Chinese. It will be done under the auspices of diplomacy and a newfound alliance. It will be packaged and sold to the public, who will buy it the way they buy everything else that's fed to them by the media. But underneath it all will be the simple exchange of money for secrets. It will undermine the United States in a way that will change history . . ."

Claiborne searched their faces. A vein transecting Vanecroft's forehead had swelled angrily and it beat a steady pulse. Reeves's reaction was less clear, but Claiborne felt confident he'd struck the right chord with them both, so he continued.

"Ford was supposed to do the job," he said. "But he failed. Our role, as I'm sure you've already guessed, wasn't to prevent Ford from carrying out his mission, but simply to monitor it. But he failed. He wavered in the final seconds. He missed his target . . .

"The target, gentlemen," he said in a low tone, "is the president."

Claiborne reached down to the floor before getting to his feet. He placed a small suitcase on his desktop and flipped open the brass latches, boldly revealing the cash. An inky scent filled the room and charged it with tension.

"A symbol of the seriousness of what we're being asked to do—one million dollars in cash," he said, eyeing the men carefully. There was another suitcase, but he was keeping that for himself in the event that these two men, like Ford, somehow failed him. One million wasn't twenty, but in a worst case, it was better than nothing.

"I have for you here the address of a safe house in Maryland. That will be your refuge once the job is complete," he went on. "From there, you will be transported by military helicopter to Fort Bragg and from there to Brazil. You'll be provided with new identities as well as the remainder of the money—another million and a half dollars apiece in offshore accounts.

"There are other candidates for this mission," Claiborne continued, picking up two bound stacks of hundred-dollar bills and handing one to each of the men. "But we're getting the first crack at it. This is a chance for you, and I won't lie, for me—if we succeed, I'll get two million as well—to cash out. It's this, in fact, or nothing. Gentlemen, this is the mission of a lifetime. If we succeed, the viability of this country will be preserved and we will be well compensated.

"Our escape is secure," he lied. In reality, he had made no provisions for these men. The address was a false one.

"If you accept, I have here the president's detailed itinerary for the next seven days. Despite Ford's attack, they've decided to stick to his schedule. He has to. It's campaign time and they don't want to give the impression that he's afraid. I'll trust your judgment as to the best opportunity for success, but I would strongly suggest you take a close look at the Acid Rain March he plans on participating in down Fifty-ninth Street in Manhattan. The size of the crowd and the multiplicity of hotel windows will provide an extraordinary opportunity. I also have the location points of the counter-sniper teams, so you can avoid falling into their direct line of fire. That's just my suggestion . . ."

Claiborne stopped speaking. He watched the two men think. Vanecroft was massaging the packet of bills. He licked his lips.

"I'm in," he muttered. "I'm in all the way."

They looked at Reeves, who narrowed his eyes and said, "I'm in if my partner here will agree to two shooters. We coordinate everything to the second, and at the predetermined time, we shoot."

"Like Kennedy?" Claiborne said, arching his eyebrow.

"Why not?" Reeves said. "It worked."

"Art?" Claiborne said, his heart beating fast.

Vanecroft nodded sullenly and said, "I don't mind if he calls the shots as long as I get my money and we take this traitorous piece of shit out."

"Good," Claiborne said, not wanting to upset the momentum of the two men's decisions by bogging them down with details. "I have packets here for each of you. If after looking over the information, you agree with my assessment, then we'll meet at Clyde's on M Street Sunday night at seven. They have a back room that will be reserved under the name of Jones. We can finalize the plans there and I can update you on any itinerary changes."

Claiborne closed the suitcase and handed it over to Vanecroft, knowing he would appreciate the gesture and that Reeves was a big enough man not to care who was holding it. He walked with them silently down the stairs and out the front door of the inn. Like strangers, they went in opposite directions.

At the corner, Claiborne caught a cab and headed back to his brownstone. He closed his eyes briefly as the cab trundled along, wondering what the odds of success were. Probably not bad. People thought killing the president was harder than it really was. If you knew his itinerary, and you could shoot a rifle, it wasn't that tough.

When he got home, he looked suspiciously up and down the street. He wondered if there had been a tail on him when he left the house five hours ago. If there was, he was confident that they were panic-stricken and still looking for him in and around Dulles Airport. Inside the brownstone, he went directly to the kitchen and mixed a drink. He didn't linger over it. In three smart gulps, it was gone. Claiborne didn't have time to celebrate his second chance, even though it was worth celebrating. He had to see to some preparations of his own.

CHAPTER 44

Jill drove all the way to Harrisburg, Pennsylvania, before Kurt would finally let her stop for the night at a motel along the highway. Earlier in the trip, she'd gone into an all-night pharmacy in a small town along the way and come out with enough sterile bandages, antiseptic salve, and Advil to keep Kurt as safe and comfortable as possible without the help of a real doctor.

The amount of blood he had lost frightened Jill. His skin seemed pallid and his lips were faintly blue. When they dressed his wound the bleeding seemed to have stopped, but even so, she couldn't help herself from fearfully prodding him awake in the front seat every half hour or so just to make sure he was still alive. After they stopped, Jill checked them in at the motel office while Kurt waited in the Suburban. They collapsed into a sagging double bed and both of them slept until nearly ten the next morning.

When Kurt awoke, Jill was alarmed at his continued pallor. He admitted that the pain was intense, but nevertheless insisted that they continue their trip. He had stocked the Suburban ahead of time with enough food, drinks, and extra clothes in case of an emergency, and Jill was thankful for his thoroughness. The less they stopped, especially during the daylight hours, the better. Jill was also happy that he was willing to let her drive while he rested with his seat fully reclined as they cruised down the highway toward the nation's capital.

Kurt didn't tell Jill where exactly they were going or what exactly he was doing. She didn't want to ask. She thought she knew, and she was going with him anyway.

"I think it's better," he had told her early in the trip, "that we don't talk about where we're going. If we're caught—not that I expect we will be, but if we are—I want you as insulated as possible."

Kurt slept most of the drive. When he wasn't sleeping, he rode with his eyes closed. She knew he was avoiding conversation and she understood. When they got to the outskirts of D.C., he sat up and pointed out another roadside motel. Again Jill checked them in while Kurt waited in the back of the Suburban where the windows were tinted.

Jill asked for a room in the back, explaining to the manager that she couldn't sleep with the noise from the passing traffic. Besides giving her a furtive, hungry look, the greasy-looking man didn't say or do anything unusual. It seemed strange to her that people were going about their lives normally while she was languishing in a world of tumultuous uncertainty and fear. The manager gave her a room on the back ground floor as she requested, and she pulled the truck right up to the door so Kurt could get quickly inside.

Jill unloaded the duffel bags from the truck. When

she was done, Kurt put the Do Not Disturb sign on the door and began to unpack. From the first bag, he extracted some dark clothes and dark rubber-soled shoes that gave Jill an unsettled feeling. But that was nothing compared to when he removed the .357 and began checking its action. Jill turned away and busied herself in the bathroom organizing the items she'd purchased for herself at the drugstore the night before.

"It's gone," Kurt said from the other room. He sounded like a father watching a scary movie with his little girl. "You can come out."

Jill reentered the room, her face slightly flushed.

"Will you help me with this?" he asked, slowly removing his shirt. His pain was obvious.

Jill helped him change the dressing on his wound, and when they had finished, her lips were pressed tightly together in her effort to keep from saying something that she knew wouldn't help the situation.

"You're scared?" he asked, touching the side of her face.

She nodded.

"Don't be," he said softly. "When it's dark, I'll go. I won't be gone long and when I come back, it will be over. We'll go up to Montreal. I know a place we can cross the border near Champlain. The jet will take us to Europe and we can start everything over, together."

With tears in her eyes, Jill turned her face up toward his and kissed him. They held each other gently for several minutes, with Jill's head buried in his chest, before she said, "I suppose it wouldn't do any good for me to ask you not to go?"

"No," he said quietly. "I'm sorry."

After a final hug, he said, "I have to get on my computer. I need to line up another routing to Switzerland for the day after tomorrow and do a few other things, but first I need to dye my hair."

"Your hair?" Jill exclaimed.

"It's a precaution," he told her. "I don't think anyone is going to see me anyway in the dark, but if they do . . ."

Jill nodded. They both knew that his picture was on the front of every newspaper and in the lead story of every news broadcast across the land. She helped him follow the directions without comment.

After a satisfied examination of a much younger-looking Kurt Ford in the mirror, Kurt removed a portable notebook computer from its case in one of his bags. He sat down at the desk, plugged it into the phone jack, and got online. Jill looked on with interest as he secured all the proper clearances for a new flight schedule from Montreal to Geneva. She didn't say a word, but watched in anticipation as he searched the D.C. phone directory online. When Kurt found the address of David Claiborne in Georgetown he glanced quickly up at Jill with a blank face. She nodded grimly and continued to watch.

Kurt went to the yellow pages and began systematically breaking into the computer systems of all the home security companies that serviced the area. The third one on the list, AST, also happened to be Claiborne's company. Getting the client list was child's play, Jill knew, but she was awed as she watched him proceed to break into the company's actual security reporting system. To do so required a substantial decryption process. Kurt's computer didn't have that capacity, so what he did was access the hardware inside Safe Tech. When she saw what he was doing, Jill realized that breaking into AST's most protected information was only a matter of time. In less than an hour, Kurt was in. Jill watched over his shoulder as he studied the layout of Claiborne's individual system. It was clear to Jill that with that knowledge, getting into the man's house and disarming the system would be an easy thing to do if Kurt went through the basement window. She said nothing, because she was certain he saw the same thing.

After a few minutes of study, Kurt let out a satisfied grunt, jotted down some notes, and shut down his computer. Without discussing the plan, the two of them shared a silent meal of crackers, cheese, slices of pepperoni, and granola bars. Jill offered to go out and get something more substantial, but Kurt argued that better fare was no reason to take any chances.

"They might start putting your picture out there too," he said.

Jill nodded in agreement. They had already seen his face all over CNN when Kurt briefly flipped the TV on and then off again.

"The way it worked out," he said through a mouthful of crackers, "with you not being there when he came to the house, was the best thing that could have happened. You're not in any of the news clips, so no one should recognize you. Still, if the media does some digging, you never know. The less you're seen, the better."

When they'd finished eating, Kurt made a feeble attempt at conversation. He talked wistfully about what things would be like when they got to Italy—the sea, the wine, the complaisant disposition of the people. Jill attempted to join in, but their words rang hollow, and like the sunlight that crept in through the shabby curtains, their talk began to fade. They soon found themselves sitting in silence.

"I'm going to try to rest," Kurt said after a while. He stretched out on the bed. "Will you wake me around eight?"

CHAPTER 45

Jill didn't have to wake him because Kurt never slept. But at eight o'clock, she helped him affix a false beard and mustache onto his face as well as arrange a body pillow, adding what looked like about fifty pounds to his frame. With his red hair, matching beard, belly, and a pair of wire-framed glasses along with a baseball cap, Kurt looked nothing like the images of him that had been plastered all over the newspapers and TV. He had planned to use the disguise at the jet's hangar in the event someone saw him, but in the present situation it couldn't have served his purpose better, enabling him to go out into the streets without exciting suspicion. Even Jill, who knew him so well, thought that he was unrecognizable.

The last thing Kurt did before leaving the hotel room was dig into his shaving kit for a couple of caffeine pills. He wanted to overcome the sluggishness that seemed to emanate from the wound in his side. He thought too of taking something more than Advil for the pain. He had some codeine left over from a back injury a couple years ago, but he didn't want to cloud his judgment in any way. Instead, he would let the pain in his side goad him like a thorn in the paw of a wild animal.

With clenched teeth he made his way toward the capital, stopping only at an Ace Hardware to purchase some tools, and then into Georgetown itself. Glancing down at the map, he wound his way through the streets until he came to a placid tree-lined lane lit at intervals by decorative lampposts. Kurt drove past Claiborne's brownstone and murmured something inaudible when he saw a yellow glow from the highest window. He cruised through the area for several minutes, searching patiently for a parking spot. When he found one, he got his bearings, pulled his cap down tight, absently patted the pistol under his arm, and set off. In his pocket he carried a simple glass cutter, a suction cup, a penlight, and a pair of wire cutters.

After strolling casually up and down the street several times, and seeing the light go out in Claiborne's upper window, Kurt stole into the alleyway behind the row of houses. Counting carefully, he found the one that belonged to Claiborne, hopped a fence, and stood plastered against the back wall with his heart banging like a dryer full of shoes. Clouds had obscured the moon, but a powerful halogen streetlight halfway down the alley cast enough light to make him feel exposed.

There was a small rectangular window that opened into the basement of the brownstone, and that was where Kurt was going in. The window sensor would go off only if he opened the window, and his glass cutter would obviate that. Kneeling on the small brick patio amid a rusty set of outdoor table and chairs, Kurt fixed the suction cup on the window and cut around the edge of the frame. Carefully, he removed the pane of glass and set it quietly on the bricks.

On the other side of the fence, a dog barked suddenly and ferociously, and Kurt's heart leaped into his throat. He jumped at the sound, but then froze and listened, straining to remain calm amid the mad din. The dog was right on the other side of the fence, howling maniacally. A light went on and Kurt scrambled in through the cellar window, disappearing from sight just as the neighbor poked his head over the fence.

"You damn fool" Kurt heard the neighbor growl at the dog. "Get inside!"

When it was quiet, Kurt stood bracing himself against the damp brick basement wall and waited for his breathing to slow. Then he moved. This was his one chance. He knew he had to make it neat and clean—get in, kill his son's killer, and get out. But he knew that if he rushed, the chance for error would double. With the small penlight in his mouth, he found the security system control box on the wall. Quickly, he cut the phone line that reported any intrusion to the security company, the wire to the internal siren, and finally the power to the system itself.

Satisfied that he could now move throughout the house with complete impunity, Kurt removed the .357 from beneath his arm and mounted the stairs. Slowly he made his way through the space, ready at every opening to find Claiborne's bedroom. Moving that way, it was nearly twenty minutes before he found himself on the third floor in front of what he felt had to be the right door. Carefully, he turned the knob and opened it.

A hint of light from the street filtered in through the curtains and the red numbers of a clock radio glowed angrily from the bedside table. Kurt surveyed the room. It was eerily still. In the bed was Claiborne's prostrate form with the sheets pulled up over his head. With his finger on the trigger and his gun aimed directly at the figure, Kurt stepped cautiously through the doorway and into the room.

In the same instant, the lights went on and Kurt felt a terrible bolt of pain in the back of his neck. The gun flew from his hand and he went down in a heap in the middle of the floor. Standing over him, in the glare of the light, was David Claiborne. In one hand was a baseball bat, in the other a pistol with a long ugly silencer. On his face was a grin that was as contemptuous as it was malicious.

CHAPTER 46

Reeves had been around long enough to know when a deal had gone sour, and he smelled it now as surely as rotten milk. His own years of experience in Military Intelligence and then with the CIA had left him in the habit of always being ten minutes away from a total disappearance. Reeves could fit his lifetime of personal effects into a small box. Besides a silver pocket watch that had belonged to his grandfather and a small framed black-and-white picture of him and his mother when he was a child, all he had were handfuls of medals, some from his days as a college boxer and some from his military service.

Now he stuffed a complete set of clothes and the trinkets that defined him as a human being all into a single military duffel bag. From the desk, he slung a thick briefcase over his shoulder that contained his computer and enough documents and passports for three different identities, excluding his real one. With the duffel bag in one hand and the small suitcase that contained the money he and Vanecroft had split in the other, he was ready to go. His apartment, a nice one-bedroom on M

Street with a terrace, contained nothing but rented furniture, and he bid it good-bye without ceremony.

Letters to his landlord, the furniture rental company, and the car dealer where he'd leased his Town Car were all prepared. He dropped them in the mail at the box on the corner and hailed a cab. After storing his things in a locker at the airport, Reeves took another cab back to the city and met Vanecroft in a mean little bar on Constitution Avenue halfway between the Capitol building and RFK Stadium. Vanecroft was waiting for him in a booth against the wall, glaring at the other patrons in a way that made even the roughest characters give him a wide berth. Beside him on the dull pink seat was his own suitcase of money, discreetly handcuffed to his wrist. After a few drinks and technical talk about the job they were about to embark upon, Reeves looked at his watch and said they'd better go.

They took Vanecroft's car, a new dark blue Pontiac Firebird, to the stadium and parked on the edge of one of the outer lots. It was nearly midnight. Reeves had told his partner that they were to meet the man who would supply them with the equipment they needed to carry out their plan: two high-caliber competition rifles, along with the kind of hand-loaded ammunition that would guarantee them an accurate shot from five hundred yards. He had asked Vanecroft to bring some cash. Each would pay for his own gun. But the way his burly partner had the entire case clapped to his wrist made him suspect that Vanecroft wasn't letting the money out of his sight.

Reeves looked around. The area was run-down and

deserted. The stadium was a sad reminder of prouder days, its parking lot littered with garbage. Weeds sprung up from the cracked pavement. Reeves took two Cuban cigars from his coat pocket and offered one to Vanecroft. His partner looked at him suspiciously. Neither of them had ever given the other anything but subtle barbs in the four months they'd been together.

"To celebrate," Reeves explained. He gazed dispassionately at Vanecroft with his unfeeling eyes.

"Thanks," Vanecroft said, smiling slightly and taking the proffered Cohiba.

While Vanecroft was busy lighting his cigar, Reeves removed the Glock from his coat in one smooth motion, leveled it at the side of his partner's head, and blasted a hole through his skull that shattered the driver's window and showered the upholstery with a bright crimson spatter. Reeves quickly opened his door and scanned the area. The pungent smell of gunpowder hung about the car, but the night was quiet and nothing moved. As he rounded the car, he removed a nasty little camp knife from his pants pocket. He opened the door and Vanecroft slumped over, hanging halfway out of the car. With the care of a patriarch carving a turkey, Reeves worked his knife through the tendons and between the bones in Vanecroft's wrist. He removed the hand and tossed it to the ground. The handcuff slipped free from the stump of Vanecroft's arm. The money was his.

From Vanecroft's jacket, Reeves removed a long dark pistol whose barrel was burdened by a cylindrical state-of-the-art silencer. It was a good weapon and Reeves hated to see it go to waste. With the gun in his belt and the briefcase in his hand, he looked carefully around again and started off across the vast parking lot, a solitary figure in the warm dark night, heading into a neighborhood that most people would have feared. But for Reeves, who had seen the worst the world had to offer, even the most dangerous neighborhoods in D.C. felt safe.

It would be several blocks before he could find a cab, and as Reeves walked, he pondered his next move. He had a flight out to Mexico City first thing in the morning. He could simply return to his apartment for a good night's sleep, but the habits he'd acquired through the years of dark plots and backroom deals told him to sweep his tracks completely clean. He didn't want to run for the rest of his life. That wasn't his style. He wanted to set up in a little oceanside place on the beach near San José in Guatemala where he could fish and drink rum and wander into town to sample the local talent on an as-needed basis. He didn't want to have to worry about the spooks from the CIA or NSA or even the people at MI with some vendetta hunting him down for the rest of his life because he was part of an assassination plot.

The problem with Vanecroft was that he had been so bitter, his judgment was clouded. The problem with Claiborne was greed. Reeves had seen that in the man's eyes. And, like all greedy people, he presumed that everyone else harbored the same sentiment. To Claiborne, half a million dollars was enough to entice them to do a monumental job, and he presumed the promise of three times that if they succeeded would carry the day. But Reeves could live comfortably on half a million for the rest of his days. And with Vanecroft's money as well? He was in fat city.

The job itself could have been done. With the classified information Claiborne had given them, they could have done the deed with limited exposure. It was the getaway that bothered Reeves. He didn't trust a military transport to Brazil. Something smelled sour about that. Now his only connection to the whole thing was Claiborne. That was the only track Reeves had left behind.

CHAPTER 47

Your boy," Claiborne said with an evil smirk, "was a pretentious little shit. But why should that be a surprise? He wasn't that unlike you, Kurt . . . So when it became obvious that killing him was the perfect way to implement my plan, I ordered it with pleasure."

Kurt stared up at Claiborne with clenched teeth and unbridled hatred. Rage contorted his face behind the fake beard. In his mind, he was thinking only of how he could kill Claiborne. He didn't give a damn for his own life. Lying there, unarmed, with Claiborne's weapon leveled at him, he expected to die. But he wanted to die knowing he'd taken Claiborne with him.

"You were my friend," he whispered, tears brimming in his eyes.

Claiborne could have no idea they were actually tears of rage, and he snickered out loud, obviously relishing the sight. "So in the end," he sneered, "it's me who has everything, isn't it? For twenty years, I've watched your company. I followed the stock! And I knew how rich you were becoming. So when I had my chance, did you think I wouldn't take it?

"What I want is for you to know, in these last few minutes of your pitiful life, that it's you who caused all this. You are responsible for what happened to your precious son. You!

"I was your friend and you shut the door in my face!" Claiborne snarled. "But after all these years of Kurt Ford getting everything and being everything to everyone, it's me who's the better man, it's me who's on top. Isn't it, Kurt?" He raised his voice hysterically, baring his teeth.

"Yes," Kurt whispered, buying time to clear his head from the blow of the bat so he could make his final lunge, take the deadly bullet, but still get at Claiborne and kill him before his own life expired. His eyes flickered to his own gun, four feet away underneath the bedside table—too far.

"Go ahead," Claiborne sneered. "Make a move, Kurt Ford. The famous, rich, successful Kurt Ford. Make a move. This is my game and it's over!"

At that moment, Kurt knew he'd have to go at Claiborne, take the bullet, and try to wrest the gun free, killing him with his own weapon, or fail altogether. But when the dark figure of Reeves appeared in the doorway behind Claiborne, Kurt changed his mind in an instant and went for his own gun. A muffled shot went off, ripping through Claiborne's torso and throwing him forward into the room. Kurt reached his gun, but instead of turning to fire, his instincts from years ago took over and he rolled. Reeves's second shot tore into the floor, kicking up a spray of splinters that stung Kurt's neck and ear.

He seemed to come up out of his roll in slow motion. His gun was leveled at Reeves and he could see the man's gun likewise staring back at him, a dark black hole in the end of its barrel ready to spit death. The two men fired at the same time. Kurt struck Reeves squarely in the chest. Reeves's bullet struck Kurt in the head.

Kurt saw stars and went down hard. Dazed, his ears ringing, he reached up and felt for his wound, a neat little trench in his scalp that poured blood out onto the floor. Staggering, he got to his feet, blood spilling from him like a faucet. Reeves lay open-eyed on the floor with a hole in the center of his chest and the scarlet stain around his heart blooming like a rose on his white shirt.

Claiborne lay facedown next to the bed, raspy sighs escaping from his nose and mouth, which also bled out onto the floor. Kurt took the gun from his hand and turned him over. Claiborne's eyes shot open, alert with fear, blood gurgling in his throat. Kurt could tell he'd been shot through the lung. With some immediate help, he would survive.

"I didn't mean it," Claiborne said in a desperate, choking whisper. "Kurt, I lied. I didn't have anything to do with Collin. Reeves did it. I lied. I wanted to get you back for everything, for not taking me with you when you made everyone rich, but I didn't do it. I would never do that . . ."

Kurt knelt beside Claiborne, his own blood spattering steadily onto the floor in fat red droplets. He smiled grimly at his old friend.

"This is what my son felt," he said, setting his jaw and jamming the gun into Claiborne's mouth. Claiborne's eyes widened in horror and his arms began to flail desperately.

Kurt spewed his words. "This is for Collin, you piece of shit!"

The gun erupted with a muffled clank. Then there was silence.

Kurt staggered to the bathroom and cleaned up as best he could, wrapping his head in gauze and tape and pulling his cap down over the wound. Quietly, he let himself out the front door, noting the broken glass in the front room where Reeves had come in through the window.

Kurt spent the drive back to the motel fighting hard to keep his composure. After what seemed like a lifetime, he pulled into the back of the lot and knocked on the door of their room. It flung open and there was Jill, her face alive with worry and then loving relief.

"Is it over?" she whispered.

Kurt nodded that it was.

He looked at her dully and stepped over the threshold wearily, shutting the door behind him. They embraced. He tried to speak but couldn't. He looked down at her through the blurry wash of tears. When he closed his eyes, he saw clearly the images of Collin and Annie. He no longer had the strength to restrain whatever it was inside of him. A pitiful sob escaped his throat. Crying, he lay down in a crumpled ball on the bed and let it go.

There were moments of clarity for Kurt when his consciousness rose up out of his sea of pain for brief moments. He didn't know what would happen. He felt certain he would die. But through that horrible night, when it seemed that dark sea he'd fallen into held no escape, he would always see her face. Tearful, but compassionate and full of love, he'd see Jill's face shining like a beacon. And somewhere deep inside him there smoldered an ember of hope.

EPILOGUE

Fifteen miles south of the small coastal town of Sapri in southern Italy, a couple sat on a secluded terrace that jutted out over the sea. Below was a private beach, its clean black sand nestled in a cove whose sides rose like the walls of an enormous fortress all the way up to where the winding road took the occasional car, truck, or bus up and down the coast. The roar of the surf explained the tangy scent that mixed with the lemon trees planted in enormous pots resting on the festive terra-cotta floor. The couple, a handsome middle-aged man with his striking young wife, sat curled up together in a large rattan love seat. They were barefoot, he in cotton drawstring pants and an old T-shirt, she in a loose-fitting cotton shift.

They sat placidly together sipping from drinks laced with wedges of lime and absorbing the mist-enshrouded mountains that fell straight into the blue-green sea. They were talking languidly about the merit of various names. The woman said she liked the name Jeremiah and the man agreed that it was fine.

The pink glow from the setting sun softened the

scene, giving it a dreamlike quality. So it seemed almost fitting when Anna Rosa announced in her quietest voice that they had a visitor. They never had visitors. They kept to themselves, treating their staff like distant relatives, doing the right things by them without becoming intimate. When they did go out to dinner, or take a driving tour to Florence or Rome, it was always in a quiet way, with both of them perpetually hidden behind glasses and hats.

They were quite unremarkable people, really, aside from the burning attraction they shared for each other. Most of their time was spent swimming, sailing, or reading the books that arrived almost weekly, delivered by the boxload to the nearby post office. They had suddenly appeared, a little over a year ago, at the modest villa whose original owner was bent on seclusion. As if to honor his spirit, they too kept to themselves.

Kurt set his drink down and stood languidly, surprised when he saw that their visitor had simply followed Anna Rosa into and through the house and was now standing behind her with the somber smile of a man whose long search had finally ended. Kurt's body went rigid and Jill turned in alarm to see Mack Taylor standing there, looking peculiarly American in his dark suit, sunglasses, and tie.

Taylor removed a gun from beneath his jacket and pointed it at Kurt's chest. A wicked smile crept across his face. Kurt froze and Jill gasped in horror.

"Bang," Taylor said.

After a few moments Kurt said coolly, "I never knew

you were one for humor, Mack. Can I offer you a drink?"

Taylor removed the glasses, revealing his lifeless pale gray eyes, and said, "Yes, that would be nice." He holstered his gun, still smiling, and sat down.

Kurt said, "I have scotch, vodka—"

"One of those would be just right," Taylor said, pointing toward the opened bottle of Pellegrino that sat on a tray beside the love seat. He took in the view and sighed heavily, taking the glass Anna Rosa had hurriedly brought to Kurt before disappearing shamefaced and frightened into the house.

"How are you, Mrs. Ford?" he said politely.

"Fine, thank you," she said, sitting back down but no longer interested in the sunset.

"How did you find me, Mack?" Kurt asked tiredly.

"I made it my hobby," he said gruffly. He continued to stare out at the sea, the mountains, and the sky and seemed to be truly enjoying himself.

After a while Kurt asked, "Are you taking me back?"

Taylor looked at him and a rare smile, born from humor alone, tugged at the corners of his mouth. "No," he said. "I'm not."

Jill exhaled audibly.

"Then what are you doing?" Kurt asked calmly.

"I'm here for two reasons," he said, taking a drink of his water and puckering his lips at the hint of lime. "First, I wanted you to know that I could find you . . . And if you had killed the president, I would have killed you."

Kurt looked at him soberly, knowing he meant it.

"Second," he said, "the president wanted me to thank you personally and to let you know that there is no effort under way in any agency to seek you out. That's his offering of thanks, and his offering of reconciliation to you for what you did for him and for what happened to your son." He cleared his throat and added, "I'm sorry as well . . .

"Of course, you need to remain anonymous," Taylor continued after a reflective moment. "That would be part of the deal. We can't have you resurfacing. What happened was too much of an embarrassment . . .

"And," he added, looking pointedly at Kurt, "the Claiborne murder investigation is still open as well."

"Of course," Kurt said quietly.

"Otherwise," Taylor said, finishing his drink and taking one last look at the magnificent view, "we wish both of you the best of luck."

Then, after standing to go and taking a brief glance at Jill's swollen figure beneath the loose-fitting dress, he said, "I guess I mean to say, good luck to all three of you."

More
Tim Green!

Please turn this page
for a
preview of

THE FIFTH ANGEL

available
wherever books are sold.

CHAPTER 1

Despite the horror of his crime, there was a chance that Eugene Tupp might go free. The legal system was a board game. Right didn't always prevail. Chance could supersede justice. That's what Jack Ruskin was afraid of.

A mist hung in the night air, muting the light. Fluorescent street lamps glowed pale blue. The scent of damp concrete and pavement floated up, mixing with the smell of cooked onions blown outside by an unseen kitchen fan somewhere down the side alley. Jack Ruskin lifted a ream of paper from the passenger seat of his Saab convertible. He tucked the bulky package beneath his long raincoat and, with his briefcase in the other hand, stumbled into the Brick Alley Café.

He stepped up onto the dining room floor and surveyed the tables, looking past the inquisitive hostess. Gavin Donohue was in the back, beyond the old wood bar and its high leather chairs, back near the emergency exit. Gavin sat upright beneath a copied

Monet. He faced the quiet crowd, a big dark Irishman with the stoic expression of an elected official. He was the D.A. of Nassau County. When he reached for his wineglass, a silver Rolex Submariner flashed on his wrist.

Jack made his way through the mill of waiters and waitresses. They were dressed in white shirts and black bow ties and moved with expedient politeness. When Jack bumped one he turned to excuse himself, jostling a second, tangling his legs, and losing his balance. His papers spilled in a gusher on the hardwood floor.

Jack cursed quietly and knelt down. He thanked the staff and even the other diners who bent down to help him collect his things. Gavin got up and came halfway across the room to help.

"Not the best place for this," Jack said, rising, his face feeling warm. He adjusted his glasses, looking through the steam and up into Gavin's face.

"I thought you'd like some dinner," Gavin said, handing him a transcript sheet from the floor. "Come on, let's sit down."

Gavin tucked himself back in the corner, still upright. He was tall and thick, and his thinning dark hair matched his eyes. His cherry face was made serious by a concrete smile. Even years ago, when they'd been young assistants together in the D.A.'s office in Brooklyn, people had been afraid of Gavin.

Jack set his briefcase on the floor beside his chair, then thumped his stack of papers down on the linen tablecloth. He took off his coat, tossed it over the back of his chair, and sat down, loosening his tie.

Jack knew Gavin had something to say to him and he didn't like the precipitous angle of his old friend's eyebrows. He felt short of breath. His heart pumped faster. He moved the brass lamp on the table and the flowers to one side. Yellow stick'um flags sprouted from the ream. Jack reached for the one closest to the top, pulling out the page. He wanted to talk, to keep Gavin from talking.

"I'm not telling you what to do," he said, "but I just don't think this Unger woman is the right one to be doing the cross on a witness, any witness. Listen to this: 'Mr. Billings, do you—"

"Jack."

"—do you think that you might have been mistaken wh—"

"Jack."

"You don't ask someone if they 'might' be mistaken on a cross, Gavin," Jack said. "I don't want to sound peevish, but goddamn."

"Jack, stop."

"What?"

"Just stop." Gavin's face turned to stone. He said flatly, "The judge ruled to exclude the van."

The quiet din of the busy restaurant suddenly sounded to Jack as if it came through a long tube. He saw the rest of the evidence falling like dominoes. The van. The blood. The chloroform. The duct tape.

Without them, they couldn't hope to prove that Eugene Tupp was the monster who had abducted his daughter. It was the kidnapping charge that would put that piece of human scum away until he was either harmless or dead. His stomach gave a violent heave.

"I'm sorry," Gavin was saying. "I wanted to tell you in person."

"You're serious," Jack heard himself say.

"Jack, you of all people knew this was a problem from the start. The cop busted into his garage with a crowbar, for God's sake," Gavin said.

"The garage was attached to the house," Jack said, accenting the point of law.

The search warrant was for Eugene Tupp's house. In New York State that meant just the house. If the garage was separate, then anything found inside couldn't be used as evidence. The police should have gone back and gotten another warrant for the garage. They were too anxious.

"Not in the traditional sense maybe," Jack said, "but the covered walkway, that could be construed—"

"Jack," Gavin said. "He ruled the van inadmissible. He's not going to change. You know that."

Jack stood. He looked around for something. Then he lifted the massive transcript off the table and slammed it down to the floor, where it burst into a flurry of paper. The restaurant went quiet. Heads turned. Gavin backed them all down with his darkest scowl.

"Please," he said to Jack. "Sit down."

Jack dug into his pocket and took out a wallet-sized photo of his little girl: Janet. She stared back at him with his own glass blue eyes, her long radiant blond hair—also his—tucked back behind her ears, a small smile on her pretty face. She was only fifteen when it was taken. Only fifteen when Tupp snatched her, and left her with a shattered mind.

"This is my little girl," Jack said in a husky voice. He slapped the picture down on the table in front of his old friend, rattling the silverware and the ice in the water glasses. A messy purple stain began to spread from the base of Gavin's wineglass.

Gavin didn't look.

"I'm going to get the max on the rape charge," he said. "He'll do time."

"Time? How much?" Jack said, his voice rising. Heads began to turn again. "Four years? Five? Six? He did time before. Do you know what he did to her? He shouldn't do *time*. He should be strapped to the fucking chair!"

Gavin removed one hand from the edge of the table and grasped the knot of his tie, shaking it loose like a dog tugging on a sock. His face was scarlet now. Beads of sweat broke out on his forehead.

"It's not a perfect system, Jack." He looked around

and lowered his voice into a raspy plea. "This is not my fault."

Jack felt his anger and disgust peak and then began to wane. His face drooped. His shoulders sagged. He felt weary, but not weary from being run too hard. He felt instead like a man who had been tied up and beaten with a pipe.

He took a deep tired breath and exhaled his words. They sounded hollow, empty. "I know that, Gavin," he said, pocketing the photo. "Did I ever tell you why Angela left?"

Gavin cleared his throat and shook his head no.

"She found this rich fat bastard from the club, but that wasn't really it," Jack said. "I was supposed to pick Janet up the day he got her.

"This whole thing..." Jack said. "It's not your fault. It's my fault."

Jack turned and stumbled back through the crowded tables like a bum. Instead of going straight for the entrance, he turned and banged his way outside through the emergency exit door and into a garbage-strewn alley. An alarm howled after him. Jack didn't care. He felt Gavin's hand on his shoulder.

"I'll get him, Jack," Gavin said. He handed Jack his briefcase. "I'll get him for everything I can . . . I wish it were more. I do."

Jack said nothing. They reached the end of the alley. Gavin stopped. Jack kept going, plodding slowly up the sidewalk through the mist and to his

car. The melancholy glow of the streetlight illuminated a parking ticket on his windshield. Jack
didn't bother with it. He drove home with it flap-
ping in protest. It stopped when he reached the
assembly of barren trees that lined his cobblestone
driveway.

His vast home was illuminated in a haphazard,
uneven manner. More than half the exterior lights
buried in the yard had burned out months ago. Still,
there were enough random beams of light to make
out the rich orange brick and the tangled gray ten-
drils of dormant ivy as they snaked their way delicately across the intricate white trim. The tall
mullioned windows were dark and empty. Many of
them hid behind ornate wrought-iron balconies.
After Jack turned off the car, he sat for a moment in
the garage listening to the tick of the engine as it
cooled.

Inside the house he found the big handgun he had
recently purchased. It lay at the bottom of his underwear drawer under a mess of unfolded clothes. Behind the purchase of the gun was a wild scheme that
hadn't fully taken hold, a rage building up inside him
that needed a vent, but now it seemed to him that the
gun's true purpose was more horrible than what he
had originally imagined. Or had he known all along
in the back of his mind that this was the fate that
awaited him?

He descended the long curving staircase with the
cool black Glock 9mm in his hand. He found a bottle

of Chivas Regal in the kitchen. A pizza box lay open on the table, exposing greasy stains, crumbs, and three chewed-over crusts. In the corner of the sticky floor was a haphazard stack of newspapers. Without thinking Jack filled a tall glass with ice from the machine and then poured in the Scotch until it nearly overflowed. He sat at the kitchen table and began to sip. The ice jiggled noisily in its bath of liquor. Jack's hands were quivering.

He thought again of Eugene Tupp and what he had done. Without the van and the evidence inside it, the man would spend no more than six years in jail, and given the crowding of New York's penal system, he was likely to be free in much less. It was so wrong. Tupp would be out and free to attack someone else's little girl and that ate away at Jack's insides.

He had taken to drinking Maalox to get him through the day. But Jack believed that he deserved to suffer. After all, this was his fault. Like his wife—his ex-wife—everyone else seemed to know that, too.

The Scotch was nearly gone when he lifted the gun from the tabletop. He brought the barrel to his lips. Tears spilled down Jack's cheeks. The gun barrel slipped effortlessly into his mouth. He wasn't bothered by the tangy taste of metal against his tongue. But when the end of the barrel tickled the back of his throat, he had to fight the urge to gag.

Jack felt himself unravel like an industrial spring. His tears were now accompanied by heaving sobs that grew in strength, sobs for Janet, sobs for himself, sobs for the injustice and the futility of life.

He squeezed his eyes shut tight, wondering what it would feel like to die.

Then he pulled the gun from his mouth and slammed it down on the table. If he was mad enough to kill himself, then fine. He could always do that. But he would be damned if he weren't going to kill someone else first.

CHAPTER 2

Amanda Lee's eyes burst open at the sound of the radio and she thought of oatmeal. She read in People magazine that Demi Moore cooked oatmeal for her kids. Amanda couldn't shake the notion that it sounded like a very motherly thing to do, and today she was going to stop thinking about it—whether it was silly or not to do something because Demi Moore did it—and just to do it. She flipped the clock radio off and slipped quietly out of bed.

Parker, her husband, moaned and rolled away from her. The ring of faded brown hair that circled his balding head was a wild tangle. Amanda sighed to herself, then kissed her fingertips and placed them gently on the back of his naked head.

She wanted to love him.

She dressed herself in running shorts and a faded Georgetown University soccer T-shirt, crept past the kids' rooms, and tiptoed downstairs. Six at six. Six miles at six o'clock. That was the resolution she had come up with about a month ago after she'd had to get into a bathing suit at Hershey Park. A small boy had mistaken her for his own mother, and when Amanda had seen the size of the real mother's rump, she'd decided to get serious. She'd been wanting to get back in shape anyway. In college she was a whip. That all faded after the kids, but she was determined.

At the Bureau women didn't worry about their looks. It was a man's world and femininity had no place. That was fine. Amanda didn't need her looks to compete. Still, there was no reason that with some effort she couldn't have both. It was like her home life. There was no reason she couldn't be a successful agent and a good mother. It was like a dual major. It just took effort.

She laced up her shoes on the front steps and stretched a little in the chill morning air. She put on her headset and tuned into Bob Edwards on NPR. Although she'd never met him, she loved Bob. She felt like he could relate. He was understated but smart, and she knew she could count on him to always be up and talking at this ungodly hour.

She ran the streets, passing row after row of squat shingled suburban homes. The sky grew brighter. Finally the day began. The sun came up and she washed away the sweat in the shower. The rest of her family was still asleep, and now she felt good. She looked in the mirror and decided to put on some makeup, not for Parker, but because she was going to see the other mothers today. She wasn't entirely comfortable with them.

There was never anything to say and she hadn't had the chance to go to lunch or out for coffee, as so many of them seemed to do. Some of them didn't work at all. Those who did had nine-to-five jobs. In her family it was Parker who did most of the driving around and the pickups and drop-offs at school. He was the one with the nine-to-five job. He sold heavy equipment for Virginia Supply and when times were good, he could come and go as he pleased.

She pulled on a black Donna Karan sweat suit. She wanted to look good without appearing to have tried. She was neither tall nor short. And while no one would call her ravishing, she knew from the woman at Lord & Taylor that a little makeup applied in the right places brought out the green in her big almond-shaped eyes, the best of her otherwise plain features. Her red hair, too, cut shoulder length, straight and styled, had become an asset—although her more inflexible friends sometimes grew annoyed at the way a certain lock always seemed to curve back across her cheek, sometimes infringing on her eye and begging to be pushed back into place. Occasionally she would wear bright red lipstick to better define her small thin lips, but only on the rare occasions that she and Parker had someplace special to go.

Finished, Amanda smiled doubtfully at herself in the mirror and went back downstairs to cook her oatmeal. The rich aroma of the cereal mixed pleasantly with the smells of spring that drifted in through the kitchen window on a warm breeze. Amanda breathed deep and sighed, considering the next three days. This was exactly what she needed, no travel, no late nights. Instead she would live the life of a normal suburban mother. It was a reprieve from the grind of her latest case.

The children stirred upstairs.

She heard Parker thump his way to the bathroom and flick on the screeching shower. Just as the cereal was ready, they all began to appear. Her nine-year-old son, Teddy, wandered into the kitchen. Teddy had the round red face of his father with Amanda's hair. He was oblivious to her, tousle-headed, wearing just his pajama bottoms and playing an electronic Gameboy. His little sister, Glenda, wasn't far behind him. She, on the other hand, was already dressed in a pink jumper. She had pulled her own brown hair into pigtails and tied them off with two pink hairbands.

"Hi, Mommy," she said. Her voice nearly chirping. "You're going to come with me to Brownies today after school, right?"

"Good morning, sweetheart," Amanda said, kissing her daughter. "Yes I am."

"And what about you?" she asked her son. "Don't I get a good morning from you?"

"Oh, hi, Mom," Teddy said without lifting his head.

"Did you do your homework last night?" Amanda asked.

"Maybe," he said. Not even looking her in the eye. She watched his face.

"Why does it matter?" he asked.

A thick lump grew in her throat. "You have to do well in school," she said.

"What was I supposed to do last night?" he asked.

She didn't know. "Wasn't it that science project?" she said. "That thing you were doing with worms and electricity?"

"Electricity kills worms, Mom. That was two different assignments and about four months ago."

"What's this about electric worms?" Parker said in his booming southern drawl. He had burst into the kitchen still working on his necktie. He was flush with the raw cheerfulness that had attracted Amanda to him so many years ago. Now it grated on her, but she let him kiss her cheek and hug her from behind.

Amanda even leaned back into him. Parker was a big man, heavyset and solid like a bear despite a stomach that was beginning to get away from him. She thought it would be good for the kids to see them that way, and she squeezed his thick hand while she stirred the pot. It troubled her to show him affection for appearance' sake. She wanted to mean it. She wanted this moment to touch her deep down. She concentrated on the sun's warmth, the smells of the kitchen, and the comfortable sound of a family.

But before she could really feel it, the phone rang.

Amanda turned and looked at it on the wall. She looked questioningly at Parker, who scowled in turn. It kept ringing until he finally said, "Well, aren't you going to answer it? It's not for me."

"Me neither," Teddy piped in.

Glenda grinned and stuck out her tongue at her older brother as Amanda finally picked up the phone.

"He got another one."

It was Marco Rivolaggio, assistant special agent in charge, her nominal boss and sometimes partner.

"Where?" she asked.

"Just outside Atlanta," he said. "Fourteen years old."